PRAISE FOR BILL GASTON AND *THE*

"Always good at sidestepping stereotypes in ....
Gaston's men live and breathe on the page. More rounded than
Philip Roth's self-obsessed womanizers, and lacking the self-
ironizing of Nick Hornby's trendy nerds, these men are not crude
caricatures of contemporary masculinity. Gaston is a careful, precise writer who creates rich, dense layers of atmosphere. . . . *The
Order of Good Cheer* is a finely crafted journey from one edge of a
continent to another." — *Globe and Mail*

"Extraordinary . . . one of the most talented writers currently on the
Canadian literary scene . . . *The Order of Good Cheer* is a feast of
nuanced writing, blessed with one of those rare endings that are
absolutely perfect. Gaston has crafted a bittersweet ode to friendship,
loss, and near-hopelessness that lingers in the mind long after the
story has come to a close . . ." — *Winnipeg Free Press*

". . . a cousin to David Mitchell's *Cloud Atlas* . . . [a] daring, big-
hearted work." — *Montreal Gazette*

"When I discover a writer who is new to me, I feel two things: bliss at
having another career to follow, and guilt that I haven't found this
author earlier. About forty pages into Bill Gaston's *The Order of
Good Cheer*, that splash of guilt and bliss arrived. . . . [Gaston] writes
like he has all the muses sitting at his desk beside him. His command of narrative gives me chills; his dialogue rings true; and the
story he tells is absolutely compelling . . . His descriptions bring
people and places vibrantly alive, and his prose shimmers with colour, humour, and passion . . . Gaston's voice is utterly and thoroughly
his own." — *Halifax Chronicle Herald*

"An entertaining imagining of people and relationships . . . Gaston's quick cuts and crisp writing help both [storylines] build in drama and depth, and both sides are fully compelling as the novel's narratives wind closer and closer." — *Quill & Quire*

". . . a challenging, provocative book . . ." — *Georgia Straight*

". . . fiction on the grandest scale. In two distinct, fluid prose styles, Gaston charts Canada since colonization from coast to coast, re-imagining history and offering a fresh vision of the modern world. . . . *The Order of Good Cheer* seamlessly unifies diverse characters, narratives, and styles . . . a celebration of the diversity that unites and nourishes our world." — *Tyee*

"[Gaston] writes with a refreshing ground-level accuracy . . . [and] takes his readers on a very long and interesting trip through both time and space." — *Vancouver Review*

"Spectacular . . . The writing is wonderful, the characterizations strong, and the premise — simple and clever and unbelievable and comfortable all in one go. It's an ambitious book, but Gaston sets his sights all the way up and pulls it up and out with panache." — *January Magazine*

"Gaston beautifully renders Port-Royal using the bare essentials of the land, sea, forest, and sky. . . . Surrounded by storms of sorrow and doubt, in the end *The Order of Good Cheer* clings to hope and believes in love." — *subTerrain*

The Order of Good Cheer

a novel by

Bill Gaston

ANANSI

First published in hardcover in 2008 by House of Anansi Press Inc.

This edition published in 2009 by
House of Anansi Press Inc.
110 Spadina Avenue, Suite 801
Toronto, ON, M5V 2K4
Tel. 416-363-4343
Fax 416-363-1017
www.anansi.ca

Distributed in Canada by
HarperCollins Canada Ltd.
1995 Markham Road
Scarborough, ON, M1B 5M8
Toll free tel. 1-800-387-0117

Distributed in the United States by
Publishers Group West
1700 Fourth Street
Berkeley, CA 94710
Toll free tel. 1-800-788-3123

House of Anansi Press is committed to protecting our natural environment. As part of our efforts, this book is printed on paper that contains 100% post-consumer recycled fibres, is acid-free, and is processed chlorine-free.

13 12 11 10 09   2 3 4 5 6

LIBRARY AND ARCHIVES CANADA CATALOGUING IN PUBLICATION

Gaston, Bill, 1953–
The order of good cheer / Bill Gaston.

ISBN 978-0-88784-816-2

1. Champlain, Samuel de, 1567–1635 — Fiction. I. Title.

PS8563.A76076 2009   C813'.54   C2008-908074-2

LIBRARY OF CONGRESS CONTROL NUMBER: 2009922049

Cover design: Ingrid Paulson
Text design and typesetting: Ingrid Paulson

 Canada Council   Conseil des Arts
for the Arts   du Canada

 ONTARIO ARTS COUNCIL
CONSEIL DES ARTS DE L'ONTARIO

We acknowledge for their financial support of our publishing program the Canada Council for the Arts, the Ontario Arts Council, and the Government of Canada through the Book Publishing Industry Development Program (BPIDP).

Printed and bound in Canada

To my grandchildren

Can we agree, the past is not dead but
the present is its surprising and complex flower?
— Felix d'Amboisee

Fowl

juin 1606

SAMUEL SITS AT TABLE, alone, eyeing the roasted fowl without hunger, when he hears the sentry's yelp.

Bonneville has but moments ago brought and deposited the meat platter angrily, perhaps because he knows he needs must deliver it again, reheated, once Poutrincourt and the others return. All day they've been off in the longboat seeking what salt marsh might be diked and drained. A wind has risen to fight their return, and Samuel hopes this is the sole reason they are late.

He nudges a bird breast with a knuckle. The flesh does not give. Perhaps it wasn't anger on the cook's face — perhaps Bonneville is shamed by his own fare. Samuel eyes the platter of five duck. That is, he tries to think of it as duck. The thin black bill suggests less a mallard than a kind of gull. His tongue knows it too, a taste more of salt reeds than of flesh. He can smell nutmeg rising from the pooled yellow fat, and also garlic, but no cook's magic helps. And one must wonder why the heads have been left on: these birds are not game, nor this the after-hunt, one's trophies displayed on the platter. These birds can be netted and broken to death by children, and are barely food. Smelling them, Samuel almost yearns — almost — for the salt beef and biscuit they chewed every day of the crossing, the mere memory of which makes the floor pitch and move with swell. The common men eat from those barrels still.

He pinches up a bird by the beak, lets it drop, stiff-necked. He takes his knife and taps a black bill. It glistens well; and its shape is not unlike the curled thrust of a talon, the kind that adorns necklaces worn by the great sagamores to the west. He must remember to snap off these bills and collect them in a pouch, for a necklace of his own, a bit of craft he might fill some hours with, to complete and save and take back to France next summer and give to...whom?

Pretending appetite, Samuel hoists a dripping creature whole and takes a bite of skin. Bonneville won't want him eating this cold, when it tastes all the worse.

THE SENTRY'S NEXT YELL has Poutrincourt's servant boy — who is one of the several fellows in this colony who can be smelled before he is heard — standing pungently at his side to tell him a lone savage is at the gate.

"Is he old?"

"Sir, I do not know that."

"Please, quick, find if he is old."

He walks rather than runs. Samuel wonders if the boy's risked impudence is due to Samuel's being the lone noble who hasn't a servant — even the priest has one. The boy would have run if Poutrincourt were here, and though Samuel will say nothing of it he guesses that before winter is out this boy will be flogged. Samuel also finds the whelp's red waist sash somehow impudent. Nor does he care for the up-tilt of the boy's nose, which allows a constant view into his nostrils — though Samuel knows one should strive to love whichever of God's designs a man is born with.

He has heard only that the sagamore is impossibly old, and that one of his names is Membertou. Membertou is the reason Samuel stayed behind today, and yesterday, and the week previous, the sagamore having sent word that he would soon come. Samuel hopes that Membertou is who it is, if only to get this waiting over.

He finds the Mi'qmah tongue twisted and mystical and often senseless, but of all the nobles he is most able at it and so his duty is to stay and make contact with the sagamore. Indeed, Poutrincourt made formal request that he do this, possibly suspecting Samuel's regret. For though Samuel knows their words he is less at ease with their ways — their false smiles, the bluster and sometimes interminably long speeches about vainglorious and unlikely deeds. Samuel is a mapmaker. He is a mapmaker who quite needs the sea and who on land is made edgy at the thought of anyone else in the longboat without him, face into the breeze, discovering even so much as the next league of mud and clams. They should have left behind the lawyer. Lescarbot could trick out the sagamore's trust with his winks and soft pinches to the elbow.

The odorous boy barely pokes his head in the door to tell him, "The savage is old. No weapon. Not very large, but tall."

So it is Membertou, and it is the day Samuel has both wished for and not, this meeting of France with New France. Poutrincourt has expressed some worry about their welcome by these savages who have for the most part presented themselves as a scatter of ghosts off in the trees: first several men, peering out, then more emboldened, standing in postures with weapons in view, and later the women, and then also children, who laughed and sometimes bent to aim their bums.

Samuel finishes chewing and rises. He plucks a serviette to wipe his lips and beard of bird grease — though some savages would veritably enshine themselves with it, with grease of any kind, in these parts preferring, apparently, bear fat. He wonders why Membertou is alone. Up the great Canada River Samuel met more than one sagamore and none of them ever appeared without entourage, braves to fetch things and to yell at, not so unlike the King's own military.

The air of the courtyard is fresh as he strides through. The westerly has some scowl to it, and scalloped cloud says rain comes tomorrow. Samuel sees that Bonneville has wedged open the door to his hot kitchen and, inside, the cook stands on tiptoes to peer out his vent, toward the gate. One door along, the smithy's clanging and rending has likewise stopped. Samuel wonders if Membertou is truly over one hundred and, if so, how well he walks.

At the barred double gate, Poutrincourt's boy leaps laughing away from the Judas hole and stands aside. Samuel hesitates and, feeling watched by the boy, says, inexplicably, "Oui." He clears his throat and stoops to peer through the hole. No one stands without. There, empty, lies the field of fresh black stumps running down to the beach and the choppy waters of the bay. To either side, more stumps, and then the dark forest. But there at the beach he spies the thin grubby beak of a canoe, aground where the longboat normally rests. But no old sagamore, no Membertou.

Now, an inch from his bare eyeball rises some dirty, greasy hair. No topknot, no part or braids — it is hair made by the wind and also, so it appears, by sleep. Now a forehead, though not that of an old man. Now eyebrows, grey and fine and glistening with grease, two narrow pelts trod upon by snails.

Still in his prank, the savage continues rising to the hole slowly, delaying the show of his eyes.

Now the eyes do come, and both they and the skin around them are deeply those of an old man. Hardened in duty, Samuel will hold Membertou's gaze, setting himself the task not to look away first. For today his own eyes are his King's eyes, and those there are the eyes of New France. They have risen full centre in the Judas hole and they widen in surprise at seeing Samuel's. Now Samuel sees the smile in them and understands that the surprise was actually feigned, was mirroring his own expression. Membertou's eyes hold this humour but Samuel sees something more behind, a strong quality he cannot put a word to. If wisdom and curiosity could become one gleam, it would be that.

In a tongue Samuel must tilt his head to know, the sagamore Membertou lisps softly, "I smell duck."

juillet 1606

CHAMPLAIN REACHES THE promontory huffing hardly at all compared to before. He has grown his land muscles again, from these weeks walking it.

Daily he has climbed to this spot for reasons other than healthful exercise. Up here there blows a harder and finer wind than that down in the compound, one that barely ruffles hair. This higher wind carves in between two mountains, in through the gut that serves as entrance to their port, and this wind smells of that true wilderness — the sea. Samuel never tires of this smell, which makes straight for his innards and draws him. But the loveless spirit of sea wind also humbles him and makes him glad to be up here for a second reason: to see his present safety, below. For l'Habitation is born. The mapmaker makes an artist's square of his hands and there, through it, captured entire, is his world:

A sheltered harbour of such size that it may one day hold a hundred of France's ships. Three rivers flow into it, and they are named the Eel, the Antoine, and the Mill. Much of the shore is shallows of mud bottom, which keeps many birds, some of which are good enough at table. Some spans of mud are dense with clam, which the men hesitate to eat, for it makes dysentery unless taken with fresh bread. From the north wind they are shielded by this shelf of mountain at Samuel's back. Everywhere lie pockets of a soil that is black and deep. Their forest boasts seven species of tree, one of which presents an unknown nut. Trout hide in all three rivers, and salmon might come late summer, sculling shoulder to shoulder in so thick a school that, says Bonneville, their future children already run across their backs. Membertou promises to show them how to catch a fish long as a canoe. A copper mine lies undug, twenty miles north, in a steeply cliffed bay. The region lacks vines.

Samuel narrows his square: surrounded by forest, a field of stumps fills several acres. In patches faintly greener than brown, small gardens have sprouted. It is late season, but the rooted crops might store under snow.

Narrowing his view farther, he frames what they've built: a sturdy outer wall of well-pointed logs near twice as tall as a man and not possibly broken by wind, beast, or savage. They have a sturdy but welcoming gate, closed to the evils of the night. Inside it, the dwellings are done, save that they wait on the carpenters' slower art to cut in windows and properly hang doors. Bringing last year's planks across Fundy Bay from the damned ruin of St-Croix saved time, though some men bear superstitions about the wood itself, not wanting death's taint in their dwelling, in particular not wanting a bed frame that cradled a corpse. They have been assured by surgeon, apothecary, and priest that the scurve that carried off last year's men is not a pestilence that itself lives in wood. (While surgeon, apothecary, and priest all deem the scurve "a failure of the spirit," it is interesting to watch them disagree on exactly what that means, for no one's truth is remotely alike.) But they have cookhouse, storehouse (with eight-foot-deep cellar this time, so naught will freeze), smithy, a nobles' house, a manor (nearly done) and a common house for the men. An inner courtyard, its freedom from stumps their most hard-won labour yet, dug, burnt, and tackled, with ship's rope, for they lack oxen. In the very centre sits their lovely well, a deep hole into earth's clean belly, the blessed wound ensheltered with peaked and shingled roof. There, the handmill (so large is its stone and so taxing the job of turning it, any man who labours there is typically suffering punishment). They own three barrels of salt beef and six of biscuit, and twenty cask of wine, three of which are superior. Two barrels of grain, one cask of salt. The sagamore Membertou boasts that within months all will have moose for the asking, for the snow will come and deepen and they will chase the hobbled moose at their leisure. And, as if God kindly noted their weariness of codfish, the first river herring have arrived up the brook west of their clearing, and though bony they are excellent stabbed through with willow skewer, mouth to tail, and touched to the embers.

The men's mood is good.

Owning the tallest roof, Poutrincourt's manor begins to look fine. Planks for the floor were sawn here, of oak. It will be near as fine a house as a gentleman's country retreat in France, though smaller. In the meantime the Sieur stays next door in the nobles' house, which, though it too will have a glass window, is made of logs and rarely will a day reach its end without a beetle or spider landing excited on one's shoulder. Poutrincourt speaks fondly — eyes shining — of the year his wife will dwell in the manor with him, and the nobles are gladdened by this dream that, with God's giving hand, indeed might come to pass.

Poutrincourt has asked Lescarbot to compose a descriptive journal to carry back next summer to read to Madame Poutrincourt, so to convince her of Port-Royal's healthful beauty. (Judging from the number of pages Lescarbot composes in a night, Samuel suspects the lawyer has aims for audiences larger than one friend's wife.)

And, there: the gentle Poutrincourt has had a path of one mile cleared to a future flower garden and trimmed woods, a place of contemplation and healthful walking. He has also had a smooth-milled cross of some ten feet erected just outside the gate so that, when a man puts his eye to the Judas hole, it commands his vision. A cross of greater size he has ordered placed atop the North Mountain, behind where Samuel stands, but twice again as high. Cutting a path there will take many working days to fulfill, not to mention the milling and transport of such a cross — and some men have grumbled (not to noble ears, of course, but one can see it in their eyes), eager to begin work on their own gardens and fish traps, always in fear for their own survival. But in the end they trust in the wisdom and benefaction of Sieur Poutrincourt, and of God.

There is a small chapel, but also giving comfort are three small cannon fierce enough to hole any longboat trying to land.

Samuel is breathing hard and, discovering himself near tears, he thrusts his hands' frame at it, at l'Habitation, three times, and declares with certainty that New France is born. He decides he will compose a proper portrait of it in map's ink as soon as he descends this hill and rejoins his brothers.

Who are one at the top: Sieur Poutrincourt, of good heart, who lacks a fortune but has been given this land by de Monts, and loves it so.

Who are eight in the middle: nobles of several kind, of birth primarily, in whose number Samuel Champlain takes a modest place. They serve God and King, and otherwise take their own counsel.

Who are thirty-six at the bottom — including cook, surgeon, gunsmith, apothecary, carpenters, soldiers, workers — men of diverse talent and good fellows all, even the several who came from gaol, their ill deeds minor enough. Some came seeking adventure, some escaping adventures past. All will earn their one hundred and fifty livres, which is thrice that for the same year's labour at home.

Who are one off to the side: Fr. Vermoulu, priest, sees that their souls stay clean and offers a food and a wine most necessary for their survival, both earthly and eternal.

Though perhaps the scurve will not visit this time.

PENETRATING THIS FOREST of mediocre trees, forearms up against endless chafing branches, the carpenter Lucien realizes how much he misses roads. Here, there is no unhindered walking except in the compound, or the path to the cesspool, or a tilted gambol along the sloped and rocky beach at low tide. Beyond that, one chooses either the deadly sea or the thick forest. At home, even if he never went another place, there were roads to allow escape, if only for the mind. Possibility is itself a freedom. Here he has the morbid sense that this lack of roads plugs his daily dreamings. And at home, when one did walk a road, one could do so without thinking. Here, to walk the forest lost in even a moment's thought is to have one's face pierced, fall off a cliff, or find oneself hugging a nest of wasps.

Though it was hours ago now, if he sucks into the depths of his teeth he can still get some faint molasses onto his tongue. The event was lunatic, truly. The brute Dédé and he had been given the labour of cleansing Monsieur Lescarbot's beloved window glass when it was lifted from its molasses. Lucien doesn't know why he, a master carpenter, was paired up with a common worker for this task—perhaps it was to match his brains to Dédé's brawn for the sake of care. Though Lucien was happy enough for it. A week earlier he'd watched with plenty of other men as that first pane of glass emerged from the safety of its molasses barrel after months of storage in it; they all saw the main thickness of brown syrup get scraped back into the barrel with sharp wooden spatulas; they watched as the first light won its way through and transparency was reborn. It was a kind of magic. Then two men were assigned the task of walking it tenderly down to the shore to wash it to its original perfection before the glass was installed into Sieur Poutrincourt's frame. Many savages arrived for this, and some looked stricken or insulted as Poutrincourt himself appeared from within, behind his fresh glass, then rapped upon it and waved. Though two older women laughed to each other, and then one shouted something.

Cleansing with seawater is what he and Dédé were this morning charged to do with Monsieur Lescarbot's glass. Dédé insisted on carrying the pane to water's edge unaided, and Lucien let him, guiding him with warnings of approaching stones or slippery clay. The huge man's bare straining calves had the size and spirit of two piglets. On the beach Lucien rolled up his sleeves and went underwater to the knees, but Dédé did no such thing. He glanced back at the compound, grunted a version of "waste not, want not," hoisted the heavy pane higher, and started licking. A few licks farther along he seemed to notice, through the tan glass, Lucien's stare. He paused in his licking long enough to say, "Yours is this other side, here." And from their clench his fingertips tapped the gummy virgin side.

Lucien considered, but not long. Simply, what harm? He liked molasses. So he would have some too. He stepped up to the glass. It was nothing but bizarre and ribald to behold the hirsute Dédé, thick black pelt framing his immense red face, his pressed and liquid tongue and madly working jaw, all so close — and then to extend one's own tongue out near it! Lucien first tasted a corner of the glass farthest from the other's face. And it was good, wonderful, not just because unadulterated but also, in a sense, stolen. Lucien relaxed to the ease of a licking puppy; on their own his eyes fell half closed. But there came a time when their two faces approached, and here, too close, was Dédé's formidable and wide-open working head, and now Lucien was aware of the larger man's noises from the other side of the glass, and the pane's slight wobble, and then they were licking, it seemed, tongue upon tongue, for Dédé had manoeuvred to place his exactly here, and it was a moment of horrible clarity. Then, when Lucien dared look and found himself perfectly eye to eye, the beast winked, and his open mouth was also a smile, though it never paused in the licking. Lucien could not tell, and still can't, what kind of wink it was. It might have said, "Aren't we the best of thieves?" It might simply have marked each other's lust for this sweet. Or, and Lucien hopes not, it might have marked lust of another kind. For this man Dédé looked to be reckless in all directions. In any event it was here that Monsieur Lescarbot caught them at it, and shouted, and strode down the bank to chastise them like boys for befouling his sacred glass, and such was the noble's tone that Lucien didn't dare offer the science that glass could not be harmed by many hundred tongues. Quite the opposite.

LUCIEN ASCENDS A forested slope. The dog picks up its pace to lead him, and under his feet there is almost a path. It is a path made by him alone, one he has trod perhaps a dozen times now, breaking the weakest of twigs, retarding new foliage. It leads to the promontory overlooking not just the harbour but out between the two mountains through to the great French Bay and on to the west. Looking west is less painful than looking east, and homeward.

Walking a half-path lets him be half lost in thought, and Lucien notes how the pains of homesickness are not unlike those of hunger: not altogether disagreeable, in that their plea augurs a future fulfillment. And a sweetness in the pain resembles that delivered by certain music. There is also some philosophy to be had in homesickness: though these trees are sadly not France's trees, in their newness is both a horror and a joy at meeting God's limitless imagination.

Lucien considers it an act of wisdom that they've brought the three dogs across the ocean, one of whom, Bernard, leads him now. Stooping to caress a dog and receive its love is the same here as it was in France, so when he caresses a dog he is wherever he wishes to be, the spirit of the act being primary, not the particular mud under one's boots. He loves these dogs with his true heart and tries to copy their humour as they sit alertly guarding doors. Their manner reveals that the very best life has been found for them: half in the wild, half at their master's hearth. Never has he seen dogs so content; they are quick to a command and yet, at rest, they sit so confident in their gazing at the vista, which they seem to feel they own.

It begins to rain and, as is often weirdly the case in New France, it grows warmer for it. At home it rained the whole week before departure and in today's rain he feels the sweet pain of envisioning his oldest brother, Albert — Albert laughing at the beer he holds in his hand, laughing at smiling women and duck farts and the surprise of a sunset. And the pain grows even sweeter in thoughts of his lovely sister Babette, closest to him in age and in heart. He will never forget the night before he put to sea. Neither of them could sleep, and for this they blamed the heat blown down on the early mistral winds. They spoke in whispers so as not to wake anyone else, and grew used to this kind of voice and the intimacy it needed — almost a touching of foreheads. They became giddy at having passed sleep by. At one point Babette took her portrait from the wall, bade Lucien come watch, placed it on her lap, and let fall numerous candle drips upon it until her face was obscured fully. Then announced, "There, I am dead." But the marvellous thing about her is that her mood was made content by this, and it was only a momentary depression, or perhaps even a purgative.

They left the scraping of wax from paint to the artistry of Charles the cook, who always boasted of his delicacy with knives, claiming in full seriousness that if they would only give him a knife sharp enough he could split and split a pig's bristle until it became a feather.

LUCIEN'S SCALP LIFTS and he leaps an inch as Bernard roars into the trees, disappearing. The dog has begun to find food of his own, though usually it amounts to nothing but a long chase. And once the noble Breton, his head half white, half black, returned to the compound with his muzzle and the brow of one eye pierced with an agony of spears. White barbed little terrors, some an inch deep, they apparently came from a fearsome creature no one wants to meet. The mapmaker Champlain, it is said, claims to know of the creature. He likens it to a beaver that launches these harpoons with its tail, but no one believes him. Lescarbot, whose camp of allegiance is larger than that of the quiet Champlain, publicly refers to the unlikely beast as Champlain's "*petit googoo.*"

Lucien continues uphill, into the rain. Bernard will find him. Perhaps because he commenced his walk while thirsty, and continues thirsty (or perhaps it is the molasses), the rain causes the foliage and its myriad greens to look lush and sweet-tempered, as if all could be eaten and enjoyed.

How is it, Lucien wonders, that the savages hereabouts know what can and what cannot be enjoyed as food? Has it simply been a process, undertaken countless years ago, of tasting?

Swallowing a slight bit, then putting one's ear in one's stomach, as it were, to listen for first whispers of illness? And had this trial by fatal error possibly taken place in France in its darkest early years too? For how else would their own knowledge have come about? The Bible makes mention of husbanded foods and of some others profane, but there is no list of wild plants, no warning as to which mushroom causes a devilish shouting death and which is as fine as meat in the stew. At home, in the forest behind St-Malo, none of these thoughts would have come to him; but on this path, amid all these glistening and seemingly beckoning leaves, shoots, cones, curls, pods, hoods, mosses, of which at least half he is ignorant, the savages' knowledge as to what here is *food* seems like wisdom of the most miraculous kind.

According to Lescarbot, a crude and somewhat bitter tuber found inland up the great Canada River has been unearthed and occasionally shipped and offered in the best dining rooms of Paris. He told Lucien he tasted of it once and said it was not special, but that its hard-gotten nature, like anything from the ends of the earth, embellished its appeal. The chefs call it, simply, "Canada." As if in the tuber they were eating the very earth of this place. Lucien pictures a fine lady, head and neck falling gooselike across the table, her cheeks aflush with culinary courage, asking, "Please, may I have more Canada?"

Monsieur Champlain, who has seen this tuber on his voyages and knows its Algonquin word, asked Membertou if it grows here at Port-Royal. While our savages have a different word for it — Champlain had to describe it with his hands — it does grow nearby, in scattered fashion, and Membertou, pursing his lips in distaste and shrugging one dismissive shoulder, said he bids his women search it out only when all are hungry.

Though the gardens are in and showing some green, Lucien hears much nervous talk of food. When the nobles speak of it

amongst themselves it is in the voice they use to discuss fortifications or ships that may or may not arrive in the spring with
supplies. And Lucien has noted what looks like a constant difference of opinion between Messieurs Champlain and Lescarbot.
(He understands that what he has witnessed is no more than
what these gentlemen let escape in front of the regular men; so
their arguments in privacy must be almost violent!) In short,
Champlain values the savages' food, and Lescarbot doubts it
strongly as profane. The pinnacle of this argument involves the
"pale, giant pine," which Champlain insists he saw cure men of
the scurvy disease in Hochelaga, to the west. And so the mapmaker looks for this tree in this region and so far he has not seen
it. He says the Algonquin use the word *annedda* for it. But
Membertou stares blankly both at this word and at the description of the tree as Champlain draws it eagerly in the air with his
hands, jumping to his toes, like a boy, to show its great height.
Likewise he describes the needles (which he says are the cure
when they are dried and boiled), comparing them with other
trees' foliage, claiming, "no, longer than that" and "yes, patterned,
a weave, but less simple." He hunts for this tree always, and asks
the rest of them to as well. Those several others who survived
St-Croix also hunt for it — one would have to say fretfully — and
Lucien understands that this is because of what they saw last
winter. Lescarbot questions the existence of such a miraculous
tree, and although like any man here he fears the disease and
would love to erase it from the world completely, he declares the
scurve to be yet another example of God's mercy, one no man
should question. He rises to anger when the mapmaker mentions
the wondrous tree, thinking it wrong to be giving men hope
while not supplying the means.

Lucien almost treads on a ring of mushrooms, which, as if
knowing his thoughts, beckon in a coy way, glowing as if to

present themselves. They are the colour of oyster — one of Lucien's favourite foods, not found in their harbour or hereabouts — a colour that despite its pale hue suggests a food of great and pungent richness. Lucien is tempted to stoop and gather but does not. He does, though, make a promise to himself to begin a course of study. It would be gauche, if not possibly dangerous, to ask a woman, but one of Membertou's sons, he is sure, would gladly walk with him after the day's work is done. Lucien will barter something for this service if needs be, and he will take the role of student, and ask questions about this plant and that.

août 1606

NOT MANY MORE weeks along, Samuel hunches over a fire made in a stump, in the crotch of its roots. In his hand is a piece of stained paper, upon which is scrawled a rumour. He is about to drop the paper in to burn it, and so do Poutrincourt's bidding.

It seemed he knew of the paper's content even before he'd read it.

Indeed this new world is one of portent. Samuel has often felt it before, always in his belly, a message sudden yet pregnant as a bulb, before he brings thought to it. It could be given him by the season's first dead leaf, or by a judgemental bird call in the distance. So it was yesterday: a monster from the depths of the mouth of the River of St-Jean.

They'd taken the longboat to last year's hastily departed St-Croix Island to search the burned and razed site for any well-wrought hasps, knobs, and latches, and iron that could otherwise go for cannon shot — a two-day voyage that might save their smithy two weeks' work. The wind sped them there, and they scavenged well, despite the men's squeamishness at putting foot to beach, let alone stooping to paw through the old settlement's waste, let alone camping overnight, which Israel Bailleul, their pilot, likened to "picnicking in the scurve's very breath."

But they found a dozen good items, as well as many nails, and on their way back Samuel bade them steer for the River of St-Jean. His stated reason was that the Sieur sought vines from that river's upper banks for transplant in Port-Royal; in truth Samuel loved the oddity of that river mouth, its cliffs and black depths and wild rapids in certain tides. After a full summer's time ashore he simply wanted the thrill of it.

Yes, he had heard savage talk of "a devil that rises to eat canoes." Last year, the young sagamore of those parts had told him of a giant yellow tree that came from the depths to leap out of the water with a roar, aiming for any man there, only to disappear for years — the savage had seen it but three times in the span of his whole life. He called it *manitou*, which Samuel knew meant Devil or, strangely, God, or something blasphemously between those two. And while Samuel didn't quite believe in so patient and conniving a sunken tree, on the several times he's pushed into the chaotic mouth of the St-Jean he's kept a wary eye. And so, this morning: he was gazing to port, at the cliff wall, marvelling at its blackness of rock, and despite the roar of tidal rapid he thought he heard something new, swung his gaze to starboard, and here it was at its peak of rising from the water: smooth, blond, naked of bark, showing twice the height of a man! Samuel's breath caught as the tree speared back down. It had missed them by twenty paces. Its end was a root-ball that had long been trimmed by rock and underwater storms and now resembled a fist; it would have stove them easy as a drunken boot does a grinning pumpkin.

Two other of the men saw it too, and screamed in their seats, and some had but half seen it, but the monster — or was it a ghost? — did not return, and then the men were all a-jabber, arguing as to whether it had truly come or not; and all the voyage back they argued still. Samuel heard it double in girth and height, and Picard assayed it was white as bone, nay, *was* a bone, and then stood firm on this. Come winter, the tree would no doubt find its way into a song.

In any case, a portent. And thus on their voyage back it was no accident their being hailed, outside the very entrance of Port-Royal, by the rotting bark full of Basques. Samuel bade them join Sieur Poutrincourt for a meal, exclaiming that they would be the very first guests of New France, but the Basque captain declined. They were on "an expedition," the captain said, but murmured it in the oddest way, gazing sideways in almost a caricature of lying, though he may just have been embarrassed about the quality of his French, or his boat. But then, pierced on the end of a pike pole, a stiff piece of paper was held out to Samuel.

A SECRET, INDEED. Standing at the smouldering stump, Samuel turns it over in his hand, reads its scrawled paragraph once more, and hisses, "*The King is a fool.*" A dangerous thought to give voice; he looks back over his shoulder at the compound, making sure he is alone.

The paper is missing its seal but might be in the hand of de Monts. If so, it is true and means that the King has again been seduced by the whining merchant class (of which several in that Basque longboat on their "expedition" were a gloating example) and has revoked their monopoly on furs in New France, held by de Monts, their benefactor.

Can the King have forgotten what happened last time? Allowing merchants to come here all-in-a-riot, to make their own barter, led to nothing but the wealth of the savages themselves. Quick to learn they could play one merchant off another, a savage held up a single scabrous beaver skin and said no to one knife, and no to two knives, and no even to a hatchet — where before, a single French knife, when proffered by de Monts alone, could win two, sometimes three beaver skins for France! Samuel himself had seen occasions where de Monts had gained furs simply for the pleasure of his Christian company.

Rich with furs, de Monts finances this settlement, this permanence, of New France. If he now becomes bankrupt, the King is sabotaging his own heart's desire, that of establishing his throne here, and growing French children here, and, most important of all, giving the word of God to a larger world. Samuel wonders how the King does not know that de Monts's original plan remains brilliant, allowing as it does the birth of New France without drawing a single coin from the royal exchequer. Simply, de Monts needs only the monopoly on fur.

If this piece of paper is true, that licence is revoked, this colony stops, New France dies, many souls go unsaved, and — *the King is a fool.* But as Samuel recalls the one time he himself stood in the court and witnessed the simpering mass of bowing dancers, all smelling of false flowers, all eager to encroach on the King's company and sweetly lie to him — Samuel wonders why he is surprised.

Again he glances back at the compound. The sentry waves to him and Samuel waves back. Ten minutes ago Samuel saw Sieur Poutrincourt weep. For now there is the question of whether Poutrincourt still owns this smouldering stump, still owns this land of Port-Royal. It was given him by Monsieur de Monts, but is it de Monts's still to give?

The nobles who know this rumour will not tell the men, who even now put their shoulders into finishing their dwellings, feeding their gardens. Seed must go in now if there is any hope of vegetables, let alone grain. They cannot slump in their labours, unsure if all sprouting is for nought.

The King is a fool. Samuel ventures these words for the third time, enough to relieve himself of a fire that almost overcrows his reason.

But now he needs must burn this crust of paper. Poor Poutrincourt, fiercely silent, then weeping, standing more unhinged by wine than Samuel has seen him. He'd read then thrust the paper back at Samuel, his look dark enough to suggest that Samuel had himself penned it, and said, "Burn this, now."

Samuel lets the paper drop. Damp and thick from too many hands, it ignites slowly. He watches until it is ash, though this seems an elaborate precaution. No one here save he and a few others — Poutrincourt and Lescarbot, and also the carpenter Lucien, so the rumour goes — can read.

Fish

AS USUAL THESE DAYS, Andy Winslow hadn't slept well but was up anyway. Deep in his morning routine and near the bottom of his first coffee, only now did he register what was happening down on the beach. Why so many people and what were they looking at? You could see in their posture an odd lean, could see care and wonder. Yes, there was that storm last night, a real pounder from the south, much howling and blow.

Andy was sitting at his window planning the drive to Terrace but so dense with thought it was like he'd been unconscious and only now did he come to the world outside himself. What woke him up truly was the sight of neighbour Sally Kitcher down there on the beach, flopping a four-foot ling cod onto a child's blue and yellow plastic wagon and trying to drag it away. At the wagon's first lurch over the gravel the fish slid off, and Andy — coming to and involuntarily standing up — could see that the wagon was already full of what appeared to be dead fish.

He also noticed that the light in his yard was different. There was more of it. He saw that this was because there were fewer trees. In fact he had a better view — more light, more harbour vista to see — and now it registered that part of his yard was gone. A corner of his lawn, where it used to meet the bank's trees and bushes, now ended at a precipice.

He threw on a stained grey hoodie and his workboots but didn't bother lacing them to stride his wet lawn to have a look at his new little cliff. He didn't stand too close in case more wanted to come down. He turned back to look at the house. Then to the lip of land at his feet. He figured that he'd lost maybe a tenth of his property. He whispered, "Holy shit," then started down the zigzag trail to the beach. Warding off wet alder branches with his forearms, getting showered, Andy wondered — absurdly — if he would ever prune this pathway.

Around the point from Prince Rupert proper, the shore beneath Andy's neighbourhood kept a wilderness feel, its bank thick with trees that half hid the houses. Along the few hundred yards of gravel beach Andy could see fifteen or twenty people, alone and in groups, all looking at dead fish and dead crabs. Some pointed a finger, some nudged a creature with a foot. Closest to him, Sally Kitcher hunched over her wagon, huffing, trying to bind her heap of ling cod with a length of cast-off yellow twine she'd found.

Andy pivoted to survey his lost yard from below. Except for one large upside-down fir, whose crown rested on the gravel, there was no evidence — no sod or topsoil or small uprooted trees. All had been carried away by the storm tide. It was simply gone!

Andy turned back to the mystery at his feet. Over the entire stretch of beach, dead fish and crab marked the high-tide line. The crabs were Dungeness of all sizes, from keepers as big as human faces to babies the width of bottle caps, and their shells did not rock in the slight waves, suggesting they were still heavy with meat. Some fish, like Sally Kitcher's ling cod, were spectacularly big, but most were arm-sized. Andy saw not just ling cod but also rockfish, and either flounder or young halibut, he couldn't tell. Gulls stood and poked, and walked rather than hopped, looking unsure where to go, as if leisurely choice was a thing unknown to their species.

He reached the water and flipped a ling with his boot. Maybe nine or ten pounds, it was sleek, firm, its eyes bright, the kind of freshness they tell you to look for in the market. The water that lapped at it, and out into the bay as far as Andy could see, appeared clean, clear, frigid. He could see no oil. He could smell nothing aside from rain on rocks, and seaweed. Weird, this lack of smell — to be standing among dead fish and not smell them.

"Excuse me?" Andy called. "Sally?"

The woman paused in her cord-tying to flash a palm, telling him to wait a sec. Andy didn't care for Sally Kitcher. They'd graduated together and she hovered near forty like him, but even at age ten she'd looked dreamless, her stern lack of humour making her seem of another generation. She had those eyes you couldn't see into, and she made Andy think "peasant stock," or "ox," despite her having gone south to university and returning with a degree in something. He'd known her all his life but he could feel closer to a stranger. Maybe it was also because he was so tall and thin and she was so short and round.

Andy approached as Sally stood eyeing her heaped wagon for transportability. The top ling cod was cinched down fairly tight.

"Slime on slime," she said, shaking her head. "Won't work."

"Do we know what's going on?"

"It's at least to the mouth of the Skeena, maybe farther. Ten miles. Fifteen miles." Sally was so undramatic, this could have been a yearly event.

"Do we know what happened? Something spill?"

"I haven't heard anything, no."

"I mean, you can't see anything."

"No, you can't."

As if to make sure, they both scanned the shoreline in both directions.

Andy offered, "Can't smell anything either, I don't think."

"No," Sally agreed.

"Was it the storm, maybe?"

"Maybe. I don't see how, though. I don't see how wind would kill fish."

"Well, waves?"

"Why would they be up in the waves?"

"Yeah." Andy shook his head. "You know, I lost a corner of my yard last night." He pointed up to his property. Somewhat incredibly, he yawned. And he realized that not only was his view of the water better, but that from the beach you could see more of his house.

"Saw that." Sally didn't bother glancing back.

"Tide must've been huge, and on top of that the waves just came in, I guess, and cut into the bank. Boom, gone."

Sally stood and tugged her wagon, testing. "It happens."

Well, no, it didn't. That land had been there for thousands of years, through countless tides and storms.

"Anyway," Andy said, toeing a small rock cod, "wonder what it could be. It sure doesn't look good."

"It sure doesn't."

"They look so healthy. Like they were alive, and suddenly boom. Fish *and* crabs. Maybe some sort of military test? Naval test?"

"I don't have a clue. No one's heard anything so far as I know." Sally regarded her wagonload again, impatient. "They do look good."

Andy realized that of course she had plans for those fish. "You're not going to eat those, are you? Shouldn't you wait and —"

"*Hell* no!" Sally glanced at him briefly, then away. "*Jesus*, no. Fertilizer."

"Ah."

"Friend in Halifax called and woke me up, she heard about these fish on the radio, said in the Maritimes they used to plow in truckfuls on the farms." She bobbed her head at her wagon. "Back when they had fish."

"It was on the radio?"

"It's been on TV already."

"This?" Andy pointed at Sally's wagon and she started tugging, a little defensively. "And they don't know what caused it?"

"I don't think so, no." Sally Kitcher's back was to him as she hauled her load away.

"Won't whatever's in them get into the vegetables?"

"*Flowers.*" Sally didn't turn to look at him. "I'm not stupid."

Andy pivoted once more to take in the tide line of dead fish, the white bellies and crab backs diminishing in the distance both left and right. He found Sally Kitcher's lack of concern stunning, but oddly enough he took some comfort from it too. Maybe this was no big deal. He noted again the manner in which the seagulls poked and pulled at a fish, or waddled to the next one, all rather listlessly, he thought. He couldn't tell if their lack of frenzy was caution or if, already full, they were bored.

He didn't feel that hungry himself as he slogged back up the path to make breakfast. It was Tuesday, so the pancake batter made last night waited in the fridge. He would still drive to the Terrace library. First he'd phone his mother, in whose house the TV was never off, to ask if she knew anything. He would also break the news to her about losing some yard. And he'd phone Drew, to wake him up and tell him. He wondered if Laura had heard about this yet. And what would she think?

MIDDAY, ANDY CAME home smelling of reeds. A subtle and creeping fug, it clung mostly to his hands but it also filled his jeans, still wet to the knees, and his poor soaked leather work-boots, which stood on their mat just inside the door.

In his pass through the living room he turned the radio on loud, though he didn't expect anything new. On his drive to Terrace and back he'd heard the identical story three times and "local authorities" still didn't know the cause of the ten miles of dead fish. It was of course worrisome, but also vaguely thrilling to hear Prince Rupert as the subject of a national story.

In the bathroom he brought his fingernails to his face. He could too easily smell the cattail's root, a swampy scent suggesting its weird pale green — and rot, the breath of turtles, the sick spirit of water bugs.

As he often did, Andy hopped in the shower with his clothes on, standing back to get his jeans into the spray. He squirted some shampoo down there, and some in his hands, and a smell like purple candy flowers rose to overcrow that of reeds. He didn't care to learn that he preferred this cheap chemical waft over something natural, but there it was. Still, no way he was going to consider those reeds food.

It was why he'd stopped in the first place, to check the cattails out as a food source. Zooming mindlessly back to the coast from Terrace (where he'd returned his books and picked up thirteen fresh ones at the college library: two on climate change, one peripherally to do with shore erosion, and the one he'd been waiting for, Lescarbot's *History of New France*), he'd really wanted only to savour the deep pep of his new car. Despite his sleeplessness, despite the dead fish and lost land, he was feeling fine, maybe only because he was going somewhere — a simple destination, A to B, contentment sometimes that simple. Then in the middle of high-torque hum he spotted the cattails in a hidden slough fifty yards off the road. He had to brake and back up carefully (people floored it along this stretch), park, and go to the trunk for his workboots. He didn't know if it was because of the mountainous terrain, or because it was merely thirty miles south of the Alaskan panhandle, but you just didn't see cattail around here.

He slogged through brush and knee-high moss and approached them feeling a little less triumphant than foolish. This was all Champlain's doing, of course; that is, the result of Andy's current immersion in his *Voyages*, skimpy and plodding as they were. Despite the blandness, and no description whatsoever of *life* in New France, some small to-do was made when a food source was discovered. Or a potential copper mine, or a stand of oak. To find a new river mouth was the biggest deal, because even up rivers he was looking for a way to China. (It was hard not to marvel at the naïveté of the era, as Europeans stumbled up against the wall of the New World and couldn't see over it.) To find a patch of decent soil in which to thumb one's seeds was good, but even better was to come upon something edible, fruit or bulbs for the taking. It meant not just survival, and reduced labour and fret, but variety, a new taste, an expanded world. Imagine, after six months of huddling in smoke and cold, nothing to eat but hardtack and unchewable cured beef, that first fresh vegetable — the first fiddlehead shoots plucked fat and clean from the riverbank mud, then steamed and lightly salted and drizzled with balsamic vinegar. *Crunch*, vital little nuggets. Funny that the French had with them a cask of balsamic, a taste North America was waking up to four hundred years later. Andy loved reading that they had garlic, mace, rosewater, dried cinnamon bark, sage, tarragon, and, yes, Dijon mustard. A different book mentioned penned pigeons, or squab, and a cask of prunes. And this was two years before the landing, some distance south, in Jamestown, Virginia. Fifteen years before the Puritans and their *Mayflower*, who from the sounds of it not only wouldn't have had spices, but would have turned from them, walking fast with heads down.

So Andy stood considering his find of cattails. The gracefully tall, somewhat haremesque leaves surrounded a long, hard stem topped by its unique brown cylinder of fur. It looked designed for squeezing, like a headless and limbless mink. There were only six of them, probably not even a meal. If he uprooted even three, maybe it would fatally injure the colony. But he squatted and worked his hands into the cold black muck and yanked one out. He held a bulb of sorts, not the true pregnancy of an onion, more the swelling of a leek. But the smell. You could imagine tadpoles suckling on this rotten smell alone. Maybe it just indicated the fecund and healthy, like the reek of a clam bed at low tide, both life and death in full bloom. In any case, stooping and examining his minor bulb, Andy realized he couldn't remember what it was you did with cattails in the first place. He'd read about it who knows when or where. It said something about making flour.

Leaving this food source to better scavengers, Andy slogged back to his car. There was something very Robinson Crusoe about it — the joy of finding a wild fruit tree, or a bent nail with which to catch fish — but the notion was more romantic in a book than it was out here calf-deep in a swamp, rediscovering the fecal smell of mud. No doubt hunger helped.

In the sunlight his Mustang's new black shone sleekly obsidian, and it was a shame to slide his muddy, reedy self into it. The car was just three months old and had its own fitting scent. He sat and grabbed the rearview to check his face for mud. He caught his eyes, his big earnest eyes, staring back. And here it was again, like waking up, like *coming to*. More and more these days it seemed that he forgot himself, for longer periods of time, lost in whatever — a book, a drive, hunting cattails, *thinking* — and then he came to. And here he was.

HIS CLOTHES DRIPPING into the tub behind him, Andy towelled off with a grimace, scraping his skin in the way he'd read was good for you, long, cleansing strokes always in a direction away from the heart. A radio voice droned from the living room, an interview, a heavy accent, something depressing about children in Lebanon.

And so what would Laura think of this showering with his clothes on? But how would she know about it unless he told her, and why would he? Unless she were here when he needed a shower or, for that matter, some clean clothes. He wasn't sure when he'd started the habit, but it was indeed a habit, since he no longer really thought about it. It just made sense to stand there under the spray and soap up your clothes while they're still on you. Then take them off, stomp on them like the tub was flat rocks and you were a bare-breasted Zambezi, and then take your regular shower, the clothes at your feet getting kicked around, properly *agitated*, and rinsed, then hung from the rod, to drip. Years ago, placing it just inside so the tub caught the drips, he'd installed a second shower curtain rod, the kind with the inner springs to hold itself up through its own endless tension (the thought of which could still make him mildly queasy).

Showering in his clothes wasn't about saving money. He had a new car that was too fast for him, he had a mortgage-free waterfront house that was too big, and if he bought a round in the bar these days he no longer gave it much thought. Nor was it about saving water, not in Prince Rupert, whose high-school team name was the Rainmakers and where, so one joke went, it rained 366 days a year. Nor was it easier than tossing his clothes into the washer. He didn't know what it was about.

But, to the point, what would Laura think? That her old boy-friend Andy Winslow had matured into a practical, innovative bachelor? Or that Andy Winslow was a kook, at thirty-nine owning eccentricities too ripe for a man his age? When he sees her, he'll resist describing the experiment where he'd stacked dirty dishes in the tub and lathered up with them too.

When he sees her.

Since her letter, since the rumours of her return proved to be true, Andy had not only begun losing sleep, he'd also begun seeing his world in a different way. His house, for instance. What (he found himself asking when he got home from work and parked and looked up) will Laura think of his house? She knew the house, had been in it a few times back when it was his parents' place, but it had been his alone for ten years now. The house centred its half-acre such that neither neighbour could be seen through strategically dense trees. It had two storeys, three bedrooms, was freshly painted a nice bone white, and of course it was medium-bank waterfront with zillion-dollar view. But Laura had seen all this, so the real question was, What will Laura think of him, thirty-nine, still living in his childhood house?

Eighteen years. What will Laura think about him still work-ing at the grain terminal? What will she think of this shrinking town? Of the cruise ship docking here now? What will she think if she hears the wolves at night? What will she think of their mothers' living arrangement? What will she think about the sushi and habanero peppers and acai juice you can buy in Safeway now? What will she think about Safeway's fancy little boxes of smoked salmon, salmon caught here, shipped five hundred miles south to Vancouver to smoke and package, and then shipped back to sell? What will she think about today's dead fish?

Though he tried to keep it to once a day, lately he paused far too often at the bathroom mirror to ask the inevitable of his face: what will Laura think seeing *this*?

HE'D BEEN ASKING that question not just of his bathroom mirror and his Mustang's rearview, but sometimes random windows on the street, hunching to get his full six-feet-four in. Tonight, he and Drew emerged from their Tuesday-night early movie (Johnny Depp really was a good actor, despite his looks) and, ignoring the rain, Andy paused at a shop window long enough to gauge his waistline. It wasn't really a paunch any more. And he had decent shoulders, and an appropriate haircut, and the new beard coming in oddly darker than his hair. He'd never had a beard before, had no clue if he should keep it, and he didn't know who to ask. Drew kept walking. He didn't appear to look back, but with the clairvoyance of best friends he knew what Andy was doing at the window. Not turning around, he said, "Be weird, eh? Laura back here?"

To this understatement Andy said, "I guess." He was grateful Drew had said anything at all. It was the closest his friend would come to saying, I'm on your side, Be careful, or What the hell are you thinking?

Yes, it would be weird with Laura back. How weird, he had no clue. He did know that, in the largest sense, it was really up to him. How seriously he took it. How worked up he got. Not that he'd be able to find the handle for either of those.

As per Tuesday's post-movie routine, Drew turned into the Legion and Andy followed. Two pints, tops. They both started morning shift tomorrow, rise and shine by five. Though with Drew these days, you never knew. Drew was capable of closing down a bar even when faced with a morning shift. Andy didn't want to think his friend had a problem, despite what Pauline had to say, despite her ever more frequent jabs in public. But Drew didn't usually miss work because of it. He generally got himself to the parking lot and in the door and punched in, sleep or no sleep. Though once he did leave his Jeep running, all day. Eight hours later there it was still purring, waiting faithfully, overheating only a little. A year's worth of jokes came from that one, as in, Drew was secretly married to a Qatar oil sheik. As in, Drew was Prince Rupert's gift to global warming, and they'd have him to thank when they were suntanning in March.

Drew aimed himself at a table full of regulars, which was loud already. That was fine, Andy wouldn't have to talk. The pub air felt no drier than the drizzly November night outside, the yeasty pong of spilled beer as familiar as his own armpit. He sat, edged the chair out from the circle a bit, not liking this corner of the bar, where you got the waft of urinal discs each time the door flew open. They'd changed those old-school camphor ones to something smelling like a really strong vanilla, which, now that he thought of it, and as long as you could ignore its raison d'être, wasn't half bad.

HER LETTER HAD been a thing of beauty, five pages long. He read it over and over and then put it away for a few days hoping he would forget it enough to enjoy anew. Because here, after so many years, was her voice again, her letter voice, a voice in which they'd found an intimacy unlike any other, even face to face. This intimacy had surprised them both. Until she left for Toronto they'd never written letters to each other before, there being no need. Then one letter led to another and it became their way of speaking for an entire year.

Andy remembered discovering his own letter-writing voice and what it could do, and they had discussed it, in letters, and agreed that it was good. There was something about being able to edit to clarify, and clarify again, and so speak the deepest truths and find the fiercest intimacy one was capable of, something the speed and lurch of face-to-face encounters often ironically prevented. It let them both talk about love. And her absence. And what it would be like when he finally joined her there in Toronto. It let her describe Toronto after a life in Prince Rupert. It let them both be funny. Then, when the time came, it let her articulate the reasons why Andy should not come after all, should no longer join her in Toronto. In this she took great care and many, many pages, as if by spreading pain's endless angles and edges over so much paper this could help ease it. And in fact it probably did.

In any case her recent letter, the first in a decade and a half, brought the intimacy back. It took only a few sentences:

This feels crazy, this letter, but when I learned you don't have email, and then picked up the phone to call you, I somehow couldn't. It felt too abrupt, or rude, or invasive, and anyway I was nervous, not that I'm not nervous writing this, but it feels really familiar, doesn't it? to be talking to you in a letter?

It was her nervousness that excited him. Made him a kid, made everything uncertain and possible, and it made him horny, right off the top. It was mostly her voice, her letter voice, the magic little leap of *doesn't it,* the assumption, the *knowledge* that he felt what she felt, that not only made him love her again, not only made him love him-and-her again, it made him understand he had never stopped.

This understanding was a ready one. If his love was a monster he'd thought dead and buried, it had been buried alive. Launched by the giant spring under its back, Laura's letter, it popped easily out of its shallow grave, and now the monster was in the room. There it was, in the mirror, tall, pale, pretending not to breathe. (Andy could joke about all this, and not. Because why did it feel like gallows humour?)

It wasn't simple, this matter of undying love. Eighteen years? Andy wasn't stupid about it. Nor was he going to be stupid when she came. Nothing was simple here, nor was it the slightest bit predictable. If love was complicated when you were with each other, it was even more complicated when you weren't. He'd done some thinking on this.

A month after Laura had gone to Toronto, if he were asked if absence made the heart grow fonder, he would have said yes. God, yes. If asked the same question a year later, he'd have given the same painful answer, but with pause. If asked after ten years, Andy would have had to look inside and then say no. After that much time, fondness has absorbed much desperation and has stiffened up. If it can throb at all it throbs a little insanely. In the long run, fondness mutates. And forgetfulness gets into the mix: memories are smoothed over and fattened up. The quick bed of pleasure grows brass ornaments and rose silk sheets; her eyelashes lengthen absurdly when she shyly blinks; her breath after orgasm is the fig-and-pepper breeze drifting in off the desert. There were no fights; she had no freckles on her shoulders. After ten years, and now after eighteen, who knows what it had been like? Who knows what even happened?

And of course her cancer added an unknowable mutation, an oddest spice. In remission, a breast removed, Laura had seemed cheerful enough in the letter.

THEY LEFT THE LEGION after Drew pounded back maybe five pints, and Andy his two. They had a half-mile to walk together before Drew turned uphill and Andy down. It was one of the saddest stretches of town, with a third of the buildings empty. Most didn't even have For Lease signs up, no point to it. A few still had Going Out of Business banners hanging diagonal inside a window, faded and yellowed. Some of the businesses still open on this stretch (Ling The Tailor, Spirit Tattoo's, and The Northern: The Best Hamburger, The Freshest Fish) were damned by their shoddy charm, the very thing tourists stared at but passed by.

What will Laura think. To the best of his knowledge, because her mother loved travelling south to visit her, in eighteen years Laura had been up only twice. Once with her hubby and three-year-old daughter, when PR was still doing okay. Then once alone, a few years later, when PR was coming apart. (Again he'd steered clear, learning after that she'd left word with no fewer than four friends to say hi to him.)

The raindrops got bigger, could penetrate hair to the scalp, so Andy took his ball cap from his pocket and Drew pulled up his hood. He looked funny in that hood. It made his long face longer, made him a horse-faced monk, lending an earnestness to an ironic man. Drew, sincere in nothing but his brooding. He'd been like that even as a kid. They didn't speak for a block, Andy guessing Drew also felt pulverized by the tavern's endless theories and bullshit about the ten miles of dead fish. Despite all the conjecture, nothing concrete had emerged. All that had been added to the radio tape-loop was that, "no matter the cause of this environmental catastrophe, Prince Rupert's commercial fishing, sports fishing, and budding tourism industries could suffer untold damage, and the only thing certain here is that this economically depressed little city on the north coast didn't need this kind of punishment."

In the bar Andy had put feelers out but nobody knew how much it would cost to shore up his property against further erosion, or what might be the best way. A young carpenter, Larry, had no facts to back him up when he said matter-of-factly, "You can go rock barged in, or you can go cement wall, but either way it's a hundred grand."

The rain eased, and now it was only the sounds of their feet. Drew seemed in no hurry, a dullness of stride suggesting boredom behind him and boredom to come. Perhaps out of this same boredom Drew asked a question he knew he'd always get an answer to.

"What you reading these days?"

"Bunch of stuff. Early seventeenth-century Canada." And the Nijinsky biography. And a thing on S.A.D., something he should pass on to Drew, who maybe could use it.

"History?"

"Well, yeah."

"Coureurs de bois in canoes?"

"Not for another hundred years or so. It's still the coast, the first settlement. It's Nova —"

"Well let's go in here then."

The non sequitur took Drew through a restaurant door, the Hickory Pit, and so launched one of his impromptu little adventures, the kind that made Andy shrink inside and want to keep walking. More and more Andy figured Drew did it mostly to bug him. In any event it was the kind of thing Drew did when bored and not sober.

Drew was at the waitress station asking to see the manager. Andy said, "C'mon, I'm not hungry," but Drew ignored him. The manager, Ken Worthington, strode from out of the restaurant's dark recesses, the question on his face turning doubtful when he saw them. He knew them about as well as they knew him, which is to say, their names and thumbnail lives. He was about five years younger and had lived in town maybe a decade. White suv, small kids. Black hair and moustache and physically capable air. He looked like a fireman, but pudgy.

"What can I do for you gentlemen?" he asked, choosing safety in the businesslike.

"I have a convention coming in," Drew announced, not slurring at all, "and I'm planning the itinerary, including dining, and a majority is calling for ribs."

"Well — we have fantastic ribs. As I hope you already know." A manager's smile.

"The thing is, I don't. Your little neon sign, the cursive one —" He hooked his thumb back.

"'Chicken, Ribs, Steaks.' It's what we do."

"And I've never had the ribs myself. If you bring me a sample to try, if I like 'em, there'll be twenty-five, thirty men in here a month from now, eating and drinking up a storm."

Worthington was caught motionless. He stared at Drew, an oddly distant look, wherein one could see cautionary words replaying between his ears.

"Okay now — so it's Drew, right?"

"Right. This is Andy."

Andy waved. "I'm fine. Not hungry myself."

Drew pivoted to face Andy and instruct him. "I'm not 'hungry.' I'm scouting locales."

"Well then, Drew — why not come in some time and order the ribs? They really are good." The manager's smile again but just the mouth this time, no eyes to it at all.

"I figured you'd want me to sample some if it meant lots of business."

"Well, it's one-time business."

"Full house, thirty-five hungry guys, thirty-five international grain workers, ordering appies, beers all night? That's not worth a sample?"

Worthington stared at Drew some more. He eventually nodded, told them to take a table, and turned for the kitchen. Andy thought he betrayed the look of someone who knew bullshit when he heard it and had decided to let himself be duped as a manager, though not as a man.

They sat at the nearest table. The only other patrons were a young couple off in the corner sitting too silent over a coffee. The lone waitress delivered two waters, and since they likely had to wait for Drew's sample, Andy ordered a small poutine. Though even a minor waistline bulge looked exaggerated on a tall, thin man, lately he'd been careful and was pretty happy with the growing paunchlessness.

"Why didn't you get a big one?" asked Drew, which was odd, since he hated poutine. He called it "triple-fat fries." Slouching across from him, Drew seemed as comfortable and distracted as possible for a man-on-a-prank. Glancing about, weighing decor choices, people, the waitress's gait, his penetrating glare focused on anything but himself. It was always a wary look. Because Drew was obviously perceptive, but very capable of misreading what was going on inside, Andy and Pauline had long ago agreed that he was outelligent as opposed to intelligent.

"I don't know. Not that hungry. Sort of watching the weight."

To this Drew said, "You know, she's had a kid and everything."

"Well, sure. I know."

"A kid. She's a different person now."

"Yeah, she probably is." Andy suspected the conversation might stay here, on kids changing your life, which would be fine. Chris leaving, a half-year ago, barely sixteen, had profoundly shaken Drew, and he didn't unburden himself nearly enough. Once at work he'd told Andy that he thought about little else these days and added, looking amazed with himself, that he'd woken up in the middle of the night and cried, and that he was pretty sure he hadn't cried since he was eight or nine years old. Trying to be scientific about it, he also told Andy that when your son, who's your best buddy, shifts from begging to shoot hoops with you to hating your guts, almost overnight and for no apparent reason, "It's a biological imperative, sure, but it's impossible to understand. Exactly like death."

But thoughts of his son didn't kidnap Drew tonight. Looking drunker than he had coming in, he counted on his fingers. "She has a grown-up kid. She had this whole career. She's had *cancer*. She's had this whole life. It's totally different now."

"Well exactly. And I'm no Johnny Depp, so I've got to be buff at least."

Drew looked away shaking his head, but on the verge of smiling.

Andy tapped an incisor. "I'm thinking the gold teeth too. Kohling my eyes."

Here Drew shifted, accepted the inevitable, decided to help. "Okay, seriously? Lose the hair, okay?" He scuffed his knuckles over his cheek.

"My beard? Really?"

"It's not a 'beard.' Remember Yasser Arafat? Remember those individual hairs he had coming out of his face? She won't be impressed."

Laura arrived in exactly a month, after first spending Christmas with her daughter, who was a freshman at university. Amelia, seventeen.

Andy decided to give the beard a few more weeks, see if it filled out any.

Worthington delivered the ribs himself. The waitress — it was one of Helen and Steve Peters' kids — followed behind him bearing Andy's poutine. Worthington set down a plate holding what appeared to be a full rack of spareribs. To one side, a dome of potato salad balanced a sprig of parsley. To another, a finger bowl of hot water floated a lemon wedge.

Drew snorted and held his hands out over the platter, a gesture of helpless complaint.

"I wanted a *rib*. A taste. A sample."

"Our compliments, sir." Worthington brought his heels together and did a slight bow. "We hope you'll choose the Hickory Pit." It was hard to tell if the manager wasn't now duping back.

In any case the ribs were awful. Upon realizing this Drew peered up from the soggy pile, lips smeared with sweet grease. He looked embarrassed and sad for the place, and for his prank, when he mouthed, "These *really* suck." Andy ate his poutine and tried to help with the ribs, which swam in far too much sauce and were chewy to boot, and maybe even a bit off, though steeped in so much vinegar it was hard to tell. They each ordered a pint to wash things down, and also to drop some money in this teetering place, which was empty when they'd arrived and still empty when they left, and the feeling upon leaving after eating free food was that they'd lifted change out of a beggar's hat.

NEXT DAY, ANDY got home from work at three and deliberately showered without his clothes on, though they were caked and beige with grain dust. It was odd at first how much the spray stung. He felt like he was an apple with no peel. Also he hadn't slept well again.

There was enough time before ordering his Wednesday pizza to settle in his easy chair beside the living-room window and finish the Nijinsky biography. It was more of a skim really. Laura's career had led him to this subject and he wanted to bone up, as it were. He'd chosen this chair half hoping he'd drift into a nap, but though the writing was bad the subject was so quirky he found himself flipping pages hunting the nuggets. What a story, what a life. Nijinsky, irrefutable creative genius, the social graces of a turnip farmer. Confused sexuality, an impresario sugar daddy, the fall of Czarist Russia, and, finally, insane asylums. Nijinsky's thighs were so thick and he could leap so high that he was thought superhuman. Audiences swore that he actually transformed into his various characters. He took to leaving the stage with a leap, disappearing into the wings at the height of his jump so that no one saw him come down, leaving the impression that he didn't. Barely able to make himself understood with words, he found sanctuary in a haughty muteness. His nickname was God of the Dance. Within a year of the height of his fame he'd be catatonic, masturbating in public and shouting in German, a language he didn't know. Andy recalled, in *Lolita*, Nabokov referring to Nijinsky as having giant thighs and too many feathers.

Andy closed his book and swivelled his chair to note the sunset breaking through and a wind coming up. In the outer harbour a scatter of fish boats punched home through some chop. (Were they out fishing already? Or hunting the tide line for more damage?) Over on Ridley Island, from the clutch of houses in Dodge Cove the wood-fire smoke rose to clear the wall of trees, then blew horizontal. But there on the horizon was some orange, some rare sunset.

It was Wednesday, tonight his weekly visit at his mother's, so he put on his one pair of dress pants, black. He had two white dress shirts, but with those pants he'd look like a waiter. The red golf shirt made him look like a waiter from some place like last night's Hickory Pit, while the dark blue golf shirt made him look like a bruise. He hated his closet. It felt not just sparse but seedy. Again there was the "what would Laura think" question, but his closet's crummy contents also asked why his social life had become so meagre. He had lots of work clothes — jeans, T-shirts, sweatshirts — and these had also become his everyday clothes. The "dress" clothes were basically old concoctions geared to satisfy his mother and the three ladies she lived with. But wardrobe demands were suddenly pressing. Not just Laura. First was next week's banquet with the Chinese Wheat People, which is what people had taken to calling them.

A shopping spree was in order, and to someplace other than Work Wearhouse. Andy felt a bit shaky imagining himself fingering fabrics and lapels. The quest was for "casual elegance" probably, but it was possible to buy something ten years out of style. On top of this was a new notion that at thirty-nine he was maybe no longer socially *allowed* to wear certain fashions, for instance whatever kind of strategic grubbiness the twenty-year-olds were wearing these days.

Andy wondered how weird it would be, and how much torture would be forthcoming from Drew, if he were to borrow Pauline to take as a guide on his shopping trip. Probably not weird at all, Andy's hopelessness with clothes being no secret. Didn't own an ironing board, smiled incomprehension at any talk of twill or raw silk. Compared to him, even Drew was a metrosexual. He'd understand.

Drew hadn't visited him up on the annex this morning, nor was he in the lunchroom, and when Andy checked the duty board he saw Drew hadn't made it in to work. He wondered if maybe he'd gone home last night and washed down those ribs with a few more. It was a problem. It actually was.

He wouldn't call over there just yet. If Drew was hungover it meant Pauline was icy and neither one a joy to talk to. Not even Andy proposing a guided shopping spree — Pauline as Sherpa for his handicapped attempt at the summit of middle-aged fashion — would raise a smile in that house.

DESPITE THE RAIN, Andy chose to walk the mile across town to his mother's. He strode quickly, intending violence to the pizza he'd just wolfed. Feeling his thighs clench with each stride he thought of Nijinsky's withering last years. To his left, though he couldn't see it, was Mount Hays, its top dusted with November snow. To his right, beyond the houses and streetlights, the dark harbour. On the breeze he could smell the ebbing tide mixed, he thought, with those fish. From several streets over, some music boomed faintly, you could tell it was all muddy on cheap speakers, and it took Andy a moment to recognize it as opera and that, since this wasn't what you'd crank at a party, something must be out of control, some loner on a binge.

On 2nd Street he passed Drew's father's pretentious place, with its fake portico supported by fake half-pillars, bought in a fit of self-congratulation during the real estate spike a decade ago. Andy never did like the similarity he shared with Mr. Madden, that of a single man occupying an entire house. In Mr. Madden's case, a near-mansion. Where next week's dinner — "banquet," Mr. Madden's word — was taking place.

Andy realized that this dinner might have been where Drew got his "out-of-town convention" last night during the rib charade. There would be maybe thirty people coming, with the mayors of Prince Rupert and Kitimat, and assorted business leaders, including the director of the grain terminal, so stratospheric a boss that Andy had never met him. In other words, all the town mucky-mucks, and all for the purpose of wooing the Chinese Wheat People. Nobody seemed to know who they were. They were representatives of government or of free enterprise. They were in town to scout, or negotiate, or finalize millions, billions, or trillions worth of grain and possibly even coal trade. The Chinese Wheat People had arrived last week and were lodged in modest rooms at The Crest. Adding to the mystery, erasing some rumours while creating others, the Chinese Wheat People turned out to be two women. (Drew had said of this, "How Soviet of them." He predicted that one would be carrying "an old carbine" and the other a hoe, and both would have shirt sleeves rolled up to reveal "state biceps.") Mr. Madden, who went with others on the Chamber of Commerce to greet them at the airport, claimed that these two women looked no more than twenty years old. He'd been announcing this outrageous fact non-stop, always followed innocently by, "But, you know, you can't really tell."

Mr. Madden had invited Andy via Drew, who said, "He says you have to come."

"Why?"

"They need a token worker. Communists expect that."

"You're a worker."

"No, I'm not." This meant that he was the host's son and didn't count. It also meant, without him saying it, that his father was still getting Drew, as much as he was able, to attend advantageous events in the hope that he would someday choose something other than the grain terminal.

"He wants me to come?" Andy asked. Though he knew. And over the past weeks, it seemed almost subconsciously, he'd picked up books on both the historical and the current Great Leap Forward, as well as one on Cantonese cuisine. It had glossy colour plates, and he'd been surprised by how many dishes looked like what you'd get at several of the Chinese joints in Prince Rupert.

In any case, he knew why he was being invited.

Especially at work, Andy Winslow was regarded as a polymath. He was enough of a polymath to know he wasn't one. More exactly, he was a reader and a repository of information.

At work he had become used to intercom calls whose only purpose was a question such as, "There's five kinds of Pacific salmon, right? And dog's another word for chum?" or "*How* much did they pay Russia for Alaska?" or "Pakistan doesn't have nukes, do they?" Maybe his answers won an argument for someone, or oiled a stuck conversation. Sometimes he'd field a question he took more pride in, for instance from a recently hired supervisor, "On those old belts, how long before a fray is a break?" A few years back, on graveyard shift, there'd been a game when packs of guys called and tested him. He heard money had changed hands.

In any case, twenty years ago, sitting his first-ever shift, alone in the tin shack atop eight massive cylindrical bins, Andy's single responsibility was to listen for the phone to ring, then punch several buttons in the right sequence, which tripped one conveyor belt over to another, flax to canola, barley to one-red-thirteen. This might happen four times over the eight hours, sometimes never. With so much downtime, he could listen to the radio, pace, or go crazy. Officially, on downtime everyone was supposed to sweep grain dust, which was ultra-flammable and everywhere. But grain dust was so fine that it was like a layer of vaguely heavy air, it merely floated up to hang awhile when a broom moved near it, and foremen seemed content if you kept your push broom propped on a wall, looking recently used.

Or he could read. Andy had always read, but he started to *read*. It ate up the time, and then it became more than that. Here he was getting paid top wage — the union was strong in those days — to just sit there. All that wasted time left him feeling not only restless, but hollow. Added up, all those empty hours were a wasted life. Magazines and crossword puzzles didn't assuage the guilt or fill the void, but books did. And so, not many weeks into his long career as casual labour in the Prince Rupert Grain Terminal, Andy decided he was getting paid to learn.

At first he didn't like getting caught reading. For some odd reason it had to do with being tall. Tall men didn't read, tall men with a book looked somehow desperate. Or hunched, or humbled, or stooped. You thought of Ichabod Crane clutching his book and striding awkwardly through a field. Six-feet-even would have been fine.

But Andy got over that and the librarians came to know him as the guy who twice weekly clomped in in workboots, late for afternoon shift and hunting books. His selections, odd for a man in this town, became somewhat known — first the Jane Austen binge, then Dickens, then the Russians, and then on into some contemporaries. Fiction fell off, and next the librarians could track his forays into geography, and biology, and psychology (clinical, pseudo, and New Age, in turn). Travel books Andy sprinkled in like vacations. He came to love extreme travel, he a vicarious voyeur of a distant culture's freakish ways.

Then the librarians stopped seeing him. The break was clean (and so abrupt that he heard of their concern for his health) and marked when, mere months after they'd begun dating, Andy convinced Regional College English instructor Rachel Hedley to give him a copy of her inter-university library card, a privilege he maintained, along with her friendship, to this day.

Lately, sitting in his hard-backed wooden chair, perched two hundred feet up, forested mountains behind him and an ocean in front, it was history that grabbed him most. History seemed an extension of extreme travel. He'd read and reread O'Hanlon stumbling in the Amazon, Matthiessen aware in the Himalayas, Goering and Coffey paddling the Ganges — there were dozens of gems. But there was no travel writing so extreme as the old stuff, those explorers who stepped on an unknown beach either to take an arrow in the neck or taste the raw, dripping chunk of some creature held out by a sincerely proud elder. Two a.m. on a winter night, rain thrumming the tin shack, nothing was more savoury than the righteous mutiny, the speared turquoise fish, the tumble with a bare-breasted maiden, all under the dangerously coded approval of villagers who thought in shapes and colours their invaders could only guess at.

History was almost by definition badly written, but even a bare-bones narrative his imagination could fill in. He would read it was three hundred rifles against three thousand Zulu spears, feel the bureaucracy in this statement and try to attach flesh and blood to both rifles and spears, and know that some on both sides were insanely brave and others cowardly and others uncertain dreamers, like him. He knew what they dreamed about — women, home, land — and imagined what woman, what piece of land. He'd Google a picture of copra. He'd investigate food and imagine the smells, the tastes, and decide that hyena tasted like a cross between cat and dog, plus the sourness of a scavenger. He would read about tropical heat and imagine the weight and feel of cloth on the skin. Hearing wind on the tin, seeing that white ice had sprung an instant pattern on the glass, he would imagine what life was like when you were always shirtless and eagerly perspiring.

Up there on the annex, where he'd smuggled a good floor lamp so he could shut off the loud overhead fluorescence, he had all-night business with the histories of Asia, and of course the Hellenistic era, and the Roman, and Spanish Latin American, and Danish, and the weirdly opaque Finnish. He wouldn't so much choose a country as he would find himself led off by a Portuguese explorer or travel the Silk Route and find himself somewhere new. He had a brief and intense time in Australia, turning to it not because of England's entertaining dump of misfits but rather because he read that the Aborigines had just been genetically traced to a region — a village, actually — in India. Prehistory was an almost guilty pleasure, since so much came off like hopeful declarations from the murk. You couldn't help but love it that a legitimate branch of Neanderthal studies had proposed partly from jaw structure that, since speech looked unlikely, they may well have communed with a crude telepathy, using an enlarged peneal under that famous big brow of theirs.

More recently, meandering his way closer to home, he turned to England and France and, only now, Canada. He read the main stuff (some of it vaguely familiar from high school) and then a coast-to-coast roll of greatest historical hits, based not on chronology but more on regional spectacle, moving from the Newfoundland Beothuks to the Halifax Explosion, to Confederation in P.E.I., to Wolfe and Montcalm duking it out in Quebec, to the War of 1812 (really just an Ontario thing but much touted in these anti-American days), to Louis Riel, to the tunnels of Moose Jaw, to various Hudson's Bay Company shenanigans, to way out west and Sir Alexander Mackenzie (who on the race overland beat by several years the more celebrated and secretly homosexual Lewis and Clark), to the Last Spike, the spate of gold rushes, and an island lighthouse not far from here that was shelled by a sub in the Second World War.

In any case Andy's work was reading, and reading was his work. Up in the shack he'd bolted a bookshelf into the tin, permanent and in full view of foremen. His workbag often sagged heavy with books. Only new guys might joke about him. To the rest he was just Andy Winslow, which meant books, just like Ralph Palmateer meant seven kids, Larry Simon meant vintage cars, and Patti in accounting meant a prosthetic right leg no one had any clue about.

Still, to be as regular a guy as possible, Andy had had to watch himself. Being asked a question and knowing the answer was one thing. Being the butt of a let's-test-Winslow joke was okay too. But socially there was a fine line between being their pet polymath and a shunned know-it-all, and the only way to avoid being the latter was to know when to put a cork in it. For instance, if the boys were onto politics, if they were huddled outside in a circle and talk turned to, *Why the fuck doesn't Quebec just separate and au revoir, assholes?* he had to learn that, even though now was *precisely* the time to mention various acts signed in 1756 that guaranteed the French certain rights, it was also very much not the time. Given the mood, given that none of them remembered more than ten words of high-school French, given that they were standing outside in pitch-black drizzle at 2:30 a.m., 213 feet in the air on a silo top with no safety rail, gazing way, way east, bitter with taxes, Ottawa, and layoffs — it was clear that the purpose here was camaraderie. Not knowledge, not truth. The last thing the boys wanted was some know-it-all setting them straight. Standing in a ring of guys, hunched slightly to be more their height, Andy had quickly learned not to correct someone who'd just put out there that all sharks must keep swimming or die, or that more guys had died in Iraq than in Vietnam, or that Greenland was owned by Iceland. He learned that you don't correct a machinist who's just said that copper is the best conductor of electricity (actually it's silver, but expensive to use). He knew you don't inform parents about parenting (especially as to immunization, circumcision, or breastfeeding). Same with race, health food, the biology of addiction, or — especially — you never tell a guy anything about his car.

The idea here was to get through a shift and maybe even have an okay time, and Andy understood that. The goal wasn't truth, it was wit, wit being the more important of the two and more *true*, in fact, than truth. Wit was here and now, vital and provable — the evidence was the laughter — while truth was none of those things. Especially when it was just more bad news. What was more sustaining, wit or truth, to a circle of guys standing in the cold, wondering when layoffs were coming, and would head office wait till after Christmas this year?

It was easy for Andy to keep a cork in it. He wasn't proud of his knowledge. He knew that most was useless and a little was a dangerous thing. He also knew that, since he never learned a subject to its cutting edge, he was an expert in nothing. Except, maybe, the physical act of reading. Which he did to get through a shift. Which he did — he knew Laura would inform him before too long — to escape.

In any case Andy knew he'd been invited to Drew's father's banquet for the Chinese Wheat Women not to be a token worker but because he knew lots of stuff and could add to any conversation, if asked. Actually he had questions of his own for them. First, their take on the rehabilitation of Tibet. Then he wanted to hear whether, with all this new wealth in their present Great Leap Forward, they thought the Dancing Monkey might make a comeback.

ANDY CAME TO at his mother's door, catching himself peering in the top of the door's three teardrop-shaped windows. He could not remember walking the last five or six blocks.

He paused before knocking. There were the four of them at the game table, intent on what looked like Sorry. There was Mrs. Schultz, Laura's mom, holding a game card close to her face, reading it with her one eye, still wearing the ugly flesh-coloured patch stuck on with adhesive. The three other women waited while she slowly mouthed the words, then just as slowly — passive-aggressively it looked like to Andy — moved her piece on the board.

He never knew whether to knock or ring the bell, wondering if it might affect how much they were startled. That sudden bustle and tizzy, four white-haired seniors in too much dither because someone was at their door. And it wasn't like they didn't know who, Wednesday being Andy's night. They'd probably been talking about him for the last hour, everything from socks to haircut, and Andy would be their focus for as long as he stayed. There would be no talk of Laura's coming, though. Neither his mother nor Laura's cared for the subject. One knew he was too good for her and the other knew he wasn't.

He rang the bell and watched three ladies check hair and scrape chairs. Only his mother kept her dither hidden. She sat calmly. Here was her dutiful son. She looked proud, if not smug. She lifted what looked to be an empty teacup and, regal, not glancing up, she appeared to ask the air that her cup be filled. She was ignored.

Sprightly Doris ran on tiptoes to open the door for him.

"Oh, look who it is," she exclaimed to the room.

"Who is it?" asked Mrs. Schultz, sincerely forgetful.

"Is that you, Andy?" asked Rita, still in her chair but trying painfully to turn all the way around.

"Hello, dear," said his mother, not looking at him.

Hanging his coat, Andy made his usual pre-emptive excuses for not staying long. He pulled up a chair to join in the game. The house smelled of onions, plus something worse, something turned. But not a dirty dish or misplaced pencil could be seen. On the counter the teapot in its cozy had been placed at perfect right angles to the cupboard. Holding nothing, the fridge door magnets — apple, orange, peach, and pineapple — were lined up on a nifty diagonal.

"The McGills," said his mother, "phoned me and said the erosion was actually very noticeable. That actually it looked to them that you'd lost quite a *bit* of yard." A faint aggression to her cheer suggested it had been somehow his fault, some failure of diligence to protect the family homestead. But surely he was imagining this.

"Well, maybe. Maybe ten feet, like I said. But just in one corner." When first telling her, to protect her he'd deliberately low-balled his description of the damage.

"Well, that can't be good. Surely it can be fixed?"

"I don't think we'll get the land back, but I'm looking into ways of not losing any more. You know, rocks barged in, or a cement wall."

"That'll be expensive, dear."

"I'm looking into it."

Rita tossed in, he thought for his benefit, "That was really quite a storm."

"It sure was," he agreed. The thing is, it hadn't been that big a storm at all and this was the worrisome part, but not something to bring up at the moment.

"Any more news?" Andy nodded at the TV, an immense flat screen over in the corner. It was always on. Tonight, two talking heads, pictures of what might be Afghanistan in the background, the sound turned off.

"Nothing yet," said Rita. She had the remote at the ready beside her ashtray. "They've ruled out a chemical spill. They're talking about a 'dead zone.' Something about oxygen."

"It's so sad," offered Doris. "Those south winds are just…" She let it trail off, looking unsure what came next.

"Are you feeling all right, dear?" his mother asked. Andy knew she'd been staring.

"I'm fine. I just need some —"

"You look awful. Are you eating?"

"Is this the oil spill again?" asked Mrs. Schultz.

"Marie, there was no oil spill," said Rita, a little harshly, perhaps repeating herself. "It's the mystery of the dead fish."

Doris said to Andy, "There were some very, very good pictures of the bears near Port Edward coming down and scooping fish up!"

"Teddy bears' picnic," said Rita. "You've played Sorry before, Andy, isn't that right?"

"A couple times now."

"Then you know what happens if you kill *me*."

Of his mother's three housemates, Andy liked Rita best. She behaved most like a friend, like a contemporary. She could relax, meet his eye, and actually be funny. It was sad how fat she was, and worrisome that she smoked as much as she did. Laura's mother he liked the least, first because Mrs. Schultz was a hard piece of work and second because she'd never liked him either. Marie Schultz was the reason Sorry had replaced bridge as the house game — a shift they would never recover from, since bridge was why the foursome had moved in together in the first place. It'd been about a year now since she lost the short-term capacity for bidding and trump and partner's signals. Then there was the habitually speedy Doris, who tried to please everyone and only say the right thing. Andy suspected that the real Doris, if one existed, had been locked away inside for sixty years or more and no one had a clue what she was really like. As for his mother, Andy sometimes wondered how much he'd like her if he wasn't forced to love her. He tended to think not much. It was hard to get through that stilted elegance.

"I'll sit out the first one," his mother announced. "Andy really needs something to eat. The winner can sit out the next. Unless it's Andy."

Andy explained that he was full, he just needed to catch up on some sleep, but his mother ignored him. He didn't like the look of that macaroni salad she was dishing out. He yawned then, some delayed proof of his poor sleep, and both Doris and then Mrs. Schultz yawned in response. Something in this made him suddenly antsy, desperate to be away from this place.

The Sorry board allowed only four players, so his mother's sacrifice was necessary, the shared attitude being that Andy had come over to play Sorry and could hardly wait. That he might just want to sit and talk was unheard of. This was a house of games. The "puzzle table" over in the corner held its ongoing jigsaw, with a lone chair in front of it, where one might choose to spend a quiet half-hour. On TV, *Wheel of Fortune* and *Jeopardy* were watched as a group, as was *Who Wants to Be a Millionaire*, until it changed hosts.

"What shift are you on?" his mother asked musically, smiling. While not playing, she would officially initiate conversation. She knew full well what shift he was on.

"Days." He had to stop himself from standing. Also, he'd figured out his restlessness. Leaving wouldn't help, he'd be restless anywhere. Leaving wouldn't make Laura come sooner.

"And what are you reading, dear?"

Andy didn't have the energy to get into the Canadian history. Plus it was something someone might know about and a discussion might ensue. So he mentioned the Nijinsky biography. He told them what a colourful mess the man was.

And after the briefest pause, his mother offered, "All are not merry who dance lightly."

Her proverbs, maxims, chestnuts. Sometimes he suspected her of having one ready for him every week, but that just couldn't be, because she typically had one at hand for any topic, as she did today. They were irritating, not because they were appropriate, or wise, as any saying that has stood the test of time tends to be. Her proverb, a month ago, to describe Drew's latest scrape with the authorities at work—"Mettle is dangerous in a blind horse"— had felt like a new glimpse of his lifelong friend's brand of stubbornness. It was her delivery that was irritating. Or that she said them at all.

"Well, he more or less invented modern dance," Andy offered.

"Nonsense," said Mrs. Schultz, tapping her piece along the board, not looking at Andy. "Modern was 'invented' by Isadora Duncan."

Amazing how Alzheimer's let a person retain arcane facts, even let them mock an iffy use of the word "invented," and yet not remember a best friend's name. Though, having been one of Prince Rupert's most notorious dance mothers, urging Laura's career on its way, Mrs. Schultz had soaked up lots about dance, especially modern.

"Ahh," Andy said, nodding as if corrected. In the book, Isadora Duncan had watched Nijinsky dance and it changed her. In fact she approached him right after the performance to insist that they make a baby together. Andy didn't mind letting Mrs. Schultz's incorrect fact stand, though he didn't like being accused of "nonsense." It was getting harder to sit still.

Rita won the first game. She laboured out of her chair to the kitchen to make tea. Andy's mother took her place and the second game started.

Mrs. Schultz asked, "What?" three times running when it was her turn and Doris nudged her. Twice she was told that the game was Sorry, and the second time she looked down her nose with the one eye, snorted, and said haughtily, "We should be playing bridge."

Andy watched for the other women's reactions. No one moved or spoke. Laura's mother looked less sad than angry. She, whose fault it was that bridge had ceased, had just berated them for not playing bridge. Was she claiming she was still able? Or had she forgotten her failing state and was giving them hell for what she saw to be their whim? Or was she in effect apologizing, and giving *life* hell for doing this to them?

He didn't like how he felt about her. But was it so unnatural to feel vindicated when life humbled someone as nasty as Mrs. Schultz? Someone whose gaze still fell on him like a sneer, someone who refused to accept that he had been loved by her daughter? You didn't want anyone to suffer, but he admitted ambivalence at seeing that arrogant stance of hers being contradicted by the growing hunch, by the fester of liver spots climbing her forearms. And there was the pink eye patch which, because it reflected absolutely no light, looked like a neutral hole into a brainless head.

Mrs. Schultz had almost been his mother-in-law. Resistance to the image lurched through his body, it was actually physical. According to Darwin, and probably also Freud, it was natural for him to want to crush her.

"Well, I have a feeling," Andy said, "that you're all playing Sorry for *my* stupid sake."

He stretched, leaned back, and smiled at his mother, lifting his eyebrows. Affirming he had done well to say what he'd said, she nodded regally, a queenly dip of the head, with soft-closing eyes. She often acted as if this were salon culture in Rosedale, or old Budapest. What had she said to news of Laura's marriage coming apart? "Marry in haste, repent at leisure." Drew found her funny. Andy found it depressing being made to wonder, about his own mother, whether her elegance was other than sane.

He moved his piece and landed on his mother's; she pretended it angered her. Doris and Rita laughed at the naughty son. Andy did generally enjoy himself here in this house. Despite the several hurdles — the incandescently boring talk, his mother's elaborate display, and now the disintegration of Mrs. Schultz — despite these things these four old women had found a kind of oasis of good humour. Maybe he simply enjoyed being fawned over, being treated like a sixteen-year-old. Maybe he liked witnessing again that his mother was safe, provided for. But he also liked being seduced by the ladies' lighthearted mood. Forced or not, a habit of their generation or not, these four creaky souls knew to keep things light. Even with the TV always on, their house seemed a refuge from the outer dark: the suicide-bomber newspapers, morose monosyllabic friends slumped in a dead town, the smothering blanket of endless rain, even the sun dragging its light away for the winter.

The women had come up with the idea eight years ago. Mrs. Schultz had been the chiding force. Andy remembered her asking them, loud and accented enough to sound angry, "Giff me one reason why not." With real estate crashing, four bridge partners bought a four-bedroom house. They drew up a constitution. Anyone could sell her quarter-share, as could their family if she died. They each cooked one house supper a week, Mondays was leftover night, Saturday they ordered in, Friday night was Go Your Own Way. When needed, they voted on things. If, for instance, Doris spent ten days in Calgary visiting her son, did she still owe her share of the monthly food bill? (The vote was yes.) When Rita was in her wheelchair for that half-year and couldn't cook, clean, or grocery shop and they had to shoulder her burden, should she in some way be penalized? (The vote was no.) Andy found it remarkable that old ladies, as a species famous for crankiness over pennies, could overcome complications like these. There'd been small feuds and pout-fests and one threat to leave, but by and large the group affirmation was that most things in life are petty. They made level-headedness and fair play a point of pride.

But you could see that their dam was going to burst. Years had added complications that no amount of fair play would solve and no one could brush off as petty. The house contained a diabetic, two iffy hearts, one hearing aid, a cane, various skin lesions, and at least one operation Andy wasn't privy to. Two no longer drove. Tonight, the smell of old cooked onions and faint garbage reminded him that it never used to smell in here at all, except maybe of too much lilac.

But Mrs. Schultz was the main crack in the dam. The other ladies didn't have the energy for her next stage. Two weeks ago she had been gone all afternoon and was found walking several blocks past the grocery store, unclear where she was. The Alzheimer's was accelerating and her leaps of anger weren't helping her case. Democracy was about to bring down the gavel. Fair play was about to pounce.

Her mother was one reason why Laura was coming back. As Laura described it in her most recent letter, it would be a case of the sick looking after the sicker.

PINCHING THROUGH HIS beard in the mirror, yawning, Andy came to when he saw his own eyes. The water was running hot and he had a mound of shaving cream in his hand.

Apparently he had decided to shave. He was getting tired of looking at his beard and applying to it the question, in that two-pronged voice of hope and fear, "What will Laura see?"

Beard or no beard it was going to be bad. Andy knew the visual jolt of running into an old friend after twenty years. So really the question was, What will Laura see in this face that's shocking and repugnant? What will look like the *opposite* of sex? Andy smiled his gentlest, calmest smile, and held it. Lots was unchanged from two decades ago. That skin was okay. The crow's feet suggested he'd been having a decent time and not sitting stewing in it. His hair was good too —hairline maybe only a half-inch back and the grey scattered, not even salt and pepper. If anything the grey made his hair look light brown instead of brown. He was still handsome enough. A neutral good looks. He knew women didn't generally look at him with hunger, except maybe in certain moods, maybe when blind with ovulation's most brute flux, for instance. The younger women he dealt with these days, the fake-nail bank tellers and push-up bra waitresses, might still call him "cute for his age." Maybe they noticed his nice shoulders, his smile. His hands were maybe too delicate for some, as they looked more suited to a deft flipping of pages than swinging a pipe wrench at a stuck lug nut.

Trying to stay objective, if he tilted his face under the light he could see the puckish angularity of a male model. Or at least a musician. There was maybe a confused relationship between nose and lips, spacing not quite right. Maybe his forehead was a bit flat. But people wouldn't think, There goes a guy with a *something*. If people ever cared to argue about his imperfections they probably wouldn't agree. He was probably handsome enough for the assumption to be that, as a longtime single man, he had navigated his way through a few women. Which was almost the case.

Anyway, his skin was too pale for these dark whiskers. Drew was right, they were too far apart and patchy. If a woman sharing the same pillow turned her face to his and looked closely she'd see too much skin.

Tonight at his mother's cemented it. First, Laura's mother stared hard at him and wouldn't stop. Finally she announced, quite savagely, *"You don't have a beard."* He knew she probably meant that she didn't remember him having a beard, and wasn't in fact declaring his beard too pathetic to be *called* a beard, but it bugged him regardless. The last straw was his mother smiling benignly at this and adding, with that limp closing of eyes, "It's not the beard that makes the philosopher."

He brought his hand up and lathered a cheek.

He'd leave long sideburns, down to the level of his mouth. He'd seen them on younger guys recently, a hip, almost '50s look except that your haircut stayed short and normal. He could always hack them off before she saw them.

He lathered up his face, leaned in close, and here were his eyes again. They appear to hold all of your knowledge, all of your *self*, but of course they're empty. They're fluid and lens. It's hard to really see your own eyes. His were an odd colour, he'd been told. A pale green, with yellow-orange near the pupil. One drunk woman had told him this yellow made his eyes look like a sad sunset. Another slightly drunk woman had told him his eyes were soulful. So apparently he had the good eyes. One defect was that they might be too big. Coming off graveyard shift they were prone to bugging out.

Laura herself had said something about his eyes. It wasn't exactly flattering, but he'd liked it well enough. She said that his eyes, when they stared at you, made you realize not only that eyes are connected directly to the brain but that eyes *are* the brain, exposed. In the hundred times he picked over her comment, he decided she meant that he looked less like Gollum than he did like a bright fellow capable of some insight.

Andy razored the foam off his face, his "beard" coming with it. He rinsed with warm water, snitched some unfoamed hairs off a spot he'd missed, and then scraped his face with a towel, up, away from the heart. He didn't stop and pose and check out his new look. Change was always awful at first, so why not skip that part.

THE DAYS WERE short and getting shorter, dark when he ate breakfast and dark as he made dinner. This morning he had already been at work for two hours and was on his third coffee when he dragged a chair from his annex shack and leaned it against the corrugated tin wall to watch the sun rise pink from behind Mount Hays in a surround of saucer-shaped clouds. Winter sunrises were rare, but this year not. He blew on the top of his coffee. He was wearing only a hoodie and felt fine, it felt like spring, though the air was cold on his freshly naked cheeks and chin. This time of year it should rain constantly and be colder—some kind of sunny-days record for November had already been set. You could hardly keep up with the weather setting records. A few months back, in Tim Hortons, a fan of global warming had argued earnestly that Prince Rupert Harbour would be decent waterskiing if the water warmed up five degrees. He was talking about water so cold that oysters stopped surviving in it about four hundred miles south.

Laura, remember how you grew up hundreds of miles not just from cities but from oysters?

How many mornings had he sat right here, taking in this view? Over the years he'd worked at new ways to see it, reminding himself that the vista was beautiful. Truly it was. Mountains, ocean. If he raised his gaze he could block out the parking lot and road that, around the corner of Mount Hays, became the

Highway of Tears. If he edged to the left and squatted, he couldn't see the coal port. Framed by this bit of avoidance, everything he could see was natural, completely not man-made, not a wire or building or road. No clear-cut mountains farther inland, or beyond no oil sands, or farther still no endless uniform wastes of corporate farms, where the grain under his feet came from. With his view, no country with its primal spirit trampled, coast to coast.

Another bonus to work: up here he could pretend it was pristine. He could still bring himself to love the place, even if it felt like the love one has for one's own arms, or feet.

Final paragraphs in her letter said:

> *I don't know if it was the big bad city that made me sick, but I do know that if I don't leave it I won't survive. I need a smaller place, like a nest or a cave, to heal. I need something simple. Not that any place is simple. But where you are there aren't many streets to choose from, on a walk. Sometimes, choice is stress. I just need to get away from here and go home. I remember how homesick I was, for years. Maybe I should have listened to that, because maybe it helped make my body sick. Moods do work on the body, over time. You were part of my homesickness. It was hard to separate you from the place. I never really knew exactly what I was missing.*
>
> *Anyway, you were brave to stay. I didn't always think that way. But you didn't follow everyone out. I remember it felt exciting and dangerous to leave. But back then it also felt dangerous — more dangerous — to stay.*

Where had he ever been besides here? Hawaii with Drew when they turned twenty-one. Trips to Calgary and Edmonton, and that one-week fiasco at UBC. If Laura asked, Where else? he

might or he might not tell her about the time, about five years
after she'd left town, when he flew down to see her perform in
Vancouver, where her small Toronto company was touring. He
remembered telling himself that the purpose of the trip was
mainly to see the new museum and a Canucks game, and hike
the Grouse Grind, all of which he did. But really there was only
one purpose. He bought the most expensive ticket but when in
the smallish hall he found himself too close to the stage he took
an empty seat at the back. She'd probably be blinded by the lights
but he couldn't risk it. The program said she'd choreographed
four of the eight pieces; she would appear in five of them. After
sitting an unbearable time, reading every word in the program,
the lights began to fall and he squirmed in his seat and, amazingly, despite himself, *giggled*, and then there she was, Laura
Schultz, hardly herself in the glare and colours and exaggerated
poses. In one piece she wore a bowler hat and a sort of tux with
tails, and there was lots of kneeling, shuffling, and rolling on the
floor. Her hair was butch and her hips noticeably wider—good
God, yes, she'd had a baby. Who was now three and a half years
old, a girl. But, though he had no right, her body, the way she
moved it, still thrilled him somewhere deep. Watching her five
pieces, awash with memories of that arm, those fingers, that
barely parted mouth betraying rapid breathing, his nether zone
was wildly abuzz. The way she thrust that cane while also holding
it back, coy in a way that was impossible to see unless you knew
her. As he knew how she smelled, right now. And missed that
smell as much as he missed anything else about her. Watching
her, the performance far, far too quickly at its end, he felt like
laughing and crying both—whatever the word might be that
splits those two right down the middle, or adds them both up.

Comedy

septembre 1606

SAMUEL SETS OFF to seek a patch of land for next year's garden plot, a clearing both deep with earth and well favoured by the sun. He deems it an unlikely find. He knows his search is in part fuelled by jealousy over Marc Lescarbot's plot, adjudged the best in the settlement. He also still hunts *annedda*, whose needles may prove thicker than he remembered them to be. He thinks now that he only saw them dried. In any case all are reasons to walk. Lately, he finds men's voices grating. Even their laughter, for it sounds like dogs' harsh agreement over some foul thing.

He prefers this rocky beach, walking the tide line, a rush of waves in his left ear and the calls of hidden birds in his right.

He will walk this shore some distance before plunging up into the forest to nearby treeless knolls — they will let him get his head high and so perhaps see a place his fellows have missed. This wind has mood and blows his hair off his collar. He is happy to be walking near water, which he can feel in his chest as a challenge, even this small turbulence of the bay, its grey toss almost a prideful dare. He feels a pang of loss for the Northern Sea itself, lying just outside that channel, and declares to himself that it is the ocean he loves the most. Its attitude is unlike more southern waters, their azure and feminine ease. The North Atlantic is heartless and wants to seduce no one. It does not care, and shocks all naive appetite for the sea. It is, simply, dangerous, and as such the test of a man. It sends men such as Marc Lescarbot to their cabins to compose fantastical verse.

Samuel decides to turn back because the wooden shoes Lucien the carpenter fashioned for him are raising a second blister — the first already grew to its anger's peak and burst. (The other nobles reject these shoes as common, but perhaps they refer to this common pain!) But in the mud they are so superior to leather. He will present his shoes to the carpenter and ask him to go in again with his chisel and make more space for that smallest toe. He must also think to ask Lucien if he can train one or two men in the simpler art of coffins. He desires to alarm no one, but it is a truth: if the coffin-makers die, any further dead will be sent to ground unprotected.

Walking, limping, he wishes for a canoe, despite these waves. The savages, even women and children, use them ceaselessly, eschewing walking for reasons that have become obvious. He wonders if the carpenter knows how to build a small boat, perhaps a coracle, some light craft very unlike the heavy woodenness of their own dories. Something a lone man could oar or pole, something he could carry on his back — something identical in all ways to the brilliant savage canoe!

Samuel turns up the bank and inland to risk a shorter route back through the woods. As he rounds a thicket he comes upon a savage squatting to defecate. It is one of Membertou's sons, the taller, unbalanced one. He had thought himself well hidden but he is startled and quickly glances up, sees Samuel. He glares and begins to mumble some incantation — *aheysoos aheysoos aheysoos* — all the while continuing his chore. Samuel turns away to allow the man his privacy and decency, but first sees how, despite his change in direction and despite the man knowing him, the savage draws a blade from his skins. And keeps it at the ready, resting armed fist on thigh. Samuel understands this, for the natural weakness of a man at toilet is such that it fires the urge to privacy.

Many strides and trees away, Samuel casts a look back and into the shadows at his sides. It strikes him now that *aheysoos* was a savage rendition of the Saviour's name! While this curiosity causes him to blink, he blinks twice more at the understanding that this man used the Holy Name as a kind of vocal talisman, a charm to ward off an enemy, in this case a Christian! And friend! But this is the unhinged son of Membertou, the one whose name is hard to say and harder to retain, and he is referred to as the crazy one, the son of split mind, to whom Lescarbot ascribes the poetic "of cliff-edge temperament."

As he hurries on his new route, recalling the brief scent of the savage's scat, Samuel has a sudden and lunatic notion of *food*. He shakes his head and laughs aloud. He is recalling, surely, the story Membertou himself told about the shameful practice of dogs when they put nose to ass of any other they meet, as it seems they must. Some days ago, seeing two dogs behave thus, the sagamore told Samuel that they were seeking news of what food they'd recently eaten, and, if the food smelled good (that is, when it entered the first hole, at the other end), the next task was to ascertain where the food had been got, by tracing the other's tracks to the source.

Samuel walks and refuses to be a dog. The savages have many such stories and perhaps some are true. Of more import is an oddity: only that morning did this son of Membertou obtain this same blade in trade with them, for two good skins. That he should be so ready, the same day, to use it, and against the very people he gained it from — is almost a picture of comedy.

THIS NEXT EVENING he is warmed by the good Lucien, who not only took time from his many labours to fix the wooden boots (Samuel still cannot wear them: to cut away any one part only makes another part rub) but also built Samuel a throne, on the shore. Samuel supposes it is because he has not tried to hide himself as he stands on the shore in a pose, most likely, of "gazing wistfully" upon the empty water. In any case, just around the point away from everyone's eyes Lucien has built him a chair on which to sit and gaze as wistfully as he might wish. It is but a fat spruce stump with a back support left on. It is not overly comfortable and likely took the skilful Lucien not much time with a sharp saw, but Samuel loves it and it is his. Mostly, it was unasked for, and a gift from a busy man.

Samuel has heard that the men already have christened it Champlain's Chair of Dreams, but he trusts it is not all for mock.

Even if it is, even if he must become a figure of ridicule, he knows it vital not to turn inward and hide. He has seen it often, both on ship and in the closeness of a landlocked winter, how a man feeling wounded will make an island of himself — this is the way to bitter humour, and worse. And it can cause others to form up as an enemy gang against the afflicted, adding to the torment, which, as a serpent eats its tail, pushes the man-island farther into a deeper, more unreachable sea.

How we judge one another! It is not unlike a beast stalking, assessing, and devouring prey.

Samuel knows that on this voyage his first error in misjudging human qualities occurred with Marc Lescarbot. He learned in all manner of books — and Samuel a mapmaker modestly well-read in science — the assumption was that they would love each other as magnets, sharing their wisdom long into the night! Not so. The lawyer finds him foolish, and Samuel in turn finds his arrogance more foolish still. (Perhaps it is their shared learning that provides them with such competing ammunition!) But curse the *googoo*. In this event Lescarbot is right. Samuel's too public belief in the savages' monumental beast was only foolish, and this he can now admit. He sees his error was to boast about it in Paris when, clearly, no beast can exist whose roarings make all, even the forest trees, frozen and incapable of motion; no beast can exist that is big as an island and carries human beings in its pocket on which to dine later. But since Samuel has admitted to his foolishness and reneged in his belief, so Lescarbot should cease his mockery, especially amongst the common men. Samuel so loathes to hear the lawyer's hissed *Googoo! C'est arrivé!* and then the men joining his mock trembling. Lescarbot himself has wrong beliefs aplenty, though he will stay blind to these even on the day Saint Peter himself points them out.

But one can correct one's wrong-headed judgements, it seems. This very morning, in fact, Samuel marvelled at how one's perceptions of one's fellows can be in error. Dédé with his swimming beetles! Today he saw anew the hirsute and beastly man. Samuel can still picture Dédé shrieking gleefully as a girl.

It was at the elbow of the brook, widened and rocked in by Poutrincourt's boy for a trout pond, where Samuel had the pleasure of finding Dédé in a hefty squat, glad as a child, pointing out this beetle and that. These beetles were of a kind unknown at home, with jet-black cloak and outsized paddling arms shaped as a leatherback turtle's is. They dashed about playfully, chasing who knows what. These beetles Samuel had seen other times, but Dédé was delighted in their discovery, calling all who would come. His honking sounded somewhat like a stag at rut, and from appearances his cheeks were blush with wine, but when Samuel joined him he was all a child, and he would point and chirp and on occasion try to grasp one. Crouched near, Samuel knew him as his typically odorous self, and part of the mapmaker wanted to take and send him into the pond for a bath with his beetles. But then, surprising Samuel (and reminding him that there really is no place for mockery or judgement here in their enclosed and intimate world), the ox-headed Dédé said an intelligent thing. He said: "Monsieur Champlain, look! On their backs you can see the sun, and twice! And they are black like lacquer is black!" He went back to his chirping and Samuel could see he was fairly drunk as he then commenced growling as he caught and burst one between thumb and finger. But in any case it was good to be in the presence of happiness and be reminded that God gives his gleam even to the eyes of the stupid. Samuel knows Dédé's fellows watch him and stay clear, judging him fragile in his moods, if not broken from his moorings, but as of this morning Samuel decides to think nothing of the kind.

THOUGH, TOO SOON, Samuel has another glimpse of Membertou's keel-less son. One of the rough carpenters, the man Simon, ate of a mushroom some days ago and only today returns to productive work. According to Simon, who speaks in fearful whispers still, said fruit was given to him in a jest of sorts, the savage Ponchonech (for that is the imbalanced one's name) plucking it from the ground under some pines and offering it playfully, and his younger brother Androch joining in, calling Simon a woman if he didn't eat it, though apparently neither of the two savages dared bite it themselves. Champlain suspects it was their man's sense of French honour that made him take the dare, he does not know. But the apothecary d'Amboisee could do nothing to counteract the weird vegetable's strength, trying *sirop de rhubarbe* and *jalop* and several other infusions besides. Simon's dwelling mates tell of him speaking loudly the first night, describing a very great contentment, and he was heard to mention an angel, though of course it was a devil, because as Samuel later witnessed for himself, he was disturbed to the quick and could not sleep and through all his thoughts ran — in Simon's own phrase — small devils. As well, he was full of devilish prophecy for this place, for Port-Royal, so Samuel is glad it cannot be true. Though Simon's ramblings did haunt some of the men, even come morning. Ponchonech and Androch have been chastised, and Membertou bade them both bring to the compound a fresh beaver's tail. Androch's tail was dead maybe a week and already beginning to foul, and Bonneville risked their friendship with the savages by shouting at them and burying it out back before they had yet walked from sight.

LUCIEN RESTS HIS HEAD. Though he lies still it feels that his limbs are at work even now, drawing the plane, and measuring, and he knows sleep is not close. Wood shavings will be curling up, unsatisfactorily and without pause, in his dreams.

He tries to imagine he is still on ship and all of this snoring is wind. Beside him, Simon was snoring in exhaustion, but now he has stopped. Two others over by the wall opposite are still eager and full-lung'd. He imagines them to be fantastical imbecilic beasts of limited vocabulary, sharing a monotonous story. Oddly, he has never heard the real beast, Dédé, snore. The big man stays quiet in sleep. It is more than queer imagining him biding his time till morning.

Lucien's pillow is only half full of feathers, for though seabirds abound he has had no time. How is it the other men find time? True, they do not take walks of such duration. They trout, or kill birds and gather feathers. A master carpenter's prerogative, Lucien scouts for advantageous wood — though now when he does so it is little more than pretence, for the first time he climbed the promontory he could tell by the uniformity of leaf colour that there would be few surprises. Endless fir with small stands of oak, and scatters of birch, from which he might one day play at constructing a savage canoe. In truth he would love to stumble upon the rusty rock of an iron mine. He has heard there are rewards for Sieur Poutrincourt if copper or iron mines are among the fruits of this exploration, and that Poutrincourt might then reward the finder himself.

Though he would rather find the den of a bear. Or see, up a tree — far up a tree, too far up to jump on him — a lion. Membertou has told them a kind of lion lives in these woods, though Monsieur Champlain has never seen or heard of it.

Well — Lucien decides, knowing in his chest — no one should be held to account for the way one fills one's time. Every style is but a solution to the demands of this place. For instance, Lucien has watched Bonneville try and try to entertain himself. As cook, Bonneville's day is more regimented, and in some sense more valued, than any other man's, and as such he is not allowed to lend even a finger to any brute work even should he want to. They could not bear their cook injured, dirty, or even tired. They go so far as to deny him exercise, for though they aren't aware of it they prefer their cook plump, perhaps because it instills confidence that he evidently finds his own creations irresistible. So Lucien has seen Bonneville on his off-hours looking rather angry and at sea. To escape the biting flies, the cook set up a bench of driftwood on a sunny outcrop that caught some breeze, but as a result badly burned his face and his lips. Then he pulled out his shoulder finding white stones with which to line the Sieur's trout pond, so that was the end of that. But it's clear the man needs to make more work for himself. Lucien shakes his head on his thin pillow. With such impatient industry, Port-Royal will be an entire village soon.

It is this industry, this mind-filling work, that keeps them all from being afraid, leaving no room for it. Lucien can stand apart and regard the hurry in their chopping and rasping and banging and barking and see too clearly that, to a man, fear is their fuel. None utters the word scurve. Sometimes a word is louder, and grows deafening, the longer it is not spoken.

Speaking of biting flies, this morning Lucien heard — and with no reason to believe it is not true — that the Mi'qmah hereabouts are not so gentle as all have been boasting. For it seems they have a famous way of torturing an enemy, one made worse through being enacted under the guise of benevolence. That is, by letting a man go free. Before doing so they relieve him — a captured Iroquois, one assumes — of the burden of all of his clothes and skins and then point the direction of his village many leagues distant and release him into the care of the woods. Apparently in any season but winter, such a man will not survive the blackflies, mosquitoes, horseflies, stag flies, chiggers, and ticks for more than two days, and it is further said that if the man does not find a pond to jump into within an hour he most certainly will be made mad, being capable by then of naught but running into tree trunks and snorting infantile noises out his nose as he tries to flee. And of course in winter the cold bites you whole.

Lucien laughs cruelly. He has far too much head for sleep tonight. Beside him, poor Simon sucks breath like a baby, seeking the health he lost over two days and nights doing battle with the purgatorial mushroom.

No, the Mi'qmah have their own especial world, one the French know only a corner of. Tonight, it had been one of Lucien's nights to join the nobles' table, and he had come late because of some smooth-planing he needed to finish before rain came. The sagamore Membertou was a guest at table, and the nobles looked well into their cups. Remarkably — and Lucien merely listened, and his opinion was not sought in any case — they were considering Membertou's proposal that some Etchemin warriors, from the south, be captured and kept here as slaves and used to grind the grain for their bread! There sat Fougeray de Vitre sombrely nodding, with Monsieur Lescarbot brow-knit, and Sieur Poutrincourt himself thinking this through. Their bread was famously adored by the savages, and lately some of them had taken turns at the hand mill — a job often used as punishment, so tedious is it — their reward being half the bread that results from the labour. But apparently their love knows earthly limits, because here was the sagamore proposing that the French with their many muskets join them in a raid south, where, seeing the French at their side, the Etchemins will be easily defeated, with slaves for the hand mill taken, and women too, if the French wish them. (Monsieur Champlain's doubtful translation of the sagamore's words left it unclear whether Membertou was boasting humorously that he already had too many women around him.) In any case, the nobles sat, perhaps envisioning all that bread and all those women, until Monsieur Champlain interrupted his own translation — for the sagamore loves to make long speeches — to tell them simply, "The keeping of slaves would not go well for us," which appeared to embarrass the rest of them, or at least bring them to their better senses. And the lawyer Lescarbot then made a joke, proclaiming slavery to be a hobby more favoured by the English. And then the Sieur bit himself on the inner cheek and shouted. Not a minute passed before he bit himself again where it had swelled, as it sometimes will, and now he both shouted and stood.

Lucien inhales deeply the smells of nocturn. It is his first week in this dwelling, and his first lying indoors in months, if you don't count that loud and malodorous ship. Here the main smell is a most pleasant resin of fir, issuing from bed slats, wall logs, floorboards, and ceiling joists. The newly violated wood smells most. It is the smell of their injury, and they bleed a perfume for the benefit of man's nostrils. For the several weeks this wood continues to bleed, Lucien will smell neither his pillow nor the breath or bodies of his fellows, all of whom are asleep but him. He decides to enjoy this night and not hurry sleep. Indeed, it might well be the best time he spends here, with the resin at its most benevolent. Nor have many bugs — the spiders, beetles, and small biters — followed them in to take up lodgings in their pillows, beds, and beards. On ship a man was bitten right inside his asshole and he had for days a fair agony of itching, and such were his intense postures to satisfy this itch that all the men laughed, and Benet finally laughed at himself too, and thereafter the unknown creature came to be known as "Benet's bug," leading to the chorus of one of the colony's first songs: "Commit no sin, lest ye be bitten within, by Benet's bug."

It is good to be indoors again. The carpenter's curse: everyone's place save his own is attended to. The nobles have been indoors for weeks. Of course, many of their planks were brought from St-Croix, place of pestilence, and though no physical evil abides in the wood, there is something of a malevolent spirit in the grain, looking like the long eyebrows of ill will, though of course this is only in the mind of observance. But better to start fresh, from innocent wood that has heard no moans, no cursing of God's own name. And still smells of sweet pitch.

Lucien realizes, in a moment of greater wakefulness, that for all the dwellings he has constructed, both from the ground up or torn down in part to make anew, he has never before built his own dwelling. Not even his own sleeping room. Of course not — his father and uncles, carpenters all, would at any hint of rot or divorced joinery pounce upon it and see it fixed. Make your own house another's envy, his father once told him, and you will never lack work.

It seems his father was wrong. St-Malo was overfull of enviable houses and notable carpenters, and even the best had often to travel miles to find the next endeavour. Lucien was trained on the rough doors of barns, and fencing for pigs, and Babette's stuck windows, when she let him. He was not the best but good enough when he put his mind into the wood, and to find employ had had to travel not miles but an entire ocean, to a new world.

Though not entirely against his will. And when, God willing, he returns, he will have the money to begin his own small enterprise, perhaps a village or two inland from St-Malo, and he knows he will not lack for work because, sadly, he will now be famous, and be expected to tell stories of exploration. To do so he will have to change his nature. Though little do the people at home know that, here, boredom soon enough becomes the biggest story, that after doing what work one can with the body, it becomes yet harder work to entertain the mind.

Children's games entertain some. Old leather gets stuffed with feathers for the invented contest of kicking a ball at a distant stump. (Men have demanded that Lucien carve them a proper set of *boules*. He may yet do so if he finds the time, and enough root-burl, which might not split.) And there are impromptu games of the most puerile: spitting, pissing, leaping to touch a nest of bees and daring not run. Always a wager of coins, a fur, rations of brandy. Almost daily there is wrestling, naked save for breeches. (Lately poor Dédé is without challenge; the last man broke a thumb; the one before, a rib; and apparently, though no one saw it, the beast ripped the hair from a poor soul's armpit.) Others have fashioned parlour games — chess in the dirt with ranked pinecones as the soldiers. Others drink and sing, and their songs have become as common as the wind in the trees. Lucien could see the boredom set instantly in Monsieur Champlain, who it seems sets foot on land only to turn forlornly and watch the iron sea. He has already taken the longboat on two excursions, one lasting two weeks and, say the men who went, almost ended their lives on the rocks of a bald and waterless island. Lucien suspects Champlain pretends to be scouting for locales of value — oak, mines of iron or copper, vines — but he is really just escaping the smell and uniform press of land.

God, what will winter be like?

On his half-pillow, Lucien weighs crude hefts of mood and decides he is still partly glad to be here, over the ocean, smelling resin, more awake than during the daylight. Though he would dearly love to have his own room, if only to escape the snoring. It is a rough irony that a carpenter is not allowed his own room here, though of anyone he could most easily build it.

octobre 1606

MEMBERTOU IS IN the mapmaker's room waiting for him. When Samuel enters, the old sagamore looks up and smiles and offers his hand for shaking — not at all a savage gesture but one mimicking and taking seriously these politics that the French perform without thought. Disturbingly, Membertou's smile brings to mind the lawyer Lescarbot's.

As they shake hands Samuel finds it funny to think that, despite so French a smile, one that Samuel duly answers with his own, they two can more markedly smell each other. He finds himself wishing that, rather than Membertou gaining these French habits, the sagamore should best remain as he would have been before, blank of face and staring proudly. Indeed, Samuel wishes he could answer that stare with a like one of his own. Two men reading each other's eyes, searching for strengths and weaknesses perhaps, but it is also a faster way to find friendship.

Of the savages, Membertou alone has free access through their gate and, once in, he takes it upon himself to go anywhere he pleases. He has been discovered sitting in Sieur Poutrincourt's chair, for instance, and Poutrincourt was on that occasion gracious enough to seat himself on the bench set there for visitors.

"In two months, or in three months, there will be moose," is the first thing Membertou says, though in a simpler way. Months are moons, and he uses no future tense that logic can ascertain. He holds his palms up and shoves them at Samuel, who wonders what the gesture might mean. The sagamore's palms are white and look soft, though they likely aren't. His hair, bound at the back, has come forward at the sides to frame his face like a hood.

"Good. We all look forward to that." Samuel decides it would be harmful to tell Membertou that many of the men, if not most of them, are dismissive of moose. All tried the dried version many weeks ago upon their arrival, and it was tainted.

"The Frenchmen continue to eat beef?"

"Yes. Beef is what we have. Barrels of beef."

"Moose is better than beef."

"We French like beef. But indeed we look forward to the moose."

"A barrel is not a place for meat."

Samuel knows not to explain salting to Membertou again, for clearly he is feigning ignorance.

Membertou visits today only on the pretence of discussing trade for fresh meat. Samuel knows the man's real reason is to once again ask Samuel to make him a Christian. The old sagamore will wait and wait. Today is Sunday, and Samuel wonders if it could be that Membertou has taken note, has counted days, and is here today because of it.

They sit erect in the room's two chairs, and Samuel flags a boy passing the open door and asks him to go to Bonneville and bring back bread, and tea. Scratching himself, hunching to glance out the square hole cut for a window, Membertou speaks casually of tomorrow's weather, then explains how one might repair a canoe even in deepest winter, by putting fire against a tree and thereby melting out — but don't burn it! — enough precious pitch. Only later, when the Sunday bell rings calling them in for prayer, does he rise and touch Samuel's shoulder to ask him the important question. Samuel looks at the floor, finding it painful to deny the man, especially when he is about to abandon Membertou for the same Christian service he is requesting. And Samuel finds it ironic that this man in front of him desires this service more than Samuel does himself.

"I am sorry," Samuel tells him and turns to leave. He knows that sorry is as difficult a word for the Mi'qmah as it was for the savages in Hochelaga. "I will ask the priest again."

He wishes Membertou would ask the priest himself, but knows he won't. The priest is the one man Membertou is shy of.

"Please." Now Membertou has him by the arm and is not letting him go.

The savage does understand that Samuel himself is unable, that he is not a priest. Membertou, though, seems to have heard of and clung to the rumour that some Frenchmen are not of the priest's religion, and that some who are not priests but pastors can also welcome a savage into the Christian family. Samuel has no intention of entering this story with the man. Last year, in St-Croix, their settlement was blessed by the presence of both a pastor and a priest, and the two hated each other so much that they twice came to blows and de Monts (himself a Protestant) was of a mind to flog them. Truly, if one said apple, the other said plum. And when the scurve saw them both in bed they still would not forgive, and when they died within a day of each other all saw this as somehow fitting, so much so that both priest and pastor were buried in a single grave, in a forced embrace. And while other reasons were given for this act (frozen ground, too few able men with enough strength to make a second hole, and such), all knew it was to end their fighting, and Samuel sensed that all approved of de Monts's ecumenical spirit.

So for reasons of peace there is only a priest in Port-Royal. Samuel has no idea as to how a savage might be made a Protestant. Nor has he nearly the subtlety of language to explain how one god can have two families.

Samuel has been to Poutrincourt for advice on Membertou's behalf. Twice now he has told Fr. Vermoulu of the sagamore's request, and twice the priest has simply stared at him, a stare too dense with opinion for him to read, but one he suspects is telling a mapmaker to mind his own business. While the King has decreed that Christianity be given to savages far and wide, it seems that the priests charged with this task will decide for themselves the timing of it. Indeed, Samuel thinks the priest a dark scoundrel, one whose selfishness surpasses any other's here, a man of scant nobility who tests the true nobles' patience (Vermoulu would call it piety) by commanding this man and that to tend the priest's private garden and fish pond, taking the men away from their many other needful duties. Using God as his emperor, he tries to be a small king here. Samuel is only glad that Vermoulu is a quiet man who prefers his own company.

Worse, Vermoulu doubts the savages are capable of belief at all. Samuel thinks he is only wrong. Twice during past voyages and summers in Hochelaga up the great Canada River, Samuel has been witness to savages who speak to the Devil. The Algonquin call these men their "God-speakers," which is heresy unheard of, but which, considering their lack of baptism, a Christian might forgive. In Hochelaga three summers past, amid several Algonquin tribes under the great sagamore Besouat, on the eve of a foray against the Iroquois, the God-speaker disappeared into an especial hut with great ceremony, the rest of the tribe moaning nonsense as he did so. Samuel watched as inside this hut the man pretended all manner of riot and fits. Indeed he may have had help — the walls shook as if he were a beast twice his size. Outside, the gathered braves pretended likewise that he had become a great beast, for they aped fear and widened their eyes, and from behind trees some of the women shrieked and wept. It was all for show, but at the same time some part of them seemed to believe in it, or at least desired it to be true. Not too many minutes later the God-speaker crept from his hut and, all asweat and as if having suffered a month of deprivation and inhuman travail, his nose looking twice the size it should and his bugging eyes hanging out over it, the man in eager and oddly childlike tones explained himself to Besouat and several others of rank, but too quickly for Samuel to understand many words, and Besouat then turned and shouted the story to the crowd of men, and to the women and children huddled listening from the trees, the gist being that, according to this man's florid exchange with his god, they would be successful in their slaughter of their Iroquois enemies. (In the announcement no mention was made of the fact that Samuel and eight musketeers were on this occasion accompanying them to battle; indeed it was in this skirmish that Champlain was to kill three Iroquois — two of them sagamores — with one shot of the arquebus. The God-speaker knew he would be fighting for their side — one wonders if he mentioned this to his god.) In any event, with this hopeful announcement the entire gathering of tribes cheered and with no interruption in the cheering commenced a riotous celebration of lunatic dance that would last until dawn. Samuel reckoned that as military strategy they could have done no worse, a good sleep being the necessary medicine for anybody about to go to war. But the dancing and singing all night indeed proved not so ill a manoeuvre. Because at dawn, following some unseen signal, the men took up their weapons and leapt into the trees and then commenced a steady running walk of some hours' duration, and then they fought the Iroquois through the afternoon and evening — all without apparent loss of vitality. They returned at the same running pace, carrying enemies' heads as if they weighed nothing.

And some time into the revelry that followed — impossibly, the braves danced some more before they slept and perhaps this irked the already tired Samuel — he drew Besouat aside and declared to him that they had heard the prophecy of the Devil, not God. Besouat asked the difference. In answer Samuel asked if his God-speaker was always right in his predictions and Besouat calmly answered no. Very tired now himself, Samuel instructed Besouat that he, his God-speaker, and his tribe were blind and deaf to the one true God, who in His mercy would give them all that they needed, if they should take up Christian prayer. Samuel then asked him how they came to be here, on this earth. Besouat told at length a story: after God had made all things, He took a number of arrows, stuck them in the ground, and in pulling them up drew forth men and women, who have since multiplied in the world up until this day.

Patiently Samuel listened and then told him that his story was false. He proceeded to instruct him in the truth, that, after creating a perfect world, God saw it needed governing and thenceforth brought their first father Adam to the Garden, and then afterwards Eve, and thence, after the Fall, the earth's children. Besouat, knowing truth when he heard it, listened as his fellows howled and leapt behind him in the clearing and all the way down to the river. The fire lit his face and he looked respectful as a child. Samuel spoke only so much as Besouat's wisdom would allow him to hear but nonetheless gave him essential news of the Father, Son, and Holy Ghost, and also of Mary. At this Besouat smiled and said their beliefs were similar: the God, and Son, and Mother, and the Sun. God stood over all, and the Mother was feared because she ate them up, in death.

Samuel went on to tell him the error of this story too, and it felt odd to be speaking in this way for, though he believed as heartily as the next man, he was no preacher. But Besouat answered that he desired to pray as a Christian, if only someone would show him how. When, seeing the long, hungry winters in Besouat's eye, Samuel tried to tell him it wasn't bread, blankets, and axes that Christian prayer would bring, but rather immortality, Besouat seemed to listen and was glad enough with Champlain's promise that next time they voyaged this far west for furs they would bring their own God-speaker, a priest who would perform the necessary baptismal rite. Samuel nodded at the darkness in the direction of the immense Canada River and told the exhausted sagamore that the priest would guide him and hold him entirely under that water. At this Besouat was frightened and did not even try to hide it in front of his braves.

So the savages do believe in that which they cannot see, and strongly. Samuel thinks they should be Christian if they so wish it. Especially these Mi'qmah here. Like the Algonquin to the west, they are of cheerful disposition, but even more so. They laugh often, sometimes for reasons the French can't determine. They too are aware of this divide, and so they are very deliberate when speaking, speaking slowly and with long pauses, waiting for Samuel's nod to continue, as if in demand that they be understood. It is obvious to Samuel that many of them are of good judgement. He believes they could be taught to read—though his saying so might see him ridiculed, or worse, if this opinion of his were to voyage back to France. Even more dangerous is his thinking not only that the Mi'qmah would make interesting companions at prayer, but also that perhaps the French, too, could learn about their own God from the savages. During one of Membertou's previous visits, as the two of them stood at the western perimeter watching the new latrine being dug, and

93

when Membertou first broached the question about becoming Christian, Samuel happened to ask about his own religion, his own god. At this, the sagamore smiled, but nothing like Besouat's story was forthcoming. Instead, with a childlike and almost dismissive flick of one hand, Membertou indicated the vast harbour in front of them. When Samuel asked him if his god lived at sea, or beyond the sea, he lost his smile, spun, and pointed at the tree closest to them, and then at the mountain beyond it, and next at the thunderclouds in the southern sky, and then at Samuel himself. Samuel was for a moment made proud, until, last, Membertou turned his finger in on himself.

Samuel marked this heresy, but another as well, his own: there might be something to learn from these people about God's *proximity*. It seems that priests, and priests especially, made much ado about God's distance. But Membertou's little dance even survived logic: were not each of God's creations an extension of God, an arm? And was not God's arm God Himself? (Samuel would in all earnestness love to call this earth *God's face*, and the sea *God's humours*, and tell no one.)

IN THE MAPMAKER'S rooms — though the old man has let go Samuel's arm and regards him with no ill will, having accepted that for today he will yet remain a heathen — Samuel has already decided not to go to service. The second bell is rung, but instead he goes to the cupboard. He turns and indicates that Membertou should sit again, if he wishes.

Recently and expertly hung by Lucien, the cupboard door swings smoothly on its black hinges. Both were salvaged from the ruin at St-Croix. Its inner shelves, though, are fresh wood, and smell sweetly of health. Samuel lifts out two goblets and the jug.

Perhaps out of regret that he could not fulfill good Membertou's wish to join him in a family under God, he offers instead the one part of the sacrament he can — wine. He stands to make a show of delivering it into his own cup by pouring it from a foot above. Then he lifts the cup in the direction of France, takes a small sip, and then, standing in formal posture, offers it to the sagamore. He knows that savages from all parts see brotherhood in such acts, just as they hold that privacy is the trait of an enemy. He knows, too, that Membertou would be well aware not only that wine is used in the sacrament, but also that in this compound each regular man receives one and one-half pints of medicinal wine daily, and also that they value it for more than its religious and medicinal properties.

The sagamore Membertou accepts Champlain's goblet with the posture and vanity of a king, literally rising in bearing to the occasion. He looks into the vessel, gazes into its depths, tilts the vessel and sees that the wine moves not at all — and there is nothing like haste in his movements. Samuel is enthralled to watch. The savage's study of the wine is only respectful, perhaps even fearful, for though he doesn't himself know intoxication, he has seen many a dull Frenchman grow bright, and then wise, and then loudly overwise, and in the end possessed by imbecility, and then, thankfully, sleep.

Enthralled, he watches Membertou take a first taste, for the tongue alone, and his eyes glance down as if seeing it. Then he has a deeper taste, for the head. Samuel watches him look inside himself, for change. Indeed, his eyes move, flitting as they would in a new forest, though this exploration is inner. At some length he looks up at Samuel with a gentle smile, in his eye the deepest sobriety of understanding. But then, hard on its heels, a merry flash of light.

They share the rest of the goblet together, and then have each one of their own, and they speak as best they can with what words they have in common. Membertou reiterates more passionately that the season of moose meat is almost upon them. Samuel congratulates the sagamore on the size of his family, and for his part Membertou sympathizes with Champlain's lack of one, despite the mapmaker's assurance that he has siblings and cousins aplenty. But it is clear that Membertou's meaning of family is that which you create — wives, children, and, he adds, brothers. Friends, he seems to mean. Membertou marvels, disturbed, at news that priests never make families. And then, after Samuel describes for him some of the dealings he can expect with priests should he ever become Christian, Membertou manages a good joke. When Samuel nods toward the blustery dark water of the bay and tells him that Fr. Vermoulu would guide him completely under the water out there, the old sagamore at first looks within, indeed as Besouat had. But instead of falling fearful, Membertou slyly casts his eyes to Samuel's and says in a quiet hiss, "Will he guide me back up?" and then tosses back his head to laugh at the ceiling.

Finished with his wine, and seeing that no more is forthcoming, laughing at unknown things, the old sagamore takes his leave of Samuel now, aping a brief French bow from the neck only, and takes his new head with him to his forest, and his people.

Samuel pours the remains of his goblet back in the jug. He hears the boots of the men as they issue from their common prayer; he leans back in his chair and considers. If a savage is eager to become Christian, eagerness alone should suffice. If the desire is rooted in a wish for the glass windows, biscuit, molasses, guns, and lace cuffs that God evidently bestows upon His flock, how is this any worse at heart than those of them who pray for a more finely appointed and easeful life in heaven?

Again Samuel will pass on Membertou's request to the Sieur, who might possess some more talent to sway Vermoulu. Though Poutrincourt seems wary of instructing a priest. Of the other nobles, Leduc wants the savages christened, while de Court dearly does not. Fougeray de Vitre does not seem to care. The lawyer Lescarbot, smiling sagely, instructs all within hearing that the Bible contains one million words, which is one million more than the savages can read.

IT WAS TWO DAYS previous that Samuel arranged tonight's visit with Sieur Poutrincourt, and he made so formal an arrangement in order to ensure this time with the Sieur alone. Samuel's plan, one he has rehearsed, is to discuss the healing nature of comedy. And then, out of that, to discuss what might be a way to survive the winter that is almost upon them.

Ironic, then, this supposed discussion of comedy! There sits the Sieur, aslump in his chair, staring through his three candles' flames, past their surround of bobbing shadow, through the blackness of the very walls and out into a blind night. He continues to raise his cup of wine with nothing akin to pleasure. Indeed, his dullness of humour speaks of one too many such cups having met their maker. Poutrincourt's boy, over in the dark corner standing ready with the pitcher, looks quite flushed himself with so much striding up and pouring. The room itself feels dull and askew.

Samuel blames this night's wind, which even now thuds its flabby paw against the walls and the window. He hates the south wind; the south wind brings with it summer airs, which gives the body false hope. It is warmth out of season, time out of joint. It is a girl's breath, to stir the nuts, and then it is a monster's, to unmast the ship. On board he hates it most, for it lulls, and therefore endangers.

But now in what feels tantalizingly close to wit, Samuel offers, "The problem with exploration is the stopping."

When his friend — Samuel is reasonably certain they are friends — moves not a muscle, only then does he remember that Poutrincourt's reason for being here wasn't exploration at all, but settlement. This gentleman had *come* to stop. That first week, striding the nearby meadows and then even helping with the lifting of the first outer wall, Poutrincourt had more than once wondered aloud at what next voyage he might bring his wife and young children along. He has not been speaking this way of late. Poutrincourt has of need cast from his mind the black rumours of the King's new whimsy of the fur monopoly abolished, and Port-Royal dying before it is fully born — and perhaps he has not fully succeeded.

Samuel clears his throat and tries again.

"That is, one problem with settlement seems to be the settling. Itself."

At this Poutrincourt raises his brows in polite agreement but there is nothing like the smile or chuckle Samuel hoped for. Indeed, his sitting room looks nothing like a place of smiles, or of settlement, for that matter. In the gloom, at Poutrincourt's side rises the staircase to his bedchambers, and the staircase lacks a railing or spindles yet. It looks dangerous, or like the painting of a maliciously vacant dream.

Samuel is again aware of the chasm between knowledge and wisdom: one can gain much knowledge and yet at the same time remain dumb to its *use*. Take the farmer who expertly raises the cow and yet remains all thumbs at the butcher's block when said cow's flesh needs preparing. Or take himself: his amateur study of musical performance and the levels of comedy leave him painfully aware that his knowledge of comic art sees him no better equipped for comedy itself. That is, he doesn't know how to lend humour to a situation. He has seen how utterly he lacks wit, save the vengeful kind that flowers in the brain slowly, blossoming some minutes too late. Which isn't wit at all but a kind of rumination, a bitter chewing on comedy's dead petals.

He simply is not funny. The elements of comedy are much like those of music, and he lacks what is probably something like rhythm. Poutrincourt has cleared his throat, which sends his boy to Samuel's side, and now Samuel sees that his own cup is empty. With pinched fingers he shows the lad that he is not much thirsty tonight.

Even the brutish Dédé has a rhythm — the coughing barks necessary for low comedy, the shouts about farts and fucking, a comedy for souls which need improvement — still it is wit and it demands a certain rhythm. Sometimes it is quick-paced indeed, an onslaught well lubricated, and sometimes its practitioners employ a knowing delay before the crescendo, which is often of a physical kind, a slap or shove or mimed explosion.

However much he would love to discuss comedy now with Poutrincourt, the latter is clearly, and literally, not in the mood. Nor, Samuel is coming to understand, did his friend have much conversation beyond his own practical dreams — the size his manor was to be, the ideal *au pair* for his children, what sort of trap would best catch these too-wily river herring. Samuel would've loved to discuss not only the reason he has come visiting this night — that being the subject of middle comedy, of men who seek to learn about and laugh at their own behaviour — but also the rare nature of high comedy, and what discovery he had just made of it, right here in Port-Royal. He would've loved to have been granted the interested audience to describe his understanding of high comedy: that it begets more tears than laughter, for it is the heart being struck with strong loving blows; it is passionate, not with yearning but with sagacious awe; it has to do more with death than birth, or more clearly with both at the same time; it has to do with man's folly and wisdom combined; it often sounds like the voice of God. He would have loved to explain and discuss all this with Poutrincourt, but even more, he would have been afterwards keen to have the man's opinion on the discovery he had just made — it is the *savages* here who, of any society he has yet seen, are prone not to low or even middle comedy, but to high.

It was the sagamore Membertou who instilled this thought in him. It was more than Membertou's nobility, of which all of them could agree he was possessed. And it was more than the elaborate theatre with which the savages embraced their dead and dying. No: it was more with their reception of daily events. The way Membertou, for instance, greeted a change in the weather — his face might widen in a kind of thanks, and awe, as if God Himself (though they have no god as high) had presented Membertou alone with a gift. Membertou's adoring face at hearing, for the hundredth time, the capture of a moose in leanest times, would similarly remind Samuel of someone sitting in audience to high comedy. It was the perfect opposite of frivolous, which middle comedy could sometimes be.

So, perhaps naively, Samuel has come to regard Membertou's life as a kind of simple but sacred opera. What else could be said of one for whom clouds meant more than the possible onset of rain? Though what would Poutrincourt make of this? Dare he tell him? For this whimsy has also changed his mind as to the savages' mode of government — which both Cartier and La Roche insisted they lacked entirely. This was an easy mistake to make, the sagamore's word being law in times of war and dispute and marriage only, while the rest of the time his people did what they pleased, save, perhaps, murder. But Samuel has now remarked that, of each of the seven or eight sagamores he has encountered in the several years he has voyaged to this world, most of them shared, at least to some extent, this nobility, this attenuation to high comedy, and it was this attitude and general bearing that the rest of the tribe could respect, and learn from, and to some extent emulate. Even when a sagamore lied to you as transparently and bald-faced as a clumsy child, you could just as easily tell that something in the man's very bones would not allow him to lie similarly to his own people. In fact it seems to Samuel that, compared to what he has seen of his own Royal Court at home, here in the land of savages a more natural hierarchy reigns — though this is something he will never dare record in his journals, published or not.

But what Samuel has wanted to do, and why he visits this night and seeks to gain Poutrincourt's advice, is to introduce to their settlement a series of banquets, with entertainment. Poutrincourt has some wit, and appreciation of wit, though apparently both had lessened as this season died and leaves fell upon the ground.

Poutrincourt listlessly raps his empty glass on the chair arm, and it takes a while for either Samuel or Poutrincourt's boy to understand that the man is calling for more wine. The boy jerks as if dragging a stuck leg and is for one moment unsteady on his feet, and Samuel hopes to God that this isn't a sign of one so young falling ill.

But Samuel begins:

"It seems, sir, that once shelter is well built, and fuel secured, and the belly filled, and God properly thanked, one needs some mode of pleasure beyond survival."

"It seems." As if to illustrate, Poutrincourt downs half of his freshened wineglass. Seeing this, his boy simply stands beside him with jug at the ready. He is pale yet glossed with sweat and truly does not look well.

"I have means in mind by which to introduce some middling comedy into our midst. That is, a way to rouse the men to a more cheerful humour. Without relying solely on —" Samuel lifts and waggles his own wineglass. On the chance he has just insulted his host, he adds, "Which has proven itself well, but which, in the morning, does tend to balance last night's pleasures." Samuel has heard enough vomiting to last him all winter.

"And then some," Poutrincourt agrees, tapping his temple, though rather brusquely and not smiling. "Please, do go on. Reveal your genius."

"No, I am no heroic figure. It is a modest suggestion."

"I was being facetious."

DEATH'S YELLOW IN these uppermost leaves is a hard sign it's autumn, but Lucien will let this gloom pass him by. Why ponder the growing cold, and future snow, when one can stay in the warm middle of this moment as it comes?

He is far up a giant old birch looking for branches of size for the spindles of the Sieur's staircase. If one can find them already grown to a near fit there is less need for lathe and measurement, all asquint in the dark of the shop. But he lies to himself — if he truly wanted made-to-measure he should be down there amongst the saplings. In truth he mostly wanted to climb this wise old tree that happened also to be white. Such a vast white tree should be the premise of a fairy story, though he isn't aware of any. In winter a huge white tree would be invisible — and wouldn't that be a good story's beginning?

He doesn't bother unpocketing his drawknife. No branches are straight. Even the youngest have taken their parent's gnarl. But he pauses for the view. He can see the whole of the bay and the entrance into it, that fissure in the mountains through which their ship brought them, a gap that's hard to see without feeling a pang inside. He strains to see the settlement, but aside from two lines of smoke issuing from a notch where there are no treetops, there is nothing marking the scar they've made in this vastness of forest.

Though it's not quite the tallest tree, such is its magic that, while in it, Lucien feels he is in the forest's very centre. He's about to descend his grand white tree when he sees them, the scatter of women and children in a meadow he hadn't noticed before. All of them are hunkered down and digging at something, lunging rhythmically as if kneading the ground's intestines. Around the perimeter the youngest of them run and play unabated. Curiously, now that he sees them, he can also hear them. There: a shrill laughing scream, and an answering young roar.

HE THOUGHT HE was quiet, but when he arrives out of the trees and into their meadow the women and children have stopped their digging and already stand up facing him, all with the identical expressionless face. Lucien cannot read if it is fear, or just an abiding caution, or even a common request that he leave. It is no meadow but a kind of swamp, and the savages are digging up white bulbs, onions perhaps, but barely the size of acorns. They hoard the muddy little globes on squares of birchbark at their sides. He smiles and waves. None moves, so he waves again and this time shrugs, and as he enters farther from the woods, wearing his largest smile, one foot sinks deep in muck and he flounders and yells, "Aghh!" The children erupt as one with laughter and, Lucien can tell, derision. Half of the dozen women turn away and resume digging. At the same time, paying Lucien no attention at all, an old woman passes him by as she comes out of the forest too, cinching closed the hide strips of her nether garments, clearly having just accomplished her toilet.

A younger one has risen and approaches him from the back of the group. She simply and easily strides up to him and stares. He could be a fish lying on salt at the market and she someone's daughter with orders to shop. Is she sixteen, or his age — twenty — or even older? Impossible to tell. He has not seen so many of them in a group before. All looked the same at first, partly because of their similar hides, and black hair, and olive skin. Now he marks their odd and differing ornaments, beads and small conical shells, and strings of coloured hemp, and some women are wrinkled around the eyes, and fringes of human winter in their hair. This present girl, eyeing him as if to determine his freshness, decides to ask him a question before she purchases him for dinner, for she begins speaking and doesn't stop for some time. Her language is full of breeze and softly snapping twigs. His instant wish is to have some language lessons from Monsieur Champlain, for he can hear clearly enough that her words offer not just facts but also shades of meaning and angles of the heart. She wears mud to her elbows but seems not at all shy about that. Lucien can smell this mud, blended not unpleasantly with a smell that is her own, one like rank apples. She's not so pretty as some he's seen but Lucien can tell she will laugh at herself. In her round face her eyes are underlarge, though he thinks he can see that when she is an older woman, she will be in some way wise.

She has stopped talking. She regards him more calmly, and now she shrugs, and it is plain to Lucien that the shrug says, "I was foolish in trying to talk to you, but I tried." He shrugs just as richly, agreeing. Her eyes flash and she smiles almost sadly now, for they are truly talking, and have entered something. Now their eyes hold, and both know how strange it is for the other in this time.

An older woman shouts something like, "*Bat*-ta!" at her. Another older one looks up from her digging and smiles hugely, missing a central tooth. The girl turns to the old woman and calls something in response, and when she turns back to Lucien, her impatient glance to the treetops is the same look from any embarrassed daughter in St-Malo.

She gives her eyes to Lucien again and her look pleads apology. But also humour at their state of affairs. For, look at the two of them! Here they are in mute collusion, intimate friends who cannot talk. He can't help but answer her smile at this. But look at us closer, she tells him as she brings her muddy hand to his chest, and with a finger draws a gentle circle. Here we are, she continues, lovers with no place to go — except the entire forest at your back. Now her palm flattens on his chest and she begins to gently push, taking him there.

Her magic overwhelms him and he doesn't know what to do with himself. He feels they are both enveloped by invisible carnal flame. No woman has ever proposed to him before. He is growing hard, and abuzz. At the same time he feels faint.

She shoves him and he is on his back, in the mud. Now the women laugh as well as the children, and when Lucien picks his head up to see her she is striding back to her onion hole, and he knows she is making comic faces to her tribe.

Yet he also knows that they will become lovers — of this he has no doubt. Her shove had been for her people. Her eyes had been for him.

Close Quarters

NOSING INTO THE terminal parking lot, Andy realized his mistake when he saw the white Hummer. The Hummer meant Dan Clark, and Dan Clark had agreed to take Andy's shift so Andy could go clothes shopping today because tonight was the banquet for the Chinese Wheat Women. Andy had got up at five, made coffee and eggs, and even read a little before driving the ten minutes to work — when he could have slept in. It was six in the morning and dark. His defrost was only now melting a hole in the ice bigger than the head-sized one he'd scraped. He was wide awake with four hours to kill before Pauline came over to "plan their attack" and take him shopping.

A pink dawn germinated behind the mountains, faint as peace. The car fan outshouted it easily, the world so hectic a foot from his face.

He put his car in reverse, reluctant to leave. He'd done all the work of getting here. But he was also aware — and this was a bit depressing — of wanting to put in a shift, like he had nothing better to do. There was no way he was one of those guys who retired and died, three months later, of *nothing to do*. No, his foot was light on the gas pedal mostly because the book up in the annex was a good one, and with this supervisor — Rogers — he'd have half the shift to sit and read. He wanted to get back to Port Royal. It was getting interesting. Amazing, the previous year on St-Croix Island, where thirty-two of sixty died of scurvy, and survivors returned to France on the single supply ship, which first disgorged fifty suspicious new guys. (What got whispered as horrified newcomers passed feeble survivors on the creaking gangplank?) Incredibly, Champlain and a few others stayed on, moving to Port Royal to be trapped not just by another winter but also by the irony that not one of them knew that, back in France, the King had cancelled their monopoly on fur trading and that their colony was bankrupt, futile, and doomed. An interesting time. Though how interesting was often hard to tell—Andy was just through the first of Champlain's journals and the famous cartographer had to be the blandest, most oblique writer in history. "... *Then I wrote a short account and made an exact map of all that I had seen and observed, and so we returned to Tadoussac, having made but little progress. Our vessels were there trading with the savages; and when this was done we embarked, setting sail, and went back to Honfleur...*" It left you asking what got traded for what, who got cheated, and did these "savages" ever have personalities? What did Champlain eat that night? If he used a plate, what was it made of? Did they have toilet paper? Andy rapped a knuckle on the clear patch of his windshield. Did they have windows to watch the snow as it grew deeper and swallowed them?

Andy had already read Lescarbot's *Nova Francia*, which was more satisfying, or at least more colourful. A lawyer, of old-school verbosity, he had to be interpreted as well: "*We... moved above all things with a singular zeal and devout and constant resolution to... cause the people which do inhabit the country, men (at this present time) barbarous, atheists, without faith or religion, to be converted to Christianity, and to the belief and profession of our faith and religion; and to draw them from the ignorance and unbelief wherein they are.*" Everything he wrote had the tone of sucking up to the King, who was a possible future reader perhaps, and his approach to the Almighty felt similar.

In any case the story was getting good. Winter had set in; men were restive, and sickness lurked in an endless night. Odd how they thought scurvy had to do with mood, with the "humours." (Lescarbot thought a humour could seep from the ground, like steam.) But a bad humour equalled, was, sickness. Maybe it was no different from today, how we literally worry ourselves sick. Stress, we call it now. Ill humour sucks at your immune system, knocks down your fortifications, and free radicals fly in like flaming arrows, doom self-fulfilled. He'd read also that voodoo, or actually vodun, works that way. The priest just has to get word out to the victim that he's been victimized and, ouch, worry's poison does the rest.

Andy flung a glance up to the silo top. Even if Port Royal was more interesting than here, it would be foolish to be caught up there on his day off, reading and not getting paid. The boys wouldn't know what to do with him.

He pulled out of the lot, laying a little rubber as he did, because he had a car that could do it and because he had come to work for no reason. He gave Dan Clark's car "the inch" as he passed it. Dan had taught them this southern signal, holding thumb and forefinger an inch apart whenever a Hummer went by, showing the driver how large his penis must be for wanting such a car. Lacking self-image problems himself, Dan Clark— some called him Handsome Dan to his face—laughed telling the boys this. He held his "inch" over his crotch and said, Hmm, yeah, looks about right. He also told them he got the Hummer for a song since they were a harder sell these days.

Andy felt bad enough about his Mustang in this regard, though it was less a guzzler than the muscle-Mustangs of yore. He turned not right but left and headed for the coal port. He wanted a closer look at the ship tied there and, a quick half-mile later, here it was, not a supertanker but a supercoaler. Chinese. He couldn't see the name (he could impress the Wheat Women tonight if he knew it), but the ship was huge. He had never seen a ship this size. Up on the stern the pilothouse looked tiny, the minuscule brain of a brontosaurus guiding an immense beast's ponderous moves. The plain of its deck was three soccer fields long. That ship would take more than one train to fill it and four or five days of highballing round the clock, lots of overtime for the coal boys before the ship's vast terracotta sides eased slowly into the sea.

Andy pulled onto the shoulder and opened his window. Lately, when the grain terminal was between ships and their own noise dropped, which happened a lot these days, you could hear that coal belt humming a half-mile away. Maybe no one wanted grain, but there was big hunger for coal. From this distance the arc of coal flying off the belt into the ship's hold looked for all the world like a hose gushing black fluid; it was easy to see it as a tanker getting filled to the gunnels with oil. Coal was basically hard oil, wasn't it? In China it would be burned to make electricity to run the robots to build endless cars to burn endless oil. It was a giant fossil-fuel fest over there.

Climate change had been in the news all week after the mystery of the dead fish was solved. Prince Rupert had suffered a "dead zone," like others that had happened off the coasts of Washington State and Chile. The cause was a huge algae bloom farther out, which died, sank, and was consumed by bacteria on the ocean floor, the bacteria using up all the oxygen in the process. Currents and last week's storm brought the lethal water to shore, suffocating any life in the shallows. One eerie aspect was that this water was pristine — perfectly healthy fish killed by utterly clean water, water that just happened to lack oxygen. The only unnatural thing was the gargantuan size of the algae bloom — nurtured by global warming. So — said the experts — we could expect more of the same. (One scientist-wag noted the silver lining here was that the fish were fine to eat, and that a big dead zone was our most efficient fishing method yet. Sally Kitcher could have had a big fry-up after all.)

Between the dead-zone news and then Raymond's visit yesterday, Andy's head was full of climate change.

Raymond was maybe ten years younger than Andy but had a natural air of authority about him. He had a Quebec accent but pronounced his name the Anglo way. Andy had called him because his white pickup, *Ray's Excavation* on the door, often parked on his street a block down. At first Raymond spent a near-silent ten minutes striding the backyard and down on the beach, sifting soil from the bank in his fingers, smelling it, pacing the exact length of frontage and noting an unfortunate lack of bedrock. Eventually he turned to Andy, looked him bluntly in the eye, and told him there were four methods available: granite boulders barged in and bulldozed against the bank; a wall of pile-driven log pilings; a poured-concrete wall; or sprayed-on polyceramic. No, Raymond didn't do the work himself, he would contract it. No, he couldn't give him an estimate on the spot. No, no ballpark figure either.

"Can you just tell me if it'll be, for instance, a thousand, or a hundred thousand, or a million?"

They both stood facing the fresh dirt exposed by the little slide. It had the sharply sour smell of construction sites. Raymond considered Andy's helpless question and he eyed Andy anew. Something in him settled down. He exhaled and dropped his professional bearing.

"Hey, I'd just forget about it, eh? You don't wanna know how much it would cost."

"That bad?"

"And there's no point. Not unless you get your neighbours to do exactly the same thing, and they get their neighbours, and you get this whole shore walled up. But even then. See, you wall just yours, the water rises, it eats into both sides there"— Raymond pointed at the McLeods' frontage and then the Wagnarskys'— "and gets you anyway. So there's no point."

Andy asked, "You on waterfront? I've noticed your truck."

Raymond smiled. "Girlfriend. You know Nadine? Nadine Dick?"

Andy shook his head, then asked, "You think the water's going to rise?" not meaning to, polar ice caps not being Raymond's line of work. But for some reason he didn't feel stupid asking this question, and Raymond didn't seem to think it stupid either.

Raymond smiled again. "It's what all the smart guys are saying. So down the road I think it's gonna to get bad maybe, yeah." He nodded at the raw earth wound that revealed nothing less than the vulnerability of Andy's property.

With the tiniest shiver, Andy knew he was letting himself understand that when the oceans rose as the smart guys said they would, he'd lose his land and his house. Even a one-foot rise would mean that, in a storm like the one they'd just had, the waves wouldn't just be pounding on the gravel beach, they'd be pounding this dirt wall that held up his yard. Apparently it was possible that he'd be alive to witness his yard shrinking with every winter storm, edging in toward the picture window he stared from, sitting in his rocker. If he'd had children, there'd be no house or land to leave them.

Consultation over, they started up the path. Neither had bothered mentioning the several gull-picked ling cod skeletons stinking at the tide line. After a few steps Raymond jabbed Andy's arm, smiled soberly, and said, "Any time you start talking walls it's not a good sign."

HE TURNED HIS CAR off. Pauline wasn't due for hours, this coal ship was a sight, he might grab a catnap in the car, and he really shouldn't be idling. The air was clean here, it was easy to forget the state of the planet, it took a dead zone to nudge you awake. Though there was evidence a bit north, and not just the polar bears losing ground or the Inuit slogging in their no-longer permafrost. It was glaciers going. Andy hadn't seen it himself — two tourists told him about it.

What will Laura think of this, Rupert as cruise-ship destination? He didn't know what to think himself. It was somehow heartening to learn you lived somewhere worthy of stoppage.

He often went to meet one, for the spectacle. It loomed over the waterfront, a fresh white office tower on its side, the largest structure in town, a line of tourists streaming out like freed ants. All wore hats, likely having been told about the rain, and all heads were up, eager to see what justified this stop. Some unsheathed cameras for the first photo op, having seen the eagles (there were always anywhere from a pair to a dozen) perched in the cedars across the street from the docks.

Many in town saved up the nuggets, those lame blurts of tourists anywhere. Some had taken to believing all tourists stupid, but Andy knew it was because one tended to hear only the blurtings of the less sophisticated. The smart traveller kept eyes open and stayed quiet until some kind of nuts-and-bolts understanding was reached. As in, from the number of empty commercial buildings, with unsteady people leaning against their brick, it was likely that this town of Prince Rupert was suffering some sort of recession. The smart tourist would generally not see the eagles and blurt, "Are those real?" Andy had heard not only that question but also a spectacular response to it, from an all-knowing dad: "Yes, but they train them."

Andy did understand his Tsimshian friend Leonard's anger over certain blurts though, acid dismissals of the Drum 'n' Dance enacted upon the municipal lawn on cruise-ship days. Smarter, quieter cruisers stood and smiled gently at the costumes, at the raucous drumming, the knee dips, the *effort*, while the ignorant might toss the dancers a glance as if they were panhandlers or some kind of ethnic booby trap trying to impede their hasty waddle back to the safety of the ship. (Andy had heard, "*That sure wasn't worth it,*" about a performance that was free.) Andy generally knew half the dancers. Some were Leonard's relatives, fresh off a village, seduced into joining the group, assured it'd be fun. Often a few did it as part of their detox, to connect spiritually or culturally, plus for exercise. But the costumes were marvellous — hand-loomed, the traditional red and black dye, and the conical hats woven from cedar bark, tight and soft as linen. If the dance looked a bit haphazard, so what? A loose choreography allowed self-expression, Leonard told Andy, it let dancers express their people's problems and wishes. Leonard, prone to spouting funny venom, went on to ask, rhetorically, What did the cruise ship expect? and proclaim that the only dance in the entire world with "that *freakish perfect unison*" was in Las Vegas or Hollywood, or maybe Les Folies-Bergère — but wasn't that for tourists too? Just like that new Moulin Rouge was built for Nicole Kidman? Who was an Australian acting American in order to act French? But didn't you *want* her most when the Oz accent slipped out? At which point Leonard laughed, as usual not knowing at what point he'd stopped being serious.

Sitting in his car, watching dawn's light bring out the name of the coal ship — *Ningbo* — Andy recalled what he'd heard from those two tourists about glaciers. It still bugged him. Just off graveyard, finding himself downtown in a fresh ant stream of cruisers, he'd tuned into a whiney conversation between a guy Andy's age and an always smiling older man who had curled, waxed moustaches and otherwise didn't look like he fit a cruise ship.

"All this way and we don't get up the inlet to see the damn glacier!"

"A shame," said the older one, smiling nonetheless, hearing what he already knew.

"Too much ice? Can you believe it? We wait and —"

"And they say the Hubbard's a magnificent sight."

"— We wait out at the mouth, you can see all the bergs clogged in there, sure, but we wait a whole day and they tell us, 'Too much ice, we're not goin' in.'"

"Well, they're protecting their investment, aren't they. Plus the lawsuits from all the relatives of all us drowned loved ones?"

Andy liked the old smiler. The other wasn't really listening.

"We came for *that glacier!*"

"And it's a shame." Here the smiler whacked the other on the elbow. "All that ice, and all this talk about global warming!"

The other said, "I *know*," and scoffed.

What bothered Andy wasn't so much that the dumb guy somehow didn't know all the bergs were from the glacier melting, calving faster than usual. What bothered him more, what made the world feel *doubly* stupid, and doomed, was that he didn't get the old guy's joke.

But that's what his yard was doing: calving.

He started his car, stepped lightly on the gas and made the gentlest U-turn. What a marvel, to have changed the weather over our heads and the ocean at our feet. Someday he was going to buy a hybrid, he truly was. He'd actually considered one but opted for the Mustang. He often visualized his trip to the airport to meet Laura. There he was in the airport parking lot standing beside this black stallion, a hand on its hood, calming it. She would step from the terminal, carrying her luggage, she would scan the parking lot for him, the clouds would part, she'd see him and his glossy black steed and — Andy had no idea how she'd take to it. Maybe, once a PR girl always a PR girl, she'd want to crack a beer in the front seat and blow her hair back.

Over the steering wheel, he eyed the mounded thrust of his car's black hood, which gave you the sense of driving in the skull of a powerful hunting dragon. He asked himself what would be sexier, this Mustang or a beige hybrid, even to a woman with cancer, poisoned by the world's pollution. He knew the answer. There was nothing sexy in a reasonable car and there never would be. When you hit the gas, that punch to the gut and gonads was something both girls and boys liked.

Of course he felt uneasy thinking any of this but he sped away, savouring the car's rumbling lust while he still could. In his rearview sat the entire grain terminal, the row of silos, the annex up on a bin top, his speck of a tin shack, book in there waiting for him. What a marvel, to think of Champlain and those men in their compound, huddled over pitchy fires tossed by breezes they couldn't keep out, how they laboured out there in the snow, chewing at logs with dull axes, stacking firewood, burning a mid-sized tree to bake a dozen loaves of bread. If you explained climate change to them, if you told them what they were starting, here on their new continent, they'd stare off in incomprehension. Or maybe cross themselves, no wiser.

ANDY CAME TO at his kitchen table when Pauline rang the doorbell, watching him through the door. He was embarrassed to get caught this way, fists clenched and breathing a little oddly, in a fantasy with Laura. Pauline could probably see it on his face. He leapt up, let her in, and on her cue they hugged, and as usual when he felt her excellent breasts against his chest he was aware that this was his best friend's wife. Pauline hung her coat on the wall peg and went off to the bathroom. It looked like she'd just dyed her hair again, that matte-black goth look. It didn't go with her hearty wash of freckles. It both did and didn't go with her health-food leanings.

He'd been fantasizing Laura's arrival. Usually it involved her emerging from airport bustle, her uncertain approach, her setting down a carry-on, and some sort of shy kiss, she usually pulling away, but then the deep and magical light in each other's eyes. Sometimes she was cool, so he adjusted by playing hard to get. Sometimes the fantasy took a more fantastical route. When Pauline rang the doorbell Andy was on his knees at Laura's feet, aware of the public spectacle and using everyone's energies of curiosity, amusement, and disapproval to add potency to his act. He an able knight to her ailing queen, resting his temple against her jutting hip bone. On his face that knight's mix of earnest sorrow, one less naive than those bystanders over there might think. His knight's sorrow came from awareness that his queen might ask him to leave her, forever, and of course he then must; or she might ask him to die for her and he would; or she might love him, but then of course one of them would be the first to die some day in any case.

Last night's Laura fantasy had been weirder than today's. Today's was pleasantly chest-swelling, but last night's was badly

119

lunatic. In real life he'd been watching a French film where two strangers meet in a tavern and go out into a dark alley. Spliced into their mostly comic sex act, up against the bricks, was a sudden clip of a sperm cell penetrating an egg, revealing the subterranean import of their dalliance. Andy had identified not with sperm but with egg. He was not sure why. Maybe it was his passivity, his lifestyle of mostly just sitting here, thinking, egglike with unborn fantasy. Wasn't there something a little womanly about his waiting for a lover to stop voyaging and come home? Maybe it was a danger sign, signalling a bad tilt to their relationship, an iffy power structure. In any case, in his fantasy here she came, flying in from an exciting life, lithe, sleek, penetrating, possibly *breastless,* a sperm to his egg. It was a dark image he had to shake his head to be rid of.

Andy reckoned he was generally excused and even sometimes applauded for his rich fantasy life. Though, sure, he was at times *accused* of having one. Accusers — those for whom pulling a spark plug weighed more than, say, reading a book on Zoroaster — saw a fantasy life to be only ostensibly rich, worthy only in a diaphanous sense, unbankable. Andy could agree that, sure, maybe he did live too much in his head.

He wasn't sure if Laura was an applauder or an accuser.

He remembered one hiking date to Stutz Rapids. It was that phase of their relationship where the main point was to find a secluded spot, unfurl a coat, and under nature's green witness make out with that ferocity known only to eighteen-year-olds who have decided that, having done it once, they are allowed to never stop. The destination was a treeless knoll Andy thought he could find. It threatened rain and they hadn't been together for a week. Andy remembered trembling with anticipation, and to cover his horniness talking non-stop. Actually she asked him to talk, to talk loud, for they'd neglected to bring some sort of noisemaker to alert any bears of their approach. And that was when Andy invented his character Haggis Chandelier — Scottish gay detective — and in his best gay Scottish accent began a racy but ultimately lame story involving Haggis falling in love with any criminal he investigated. (Accosting one freshly handcuffed scowler, Haggis asked in the softest voice, "Be ye not even a wee bit remorseful then, big laddie?") There was nowhere to go with that one, so Andy launched into a description of how great this hidden knoll was going to be, how *enchanted*, with fairies you could sense but not see, spirits who protected you from all harm so long as your mood stayed good, because that is what woke and sustained them, the good mood of happy humans, especially horny ones. In fact the famous capriciousness of fairies was a backward interpretation, it was happy human mischief that brought them to life in the first place. Andy kept it coming — when they found the knoll he pointed to the invisible ornate oak bed waiting just for them. Though smiling, Laura said, "I hope you like me as much as all the stuff you can't really see." With her face lit up by a sun just now breaking through clouds, and further perfected by this coy humility, he almost died right then of love and horniness, and all afternoon took the greatest pains to show her how much more he liked her than the stuff he couldn't see.

But he couldn't tell then, and couldn't remember now, if what she said was accusation or applause.

"Um. Earth to Andy. Can I make more coffee?"

Andy nodded; Pauline knew where everything was. He told himself it didn't matter what Laura thought. He really shouldn't care. He was tired of these unmanly poses of his. Here in front of Pauline it was almost humiliating. If she could read his mind, this morning she would have seen him kneeling, and last night penetrated by sperm.

So why was he scared of Laura? Why was he picturing her as the top dog? It wasn't that way when they were together. They'd had balance. They'd seen eye to eye. Their yearning appeared to hurt about equally.

"Hey, that's not so bad," Pauline said, pointing out the window at the backyard. "Drew said you lost a major chunk."

"Maybe I exaggerated when I told him."

"But, jeez, you lost some trees too."

"Can see more water now."

"What are you going to do? You going to put up a fence?"

Andy couldn't tell if she was being funny, or meant a fence to keep kids from falling off the new cliff, or if she'd just spoken mindlessly, which she could do. But she changed topics.

"So what we need to do," she said, taking a pad and pencil from her pocket, "is make a list. We're going to get you at least three outfits. Outfit number one, something for the banquet tonight, right?" Behind her, coffee burbled in the maker.

He was afraid of Laura. Laura was coming back and he was afraid. Of the unknown. There. He'd just shucked the Andy Winslow oyster: he was afraid of anything new.

"You still going to that tonight?" Pauline asked. "You even listening to me?"

"I'm going. I'm listening."

"Number two, something for basically 'going out.' You know, even to the pub. Even"— she made a beaverish show of teeth, meant as disgust —"hitting the bar with Drew. Okay?"

"Okay."

"And three, something for when Laura gets back. You want something maybe just a bit souped up for that, right?"

Andy could see Pauline holding back, keeping her excitement in check on this one. She had long ago given up any matchmaking on his behalf. Just as, like Drew, like everyone else, she had long ago stopped telling him to go somewhere, find someone, do *anything new*.

She asked again, "Right?"

"Why not." This concept of getting "outfits" was novel. It sounded so female. Guys had pants and shirts and the colours matched or didn't. Maybe metro-males had been wearing outfits for years and he hadn't noticed.

"You doing okay?"

"Yeah. Why?"

"I dunno, you look really tired."

"No, I'm okay."

"Drew told me you looked really tired too. You sure you're okay?"

"I don't sleep well starting day shift, or something."

"I like the sideburns, by the way. Way better than the beard."

"Thanks." These sideburns were always here. I just had to envision them and sculpt a way in until they were revealed.

"For some reason, those sideburns, I think Johnny Cash, even though you don't look anything like that. But maybe one outfit let's go for a man-in-black look." She splashed herself more coffee, spilling a bit. "This is going to be fun, right?"

"Right."

"God. Andy. What's it going to be like with her back here?" She was looking at him, guileless, innocent, the question rhetorical. She was including herself in it and minutely shook her head in wonder. Pauline and Laura had been friends. The four of them had been two couples together, tight all through the last year of school and that next summer.

"And I heard you're going out to get her at the airport?"

"That's right."

"Well, *I* think it's sweet."

Unlike your husband, Drew, who thinks it's pathetic. Who thinks it's naive. Who thinks it reveals a desperate friend he never knew.

"What do you think is sweet?"

"That you're this excited after twenty years."

"Eighteen, actually."

Pauline began her list and Andy half listened.

How could something *sweet* threaten everything? In thirty-nine years, he had built the cleanest, safest life of anyone he knew. He owned a house and land, albeit shrinking land. He had a job he didn't take home at night, paying him more than he could spend on gas, groceries, CDs, books, the weekly shiatsu, even outfits, and he would not be fired because he had been there forever. He had a great new car, he had a double kayak he never used. He had a mother who was healthy. He had no girlfriend, wife, or kids. The worries, knots, and complications that filled his friends' lives were precisely what he was free of. He did his shifts, read books, watched a popcorn movie with Drew every Tuesday. He walked a lot for exercise. He didn't have abs, but he could feel them under a forgivable and recently shrinking belly.

More and more he was thinking that, boring as it sounded, maybe consistency was the *definition* of comfort, or peace. Maybe stability was the hearth to warm one's feet at. Maybe sameness didn't mean one was stagnant. Maybe self-betterment was more subtle than people thought. Maybe it involved modesty and patience and had nothing to do with the extreme shift, the panicked search. Maybe breathing like a metronome was the most peace you could hope for.

Andy even knew when his life was going to end. His father had died of heart disease at sixty-three, and his grandfather at sixty-two of an identical condition, one with high genetic predictability and a long name that Andy purposely did not commit to memory. Neither father nor grandfather was obese or smoked, so Andy was more or less a ticking clock, and the doctor he'd joked with about not making any plans after 2033 had only smiled and, apparently serious, said that twenty-five, twenty-six years was still a long time.

Yes, he was alone. He felt depression's inevitable attacks, and worked to blunt the triple prongs of no love, no children, and a non-career. What helped was the suffering of friends — those with love, children, and careers — and the daily pain on their faces. Their lives had high points, bubbles of bliss he had no clue about, but these friends were burnt and tossed and soured by care. (A walking sandwich board of pain, Drew had been a huge help in this, for years.) Andy took from all of it that, while he had no keys to happiness, they sure didn't have any either. In thirty-nine years of examining the evidence, it seemed that no one, anywhere, had any of the main questions figured out. So in this sense at least, Andy had lots of company. Read history, turn on the news, talk to a friend — you encounter more floundering. If anything, for all this shared confusion the world felt crowded and familiar. He wasn't alone at all.

Breaking the pencil lead dotting her exclamation point, Pauline finished Andy's list. They put on their coats, she led the way out the door into snow flurries, and since Pauline hadn't driven his Mustang yet, Andy decided to give her complete control of the day and suggested she take the wheel. Pauline was anything but a car person but she pretended to be excited to drive his cool car. She had always been kind that way.

IN THE CLOSET's full-length mirror in his parents' old room, Andy checked out one of his four new outfits. Tonight he would be a man in black, though the belt was more a deep purple. And the shoes dark brown leather. They seemed too thick-soled and somehow nursey and he still couldn't find a way to like them. Downstairs, some Vivaldi was playing too loud. That music and this clothing didn't mesh at all. His mood had bifurcated badly, maybe permanently. It was easiest to change the music. Though he had no Johnny Cash. He had nothing new either, nothing he didn't know every note to. He'd try some latter-day R.E.M., some of which he didn't like very much — maybe he'd hear something new in it. The banquet began in an hour. Maybe he should nudge his humour with a beer.

On leaving the last store, when Andy moaned about spending seven hundred dollars on clothes, Pauline gently reminded him that most men his age with his bank account had no problem spending that much on a leather coat, or two new truck tires, or a charter on Leonard's boat. In Vancouver, she continued, four people could drop that on a nice meal. Especially, she said, if Drew was there and you included the bar tab. It was here she added somewhat casually that it looked like she and Drew were splitting up.

Almost in a panic, Andy asked if they were both still coming tonight, as if checking to see if they'd broken up yet — because if they had, maybe they wouldn't.

Pauline said they were coming. She added that it wasn't just a fight, it was bigger.

"But this is — I knew you guys were sort of, I don't know what, but I hate hearing this, this is awful." Andy had watched Drew and Pauline go through puberty holding hands. You couldn't imagine them apart.

"Well, it looks like we can't stand each other any more."

"That's hard to believe."

"Nope." Pauline was chatty, ready to break out in jokes. "He can't stand me, I can't stand him."

"How? I mean, I know it's probably complicated, but how did this happen? *When* did this happen?"

They were passing the mouth of an alley next to the Elks' Lodge, and there nestling up near the base of the cinder-block wall was what had to be human feces. Last night, someone had taken a mere two steps into the alley and yanked down their pants. What was that about? Why not go ten more feet and turn that corner? Why not run into the bar?

"Well, he's been depressed — Andy, he's been depressed a long time now. Not *depressed*-depressed, but just really sort of down. And when he gets depressed he gets critical. Of me mostly." Pauline's voice got thin here, almost shaky. "Drew gets mean. I get mean back. That's what's been going on for a while now. You try to be kind, and I think he tries too, but it doesn't last long. I mean, he *mocks* me for trying to be nice to him. C'mon, Andy, how bad is that?" She looked up and watched him nodding. "So — we can't stand each other any more." Staring at her feet, shaking her head, Pauline was feeling her words. She added softly, "So why fucking put up with it for the rest of your life, you know?"

"That's really sad to hear." Andy shifted all his black plastic bags to one hand and took Pauline's in his free one. She was his friend too, and this was allowed, this was fine that he be her girlfriend for a bit.

He couldn't imagine them splitting. They weren't an ugly, bickering couple. Maybe the one time he'd seen them truly angry with each other was back when — ten, twelve years ago? — Drew built an English pub in the basement despite Pauline's pleading with him not to. He built it anyway, their marriage survived, and two or three good parties followed, but it never became the hub of social gaiety Drew envisioned, and then it became Chris's bedroom. Andy remembered joking to Drew about the wisdom of giving a boy a pub for a bedroom, a sad irony now, one Andy was careful to avoid pointing out, given Drew's worries about Chris.

"Drew drinking lots?"

"Not really. He doesn't drink at home at all any more." She turned to him with a mischievous deadpan. "He's too depressed."

"What do you think he's depressed about? I'm asking because you seem to be thinking this is where it started."

"You name it." Pauline said Drew couldn't watch TV news any more, or read newspapers. Andy said that didn't sound good, and she said it wasn't just that, it could be triggered by anything. For instance, she said, last night, Drew got depressed reading *The New Yorker* cartoons. His dad had started their gift subscription to *The New Yorker* again and their first issue in years came yesterday, and Drew scanned the cartoons first, as always.

"You know that R. Crumb? The old hippie cartoon guy?"

"I *love* R. Crumb." He hadn't seen R. Crumb in a while, except that film about him. He and Drew had seen it together.

"It depressed him."

"It did?"

"I think because R. Crumb was in *The New Yorker* at all."

"Huh." He could see being disappointed by it, but not depressed. And why not spread the dark joys of R. Crumb to the conservative masses? Still, you could understand the nostalgic underground strand Drew was clinging to.

They walked a few more strides before Pauline asked him what he thought Drew was depressed about.

"I don't know. He does seem sort of down." "Down" had always been Drew's way, though. Andy pictured, maybe they were twelve, Drew pulling his face back from a new microscope, having had a gaze at hairy scooting things, and on his face was knowledge that all life was hungry in a dangerous way, malevolent, and fundamentally wrong. "Down" was something Drew generally brought to the table. Though maybe he'd been farther down of late, come to think of it. He'd been meaning to lend Drew that book on S.A.D. It said excess melatonin might be the culprit, which was surprising, as was the fact that northern latitudes didn't appear to cause it, despite the twelve percent of Inuit who —

"And if he's suicidal," said Pauline, "me being there won't make a bit of difference."

"*What?*"

"Okay." Pauline stopped and threw her hands up as if warding off a crowd. "Forget that. I didn't say it. Mistake."

"Jesus."

"You can't help thinking about everything, you know?"

"Has he said something?"

"Forget it. *I'm* more likely to kill myself."

"Are you thinking about his mother? Because —"

"She fell asleep at the wheel."

"True." Who knew what Drew thought. He wouldn't talk about his mother, and what could be more telling than that?

"It's funny but —" Pauline was suddenly quite cheerful now. "It's not *funny,* but he thinks you're depressed too."

"Me?"

"Maybe it's, when you're depressed, you think everyone's depressed."

"He thinks I'm depressed?"

From Pauline's look it seemed she was going to ask, Well, aren't you? Instead she said, "He calls it 'your rut.' I think it's the solitary life you lead that worries him. Actually"— Pauline squeezed his hand, though it was more timid spasm than squeeze — "I guess we both worry about you sometimes. But hey —" She turned to him and laughed. "This isn't about you!"

He spotted his car a block away looking too wedged in between a white pickup and a yellow hybrid taxi. They were done talking, but Pauline quickly asked him not to mention the breaking up to anyone because they hadn't told Chris yet. Andy said he'd thought Chris was still in Calgary, and Pauline said he was but that she didn't want him hearing it from friends over the phone. Barely sixteen, a month before grade eleven exams, Chris had driven to Calgary with an older friend who'd taken his father's truck without permission. When the father threatened to press charges the friend came back with the truck, but Chris stayed. He was flipping burgers, or that was how Drew described it to Andy. "Doing anything he has to do to stay away." According to Drew, Chris might have got a U.S. scholarship in either hockey or tennis, and Chris's response to this kind of encouragement had been to drop competitive sports. To hear Drew tell it, his son dropped sports *because* of Drew's encouragement. Now even high school was a question mark. Andy liked Chris. He'd met him when Chris was a day old, and Andy was probably the closest Chris had to an uncle. He'd been Chris's fellow student when Drew taught them both to fly-fish. And Drew was right — Chris had been the normal little kid, eager for Dad's attentions. Andy had watched him hit puberty and grow into a wise little cynic, not unlike Dad, but even Dad fell under his freshly baleful gaze. Andy didn't know if Chris had drug issues, but he looked the type, with his knowing eyes and careless hair and acid-wit T-shirts. In any case, Chris was probably the main reason for Drew's depression and no need to state the obvious to Pauline. If Andy had seen Drew tear up on the subject of Chris, imagine what she'd seen.

Before they climbed into the car, Pauline smiled at Andy over the black mirror of the car's roof. "Anyway I don't know. It just might be better to be away from each other. We're both wondering what that might feel like."

Pauline didn't care to drive the Mustang back to Andy's.

IT BEING WEDNESDAY, on the way to the Wheat Women party Andy dropped by his mother's for an abbreviated visit. He was ready for her to see him in his black clothes, disapprove, and pronounce something in singsong like, "But clothes don't make the man," absolving him.

He was hardly noticed. Laura's mother had gone for her walk but failed to return. She'd been gone two hours, it was dark, and now raining. They'd all been out looking, and Doris's daughter's husband still was, and they'd just called the police. The dining table was set for four and centred by a bucket of chicken, its famous smell of spiced fat thick in the room. Coleslaw and French fries had been put into bowls and serving spoons laid out, but nothing had been touched. Andy's mom seemed particularly stricken. She looked grey and her eyes betrayed that she'd been crying. Andy didn't think he'd seen her like this since his father died, and this bothered him, the similar weight given his father and Mrs. Schultz.

He wanted to ask if Laura had been called yet.

"Is this the longest she's wandered off?" he asked instead.

"I think so. But it just feels wrong. Something's wrong this time."

"Well let's hope she rolls up in a taxi at any moment."

"It feels different. We all agree." His mom looked over to Rita, who said "Mmhmm" without looking up from leafing through the phone book. Doris agreed from her living-room chair.

"We drilled her," said Andy's mom. "We made her promise and promise to call us. Her coat pocket has our phone number, her purse has our phone number, her wallet has our phone number. We told her to phone, phone, phone. If she forgot that, I swear she'll forget to breathe."

Andy didn't know what to say so he said nothing.

"But you look very nice, dear." His mother was looking at him down her nose. "Very 'of a sort.' For your party. Your shoes especially."

"Thanks."

"Doesn't he look good?" His mother didn't raise her voice but aimed the inflection at Rita and Doris. Doris responded that he looked very nice, and Rita said so too, but without looking up from flipping her Yellow Pages, which stung Andy a little.

"Maybe I could go back for my car and do some looking too."

"No, dear, you have a party to go to. We've checked all the places we can think of, and now the police are checking . . . some of the 'other' places."

Places a body might be found, Andy understood.

"Well, this is really a drag."

"It is, dear."

He watched his mother shake her head, for herself only, not performing. She said, barely audible, "Either way, it's the end."

Doris scampered up to Andy apropos of nothing and, smiling, asked if he wanted some chicken. Andy thanked her and explained that he'd be eating at the party. Rita, funny and his friend again, did a voice to ask Doris "why would he want trailer-trash chicken when his party's hoidy-toidy catered?"

But the room sobered quickly. Not even tea was being offered so Andy decided it was time. He wished them luck in finding Mrs. Schultz. He said he felt guilty going off to have fun. He added that he had spoken with a contractor about building a seawall. His mother nodded and said that was good to hear, but she was plainly bound up in her worry. Andy hadn't seen her like this. He went to hug her but she didn't get up. She raised her cheek for a kiss, distracted, hardly aware of his lips. To his back she said, "Even the best of friends must part."

THE TWO CHINESE women did look twenty. Andy sipped a glass of ice-cold Aussie shiraz and watched them, surrounded by a circle of smiling older men in suits. It was funny to think that commerce fuelled this swarm and not the expected other. One was very cute, though her face was big and almost perfectly round. Like a poem that rhymed, she was pretty but seemed limited. The other had a horse face but she looked kind, and you could see her sense of humour. They both wore a skirt and matching blazer — the pretty one's navy, the other's tan. Both up on high heels. Neither tapped a foot to the Eagles song "Hotel California," a bizarre selection Andy thought at first, but then not, given the makeup of the crowd. Counting back, he realized the song was as old as he was, and offensive to none.

Though all the other men kept their shoes on Andy had taken his off by the door because after his walk in the rain he pictured the odd spongy soles of his new shoes retaining a dirt stew and depositing it into Mr. Madden's cream carpets. And shoeless he would loom a little less over the Chinese women. He sipped and watched them from the edge of the foyer. He heard "beautiful city" in a tortured accent from the cute one, while the other — who wore a wooden Haida comb in her hair — kept saying "shipping."

Andy would approach the women soon. If they asked him, he could tell them about Prince Rupert. It wasn't like he'd boned up but, sure, he'd gathered his thoughts. First he'd ask them, Did you know that Prince Rupert *exists* because of Asia?

133 ❧

He'd say that even as a boy he found it funny that on maps of the west coast of North America, the only dots were L.A., San Francisco, Seattle, Vancouver, and Prince Rupert. Sometimes Portland would be there, sometimes Anchorage. Why Prince Rupert? Because — and the funny one might like this — Prince Rupert was *supposed* to be big. Mapmakers were *anticipating* PR to earn its dot. Prince Rupert was supposed to be Canada's grain spigot. There was supposed to be a giant lineup of ships out there.

He'd enjoy telling them that Prince Rupert was an invention, born in 1908, when Mrs. Eleanor M. MacDonald of Winnipeg, Manitoba, won the $250 prize for her suggestion of "Prince Rupert" as the name for the town being built at the end of the new national rail line on Canada's northern west coast. She chose the name because Prince Rupert was the first governor of the Hudson's Bay Company, a cousin of King Charles II, and also she liked his looks.

Andy would add that Charles Melville Hays built the rail line after noticing, on a map of the world, how British Columbia toppled westward the farther north one went, meaning northern B.C. was hundreds of miles closer to Asia, miles that would lure any shipping company wanting to save fuel. In 1904 his engineers declared the base of Kaien Island, ninety miles south of Ketchikan, Alaska, to be one of the world's finest deep-sea harbours — ice-free year round and a minimum channel depth of one hundred feet. In 1908 the rail line was finished, two hundred white people lived on-site, and Mrs. MacDonald won her contest. In 1910 Prince Rupert was incorporated as a city. In 1912 Charles Hays died on the *Titanic*.

Andy would ask the Chinese Wheat Women if they'd seen the ten-foot-tall sign perched five miles out of town on a scenic bluff overlooking the Skeena. Perhaps the distances were a little pathetic for being hand-painted.

> Tokyo, 3830
> Vladivostok, 3928
> Panama Canal, 4303
> Shanghai, 4642
> Hong Kong, 5286
> Halifax, 6641
> Sydney, 6671
> Calcutta, 8332
> London (England), 9104

Andy could explain, if they were still nodding, that these destinations remained dreams. In 1990 Prince Rupert had a population of twenty thousand. Today there were seven thousand fewer. And if they were at all intuitive, the Chinese Wheat Women might already have noticed how, despite the smiling and laughing, every guest here looked hungry. The Wheat Women, especially the non-cute one, might link it to *all this rain*, and she'd be partly right. She might also notice another shared feature, an impatient lean to the body, something like a pugilistic barfly's chin sticking out. The Wheat Women would do well to prepare themselves.

Andy's glass was empty, a perfect excuse not to approach them just yet. He pivoted on new socks in the direction of the bar. He wondered if they knew about the Highway of Tears. Probably they did, probably they read the local newspaper and knew the death count had just risen from twelve to thirteen, all Native girls — who didn't look that unlike the Wheat Women — who had disappeared on the highway to Prince George after sticking out their thumbs not more than a mile from this house. But they might not know about the Iron Chink, not unless they'd toured the Cannery Museum. A hundred years ago, when the salmon were limitless and Chinese cannery workers stood shoulder to shoulder moving fish down the line for one to gut, one to scale, one to fin, one to cut in chunks, and one to stuff in a can, along came a machine that could do the work of all of them. And, as the cannery owners congratulated themselves, they didn't have to feed it. But they did give it a name.

ANDY WAS STANDING in a small line for a refill of shiraz from the bartender, a sad-eyed and shirt-and-tie-garbed Tsimshian girl nearer fourteen than nineteen, when Drew, Pauline, and Leonard arrived. Seeing Leonard, Andy recognized the girl to be one of his innumerable nieces, and now he understood Leonard's presence here too. Leonard sometimes used events like this to get loud about the white man's corporate intentions, and Andy hoped he would keep his mouth shut. With the Highway of Tears again in the news, things could escalate. In any case, as the Leonard-niece awkwardly topped up his glass, Andy supposed this girl got her job in the first place because of Leonard. Further evidence that this girl got her job as someone's favour was an ice-tub full of not only white wine but also the red. Andy tipped forward to whisper that she should get those reds up on the table because they should be room temperature, and the girl complied, dead-faced, as she likely would have had he been a strange man in a bathrobe in off the street, asking her to hand over ten bottles of wine. He saw that her earlobes were freshly pierced and the holes, one of which was off-centre, were inflamed and swollen closed.

Drew didn't hang up his coat before striding into the living room to kneel at his father's stereo. The Eagles disc was near its end but Drew took it out to put in — Andy could see when he reached his friend's side — a Miles Davis. Drew knew that the legs beside his head were Andy's.

"He won't even know the diff," Drew said quietly, but with the weight of judgement. "Nice duds," he said to the new black pants beside his face, this judgement a little harder to gauge. From the speakers a trumpet opened with strangled *poop, poop, poop*s, that Davis sound.

Funny how, kneeling there, Drew looked the teenager again, easily playing the role of intolerant son in Dad's house. Andy couldn't help but think of Drew and his own son, Chris, and what goes around comes around. Though it wasn't the same — Chris wouldn't even talk to Drew, and here Drew had willingly come to his father's party.

Andy deliberately kept his eyes from the mantel and its central picture not three feet away, a depressing photo if you knew what to look for: a blowup of Drew, Pauline, and twelve-year-old Chris posed outside Arthur Ashe Stadium in New York, Chris holding up the tennis ball Pete Sampras had smacked into the stands. Apparently Chris, who it turned out liked playing tennis but not watching it, had never not been a jet-lagged and whiney mess the whole trip. In this picture, much celebrated by Mr. Madden because the trip to the U.S. Open had been his gift to them, Chris glowered. Drew looked only wary (he'd told Andy the guy taking their picture was weird and Drew was wondering if he'd get his camera back). And there, with her arm around his waist, was Pauline — her smile way too happy, inaccurate.

Andy hadn't seen his friend for a week, what with Drew's absence from work and then a shift change. He cupped Drew's shoulder, said hi, and offered him his untouched glass of merlot.

"Ah, man, I'm on the wagon." Drew shrugged, smiling, and here his judgement was directed at himself.

"Holy cow. This is a first."

"It wasn't helping the situation." Drew met Andy's eyes and it passed between them that he knew Andy and Pauline had talked.

"Well, maybe it will," Andy offered, nodding. Surprising himself with an expression at least ten years gone, he added, "Gotta listen to the head-Betty, I guess." Somehow the Betty Ford Clinic had joined your inner voice of guilt to become your head-Betty, who kept tabs on your drinking.

"Yeah, well, who knows."

Andy snatched his wine back to his chest. "Can't have it anyway because it's mine." He took a sloppy sip. In the middle of this little gesture he knew he'd wanted to have a beer with Drew, and a chat, a heart-to-heart. A beer would've been the only way it would happen.

"Andrew! Good to see you!"

Drew's father was at his elbow and they shook hands. Mr. Madden was the only person who called Andy Andrew, save for his mother, who might use it on occasions like his birthday, as if to remind him of his actual name. Drew and Andy were both Andrews as kids, and everyone agreed that because of their obvious close friendship, to avoid confusion one must became Drew and the other Andy. Apparently he and Drew chose. Neither had recollection of any of this, and neither got excited when any parent hauled out the anecdote. And when Mr. Madden called him "Andrew," Andy always got the slight sense he was being reminded that his own son had been made to change his name furthest and that Andy had been done a favour.

"Nice spread," Andy said, smiling at the cloth-draped table holding platters of hot and cold hors d'oeuvres. (He saw one was chicken à la king in puff pastry, which he hated.) A longer table was just now being set up with warming trays and Sterno pots. A Native man of about twenty-five, with one of those bodies that is wide face-on but almost skinny in profile, wearing white apron and tall chef's hat, lugged a stainless-steel bin and placed it in its cradle over the lit flame. Andy recognized the man as another of Leonard's relatives.

"It's the Chamber of Commerce," Drew's father explained. "I was only happy to provide the space." He smiled and, house-proud, with a hand indicated first one end of the long living room, then the other. He leaned into Andy with a stage whisper. "Maybe I'll get to keep the leftover hooch," then he gave both Drew and Andy a stage glare. "Not that there'll *be* any, with you two here."

Mr. Madden had bright eyes, and charm. Andy figured he was PR's most successful realtor largely because, like some politicians, he'd got so good at trying to act like a nice guy that, over the years, he'd actually become one. Drew's mother had died twenty years ago when her car went into the Skeena as she drove back from Terrace. It was a straight stretch, no ice, suicide an unstated possibility. Drew had inherited his brooding nature from her.

Mr. Madden cheerfully asked Drew if he'd be "stereo master" for the evening, and his son said okay and walked off, up to the bar, and got himself a bottle of beer. Andy watched him tilt it back for a long first sip.

THE CUTE ONE'S name was Li and the other's May. May was the more interesting to talk to, and not just because her English was better. Andy had been right in guessing that she had a sense of humour.

Still standing in front of the couch, the Chinese Wheat Women hadn't left each other's side, and now Andy and Pauline chatted with them, just the four. The various town dignitaries and businessmen appeared satisfied for the time being that they had done their duty.

May drank beer out of the bottle and Andy another glass of wine. To break the ice he asked her if she could stand the weather here. She told him she came from "a raining city" north of Shanghai and she found the weather here "okay." He asked her if she'd ever heard of Dancing Monkey.

"It's a dish, a meal, that royalty would eat," he explained. "I think in the south. Canton."

"It is monkey that they ate?"

"Yes. It's the most decadent thing I've ever heard of. I was wondering if it still might exist in, you know, certain circles. They'd have to be very *corrupt*, I think."

"Corrupt to eat monkeys, yes."

"Yes."

"But, no, I have not heard of this, ah, dish?"

Andy asked her about her last name, which had sounded like, simply, E. He asked how she spelled it, and May told him that in her language she drew it with a character, and in English it was for her to choose.

"I could spell it one E. But then I have a curious name. I think it would be a very 'hip' name, like the name of a rock star."

"I guess it would."

May's eyes shone above her constant smile. Prone to the word-play that non-native speakers sometimes are, she enjoyed her own humour. "I could spell it a single Y, which would be phonetically more correct, I think. You have 'sill-y,' and 'Bill-y,' and 'y-clept.'"

"Holy cow!"

"Yes. 'Hol-y.'"

"No — you said 'yclept.'"

"This word is not so common I don't think."

"People actually only say it to be funny." She could be a friend, a PR girl, except for the way she kept nodding, almost a bow from the shoulders, every third or fourth word, a gesture of subservience maybe, even if it wasn't felt.

"But if I spell it Y, then people I think will pronounce it 'why,' which will be curious, to have a question for a name."

"May Why."

"Yes. I am being asked a question every time I am spoken to. It is like a joke. You have a very famous joke about the word 'who.' It is a baseball joke."

"You know that one?"

"Yes. It is very, very funny. I think so. My English teacher used it in his class. He was from Canada, from Halifax. Grant. He told us his name and home were all we needed to know, to speak English. Glant flom Harifax. It took a very long time to teach my ear to teach my tongue." Saying all of this, May had gently turned away from Li and dropped her voice, and Andy understood that she didn't want to embarrass her friend, whose tongue was not as well taught.

Li would likely not have heard in any case because she was talking with Art Tanner, an ex-businessman who now worked in government, keeping alive the province's tradition of selling all its best trees to other countries.

Tanner was talking loudly to her, as one does with foreigners.

"So let me get this straight. Li? Yes, Li. Now, Roger over there — Mr. Sorenson over there says — You say you're 'a student'?"

"Yes, we here studying nature of sistah city." Li's foreignness had her bring a hand to her mouth and shield it when she grew unsure. "And shipping, to China. Ah, relationship of—"

"You're a student. A university student."

"Ah, yes. University in Shanghai. Study of relationship, for instance, hypothetical, of drought in Alberta, plus market price grain, equal amount of tons shipping to China. Many factor. Very very many factor."

"You don't work for a corporation then?"

"Ah, no no."

"You don't work for your government either?"

"Yes. Our government, Chinese government, give us grant, to study these, ah, relationship." She pronounced "Chinese government" as one fast word. "You know, Prince Rupert is seven hundred eighty kilometres close, more close, to ports in China than —"

"We're aware of that. So you're here to — While you're here, is there any way you can, let's say, influence —"

Art Tanner had turned two shades darker during this exchange. Andy could see that all he really wanted to ask was, Is there any point in any of us talking to you?

"Let me try this. Will your 'study,' possibly bring, an increase, of business, of 'shipping,' to Prince Rupert?"

"Ah-yes. If our work is, you say, 'publish,' and Chinese government see, then, yes, more shipping very possible. Very good."

Meanwhile, May E was trying puns on Pauline, and Andy decided she was mostly frivolous. Li was mostly shallow, and Art Tanner mostly selfish. Andy wondered what *he* mostly was. He knew he was gazing at the wall of beige drapes and that he couldn't pull his gaze away, staring so thoroughly into the wavy scalloping that he could feel his brain move with it. He was wet with perspiration. Maybe it was these new clothes.

Art Tanner regarded Li as if gauging whether she might still be in any way worth his while. Apparently she was. His face collapsed then rebuilt itself to smile in an altogether different way, a less businesslike way, and he asked if he could fill her half-full glass.

SOMEWHERE IN THE thick of the evening the banquet developed a ragged and angry feel. It had lost dignity, if it ever had any, so as to be almost fitting when someone threw up in the hall bathroom. There was little laughter now and people started trickling out. Andy couldn't say if it was the fault of Leonard's yelling at Worthington, or if the Wheat Women's impotence had blunted the horny commercial spirit. Or it might just have been the food. Andy had already decided it was the food. It wasn't horrible but it was supposed to have been good. Food could make you groan and laugh. Staring at the half-full trays of chicken à la king and dry meatballs, Andy thought of yesterday's reading, of Champlain, of changing a colony's mood with brilliantly strange food, with celebration for its own sake. And he might have cured scurvy! The livers of seal and porpoise had vitamin C in them, but only if freshly killed, and they also ate the green stomach contents of moose. In a fantastic accident, Champlain had unwittingly also cured their plague.

Leonard had started yelling when Andy was in the kitchen phoning his mother. She'd called the party with a message for Andy, simply that "they found her." Andy wanted to make sure that they found her healthy, and to see about his mother too. He was calling just as Leonard came into the kitchen, seething, followed by Ken Worthington, the manager from the Hickory Pit. Andy had noticed Worthington flitting in and out of the party, checking on the food table and beer supply, and not only whispering admonishments to the guy carving the baron of beef but straightening his chef's hat. Apparently Worthington was the caterer. In fact Andy thought he recognized the rib sauce smothering tonight's "Barbecue Winglettes."

His mother answered and, yes, Marie Schultz was alive and well. Behind him, Andy heard Leonard saying something about the toughest roast beef he'd ever had. Then something about his niece and nephew. Andy suspected that Leonard mostly used "niece" and "nephew" and "brother" in their idealized sense.

"But no," Andy's mom said softly, "she's not well and she's not the same." Laura's mother had walked all the way out to Oliver Lake Park, where the police found her sitting at a picnic table, under that new shelter the Rotary Club had built. They didn't know how long she'd been sitting there by herself in the dark, frightened, and she didn't know either.

"You sound *really* tired, Mom. You should try to get a good sleep." Behind him, Ken Worthington and Leonard were debating the ethics of minimum wage.

"We're in a dither here. Poor Marie was just happy to be home, and we've upset her."

Andy asked her what she meant.

"We're angry, dear. And we've told her that we don't know what to do with her." She allowed herself a long pause and then spoke slowly but with the weight of a milestone in her voice. "We've told her, that we don't know, what we're going to do."

Andy said nothing could be decided tonight and at least they'd found her and they all needed sleep. His mother pointed out that tomorrow was another day. They said goodnight.

"Andy." Leonard was not looking his way but he was being hailed. "We need your opinion on salmon. Come settle something."

"I'm no foodie." But Andy went to stand by the two men, both of whom were portly, and black-mustachioed, but while one was unidentifiable in an off-the-rack grey suit, the other wore jeans, a Tibetan felt vest, and what he called his "headdress," a single eagle feather attached to his ponytail, that bounced against his back when he got this animated.

"Tell me," Leonard said to Andy while he looked Worthington in the eye. "Would you say the Chinese are famous for fresh fish?"

"Um. I guess." They were a people largely lacking refrigeration, but sure. They kept carp in pools. Actually they dried most of their fish. And there'd been a nasty taint to some squid he'd had at the Jade last month. Likely Leonard was thinking of Japan. "Sure," he added.

"So if you want to impress Chinese dignitaries with fish, would you say that freshness is something you shoot for?"

Worthington snorted at the "dignitaries," but chose anyway to address Leonard's logic, namely his failure to mention the closure and ban on fresh seafood until the mystery of the fish-kill had been solved.

"Whoa." Leonard pointed both hands, like six-shooters, at Worthington. "Closure was lifted two days ago. You had time to —"

"One day. The boats haven't even gone —"

"The salmon are *in the rivers*. You want fresh salmon, you talk to someone like me. You going to make this thing work, you need fresh. It's your *job* to get it."

"Don't tell me my job."

"That *frozen* sockeye was cooked *dry*, and putting a *sauce* on it, that slippery fuckin' hollandaise —"

"Béchamel sauce. Gimme a break."

"— only makes dry fish feel *dryer* and doesn't fool *any*body, and those fuckin' frozen prawns were *farmed ones from China*."

"And was a nice touch. You know, 'China.' Trade. As in, we're already doing it. 'Trade.' As in, yes, we catch prawns here too, but look what we eat: yours."

"*Frozen, farmed, Chinese.* You know why they're the cheapest ones in the store? You know there's health warnings on that shit? They use shit water, and to keep the shit alive they pump in crap galore, unbelievable, they inject the fuckin' *hormones* with antibiotics to keep the fuckin' crap out of the — You know what *night soil* is?"

"All imports are —"

"They use *human shit* to fertilize *every*thing. The fish farmers and all their fat drunken uncles stumble out at night and reef down their fuckin' black pyjamas to take a dump in the family prawn tank."

Ken Worthington lifted a single hand by way of goodbye, or maybe "I've had it," and turned to leave. Andy felt bad for him. He was in the wrong business, because he had less a feel for food than for money, and here he was moonlighting to make ends meet, cutting a few corners. Palming his way out the saloon-style door, Worthington looked mostly tired.

Leonard seemed tired too as he grabbed a beer for both of them from the fridge. Side by side they leaned back against the kitchen counter.

"What's with Drew?" Leonard asked, mostly to the floor. "He looks messed tonight."

Andy said he didn't know. He could say he was ignoring his head-Betty, but didn't want to explain a word game. He asked Leonard why the tilt with Ken Worthington, and Leonard said he'd arranged the jobs for Grace and Neil — his niece and nephew — and this catering business could really work out, it could get bigger and make jobs for more kids. Leonard tried to get Andy to agree that the food was abysmal.

"It's not memorable, no."

"It's fuckin' sad. There's no excuse. You try that barbeque sauce?"

"It's sad."

"And Grace needs something good in her life right now."

Andy pictured the dead-eyed girl out there, clumsily tilting wine into businessmen's glasses. "She from the north?"

Leonard nodded. He had relatives in the villages to the north and south, both accessible only by boat. The village to the north was worse in terms of what Leonard generally called "family values."

"Know what they're doing there now? They get cranked on meth and—You know extreme fighting? Those shows on cable?"

Andy asked if he meant that caged fighting with no gloves, where you could knee and elbow and they got all bloody, squeezed up against the chicken wire. It was sometimes on at the Legion if there was no hockey.

"They get high and they extreme fight. With their *friends*, man. They do a fuckin' fight club." He implored Andy with the saddest small eyes, and Andy could see the niece in that face. "They try and beat up their brother. Their best friend. They do meth and try to kill each other. *Brothers*."

"Jesus."

"It's gotten fuckin' primitive, man. It's that satellite TV. Bad news."

"Where's Grace stay?"

"With her aunt." Leonard began violently shaking his head at the next thought. "You know, her brother, sixteen, seventeen, he's cooking meth in his bedroom, almost killed them all, and his father doesn't give a shit? Does *nothing*?"

"Did it catch fire?"

"I don't know, it was fumes or something. The thing is they don't care. Father's a selfish asshole. Mother doesn't metabolize."

This was Leonard's term for a drunk. He liked seeing alcoholism as purely physiological, to remove all judgement.

"Speaking of which"— he brought his empty beer to his face and peered in —"to beer or not to beer, that be the question."

"Charter tomorrow?"

"Bears."

Taking tourists on the long run up-inlet he didn't have to leave as early as with a fishing charter, but still early. He didn't care much for grizzly watching. It demanded noiselessness once within two hundred yards. The Khutzeymateen sanctuary had the world's densest grizzly population and you could generally count on some to be feeding on the shore grass, but you had to be delicate. Leonard had to cut the engine and drift in with not even a *clink* from binoculars set down. Andy had come along a few times to help, basically to make coffee and hand out sandwiches. He didn't love grizzlies himself. They hated humans and were kind of insane, as animals go. Through a complex lineage tree they were related to a large, evil pig. He suspected Leonard needed his help less than his company, so he'd feel less lonely when the tourists complained among themselves that this "close encounter" with the bears just didn't seem that close, nothing like what you could see at home on high-def. Leonard once told Andy that most people with the money to afford his charter were automatically a bit afraid of him not only because he was Indian, but because by rights he owned everything they could see and deep down they knew it. He'd also told Andy, somewhat dramatically, that when passing Metlakatla he wouldn't announce that the abandoned village was once the site of the largest church north of San Francisco and west of Chicago, because he didn't want to reveal where his people had first been enslaved.

"Texans," Leonard added, about tomorrow. For some reason Leonard liked Texans.

Andy remembered Leonard's words to Worthington, "You talk to someone like me," and had an idea.

"Len, could you get some wild food, no matter what time of year?"

"Sure. Maybe. Like what?"

"I'd pay for it and everything. I'm thinking mussels, the big—"

"West coast of Haida Gwaii. Where it's crazy stormy they grow the size of dance slippers. Read that in a book, 'mussels the size of dance slippers.'"

"Great."

"But they'd have to be flown in. Which shouldn't be a problem. I've got a buddy supplies a resort out that way. How many pounds you want?"

"I'm just thinking. How soon would you have to know in advance?"

"I dunno, a week?"

"How about a moose?"

"You want a moose?"

"'Some' moose."

"Well, it's out of season, you know."

"That's why"— Andy smiled —"I'm talking to someone like you."

Leonard nodded sombrely at this. "Okay."

"But it would have to be fresh. Not frozen."

Leonard glanced his way and looked down again, nodding. "Hmm. Okay."

"You think?"

"They're inland, you know. Gotta go past Terrace. Where we're talkin' deep snow."

"Right."

"And we're talkin' poachin'. Just so you know."

"I thought you guys had rights all year round. You know, for cultural reasons. For Aboriginal sustenance."

"Sell it to whitey, it's poaching."

149

"What if you give it to whitey?"

"Touché."

"But you can get me some?"

"I'd need at least a week for that too."

"Actually," and here Andy hunched down with eyebrows raised to peer into his friend's face, to let him know he was serious when he said, "I think I'd mostly want the nose."

LOOKING FOR DREW, Andy wandered out into a party that felt thin and faintly poisonous, in the way of parties that have passed their peak. Leonard's niece and nephew ineptly packed food and equipment under the sober direction of Ken Worthington, who kept an eye on the kitchen lest Leonard leap from it. Andy could have told him that Leonard had left through the back way, but instead shot Worthington a smile and shrug of commiseration at having to work while everyone else was playing.

Drew was over by the stereo, bumping one hip to a song Andy recognized, some of Drew's old funky fusion. The volume was too loud in the half-empty room and added to the night's desperate quality. Drew's goofy dance — he lifted a leg high to lightly stab down a big toe as if popping an ant — made Art Tanner's wife laugh and, off to the side, Pauline smiled despite herself. For a couple about to break up, she hovered close. She looked never not aware of him.

Andy watched his friend, who evidently had his head-Betty locked away in some closet for the night. As always when Drew was drunk and moving, his hairline sprang with sweat and little talons of hair clung to his forehead, that Roman emperor look. He had a fancy-frilled meatball toothpick in his mouth and seemed to enjoy being watched. It felt like Drew had avoided him tonight, perhaps feeling Andy's intentions from afar. When

Drew didn't feel like talking, no talking took place. It was sad to so clearly see the twelve-year-old in his friend bouncing there, older bones in older flesh, a guy not too happy about anything any more, it seemed. Andy wondered when it was they'd last truly talked. When had they ever talked? There was that notion of best friends not needing to, which is why they were best friends. But that no longer seemed true. It felt like something had shifted, or faded. It felt like Drew could move away, could just suddenly leave without even telling him.

May and Li were still surrounded, but by a more motley clump of men, despite their suits. Andy found it telling that no formal introductions had taken place, no gesture of civic welcome. It seemed no one had found out who they were, exactly, other than who they weren't.

Art Tanner was drunker and still cozying up to Li, who stood trapped in the L of the cream couch and chair set. May was nodding at a couple of men, a baby oyster poised on a toothpick, listening so politely that she couldn't pop it in. If May asked him, and he hoped she would, Andy could tell her that oysters, just like the one on her toothpick, couldn't grow up here.

This should probably be his last glass of wine but he was also going to tell her how in Prince Rupert, after a late-night tureen of pho or a pomegranate martini, you could go home and sit with your window open and hear wolves trilling. They never used to come this close, but since they built the dump a decade back they came for the rats, Andy had heard. Then got good at picking off pets. May, his neighbour two houses down was walking her old black lab up near the hospital last spring when, completely ignoring her, two wolves were on her dog, which they "disembowelled in about three seconds." Only a month ago somebody's poodle was gobbled in the industrial park and now there are signs posted there, May. How cool is that?

Sweating, weaving the tiniest bit, Andy knew he wanted May to understand why he'd never left. He also wanted to tell May about Laura, and that actually he wasn't alone, despite appearances. He'd ask May if they had modern dance in China, or if it was still all traditional posing, or Cirque du Soleil plate-spinning.

May got her oyster in and chewed it, nodding to someone's lecture about the Beijing Olympics. Leonard's niece walked by with a bottle of red in one fist and a white in the other, filling glasses, and how could May not want to know about the Tsimshian people, who came from Asia but hadn't strayed far from the land bridge just north of here. In 1906 when this was a tent city a bunch settled here for white man's commerce and poisons, and the influx continued still, which was a problem, May, which you can see.

"Hello! Andy!" May was waving him over. He hoped he hadn't been staring.

Leonard's niece drifted back, saw his nod and filled his glass with white wine. Which, mixed with the dregs of shiraz, turned pink.

But, the Dancing Monkey — was May *allowed* to know? He'd read that the rich could still arrange it in one secret Hong Kong restaurant. So inhuman was this meal it was hard to contemplate without feeling shame for your species. It used a special table with a hole in its centre, a harness beneath. From this hole the top of a live monkey's head protruded, the top half of the skull surgically removed, the living brain exposed, into which eager diners would dig, lifting out tasty bits of grey matter. Below the table, the monkey "danced," as now a left leg was triggered, now an elbow. But, horrible as this was, wasn't it maybe the outer limits of an honest instinct — faint now — to eat the strongest, smartest thing? To take it in, absorb it? To chew the pounding heart of your enemy? To eat vitality itself? To eat *worth*? Wasn't this the idea in health-food bars where they scissor a bunch of growing wheat grass then shriek it through a juicer so you can gulp down the deep-sparkling cells? Wasn't sushi in this ballpark too? May, your enemies the Japanese have an even fresher sushi — fish that's still alive, eaten to gain the creature's living essence. What was the word? He would ask Leonard if he could deliver a salmon that was still alive.

With Andy at May's side the fellows who were being loud didn't get any less loud, and Andy saw that the Wheat Women were being mocked. He could also see, over in the far corner, on another set of couch and chairs, Mr. Madden sitting in a square with the mayor and two other like types, perhaps agreeing that though tonight had performed below expectations, steps could still be made in the eventual emergence of the Port of Prince Rupert as a global superport. The future is now as we step into tomorrow.

The main mocker was red-haired Dan Boyd, who told them, "So, tell the chairman to, you know, turn the country on to —"

"We no longer have chairman. Is now a —"

"— *canola*, right? Tell the chairman we'll sell him a *billion bottles of canola*."

"Yes, canora," Li said, turning from Dan Boyd's wolfish mouth to Art Tanner's wobbly stare. "Is Monsanto, yes?"

Dan Boyd was a supervisor at the terminal and a man with whom Andy had frail relations. They'd been childhood friends but weren't any more, so there was that slight embarrassment. There was the other embarrassment, that Andy could have been a supervisor if he'd only wanted to but had shunned it, and now they played the roles of boss and underling.

Boyd pointed at Art Tanner's dog behind the couch, shaking his finger at it. "Watch it, Art," he yelled. The dog was medium-sized with a sheepdog's face, groomed to show-quality, and Andy bet Art Tanner brought it everywhere less out of love than from wanting to show off how well behaved it was. "Watch it, Art," Boyd yelled, making the dog raise its head. "They might eat it. They might think it's some kind of giant chicken."

The main reason Andy thought ill of Dan Boyd was because of his children, and how he didn't want them.

IT WAS RAINING as he walked, which felt ordinary and good. Rain and this wind would make his open door, warm kitchen, and then bed a string of comforts he would try to stay awake to.

He'd left the party in a bluster. He'd grown irritable and, not smiling, he'd told Dan Boyd to "be nice," and then told Mr. Madden that those two women should be looked after and sent home in a taxi, eliciting "ooooo!'s" from the men, including, Andy was bugged to see, Drew.

He chose a long route in order to work bad food from his legs and wine from his head. From ghostly habit he headed to what was once Central Park, which disappeared five years ago when the several acres of woods in the heart of downtown were razed and a tin-sided mall erected in its place. Now, out of the rain, were a Zellers and banks and a Superstore and discount clothiers with racks of off-gassing shirts sewn up in the sweat-shops of Asia. (They arrived by truck after being unloaded in the port of Vancouver.) Many mourned the loss of Central Park but at the same time admitted it had become a hazardous place. Lots of drunks passed out there and who knows what other gar-bage ugliness went on in the dark and wet. Drunks still tried to get comfortable inside on the mall's benches, maybe attuned to the ghost forest they thought still surrounded them, but it was easy for security guards to patrol a mall.

A few blocks along Andy strode past his mother's. All looked dark and peaceful. For some reason Andy always felt good when he knew his mother was asleep.

Then he found himself on 6th, and here was the Northwest Academy of Dance. Despite the rain, he stopped. The home-lettered sign, its font verging on Olde English, worked hard for elegance, a suggestion that everything inside was Old World and not from here. Which was true, perhaps, if you considered the origins not only of ballet but also jazz and tap and modern. Here, the only dance was Tsimshian — even Haida dance was considered a bit of an incursion. In any case, the Academy had been Laura's ticket out.

Andy had spent a lot of time in front of this building waiting for her to finish. (Occasionally her mother would waltz out first, having watched the session, her eyes' icy warning serving only to give his Romeo to her daughter's Juliet all the more tang.) Out she'd race, to stop short two feet away, embarrassed by "how I must smell," and it took Andy months (afraid she'd think him an animal) to let it all out and tell her that not only didn't he care that she smelled but that he loved it, one smell in particular. "I have multiple stink?" she laughed, and he told her about the three fairly distinct smells, the only one he didn't care for being the one that smelled like Campbell's chicken soup. (Sometimes he could smell her feet and that was no treat either.) He said he'd noted no pattern to her smells and had no idea if they were linked to diet, exertion, or, "you know, your hormonal stuff." He explained what little he knew of pheromones and how they maybe dictated his preferences. He probably talked too much and revealed too much about himself, and it didn't get her walking any closer but he was brave enough to insist that "one smell in particular" drove him crazy. Plus he loved those leg warmers bunched on her ankles like that, and how her black terrycloth headband framed her face.

"Laura Schultz." Andy heard himself actually whisper this, standing in the rain in front of the old Academy. Back when he was so in love with her, especially when she was newly gone and he missed her leg warmers and her smells, he fell in love with her name. He remembered driving to Terrace and back, just for the hell of driving, when he enjoyed a kind of fit of saying it — *Laura Schultz* — into the echo of his small car just to hear it again and again. He remembered a day on Leonard's first boat, a rotting old crabber that lacked even a winch for lifting the traps, back when Leonard was wild and would raid competitors' traps and replace the crabs with a bottle of something if he liked them, or nothing if he didn't, and Andy spent that day in sleet pulling line and saying "Laura Schultz" over and over. Laura Schultz, Laura Schultz. He remembered reaching into a pot to wrestle out a stubborn crab that wouldn't release its stiff legs from the mesh, as if knowing things would get worse for it outside this cage, and when he pried it free and rattled it and yelled "Laura Schultz!" at it, Leonard asked him why the fuck he just didn't buy a plane ticket. Laura Schultz wasn't a pretty name, and he heard nothing much good in the German part, but it was an earthy name, with a visceral tug to it, butter and warmth and promise, a warren of good-smelling animals. Sometimes just saying it to himself was enough to make him horny, horny past the point of not-doing-something-about-it horny. Laura Schultz. Laura Schultz.

"Laura Schultz." That was the year he'd walk by this Academy on purpose for the yearning leap it gave his stomach. By then he was in solid at the grain terminal and getting lots of overtime and he was saving up for Toronto. He was really going to move there and join her. It wasn't just to join her, it was to go to U of T, it was to get out of PR. Some friends had already left. He would look up at the black lettering and feel that, indirectly, the

Academy was his ticket out too. Who knows if he would have been making this move without it?

Andy saw no light coming from any upper window but he guessed Helen and Michael Smythe still lived up there. They'd come from England and taught everything themselves, occasionally letting star pupils like Laura teach a beginners' class. Michael was ludicrously effeminate and everyone agreed theirs was a lavender marriage, a cover for them both. Andy thought Helen odd, almost dim-witted for never changing her loud manner no matter who she spoke with — a six-year-old tap dancer, a parent, or husband Michael.

Five or six silent shadows, teenagers probably, were moving in his direction from a block away, so Andy spun and walked. You never knew. These last few years, you just didn't. Though this street had long felt dangerous to him for other reasons. After Laura's final letters, to get home from downtown he walked along 3rd in order to avoid seeing the Academy. It and all things dance were dark, seductive, and took advantage of the innocent.

They were both just nineteen when it took her away again but this time dragged her farther than he was allowed to follow. She'd been in Toronto one month short of a year when the first of her final letters came, and it began:

Andy everything has changed. I don't know how to start or make it easier for you so I'll just say it. I'm having a baby about six months from now. The father is a dancer, Robert, who leads the company. We started seeing each other only a few months ago. I never lied to you, and I still won't. I still love you. I don't know if I love him. But I'm going to have the baby, so I want to love him. He says he loves me, he says he'll get married if I want to, but I don't know about that yet. I don't know how much to say about Robert, because of how this must feel for you.

Everything I do and think has to be for the baby right now. This feels selfish and maybe looks selfish because I don't know this new person at all, and it's still more me than anything else. But I can't even say I'm sorry to you, because I can't let myself go in that direction even for a second. I've decided to be happy (such a silly word, but it's the one I'm shooting for) and I can see that happiness is a decision. Once I decided to have the baby, I also decided that everything is in service to it, even my moods. I can't look back. I can't be sorry. My career is also going to take a backseat. Maybe it's finished forever, even before it began. Like us. But I've decided to decide that that's only good.

I can say that I'm sorry about what you must be feeling now. And for me to say that I still love you, might be a kind of torture, but I can't not say it, because it's what I feel, and I've also decided that it's good, it's only good, to love. Mostly, to love a baby. To love two men. To love anyone, everyone. To love the world if you can. That's what I've decided. If I turn back, if I have doubts about any of this, if I look in any direction other than the one I'm looking in right this second, it's only dark.

Wet to the skin and tired, Andy passed Moose Tot Park, its carved wooden sign and name not charming tonight but absurd. He turned onto his street. He did feel healthier for the walk. It was darker on his street, with fewer streetlights, and patches of forest between houses each on their half-acre lot, and he could hear what were probably foot-high waves breaking on the beach below. He knew in his childhood bones this darkness and this sound, knew it more than he knew the town, its density and fret, and he felt more comfortable here than anywhere. Why then did it feel like a wraith could fly up from behind and take him by the neck and fling him way out over the black waters of the bay, where he'd drop and drown alone, anonymous, no trace?

Andy shivered, told himself that aloneness was no cause for fear of any kind. Striding his driveway, in a further act of bravery he forced himself to walk beside his house, trailing fingers on the wet siding, to the even more complete and windy darkness of his backyard. Careful to stay well clear of his new cliff, he stopped somewhere in the yard's middle. The wind carried the raw-earth smell to him, his property's wound. The wind felt fine on his face, actually. It woke him up further. He still felt angry in the gut.

He'd hated seeing red-haired Dan Boyd in his happy mood of attack. He was what drove Andy from the party in the end. A decade ago, because of drinking and a jail term for a hit and run, Boyd's wife lost custody of their young boy and girl. Out of prison, she kidnapped them and in a feat of disguises and stealth stayed free — and by all accounts a sober, doting mother — for seven years. They caught her in Nova Scotia; she went to prison again and the kids, now ten and twelve, were returned to Boyd, whose string of nannies were as mean to them as he was. People said the kids should have been left with their mother, and laws should be more common-sense human. For instance, they didn't even ask the kids what they thought. A social worker had told Leonard they were clearly afraid of Boyd, and that Boyd took as many shifts at work as he could. And once when drunk Dan Boyd said this to Andy: "Parents don't like their kids. They actually don't and they're too chickenshit to admit it."

Andy had left the party if only to be free of Dan Boyd. Then, after avoiding Andy all night it was Drew who caught him as he fled out the door. Drew ran up and grabbed his arm and spun him round to face him. His friend was dripping sweat and he looked pissed off at everything and nothing. Laughing, Drew told him in a kind of hiss, "It's *all* sinking, man — don't worry about it." He was being only mean. As if Andy could think of nothing but his yard. Drew was beaten down and poisonous and wanted to spread it. He laughed again, shoving Andy to launch himself back into his father's rotting party, and Andy had never seen his friend quite like this in all the time he'd known him.

Wind in his face, seeing absolutely nothing, Andy felt better, and fully sober. He'd jump in a good, hot shower with these new clothes on. They felt tainted now, like the dirty filter for one lousy party. Tonight had put him in mind of a different sort of party altogether. Mussels. Moose nose. And odori. That was the word — *odori*.

Andy turned and had a fright when he understood he couldn't see his house, and that in one direction lay a cliff. But the wind, now at his back, was a sure guide, as were the waves' gentle crashings on the gravel. He began to walk precisely away from that. He walked slowly, in the grip of his senses, walking mostly with his ears, so wide awake now. Then, as if toying with his attention, the wind shifted. There was a brief hitch in the rain, almost like an in-breath, and it began to snow.

A Little Necklace

novembre 1606

IN THE MUSIC of settlement, boredom is a melody that begets foul, discordant strains. Twice now Samuel has seen men making onanistic use of themselves in the forest. Unlike the first man (Samuel thinks it was Simon), who scurried away shamed (one hopes), the second merely turned his back, paused in his devilish fever and waited insolently for the mapmaker to pass.

Last year before he fell sick with the scurve himself and ultimately perished, the priest said some words with which Champlain agreed. As they watched men fall to unease and listlessness and then to the disease itself, the priest contended that idleness and boredom were themselves the cause of the scurve. Samuel found himself agreeing with him (though he still believed, and believes, it is also bound up in one's intake of food. But is this entirely different? Don't we manifest the humour of that which we take in and make our own? That is, mightn't food be a cause of boredom?) The priest termed their malaise "a fall in spirit" and it angered him such that he seemed to withdraw his compassion for the ailing men. At this Samuel no longer agreed, because the priest went so far as to ask, how *dare* one be not always excited, having been given life by God and placed on earth amidst all of His wonders? (And Samuel was amazed that, when the priest fell ill himself, he didn't appear to change his views about any portion of this. In fact he faulted a loss of faith for his illness, going so far in his arrogance as to *lose* faith to prove his point. Even on the day of his death, the priest's nostrils never did lose their ability to flare.)

It isn't the first autumn that Champlain has found himself pondering this: settled and safe in their sturdy compound, so much of their task done — all save the real and most onerous task called winter, and waiting — how were they to keep boredom at bay?

Unlike a storm at sea, when one is busy keeping the ship's masts pointed heavenward and the bodies of all one's men alive; unlike landing at an unknown shore and declaring it New France and then with all one's will building a shelter with which to block the wind and digging furrows in which to sow one's precious seed — unlike these most vital pursuits, the act of settling allows a routine akin to stagnation, in whose water blooms a thickening sea of bad humours and irritants.

The odd stench of one's shipmate is utterly of no matter in a storm.

The fights have for the most part stopped, the combatants finally seeing no reason in fisticuffs when the fight would only be compounded with a flogging. But there continues the whispered bullying, and mental tortures of a grotesquely subtle kind. For instance Samuel has twice seen Dédé walk past Lucien sitting at table and sink a foul thumb into the moist heart of the carpenter's supper, and from the undisturbed look on both their faces it looked to be ritual now, or even mindless habit.

One game appears to have ceased, and Samuel is only glad for it. Soldiers and nobles alike, while sitting on a ring of stools outside the east wall, play their parlour games in the dirt whilst waiting patiently for hummingbirds to come and suck, some thirty paces off, at the bits of red satin sash torn and fastened as false flowers upon staves set into the ground. Taking turn, they train their muskets upon the flitting mirthful jewel, and fire. At first a hit was rare, but then some men got expert at it, and bird after bird met its end in a burst of shards too small to be deemed feathers. When questioned by none other than the Sieur of this land, Poutrincourt himself, the men, only half in jest, asked him back if there were another form of shooting practice as ingenious and beneficial as this, and added that they were training for the big war to come, and fell to laughing — Poutrincourt laughed too — about whether this war would be against Indian, Spanish, or English. No matter, they agreed, since we French can shoot hummingbirds out of the sky! Samuel wants to say that the real war seems to have been against these very birds, who seem now to have disappeared, so we have won. He wants to ask too that, if we have indeed killed them all, what kind of victory it is. He is reminded of his good uncle's caution: When you capture all the fish in your pond, you have in fact lost them. (In fact he suspects that these birds are amongst those that fly south to sip flowers still in bloom.)

But the days march, apace. This evening after supper, several of the men complained to him and asked if, during the savages' next session of bartering, it could be held outside the compound, "and when there's a stout wind." True, some furs do carry a bad stink, and the savages do not smell as the French do, for they lack perfume and use no salt in their diet. For almost all of them it is a first encounter with the natives of New France and so their smell (which is really no worse nor much different than the flats at ebb tide) is highly noticed by them — but this is the kind of petty irritant he ponders. He promised them that smell will not matter come March if they are near starving; he declared that all the peculiar smells of New France, not least the savages', would be drawn hungrily into both nostrils as if it were food. And he told them last what Membertou had only very recently revealed, that the savages hate their smell just as well! Membertou told him that, often, before these same meetings to barter, his braves will draw a mustache of pine resin under their nostrils! (In fact Samuel had wondered why it was that, by the time the savages left, especially if the fires were smoky, their upper lip would sport a new mustache of soot.)

Samuel believes the men then went next to Lescarbot, to see what *he* might say about bartering, and stink, and a stout wind. Sometimes Samuel thinks the men see him as Poutrincourt's right ear, and Lescarbot the left.

But in any case it seems that the problem with exploration lies in the act of *stopping*, in the lack of forward motion, in the compass being stowed, in the encavement of vigour within the walls of routine. Once shelter is built, and fuel secured, and the belly filled, clearly one needs distraction beyond the wants of survival. One needs now to explore the smaller maps of pleasure. They have no women, but they do have wine, and so they also have song. And though Samuel has not much ear for it himself, he will continue to encourage poetry from one and all. If only to suggest that exploration can be within. (And if only to give pause to the endless poetry of Lescarbot, which flows out unimpeded by competition. He has succeeded in making Samuel forevermore tired of the words "wondrous," "France," "lark," and "king.")

And, an idea he has been pondering: they have spice, they have meat in the forests untried. A day barely goes by without rumours, often from Membertou, of intriguing food — the egg mass of an immense armour-plated fish; mussels smoked under resinous pine needles; even the entire humped nose of a moose in its own especial gravy. So perhaps they might engage in making more poetic with their food? Even Lescarbot agreed with him in this when together they witnessed once again the saddening sight of the men chewing at their salt beef, in their eyes nothing remotely like cheer.

CHAMPLAIN IS LATE to rise this morning, though even from his pillow he's heard some commotion without. At first he thinks it a joke, these tidings that Dédé has found three dead bats in the courtyard. (The first joke being that Dédé, so vast and bearded of body, owns the wit to find anything at all.) But to hear that he has found not only the Devil's creature, but in the number of the Trinity! Israel Bailleul, who has brought the news to his door, speculates while Samuel pulls on his breeches and coat that this very number cancels the harm of the Beast itself, and that, because Each of the Trinity had killed Itself a bat, instead of an omen of evil it was a reminder that God works in their midst in New France and has sent them a sign of exactly this wondrous fact. Bailleul adds that this explanation has become Lescarbot's official decree on the matter.

Samuel goes out to see them himself. All three are on the ground, two of them some ten paces from each other, the third being some fifty paces distant, lying over by stores. The morning is warm enough, and with the dew off them they look rather fluffy and innocent, and the pleasant deep brown of sable. Dédé is still promising to all who listen that he has not moved them (save to crush the first one's head with a foot, "to see if it was dead"!) Yet each was in the identical position, that is, on its belly with wings folded tight against its sides, chin flat out upon the ground.

Samuel hears more murmurs. That they had chosen to die as one is taken as evidence of either Grand or Evil design, and so he takes it upon himself to protest and offer a less exciting alternative, that, for example, they might all three have been blown down by a single tremendous gust of wind, or eaten a similar noxious food. (This second argument of his is a poor choice, in that the men instantly counter in one voice that it is well known that bats do not eat.)

Their priest, Fr. Vermoulu, has been pulled out into the yard as well. He appears woeful and silent on the matter and indeed he looks afraid himself. That the priest comes from the hidden low mountains east of Gap, where they are more superstitious than good Christians should be, Samuel has kindly never pointed out to the men, though perhaps he should have, and perhaps some day will have to. Fr. Vermoulu strides about in that heavy manner of his, as if fuelled by duty but weighted down by the Lord's own knowledge. He stands over the first beast, makes as if to nudge it with a foot, then seems to think better. He now makes a strange motion with his hand, strange in that it began as a blessing and then crumbles into something unknown to them, almost as if the man lost himself. And it is this mistake, this hesitation, that gets the men grumbling and crossing themselves in a mass, and for this Samuel is rightfully angered by Fr. Vermoulu, who is young, and foolish, and in any case very much just a man.

Risking trespass of the priest's authority in this matter, Champlain approaches the bats himself. For indeed the priest has failed to take authority in assigning neither Divine nor Evil machination to three bats being identically dead in their yard. Instead he has half inserted his hand, so to speak, and withdrawn it half burnt; and he has caused everyone, even Poutrincourt — the good gentleman almost as agitated as the common — to regard these fumblings with fear and to cross themselves like widows in a boneyard. (Samuel dares admit to himself how much he sometimes does dislike priests; this dislike happens whenever they fail to remind him how much he loves his God.) Superstition — of which he himself has been accused, yes — must not be allowed to take root here and own them all.

He picks up the first bat by the wing. He himself is startled — but tries not to show it — by how shockingly little it weighs. Though far bigger they weigh less than an acorn, he'd guess. They weigh so little they are like not to exist at all. And yet they do, they marvellous do: half bird, half beast, they are almost pretty of face, yet so hideous in arm and wing and claw. It is their misfortune but not their fault to look like the Devil Himself. And they fly at night, getting into what sorts of mischief no one knows and, yes, perhaps they do not eat. If they do, they do not eat much.

"A bat," Samuel states, then flicks the poor imp at a bush. It catches and stays like a sick leaf.

"There are three?" he asks cheerfully, and at this the men nod and mumble, amazed and afraid, though he can see a few men, Lucien in particular, smirking. Lescarbot smiles too, but with hatred for Samuel, who alone among the educated has thought to use the tack of reason. He has also made an enemy of the priest, but that does not bother him as much. There is a priest back home in Brouage who likes him, and that is where he intends to die.

"If Dédé was to venture outside the walls I'm sure he'd find a fourth, and a fifth," Samuel offers. "Someone go ask Membertou if he has ever found more than two. Maybe out in our bay last night a fish died. Maybe all along the shore are some dozen crab lying on their backs."

Some men shrug and some nod in allegiance to his sarcasm and he thinks he has changed the course of some minds, at least on this day. For he does own the authority of having lived longest in this New France. He has seen some of its strange creatures and he has been misled and been made afraid, and then ashamed of that fear. He has never made secrets of this.

He wishes he had more talent to say what he wants to say, something that would incur the priest's wrath all the more, for the words should be his: that watching them here is the same God who watched them in their cradles at home. This present wilderness might be without religion, yes, but there is no place a man can step that is without God.

THIS SAME MORNING Membertou announces himself in the savages' traditional way, shouting "Ho-ho!" from a distance, and he pushes into Champlain's chambers so wild of face that at first he wonders if the old sagamore wishes to do him harm. Membertou looks the buffoon, yet wily, as Samuel sees in his countenance some sly intent. But so drawn is his face and so distended his eyes that Samuel now sees he is excited on top of being very tired. Even from the door Samuel can smell him, and underneath his usual odour the old man smells like the sourest of mud.

Wearing this agitated look he approaches while holding his birchbark quiver hidden behind his back—another reason Samuel wonders at his intent. Then he brings it in front of him and holds it out between them and shakes it. There is no evidence of arrows protruding, but something makes a dense rattling from within. Then he holds the quiver in front of his chest and now lifts it farther up, regarding it with his eyes, then thrusting it out in so noble a position that one might suspect it holds the waters of eternal life.

Membertou says, "Sir!" and spills the contents of his quiver onto Samuel's table.

Oh! Escargots! The snails fall out and fill the tabletop. Shiny-wet with dew and their own lovely excretions, the sound produced as they issue forth is a thousand moist clicks at once, more rush than clatter, almost a hiss. He is instantly excited by these beings, this beautiful food. They are slimmer of shell here than at home, but they carry the same pattern of beige and black lines. Wet and made brilliant in the morning light, they are lovely.

"Eat!" the old man announces, and then laughs, as he often does at his last word when there is nothing more to be said, though no joke has been told.

And so Samuel learns that his savage friend has been up before sunrise three mornings running, gathering this surprise for him.

He hadn't been aware that Membertou was listening, some nights earlier, as some of them were going down to supper, when Samuel had moaned, dreamlike, that what he craved most was a feast of escargots. He does recall Membertou asking after them, and someone thenceforth describing their shell and nocturnal habits, their slow nighttime journey, their glistening trail, and their escape to hidden dens before the sun. But listening he had been, and Membertou has been out hunting the forest floor under the moon, plucking these treasures up.

Samuel thanks Membertou, who bows his head. Reaching into this private bin of stores he brings out not just a knife but also two iron nails, placing them on the table apart from the snails, some of which have made themselves upright and begun to move. Samuel hopes it is not a flash of disappointment he sees as Membertou hesitates before placing the barter in his wet quiver. The man had worked very hard for Samuel's pleasure and had seen his joy, and Samuel wonders if perhaps he shouldn't have given him more nails. Or perhaps even a hatchet. Or it seems perhaps Membertou would be happiest if Samuel had given him nothing at all; perhaps what the sagamore wants most is what he asks for now: nodding his head and walking backwards while leaving, like savages do, Membertou mumbles quietly again that he wishes to become Christian. But most of all he looks ready for sleep. It is easy to forget the man is past one hundred years old.

In any case, though Membertou already knew of the escargot, it seems the savages use them only as forage in difficult times, eating them uncooked and without salt or anything else. No wonder escargots are not savoured by them, for salt truly opens the gift of their flesh. Even as Samuel counts the several dozen on his table he imagines their many brethren that still roam the woods, unaware that no longer are they safe! Still, if in three bouts of searching this agile old hunter found but sixty-three snails, it does discourage Samuel somewhat.

He likes them as a favourite aunt made them, with shallots and fennel, and of course salt. The fennel is perfect, for are escargots not like fish who carry an encaved pond on their backs? More like fish than flesh in any case, in the same way that the dolphin-fish they speared during the crossing was more flesh than fish — indeed, it was more rich even than beef, and consequently some men were startled off their enjoyment of it. That it blows foul mist and noise from the top of its head is unsavoury enough.

Sadly, they lack fennel here, though there are rumours of a fern-root that approximates its taste. In the meantime, they have in their gardens some garlic that, though still green in the bulb and the size of a pea, will grace the butter, which will grace the salt, all of which will grace the snail. Tonight Poutrincourt and he will eat escargots. Having for so many of these months been fed on ship's rations, food that is really not much more than common fuel for a body's basest fire, he finds that the anticipation of beautiful food is the rarest and best thing. He rolls a snail, in its slime, between thumb and forefinger, and wonders if exalted food, that is, unnecessary food, isn't, in fact, necessary. He means no disrespect to God when he wonders further if humble men like him are not honouring their lives simply by being, when they can be, magnificent eaters.

TODAY IS THEIR Sieur's birthday and on the cook's shout Lucien along with all the other men is invited to gather in the court-yard, around the flagpole, to enjoy two fingers of brandy and toast the noble birth.

He has the shutter open just enough to let a beam in. Lying abed he savours the day's section of Homer. Each time he turns a page he regrets his fingers' calluses, the rough stain of his trade. It is Lucien's second time through, and he anticipates Odysseus encountering the cannibal Laestrygones, a thrilling and favour-ite part. He wonders if he could simply remain here and not be missed. Depending on the noble's mood it is an insolence he could be flogged for, but the risk of being caught is small, since no one would expect any man here not to gallop like a horse in the direction of a whiff of brandy. Lucien does not care much for it except as a digestif to ease heavy foods. In quantity, the joy it brings comes on too quickly and then all turns simply com-mon, where the cause of a song or a fight could be one and the same. Though one cup of brandy will not lead to this. Lucien presses his book flat under the mattress and rises.

The courtyard is bathed by the richly oblique sunlight of four o'clock on a November afternoon, a falling but vivid light which Lucien suspects must exist wherever one journeys in the world, the sun being the sun. A heavy and liquid light, whatever it touches invites description in poetry. Even men's faces gain depth and beauty, even the harmed ground at their feet. Lucien sees, there, a friend's cheek and thinks of the word edible, then understands he has been reminded of the gold of an egg yolk. In the forest behind he sees the deeper green a vegetable gains when blanched. Lucien takes some comfort in knowing that this is the very sun that falls even now on his backyard at home, illuminating the ground for the chickens as they peck, bathes his sister Babette's face as she pauses from unhanging the dry linens. Perhaps, as if hearing something, she turns and gazes long to the West. And it is good to know that, in the sun's own time, he is only one half-day distant.

Lucien pushes in between two others and extends his arm to receive his cup, which is followed hard upon by Poutrincourt's boy pouring brandy from a jug. Lucien is perhaps the only man who makes no noise at getting his. Some men supply a whispered joke, "Come, boy, don't be so mean now." Some loudly sigh and smile. When Fougeray de Vitre shouts a simple toast to the triple hierarchy of God, King, and Sieur, Lucien tilts some brandy onto his tongue and tastes it up through his nose. He will wait till the sensation passes before taking another taste. Those on either side of him throw the entirety of their cup back against their throats and as it goes down hot they cough.

Lucien joins in weakly as all the men chant Sieur Poutrincourt's birthday praises. Looking already flush with drink, Monsieur Champlain calls waggishly for a speech. Sieur Poutrincourt is flush of face too but is too contained a man to concoct a speech, least of all about himself, so Monsieur Lescarbot performs one for him. Lescarbot loves to speak and relishes his own talent when he does so. He has the deep voice of a larger man but he is small, his tight body reminding Lucien of oars strapped hard together in the shape of a man, and though he always smiles he seems dangerous in the way some small men can. Speaking so well that Lucien suspects he has come prepared, Lescarbot begins with a fantastic anecdote about the nobleman's very birth, and how the midwife grew uncontrollably amorous at the first sight of him. Lucien sees that the nobles have been making merry all day long, so raucous is their laughter. It isn't often that noble laughter outshouts the rough kind of the regular men.

Lescarbot's speech turns to serious praise, that New France could wish for no better soul to plant its first flag, et cetera, and while it might be true, Lucien looks for creatures in the clouds that tumble overhead, though down here in this valley there is not more than a whisper of air. Such it is when the wind comes from the north; come the hard winter, that wall of young mountains will prove a most kindly friend. No — small mountains are old mountains, he has learned this in his reading. Mountains don't grow as trees do. They grow smaller, wearing away like Roman steps, losing perhaps a pebble-height each noble birthday. Lucien sees a hare, with ears that drag far behind him, as though with his ears pinched in a cook's hand he still runs to escape. One ear separates and becomes its own dolphin-fish —

Lucien startles badly at the firing of the first cannon. He half heard the finale of Lescarbot's speech, something about "the declaration of all cannon" because Port-Royal, and New France, was celebrating the birthday of none other than its first king. If any a man thought about this near-heresy it was blasted dead by the final shot. Lucien thinks he has witnessed the worst case of currying favour ever in his life. A man can truly shrink himself through trying to bolster another. Sieur Poutrincourt neither smiles nor moves as his eyes vainly try to penetrate cannon smoke to take in the bay. Lucien braces himself and lets his mouth hang open for the next shot. For some reason the ears hurt less if you give your head another hole.

LATER, THOUGH SUPPER'S bell has rung, a clutch of fellows including Lucien remain leaning against the storehouse wall. Two men smoke savages' leaf, one in the foreshortened pipe he'd carved from the crotch of a root, and the other, Champdoré, from a more ornate affair received through private trading with savages to the south: the bowl is fashioned from an immense lobster claw, and one long claw-tip curls out bright pink in a rather elaborate flourish. Champdoré is proud of this device and will not lend it around. But Lucien will take the wooden pipe when offered him, as he hopes it will be. He has tried it before when the savages last came to barter skins and he likes it well enough, or rather it is one more different thing to tell his children about, should he ever be so blessed.

And at this thought of children his hair near stands on end, because such a miracle is suddenly possible, however much it flies beyond all thinking. Ndene. She is still all the miracle he needs to see. And he can see her so vividly at will: how, after a fortnight of placing himself in spots she frequented, suspecting she did the same; how, in the company of others they could only smile, though on one occasion behind the north wall quickly find and squeeze each other's hands; how, only three days previous, she is laughing gently as she surprises him out of the trees! Her intention is clear, and marvellous, and there is no need — nor, it seems, time — for words. For so it is that her hand is on him, between his legs, feeling for what is there, when Lucien finds he needs must stop and he stays her hand. He has imagined just such a time, of course, and he has wanted nothing more — what then is this that freezes him? It seems that, rising up, thudding behind his eyes with his own blood, is the blurred whole of Scripture, its ensnarling words about sin without marriage.

Also staying his hand firmly on hers is the sudden tempest, that blows inside him like wind, made up of combined indistinct echoes of Poutrincourt, and the King, and the gallows, and even of his own mother, and the one talk they had about the nature of this very thing that is upon him now, and his promise to her, one that he has kept.

Ndene's first look is incomprehension. For indeed Lucien's own bearing had countenanced this day — it had hoped for and asked for it. Her second look is anger. She gestures in question, and waits. He tries to explain, using the word God, which she knows, and also he makes clear that his own sagamore, Poutrincourt, does not want them to do this. It takes not a moment for Ndene to ask, and get his answer, as to what *his* desires are. In the end she cannot abide his hesitation. Again he tries to explain, and again she cannot find any sense in it. Why not do this thing he so dearly wishes to do? And in the attempts to explain, Lucien comes to question himself. And then for him a doorway through his wall of fear, or guilt, or whatever is its name, opens with these words, *there is no sense in this inaction.* Whereas his senses are full of her, of her and him; absent of *any sense* are the many words, and paper, and the past. There stands Ndene, laughing at him and shaking her head as if he is the dullest fool. Until he laughs too and goes to her and embraces her, because now he understands her freedom.

And then, as if their conversation had not taken place, again she works like there is no time, all is haste. And soon all restraint's undone. The very land tilts under his boots. Beneath harsh deer hide lies her impossible softness, her breasts, her round belly. Their clothes come only half off and work up into a knot and the cold is instantly on them, making them laugh grimly and hastening them on and serving as though to lift their desire higher. In his ear, her sounds are not so different than those he's heard drifting from haylofts, from bedchambers, in St-Malo. It is a wondrous union and after, breathing, they meet eyes, and he knows he loves her exactly the same as she loves him, even for her smell of turned apples. Dressing, she points to the rising afternoon sliver of moon and counts seven fingers, and with these same fingers shows that she and her people will be trekking south. Only while walking back to the compound, whistling in amazement and stubbing his feet on roots, is Lucien stricken with the question of whether she meant seven days, weeks, or months. Or whether she returns in such a time, or it's that long before she will be leaving. In the meantime he has searched for her and it seems that she has already indeed gone, which explained the haste. He has thought of little but Ndene for these three days now. He dearly hopes she didn't mean months. Doesn't a moon signal a month? God, he hopes not.

But in those three days he has listened with new interest to the constant moans of those stricken by the lack of a woman, as some of the men so claim to be, for more than a few are married. Dédé has bragged how he is going to take himself a savage woman and risk the penalties it will bring, and at mention of these penalties Lucien's ears perk up further. The threatened punishments are vague and there is argument about them. First, there is the crime of relations with a woman not baptized, and then there is the crime of relations with a woman before marriage. That one is not allowed to marry an unbaptized woman seems not to contradict these crimes, nor provide an excuse to have sexual relations, though some of the men have argued this logic. Nor is there consensus on the penalties, which would certainly include flogging, but if one crime were added to the other, perhaps imprisonment as well. Lucien's stomach fell when Fabrice, who does not exaggerate, claimed that in Hochelaga a man was hanged for it, but perhaps only because he had forced himself on the savage, and she was the young daughter of a sagamore, or a sagamore's niece, but in any case the severity of the penalty had to do with quelling the anger of the neighbouring tribe, which numbered in the hundreds. Some men claimed that any taking of a savage woman means, at the very least, a voyage to France in chains. It seems that much would depend upon the priest, who would identify the sin, and then it would fall to Sieur Poutrincourt, who would decide on the punishment. Some men have sneered that relations with a savage would not be considered human, but bestial, and not merit mention beyond dismissal and disgust.

Lucien scratches the back of his neck waiting for Simon to refill the pipe. He pictures Ndene again, and the small meadow she knew of (how well? he is beginning to wonder), sheltered on two sides by mossy rocks, her eyes, her smile before, and then after, and the quieter way the second smile included him. He knows that, if she comes to him again, he will not care about men's laws. And if any man or priest tries to tell him of God's laws against Ndene, or against them together in the meadow — he won't listen because naught in it will be true.

Lucien feels emboldened when the pipe is passed to him. Pulling in a lungful of smoke, he tries a savage trick, which is to blow the smoke out from his nose. He didn't think he could and is surprised at how easy it is. One of the men spots him and calls, "Lucien!" and the rest look his way just as two rich streams pour out, fully like a dragon. The effect is to bring water to his eyes. He doesn't cough but his nose burns and then he has to go hands on knees as a whirlpool of sense overtakes him, worse than the day of seasickness he survived. His nose chokes up with snot. The men laugh and then question him. Lucien simply says, shaking his head, "I'll not do that again." Amazingly enough, two more men try the same trick, and succeed, with the same result. The second man, Henri, lurches unsteadily around a corner and vomits, but his head was also more filled with wine. The robust Dédé calls in a foul woman's voice to ask Henri if he would care for some more leaf.

"I am glad," says none other than Monsieur Samuel Champlain, who takes a turn at the pipe, exhaling gently out of his mouth, "that young Lucien did not instead shoot a lead ball into his brain. We would now have three less men!"

The men laugh politely. All can tell that Monsieur Champlain is not given to wit. But he is standing out here with them, the regular men, drinking from the common cask, and they appreciate this. Lucien thinks that the cook Bonneville, though, appears to be in cahoots with Simon to top the nobleman with wine and watch him grow foolish. Lucien has seen the two trade eyes, and Bonneville raise his brows in all innocence as he brings the jug of wine to Champlain's cup. The nobleman, as if ashamed to be slow of thirst, drinks off his cup so that there will be some room into which Bonneville can pour. And then Bonneville and Simon have looks again.

"Lucien?"

The mapmaker is addressing him alone.

"Sir?"

"Like this. As in all first voyages, at first make small."

Lucien watches Champlain draw moderately from the pipe, take the smoke not so deep into his body, and then blow two faint streams from his nose.

"We need not be as savages in this," he says when his nose ceases its blow. All have seen the savages hereabouts commonly try to best each other not just in wrestling and eating and running but also in heartiest smoking. Lucien wonders if indeed it is this very smoking that could have given rise to the rumour of dragons in this new world — later disclaimed by Cartier — but

Lucien won't let himself ask this of the noble. It is something he can ask Ndene.

Lucien notes that Monsieur Champlain is with them and not at the birthday feast, to which the regular men are not invited. Standing where they are they can hear the nobles bellowing at table. Worse, they can smell the joint of fresh venison. Lucien thinks he can detect a sauce made of berries. That is, he thought so before he injured his nose with smoke.

And there is no doubting that Samuel Champlain is a famous man. He was navigator on early voyages and he has had his own command. He has been up the great Canada River twice and is known to the great sagamores there. He has killed savages with an arquebus. He has seen creatures and wonders untold. He has a volume of journals and maps published and well read. He has thrice been received by King Henri. Yet he stands here with men who will never in their lives see let alone speak to a king. Still flush with wine — he has twice apologized for being drunk, though he isn't very — Champlain now does most of the talking. Indeed, the men want it so.

"And yes there have been storms that have taken lives offshore here. Well, off the great banks. Mostly Basque lives. I don't know why the Basque so stubbornly stay on the water. But it's not the storms, it's the *lack* of wind that kills on the banks. How?"

The men know how. They know these stories but they allow the man his rhetoric.

"Fog. Fog, shielding mountains of ice from man's eye. To strike an iceberg is to strike a continent. It does not move. What moves are the planks of your bow. What moves is the spine of your keel. Your only hope is for the ice to own an overhang, a ledge — and many of them do, the water being warmer than the air — that first strikes you above waterline. Then you have some small chance of repair..."

Lucien watches Champlain. Compared to the others, this noble seems not so aware of his face — his moustaches and hair are often loose. Perhaps, so much at sea, he lets himself be wind-blown on land as well. Lucien knows, as do all the men, that this noble is not so high-born — they can see this not just in his bearing but in the other nobles' regard of him. Lucien sees in their treatment a chance to vent their jealousy, especially Lescarbot, who has hardly ventured outside of Paris and who works the hardest not to show his fear, generally with an ornate humming of tunes. Still, Lucien cannot tell whether Champlain's slightly tawdry presentation stems from not knowing or from not caring. This evening, for instance, he wears a thing new and peculiar — strung on twined hemp after the savage fashion, but looking like a child might do it, a little necklace made of black seabird bills. It appears as though the twine were strung randomly through either of the two nostrils but not both, so the hang is not even and the assemblage looks bumpy and ajumble, even silly; and if one thing can be said for savage work, it is always even and true, with the sizes of fang, or claw graduated like pearls. He seems an odd man to be otherwise expert at the precise fitting of measures and lines upon a page.

The mapmaker continues to talk, much like a man who needs to. But the men are eager to hear, even stories they have heard before. One story that has most affected Lucien, and affects him still, is of Sable Island. He first heard it, in part, years ago in St-Malo, but Monsieur Champlain has landed on the island himself, and knows its qualities, and so he fills the story with details that give it life for Lucien. For instance: not a tree stands on Sable Island though it is forty miles in length. At most a mile in breadth, it is one long ridge of sand. It has grass and some shrub. It sits two hundred miles off the coast of New France, at the height of the Strait of Canso. Surf pounds it from the east.

The wind there does not stop and the grass stands up straight but a few days of the year. Nine years ago, an expedition similar to theirs, to monopolize the fur trade and settle New France, was bankrupt even as it began. The captain of the ship, informed of this and infuriated that he might not be paid, dropped twenty men, six horses, and twenty hogs upon Sable Island. The nobleman in charge (who Monsieur Champlain out of delicacy would not name, though Lucien recalls it to be a Monsieur Caron) instructed these unfortunate men to found a way station to replenish ships making the voyage to New France. He promised a ship would call for them in a year's time. But Caron was imprisoned back in St-Malo and for whatever reason no ship was sent to Sable Island for four years. The ship arrived to find six of the twenty still alive. Only two had died of the scurve. The rest, said Champlain, "had such disagreements that they cut each other's throats."

Lucien wonders at these "disagreements." It was simple madness, surely. Though it's possible that in a simple place the madness is made more complex. Not a tree on the island. Constant wind. No desire of being there in the first place. No woman, no child. Driftwood to make one's tangled dwelling. Only beef and pork to eat, as well as, said Champlain, clam. No boat to row out for fish. Fresh water was no problem because it rained two-thirds of the year. One no doubt caught it in barrels, but Lucien pictures a lonely soul — it is himself — standing with mouth open, catching windblown drops, nothing better to do. Did they form enemy camps? Did they take each other as wives? Did any ask a friend to cut his throat as a favour?

On Sable Island remain the pigs and horses, now gone feral. There have since been two wrecks blown onto its beach — again Basque fishermen — and the hogs have come to good use. So a way station of sorts it did turn out to be.

They keep asking Champlain to speak of calamity. Of the very worst he has seen in life. As one tale stops, they smile nervously and shake their heads, then ask for another. Or they remind him of one they already know, for many stories were made famous during the crossing. Lucien knows why the men ask, and he knows why the mapmaker does not mind telling. It is so they will feel lucky and safe tonight in this world where luck and safety might not last. Tonight, their legs are steady on land. They will go to sleep knowing they have three cannon and thirty-odd muskets, and that the savages hereabouts are jollier than those to the west. They have sweet water to drink and a new, deep cesspit downwind. They have casks of wine and of biscuit and of salt meat. Certain leafy crops have grown well and taste as they should. They have many songs, and two new ones have been composed and learned and enough men are harmonious to drown out those who aren't. They have a Cross outside the gate and soon, they have been told, a larger Cross will stand atop the north mountain. Their lives all continue and indeed Sieur Poutrincourt is having a birthday. In a year or two his wife and children will live in the compound, and perhaps some other noble families too. Most of all, the men know a ship is coming in the next summer. It will take, back to France, whoever wants to go. Or, perhaps, whoever remains alive. It is November now, and the men desperately do not speak of this ship. Those who do are told to shut up.

Lucien knows why Champlain will not speak of one calamity, though he has been asked by indirection. He will not speak of last winter, or of the Island of St-Croix, at all. There, men just like them built a settlement just like this. Mistakes were made, and they are now famous mistakes. The island had no water of its own, and men had to row to the mainland, about a mile, to refill the casks, and winter storms sometimes prevented this. As well, there was no shelter from the winter wind, nor was there handy wood to build wind-walls. These mistakes led to a new search, and that search led Champlain here. He is one of only three men amongst this present company who spent last year on St-Croix. Everyone knows that of those seventy-nine men exactly one beyond half — forty souls — died of the winter scurve. And now, standing out here, leaning like an oaf against the storeroom wall, the nobleman has been asked gently and respectfully to describe it, but the mapmaker declines. The men no doubt think he is still too saddened to bring the details to mind.

Lucien has noted the navigator's star winking at him between trees as it cleared the north mountain. He knows why Champlain is refusing to tell the story of St-Croix. It is because, despite this being a warmer spot, and despite there being fresh water at their door, there is no reason why St-Croix won't happen here, this winter. Why should it not? These men sharing this pipe and this wine pray to the same God the forty men of St-Croix did. The scurve is said to be the ugliest dying possible, its one saving grace being that, near the end, the dying do not care... but Lucien will entertain it no more tonight. Instead he shakes his empty cup at Bonneville, distracting the wine-monger from yet another attack on the noble mapmaker Samuel Champlain.

SAMUEL HAS TONIGHT become drunk on common wine and, having guzzled like a lout only moments ago, he grows drunker still from it. Sitting in his chambers, trying to put thoughts to his journal, his pen wobbles and is impatient to end each present word. He has enjoyed the evening nonetheless.

He edges open his sliding shutter, but not too much, as the night cold streams in to sit under the table and embrace his legs. His fire is stoked, his face and hands are warm enough, but he sees that come winter he will not be opening that window at all. Apparently, sitting in stores, there is a glass for his window. Of the nobles, only his and Lescarbot's glass remains uninstalled, Lescarbot having trumpeted to the whole encampment his selfless desire that "more needful things that ensure our common survival" take place before the fixing of his trifling window. Samuel knows it will seem mean of him to complain just yet, but he will, for he so loves to gaze out, even at night, because of the rising stars — and because there! across the bay, even now, is a light. It flickers once, then sinks, then dies. A savage fire, no doubt, but what is its story? Was it doused for some reason? Is it a fishing party, encamped by the Eel?

A storm builds between him and Lescarbot. The other man must know it too, for he's lately kept his distance. While in the same room he gives Samuel his shoulder and rarely his eyes. Today, hard upon Samuel wishing the Sieur Poutrincourt a good birthday and offering him escargots for later and then simply shaking his hand, Lescarbot launched his own birthday speech and shook the heavens with his oversugared words. And then came all seven bombastic — and traitorous! — cannon. The first shot put Samuel deep into a cave of disgust and he did not care to see the man again this night. So he did not.

Yet still he grips his stylus too firmly, due to Lescarbot. The man had the giddiness of soul to dare tempt fate. In a toast that went on and on, the lawyer added, while glancing and grinning into his brandy cup, that they had with them "in this November liquor, the sovereign prophylactic against the ravages of scurve." How the man makes light of a terror he has never felt chew his own bones nor seen put a fellow in his grave. His accompanying smile is like a syrup spooned daintily yet mistakenly into beer. What Samuel hates most is Lescarbot's poet's way of joking: in October, anything he drank was "this October liquor," and in September, the same. This brand of wit of his is like a flower that has no meaning and lacks any good smell.

The regular men are a mixed sort, of course, but all are agreeable enough fellows. The cook Bonneville is a scamp who tried to get him drunk, and he won that game, though he thought it secret. The pilot Champdoré, with his pretentious royal-pink lobster pipe, has no friends because he is always on guard — against what, who can say. The brute Dédé smells so and has little of God in him, but Samuel would gladly stand behind his buttocks in a fight. Young Lucien, the fine carpenter (he is an able one too; Poutrincourt runs his hand over the joinery of his new staircase railing as though it were a woman's arm), is a quiet wit, and too shy to befriend, but it is said he not only can read but does. The handsome Pijou will meet no one's eye, but he is amongst the wittiest of men. Samuel would love to hear what sport he makes of the nobles, including himself, when no nobles are there! And the farmer Claude Medoc, no one hears a word from him, and his eyes are as forlorn as a puppy's, and Samuel is thinking he should not have come. He has a young wife, and he came aboard on the misbegotten notion that here he will make his fortune! Did no one tell him that all bartered skins hereabouts belong to Monsieur de Monts, to one man? That Claude Medoc would be thrown freshly into gaol if he went ashore at St-Malo holding a single ragged fur to give his lovely young wife? That not even Samuel Champlain can give a knife and receive a skin unless the good Monsieur says that he can? (Samuel recalls that the last time their deluded King allowed the merchants to come and trade here, de Monts bade Samuel erase several strategic tidal rocks on his popular map so that said merchants might flounder and die upon them. Samuel was more than a little glad when they did not.)

Samuel sees he has begun to draw a beaver, beginning with its hind legs. It stands at the paper's bottom, and now holds up with forepaws his square body of sentences, as though his words were a map. He adds a cross-stitch pattern to the tail, and begins to shade the fur, as if it were indeed a proper beaver, and this a proper map. Why not?

Like dry rags, the men soaked up his tales and wanted more. Samuel almost startles at the notion that he might be of more comfortable mind around these regular men than his own kind, and it isn't just because these lesser men honour him. Indeed he had become aware of this tonight even while speaking. With these men he didn't care that his southern accent showed, or that he has not read the book another noble has, or says he has. With these men he doesn't care who knows that he has but a modest fortune and is at some lord's mercy when undertaking a voyage.

Tonight these men wanted tales of horror from him and he gave them what they wanted. Except St-Croix. He does not believe in dreams' portent as some do, but he does note the manner in which a strong dream will shadow one's waking day. How could he tell them he had just dreamed of that place? Not St-Croix exactly, because these men he drank with tonight were themselves in the dream. The dream had begun with the St-Croix men, who then became the men here, as it is with the currents and eddies of dreams. In it, Dédé's scurve came on in an instant. He was one minute laughing, then the next his mouth was full of putrefying flesh and his voice thickly muffled and he choked and then spat out his inner cheeks. But still he laughed, neither scurve nor death of any concern to the man he is, and of course the scurve went away in him, as if he'd chased it out with scorn. But not so the other men. Lucien had no teeth and, discovering this in the looking glass, he ran off into the night snow. Samuel himself discovered sores on his legs but then on closer scrutiny they were nit bites. And then Poutrincourt's own children, beautiful twin girls, were there mewling and dying this foulest of deaths, all the while dutifully placing their bloody fallen teeth into an ornament box, as all chaste girls will keep things, whispering over them as over a dowry, and at this juncture Samuel was shocked awake and it was morning, and in the way of dreams he was disturbed long into the day, tendrils of it clutching and befouling his moods — until he became drunk. And he did not care to speak of such events this evening. Not that he believes in dreams.

Yet he fears for these men. In truth he feels himself wanting to draw apart from them, not wanting to love them as he might soon do, for there are some he loved that lie underground on St-Croix. He has heard that in times of war the wiser soldier finds no friends.

He knows he will not die himself, though he does not know how he knows this. Perhaps all men know it, even those who then die surprised! But on last year's black island, not one noble died. And he still believes he knows why, and feels in his deepest sense that it has to do with what is eaten, but even more with what is not eaten, though Lescarbot thinks him a fool in this too. (Let him cure this year's dying with some February liquor!) And as proof Lescarbot reminds him that their priest there died too; and when Samuel answers that the priest died because he wanted to, Lescarbot looks at him, wonders if he's blasphemed, and keeps any more words to himself. He was not on St-Croix. How could he know? And how could he know that here in these tight quarters, surrounded by this vast closeness of trees, it is best to leave one's logic back in France?

STEADIER OF PEN, Samuel sets to his journal, the one he will see published, marking the day's weather, and moon, and the tide's neap and ebb, and notes Poutrincourt's birthday, but he is tired. His gut strains at its buttons and holds its swell. So none will hear him, he goes outside the gate to purge himself and at once feels better for it, though on his return and once seated again, he believes he needs must creep back out to do so again. He has been told by more than one master drinker that purging so, plus much water taken before sleep, becalms the next day's angry head — so this time he will fall to his knees at the stream. Thirst has always felt to him more honest than prayer. Perhaps he is too scientific a man, or perhaps he has never learned how.

ON THE SEVENTH DAY, Lucien returns to their spot. The very chill and silence of the place — a toy meadow lying soft between a rock outcrop and three stout oaks — is so complete that he knows in his body, somehow, that she will not come today.

The ground is damp so he sits on a fallen tree. Its angle of repose and the spikes of its many broken branches make it hard to find a patient seat. Again and again he closes his Horace and stands and tries another place on the tree. In the end, he climbs and sits up on the rock outcrop, which also gives him a better perch from which to penetrate, with unceasing gaze, every direction of the forest. *Ars Poetica* he keeps closed on his lap. He had wanted to show her letters, words. It would make her understand him better perhaps, though it also carried the danger of showing her their impossible distance, and driving her away. He is wary of his desire to impress her. There is something troubling in how confident she is with him. She is not in awe of the French, or of him. Though neither is Membertou, who is possibly her uncle. None of them seem to be. Though they love — love — their bread, and would indeed trade meat for it in equal size.

It begins to rain and, looking up, Lucien thinks the clouds are swift enough to pass in time, so he will stay. Tucking Horace into his middle, he doubles up over it. He wants the three books he owns to last, and this bound paper held tight to his stomach feels like the most mortal thing about him.

A HARSH AND ODD wind blows from north-northwest, bringing with it a thin bitter smell from the hills that lie unseen there. It is hard even to lift one's eyes to it. The dark season has settled in hard, leaving no more hope for warmth on the face, save that gained by leaning at a fire. Samuel hates and cannot shake an image, though it was many weeks ago, of salmon-trout drifting, soft and dead, back down the stream from out of the impenetrable forest, as if they were poisoned there. In the garden's deepest soil only the most stubborn root vegetables survive, withering to protect themselves against the cold. He is familiar with the tone of this November month, its unease, its blooming restlessness. With the coming of snows the men find abundant time on their hands, time to fill with whatever entices, however limply. For most, unoccupied time feels more like burden than bounty.

For Samuel, he seduces himself these days with conversation, not with his fellows but with the regular men. This particularly foul and blowing Sunday, after midday meal he decides to forgo the brandy and leaves the nobles' table to circulate amongst the men as they are in the business of dispersing. The question he pleasantly puts to them, each in turn, is, "Please, tell me: why did you make this voyage?"

What he finds oddest as they make their responses is that so many of them seem incapable of telling the truth. That is, of turning their gaze within and questioning themselves truly.

There are few answers in the direction of "I wanted to escape my dull and brutish life for one of adventure" or "I am third in the line of heirs and have no chance of fortune at home — the one hundred fifty livres I gain here is some slim chance." From more men than he can count comes such an answer as, "To help colonize New France." Or "To aid in spreading the realm of God, and our King, and our country." In short, parroting the King's own mandate, perhaps in hope of finding favour with a noble. Or, more likely, in fear of speaking otherwise in case a noble might find fault.

Even when Samuel presses, and pleads, "*Vraiment?*" he more often than not gets a "*C'est vrai.* To aid in spreading the realm of etc." And as they repeat themselves he receives now a look that admits to the lying. In fact, he sees in this look a fundamental right demanded by the common man: that he be allowed the freedom, in saying the expected thing, to lie to the nobleman. They consider it their right, and an allowable insolence.

Only the carpenter Lucien is willing — blandly willing, but willing — to converse more freely with him on this subject. In all, over the past weeks Lucien has grown less shy. This noon Samuel has him pinned as he remains at the common table, cleaning bark and such from his supply of tobacco, which Lucien has in suspicious abundance these days.

Samuel considers Lucien an odd man in that he doesn't fit his lot in life; that is, though he has rightly taken his family's trade, and does a fair job of it, he is not large of frame or thick in hand and seems more suited to the arts of the better-born, those of music or poetry or painting. Even his skin is clean, and fair, and his beard of a finer sort, such that his cheeks are almost bare. Samuel himself has seen Lucien reading, and Poutrincourt suggested that the subject of his book is sometimes poetry. In any event, to Samuel's query about his reasons for coming here

Lucien speaks chiefly of "having naught but one choice" but also of "wanting to test myself, against fear." Not looking up from his leaf, Lucien picks through it like a squirrel.

"Of what?" Samuel ventures, noting the whimsy playing on Lucien's face.

"Of the sea, and its weather. But not so much now. Being on land."

"Of course. And?"

"Drowning. Though, again, not so much now, sitting here. But, death. In general."

"If God had wanted us not to fear death, He would not have made this fear so natural in us. And what else?"

"The savages, at first. But now, not at all."

"I concur. And?"

"And men. Who have nothing at all to do."

"The men?"

"Yes."

"Surely you don't feel unsafe at their hand?"

"I also include myself in the collective noun."

Lucien smiles so as to show his seriousness is tainted by irony — wit's slinking cousin — but Samuel can see his point. Who isn't a bit afraid of oneself in the wide basin of unfilled time, with no known tide coming to fill it? It makes men do... what? He, for instance, has been driven by his own unfilled time to question random men this day, naively expecting not just truth but some measure of friendship.

But Samuel is not sure friendship is possible even with the likes of Lucien, even if they were both to desire it. Doffing the cloak of one's class is always uncomfortable, a nakedness, even if neither one fully believes in the cloak from the outset. Harder still to engage in such nakedness when in full view of other men. And Lucien's ways are unknown to Samuel in any case. It seems he has his own adventures, indeed his own colony, in his cranium. Off by himself, or thinking himself unobserved, Lucien frequently whistles, yet they are airs not of jollity but more like sadness, and also very strange, a music not common to the rest of them. Its melody leapfrogs out of time and takes up an oblique new measure, and sometimes suspends itself in no sound at all, where the silence is itself part of the lyric and poses a question or a mystery — and then the whistle begins again as if to give silence its singing answer.

"Lucien. Would you like to leave here if you could?"

The carpenter looks startled by this, perhaps wondering for a moment if it is indeed possible. His eyes glance this way and that, as if to review a calculation of that which is good in New France against that which is not.

And of that which is newly and secretly good. Lucien's reply, "Sir, if someone could leave with me," is humble yet a boast as well, and it is more answer than Samuel wants. The carpenter's open-faced honesty is not so much impudent as it is reckless in its trust, which Samuel knows is his own fault, for offering such friendship. In any case, it makes the rumours true. And Lucien takes another bold step toward a common intimacy by asking Samuel now if he, too, would not return home if given the chance.

"No, but I would like to be at sea," says Samuel. "Or up a new river." He thinks a moment, and then voices a favourite notion. "It is with their canoes, not our ships, that we will get to see China."

Samuel notes Lucien shaking his head at the wonder of this. But then sees that the carpenter is merely disagreeing.

"No?"

"Not 'we,' that's certain. Perhaps you. Never me."

"Well, likely not me either. I meant France, of course."

"Of course." Lucien appears to remember something and then begins to laugh quietly to himself.

"What?"

"It might be me after all, since I'm the only one who's learned to paddle." Lucien is beaming at him, staring him openly in the eye. "I got well wet the first time, but since then I've got rather good. I didn't come last in a race."

Samuel forces his own smile down. "You must take more care."

"I'll ask for another lesson, yes." The carpenter smiles with irony again.

"I believe you know I am not discussing canoes. You must take more care."

Lucien studies Samuel's face the briefest moment before dipping his head in a simple bow. "Thank you, sir. I will."

Samuel takes this as cue to turn and walk away. Indeed he felt it was an act of friendship as much as his station to make such a demand of Lucien. The man was near foolhardy. Though Samuel would have much rather stood longer and spoken of paddling and its art. Indeed he would love to paddle a canoe and then own one. In Hochelaga he'd been in a canoe, sitting in its centre while a brave at either end paddled him about like a little king.

LUCIEN RETURNS TO their hidden meadow every day, just in case. Eight and nine and ten days pass and he tries to resign himself to the truth that she had spelled out weeks, not days, on her fingers.

But now, on this the twenty-first day, Ndene steps out of the trees. She is neither laughing nor smiling, and Lucien is at first wary of this until he sees that she has been waiting for him too and that her face is severe with missing him.

Their clothes are more and thicker but they come off as quickly, and though there are no bugs there is the broader bite of the cold. In the corner of the meadow where wind has forced a bed of oak leaves into a nook, they lay her cape, and they draw his coat over them both.

Soon they are made perfectly warm in their lovemaking. When they finish, and rest, and begin to cool, they have only to begin again and it is like pulling a weightless quilt over them.

Even when they have paused in their lovemaking they don't try to talk. It is Ndene who seems assured that there is no need to. Her manner of resting, of staring off over his shoulder, suggests that whatever thoughts or words they could arrive at are of no matter at all. How could one better this? And so Lucien relaxes into this posture as well. He doesn't try to think, or to speak, or to meet her eye. To do so, seeking some kind of reassurance, would be to doubt their growing bond and by questioning hurt it. Her manner tells him that, at least for now, lovemaking is all they need do. And how can he not agree? As her loveliest body, her perfect shape, takes his in, it is only obvious that both of them have been made for this, for this most of all; that in their perfect wrestling they do none other than unwrap God's gift and witness its sacred brilliance, and in doing so carry out God's will. That God had them snorting and yelling like beasts could be seen either as comedy or tragedy, should one care to ponder this, and Lucien does not.

IN TIME HE SLEEPS, but when Ndene shakes his arm he sees the light is unchanged, so he hasn't dozed long. They rise to dress. Partway into pulling on clothes, Ndene stays him with a hand, insisting that she help him. She rolls on his second legging, helps him pull on breeches. Lucien smiles with warmth when he sees her secretly fondling and turning the clothes, checking the build of each garment, picking at a hem, perhaps with the goal of someday making such clothing herself. Finally, she stops, turns, and demands that he pluck all the broken leaves from her hair.

It is obvious that Ndene is thinner. Perhaps from all the distance walked. Perhaps they didn't find the food they were seeking, if that was the nature of their journey, as apparently it most often is. When birds nest in a certain bay, or fish gather at a stream mouth, there her people will gather too, bringing with them or building on the spot the simple but ingenious machines to harvest the creatures and then prepare them for eating. He has seen her family cook a seal in a hollowed-out stump, the bowl of which was filled with water and the stump below set on fire, causing the water and the beast both to boil.

She has lost any softness or roundness of belly, and she is almost without breasts, and when Lucien shows her this with his hand, she does the same at his waist. He has lost his small belt of fat too, and hadn't noticed.

Lucien has practised and saved up some sentences for her. Dressed, hair free of leaf, they sit back down, leaning against each other for shared warmth. He tells her, in what he hopes sounds like Mi'qmah, that he has a sister, Babette, a brother, Albert, and that he lives with his mother, father, and paternal grandmother. He lives in the seaside city of St-Malo, famous for its building of ships. He tells her that, to make his living, he fashions things out of wood. Ndene doesn't seem to understand this last part, and it begins to occur to Lucien that this might be because, in her world, all men do identical things. So Lucien tries as best he can to explain that d'Amboisee, the apothecary treats the men with herbs and potions, Bonneville cooks their meals, the soldiers protect them all with their guns, and Lucien builds them all a place to live. Ndene regards him a moment, understanding, and then points to her chest, stabbing it again and again, while with great humour explaining to Lucien that she, Ndene, catches fish, cleans the fish, cooks the fish, digs onions, makes clothing, salves men's wounds, builds houses, finds the bark to build the houses, snares a rabbit, cooks the rabbit, mends the — and Lucien has to put his wrist into her open mouth, whereupon Ndene keeps talking, muffled and comic, knowing, a clown.

SAMUEL HAS SUFFERED the kind of day that, though bright with sun and cloudless, still appeared dark to him. Of course it is but his inner humour that so tints the heavens. Not helping is his suspicion — no, it is less a suspicion than a truth, even if the men don't know it — that the disease is upon them. He has seen the vague limp, and the dull glower, taking over a half-dozen of the men. So, it's here — but when was its arrival ever in doubt? There's no surprise in it at all.

As he often does at such a time, he gathers his pens and ink about him, unfurls a precious fresh sheet of better parchment, and sets to work.

Yet, hunching over the page for minutes, and minutes more, nothing comes. He has also pulled out various sketches he has yet to commit to ink — the midsection of the River of Saint-Jean, the coastline some leagues below St-Croix, as well as ideas for adorning the finished maps, such as Indian maize, a beaver, a sturgeon — but he does naught but stare at these unmoved. And remains melancholic.

So he turns from his possible art and ponders this mood in hopes of manoeuvring out of it, as sometimes works, casting words as soundings to keep his heart off the reef. The first coil of logic he tosses to himself is simply to announce that reefs are always here, are in everyone's own sea, and are a part of all voyaging. Yet how is it then that some intelligent men always forget these reefs and always founder, surprised? Why, too, do some of the dullest have such apparent talent for mirth? Having run aground, any glowering genius would be a fool not to want some of that skill. Even the witless Dédé laughs more than most, roaring broadly when a fellow trips and pitches into the mud, or smiling like a lover when he happens to witness the flexing of his own hammy arm in lifting a water bucket over the high lip of the well. Or, give Lescarbot one tankard of good wine and he is at carnival: he sits taller, and life could not be better for this *roi de flan*. Another, the carpenter Lucien, who likewise seems prone to melancholy, returns from his walks unsmiling but eyes full of soft light, content, it seems.

How can it be that, when hit with the first cold drops of rain from a surprise cloudburst, some men curse, and *some laugh*? For some, one cold drop of rain might deliver the final insult, the tipping burden, and send a man to take his own life. For others, a cold drop of rain might cause them to shout for more, as if it has shocked cool their hot captivity and relieved them of a load.

He picks up a pen and dips it, to try again. Indelible ink can be his fresh rain. It can be no cause for gloom, this committing the unknown world to parchment. No burden, that he be certain enough of his marks to apply indelible ink to these empty wastes. He can, with a full heart, give new, human truth to God's landforms and to His sea, making them usable to all the men yet to come to these places.

So he adds lines of shading to the southern shore of the River of Saint-Jean. Some trees, to show where timber can be taken.

He feels a swelling gladness in his chest. And he will confess here, to the sad silence of his candle, that as he makes these marks that show the very growth west of New France, and of their King's lands, he thinks neither of men yet to come nor even of New France. As he moves his ink, hearing the scratch as he wounds the fresh sheet with black blood, he is thinking only of himself. This — he says to his heart — is where we have been. He thinks of himself as *we*, though not as one who is royal. He refers to his hands, and his vision, and his body, and his memories. All of it feels like we.

Perhaps because he lacks family. In any case, he draws, from the sketch, the westward push up the River of Saint-Jean. He is careful to show any fatal rocks, and shades them well and with respect. He adds some smaller rocks in their likely yet hidden locations, though he isn't as certain they are there.

4 *decembre* 1606

STILL STEADY ON his course of getting to know these men, whether or not any wants to be known, he contemplates each in turn. Tired of the guilt he feels at learning, yet again, that here is another fellow whose qualities he does not like, he wonders, Whose fault? But he doubts that fault is the issue. Like a divorce of magnets flipped, dislike seems more a force of nature.

He also tries to find no fault in himself when he understands something more. Since he himself is lately bored, melancholic, and even verging on despair, it stands to reason that the other men are as well. Indeed, he can see it in them. And yet shouldn't this understanding make him feel for them, forgive them, love them? It does not.

In any case, the men. For instance the apothecary d'Amboisee. Though of Samuel's own age and soft-spoken, d'Amboisee is an irritant largely because of his superstitions, which have gotten worse. Perhaps superstition is not the word for his affliction, which is definable only through description: upon entering a room he will eye every corner of it with pronounced wariness.

He will eventually make a judgement of some sort and then go and stand or sit in only one area. Sometimes this makes him crowd absurdly with other bodies already located there, and other times this makes him sit altogether alone. But where he places himself has nothing to do with people, and all to do with what the rest of them cannot see. He neither apologizes nor explains, but from what Samuel has gathered, the apothecary's irritating sensitivity is attuned to such things as the time of day, the moon's arc, the humour, and sometimes even the *birthdate* of those who have been in the room and those who have yet to arrive, et cetera. He owns a suspicious and irritating vision. Perhaps it is the laudanum cordial Samuel knows the man takes in some quantity; but more likely it is the man himself.

Perhaps Samuel's problem — as Lescarbot gladly points out to him — is his attempt to leap the walls that naturally keep the classes of men apart. The lawyer could well be right. For Samuel's search for affinity within the common class has for the most part served him up irritants of a ruder kind. When the foul Dédé belches and then slaps the nearest surface, seeing him as a simple carnivore does help Samuel refrain from judgement, but this understanding does nothing to cushion Samuel against the sharp sense of the man, and the actual smell of him; much as, though one might *understand* a fowl-house not properly slopped out, one does not want to stand within it and breathe deeply. Thus, understanding is not love, though Samuel has heard in some philosophies that it is.

He finds it worth noting in this regard that not many savages irritate him. Perhaps this is because he does *not* understand them and, so far, can find them mostly fascinating. Even the savages far to the west: they commit such horrors upon one another, true, but their tortures don't concern him and their thievery is for the most part ingenious. That time he found his best knife under the woman's foot — how did she get it there?

And some of them, especially the Mi'qmah here, can be delightful. So openly loving are they when they trust.

Membertou, last night at table, referred humorously to his age. Samuel believes that's what he did. At one point, he playfully grabbed for Poutrincourt's boy as he walked past with the wine jug, which Membertou wrestled away from him, mostly in merriment. Membertou was bare-armed as always, and, wine jug now in hand and poised to pour it around, he stopped to regard the crepey underskin of his own arm as it jiggled, noticing his aged flesh, it seemed, for the first time. Perhaps he was self-conscious, for he looked up at the nobles seated with him and he on purpose jiggled the flesh anew. With his other hand he pointed to this offending wrinkled skin, laughed, and said, "I have arrived in this body too early!"

Samuel believes that is what he said. His Mi'qmah language improves. He has begun giving informal lessons to Lucien, who requested it of him, which deepens the trust between them. Indeed, Samuel believes the carpenter would have told his reasons if he had been so forward as to ask. So they both remain safe for leaving it unspoken. In all, they have had several sessions during chance meetings outside the walls. Samuel has taught him words on the subject of weather, and seasons, and animals, as well as some nautical terms. Last meeting, Lucien tilted his head as will a pup to learn that the Mi'qmah sun, *nakuset*, and moon, *tepkuset*, are to the savages to the west one word alone, *gizos*. He then claimed he could not decide if, in having but one word for these two heavenly bodies, the western savages were stupid or strangely wise. Sometimes he asks Samuel words he does not know, or knows only in the western tongue, and sometimes Lucien will offer up his own Mi'qmah word unknown to Samuel, almost as in friendly trade. The first time, Lucien somewhat boastfully and with eye aglint counted to five — *newt, tapu, sist, new, nan* — and it wasn't till he was done that Samuel understood it wasn't he who had instructed him in this. But generally they are words of little use: words for the items of clothing Lucien himself wears, words for domestic utensils, and some for the minor plants, and for certain spirits that govern the savages' lives. They also have the word *googoo*, and it is also a monster, but hereabouts it is not thought unfriendly. Last meeting, Lucien taught him tongue, *kilnu*, and belly button, *kili*, and Adam's apple, *joqlem*.

TONIGHT, PERHAPS AS a purgative, and to work off too much wine, Samuel writes as if in his journal, but this time at length, holding back nothing. He uses the back of a sketch he no longer has use for, and thinks he shall burn it after, and this gives his pen a quickness and freedom:

15 *décembre* 1606 (*to burn*)
Regarding us and our neighbouring savages, and our taking of food: if our way is up, theirs is down, if ours right, theirs left — so many and so large are the differences. Note but one: they eat as if no tomorrow is coming, verily stuffing themselves until the joint of moose (for instance) is clean bone. Even that bone they'll crack in the fire and suck for dessert. And then — pardon my fancy — sleep now attacks and sucks *them*, all greasy-faced and overcome with meat as they faint like dogs and fall snoring onto their own arms. We, on the other hand, nibble and fuss at our biscuit and salt beef, ease the swallowing with some wine. Note another:

they eat their meat unadorned. And indeed it is often naught but meat in their meal — they eat a beaver, or a stag, or a fish, naught else, not even salt! We, as if covering God's offering, salt it, clove it, mace it, pepper sage thyme sugar it, or soak it in vinegar until vinegar is what it is. Excuse another fancy, but a rakish poet might suggest that while we dance with and court our food overlong, they marry theirs directly. One might also add that the savage palate never lets a lack of fire get in the way of their more hasty love either. I propose that raw flesh is less charming to them only because it remains flexed and is less submissive to their chewing and their swallowing.

This evening Lescarbot, in mocking their food and their manners (it is a wary mocking, for he is still afraid of them), remarked on their ignorance of "God's etiquette," as if there is such a thing, as if He wastes His evenings sitting in judgement of whether one stabs with one's fork or eases it under. Lescarbot is a fool. God doesn't dine, except perhaps on our good sense and cheer, which works to alert rather than tire Him, if He deigns notice us at all.

In any event I would now propose a hybrid menu, a way to get the men to eat of the savages' fresh food, especially their strange berries and herbaceous small vegetables, most of which they save by drying. I claim it is no accident that, for want of fresh food, our common men sicken — as several seem to be sickening now — while the savages do not. Nor do we nobles sicken who sit at Poutrincourt's table, a table adorned more often than not with whatever the savages have killed and brought to us, fresh, for barter.

I have seen the equation too often to ignore it yet longer. It is now not a question but a truth. Lescarbot laughs at the idea and, since he owns wit, he also owns Poutrincourt's ear.

Through this whole talk, our priest Fr. Vermoulu does not blink but rather chews along with the rest of the cattle. He continually pronounces savage food as *profane*. And so the men turn away at the thought of savage food — the thought, more so than the food itself. But nor are the savages themselves free of lunacy, for of all the world's food, they savour most our dry biscuit.

Not many deserve the tongue God gave us.

After putting down and cleaning his pens, Samuel finds he is breathing almost hard, and needs must rise and walk, though it is late. Striding the courtyard, and passing through the gate, and even so long as he is in sight of the walls, he feels that every man awake knows the words he has written and carries in his pocket, in a crumpled ball.

SOME THREE DAYS before Yule, Samuel's friend the good sagamore Membertou is finally granted his wish. He and his family (and some whom Samuel suspects are not his family) are invited into the Christian faith.

The politics of this manoeuvre have not been simple. Membertou has all along piped his plea loudly and like a boy to any who would listen, even the common men. But of late Lescarbot — who now maintains that, in the eyes of the King, the more savage souls saved the better (that is, better for them and their enterprise here) — has been seeding the ear of the Sieur. Samuel cares not one way or the other, except that he finds it repugnant to witness Lescarbot's entreaties for they are based solely on connivance, and only a little on religion. Lescarbot clearly believes the savages are no more capable of holding the Scripture's truth than an unbunged cask can hold wine. And now Poutrincourt has beseeched the unsmiling Vermoulu to carry out this conversion and give birth to two score of new Catholics. Poutrincourt's motivation here is that the priest has fallen ill with the scurve, and so the good noble thinks to do it now, or do it never.

At the door to the dining hall, Fougeray blows a trumpet and pulls the horn away to reveal a smile of condescension. So much for the earnest solemnity of saving New France's souls, thinks Samuel, sitting at table, watching the Mi'qmah troop in. Though some would argue that what matters most is the power of the rite and not the readiness of the supplicants.

The evening is cause for merriment if nothing else, and some of the Mi'qmah, the children in particular, seem transported and have been made marvellously happy, jumping up where they are and laughing at the ceiling, and so maybe this is justi-fication enough. Barging in bellicose, and wearing a live bird attached in his hair, Membertou himself is like a child oaf. Samuel would dare say the old sagamore has lately come to welcome the next goblet as heartily as a common French sailor; indeed he knows most of their songs now and is in a hurry to lead in their singing. At the same time — something Samuel has noticed before tonight — even at the height of his bellowing, Membertou steals knowing and capricious glances at his wives and sons, and though their bodies' vocabulary does not include winking, his bemused eyes flash the equivalent. It is as though he is suggesting to his followers that it is the French who are the children, and he their guide, and moreover that his manipula-tions take place without their knowledge.

Membertou shouts his habitual "Ho-ho!" to the table of nobles, and greets them first with an upward flourish of a hand, pausing in this savage salute, and then moves to them each in turn to shake their hand.

Vermoulu stands before them all, seemingly at the ready, and yet also unclear how to proceed. He is young, and how many conversions, or even baptisms, could a young priest have conducted in a land of priests? Vermoulu has said nothing about his health, but he was spotted two days ago leaving both the apothecary's and the surgeon's quarters, his countenance glum. Samuel can see the signs. The priest appears dizzy on his feet and walks with pain, as if his legs feel twice their bulk, and he chews timidly, in fear of eating the swollen meat of his cheeks. More and more, Samuel marks the marriage of food and ill humour — this is a man whose privilege allows him to have his own garden and eat at the nobles' table but he won't. In a gesture of humility and poverty that appears only prideful, he insists on nothing but beef and biscuit, and not much of it. Moreover, his condemnation of many of the savage foodstuffs as profane has put many of the men off these good, though strange, foods too. The deer's stomach, for instance, which was one fortnight ago boiled in its entirety and the green contents divided and eaten, and which tasted near as good as a spinach purée, was declared by him a blasphemy because, in his words, "it is food already swallowed, and therefore almost excrement." It was the only green stuff they had seen in two months, save the skins of some small tubers. Samuel lightly challenged and queried him, and Vermoulu could not substantiate his claim with a citing of book and verse. Samuel has seen other men of the church become as this one: to them, their own insight becomes dogma. Indeed it seems a perversion common to all leadership, especially, Samuel would venture, in an isolated settlement.

Smoke from the abundance of celebratory candles, lamps, and an overstoked fire stings his eyes as he watches the savages line up. Apparently the children will become Christians first. Poutrincourt sits to the side, smiling regally, a proxy king. Samuel does not know why he is finding this distasteful, seeing as it is all meant to quench Membertou's thirst for God. But when Lescarbot, who looks dressed as for his own marriage, stands and begins to speak, Samuel drinks deeply from his goblet and then with nary a pause lifts it to catch a server's eye. He refuses to listen to the speech but does note the lawyer's skill in giving the words King and God and Poutrincourt equal measure.

Father Vermoulu, glaring through the damp cowl of his dis-ease, spills water on the savage children's heads in turn, whispering what Samuel assumes is proper Latin while, seated centre stage at a desk with pen and parchment, Lescarbot announces and records the new Christian names. Brave with brandy, of his own accord he chooses the names of the French Royal Family to bestow on the savages upon their birth as Christians. Membertou's grandchildren are now Prince Louis, Princess Charlotte, Princess Marie. Membertou's eldest son, perhaps because of the shape and posture of his skin headdress, is given their Pope's name, Paul, and for this Fr. Vermoulu gathers enough energy to send the lawyer a withering look. (Samuel is mostly relieved to see that the other son, the keel-less one, has chosen, or been forced, to be absent.)

The gathered men drink with purpose, and they cheer and toast each new Christian in turn. The savages drink too, and they arrive now at the stage willy-nilly. Membertou's wife gets the name of King Henri's present wife, and she is announced as Queen Marie, and while none of the savages are any the wiser, the men know the name's import and cheer this new queen. One of Membertou's younger daughters — Samuel thinks she is a daughter, but in any event she is the carpenter Lucien's paramour — is given the name of King Henri's earlier wife, Queen Marguerite, and her response is to glare at the supercilious Lescarbot and then say something bold and harsh-sounding to Membertou, whose own response is already Christian, for here he turns his cheek. At this juncture some of the men call out such as, *Hear Lucien's lady!* and, *Aha for the carpenter's bitch!* at which Poutrincourt perks up, and then looks concerned, and also perhaps embarrassed to be apparently the lone one in the room to know nothing of this affair; and then he turns this way and that to ask quick questions. Samuel wonders what will come of this, for the Sieur is one who lives by, and indeed believes in, the word and rule of both Bible and King.

Samuel checks, but cannot locate Lucien's face in the crowded room.

For the most part the evening moves apace, and each child, young or old, receives their religion and their new name with a pride that is defeated by wonder, for they would hear their name, a kind of gibberish to them merely, and instantly look to Membertou for confirmation that something good has just been done. And their sagamore, kingly himself tonight, uniformly nods and smiles, and with raised goblet toasts them like a Frenchman.

For Samuel, the Mi'qmahs' innocence and wonder help this evening by giving it honesty and, he confesses, a kind of entertainment, the likes of which they have not yet seen in their modest compound. But at the same time there is taint to it: each time Lescarbot says a name his posture is the caricature of a king granting favours, and his smile is as curved as his hair. He is patronizing even to Membertou, who at last has now stood and come forward. Lescarbot delays, sensing everyone's wait, the sagamore's most of all, and when he finally says, "Henri," he shines with a look so self-proud it suggests that he, Lescarbot, owned the power to make kings.

Good Membertou leaps to leave his feet with earnest surprise and happiness when learning he has been given their French

King's name. And not just his age makes this a lunatic sight, for it looks like the finch tied to his hair is trying once more for heaven, and this time succeeds, if but for a second, in pulling the old chief up. At this same time all the men break into a sonorous Te Deum, giving the hymn their full lungs and hearts. And the sum of all this catches up the hairs on Samuel's neck, and swells his throat, and makes him smile and wonder if perhaps this is not a most fortunate evening after all.

But then it is unfortunate that the new king now begins to act rather too kingly, as though the name he now owns has some serious import beyond being merely a name. Even before the men have stopped their singing, and then their cheering, first and instantly Henri Membertou loudly seeks wine, and Poutrincourt's boy reluctantly scurries to do his bidding. But when the sagamore calls loudly that a chair like Sieur Poutrincourt's be set beside the Sieur's, no one seems to heed him, and Poutrincourt merely turns away. And Lescarbot's smile loses its curl.

Samuel turns away himself. He feels unsteady in mood, and he has sought more comfort in wine than is usually the case. He can pretend it is tonic for the blood (as the surgeon, though not the apothecary, insists it is). But the night lifted his spirits not a bit. The winter weather is hardening without, and all of their lamps and candles seem innocent of this fact, as does their raucous and hypocritical glee. He is not the most religious man here, but he feels that something is dangerously wrong, this room filled with the face, but not the heart, of belief. One should not tempt God in this way. With the priest, three men are now ill, though they are still on their feet. Only Samuel and some few others know what their death will look like, and again tonight's naive jollity seems ill-advised.

And one wonders what will be the effect upon their Mi'qmah friends, this conferring of the name, but not the sense, of

Christianity. The rites being done, the no-longer savages stand with dripping heads listening to the last of Lescarbot's florid speech about the Trinity, Christian duty, responsibility, and privilege. The speech makes up for Father Vermoulu's lack of volubility and then some.

Now, striding forward to stand an inch from Lescarbot's small shoulder, beginning with *Ho-ho*, Membertou respeaks the lawyer's words in his own tongue for the benefit of his tribe; and what strikes Samuel is this: customarily, the savage tongue needs five minutes' time to explain what the French explains in one. Why is it, then, that Membertou's speech to his people takes but one minute, when Lescarbot's took five? Possibly the answer is that the chief speaks of privilege only. Why else would they help themselves to all of the bread, as they do now, from both bowls? Little Princess Charlotte, bread stuffed in both cheeks, fills the front of her skins with more. Likewise, Membertou's son, his face newly hardened, demands wine from the good jug. Samuel is not certain if Poutrincourt has noticed this. Clearly Lescarbot has, for he laughs, but he does not care. In future he will simply deny them.

Samuel knows that these new Christians will never darken the door of church. And they still have not been taught how to pray.

LUCIEN WAITS FOR HER in the courtyard cold, pacing by the well, and it's his good luck that Ndene is the first to emerge, appearing black in silhouette to all the celebratory light issuing from the doorframe.

One arm is up, her hand moving on her head, and Lucien sees she is trying to rub her wet hair dry. So the priest has baptized her with water. She looks severe. Such is the chill this night that she should not be out with wet hair.

Lucien steps forward and offers Ndene his hat, but she aims her head away from it. She mumbles something and Lucien believes he has been told not to worry because the water will freeze. He smells wine on her breath, and she has never had wine. He notes that, while the other women and girls, some of whom he saw go in, are wearing especial finery tonight, Ndene wears her skins unadorned. They walk the distance of the courtyard, then approach Poutrincourt's boy, who has preceded them and is already at the gate. Under the smoking torch he looks miserable and sick, and he shoves one stuck gate door open for them with a frustrated bellow of breath.

Lucien and Ndene walk the trodden snow of the main path for a time without speaking until Lucien feels it might be time for the game they play, which is to nudge her with his shoulder, gently breaking her stride, a trick that always makes her laugh, or at the very least smile, and shake her head at her own stupidity for being so clumsy and foolish to have been taken by surprise yet again. And then wait until he has forgotten his jest before taking her turn to put her shoulder to his and send him into the brambles, or a drift.

This time, she merely regains her stride, takes his arm, and squeezes it, as if to say that no such jesting fits this night, please stop, it is enough merely to walk.

So they walk, the half-moon on the snow more than ample to guide their eyes, for it makes the snow almost bright and the tree trunks black. There is a breeze, adding a double cold, but the walking quickly warms them. In all likelihood they won't make love on the ground tonight, though Ndene has surprised him before. And perhaps she is leading him to another of the hidden barked domes that appear, it seems, everywhere, not that Lucien likes them. They smell, even in winter, because those that stay upright through five or ten or however many winters have been used for every human purpose, time and again. Though, in winter, at least the bugs are dormant. (Repugnant as it is, Ndene has told him that sometimes during the very leanest times these domes are ripped apart and toppled in clumsy attempts to get at these insects' frozen nests, which are plundered as a scant meal.)

They walk on in the night, having instinctively taken the fork in the path that turns uphill, away from the bay, for it is coldest next to water. (He has touched her head and those newly sacred strands of hair are indeed frozen. Long, bendable twigs.) They walk some more and now Lucien feels her shoulders ease down and her breathing slow. At long last she pauses beside a sheltering wall of rock and speaks, and what she says has some humour to it as she tells him that her new French name is Queen Marguerite.

Lucien laughs and falls to a knee, takes up one of her hands in both of his, and kisses it. "My Queen," he says, in so honeyed a courtly French that she may be able to distinguish it from his ordinary voice and know that he is play-acting. She does seem to understand the entire gesture, for she is queenly in manner as she pulls him to his feet. She leans against the rock wall and she is nothing but royal in her command that he lean in against her. She moves quickly with both of their belts, and he can tell that it will be fast, even beyond the need for haste demanded in such weather, and that there is still anger in her.

WHEN LUCIEN HEARD that Membertou's request had finally been granted, and that the sagamore and his family would be made Christian, he was surprised only to learn that this conversion would include his own Ndene. Up until that time he had no knowledge that they were related, let alone closely. He still is not clear on it, but Ndene is either the sagamore's niece or great-niece. According to Ndene herself, Membertou favours her like a daughter because she is honest with him and tells him what he is doing wrong, a quality he either likes or doesn't like in others, or perhaps just women. It is hard for Lucien to get these sorts of things clear, and eventually he and Ndene give up trying. Tilts of the head, widening eyes, encouraging laughter, fingers sculpting the air: this language works better than the spoken, but it travels down the road of subtlety only so far, and accuracy is never a certain thing, and often they fall to a silence unsure of what, if anything, has been understood. Had she *seen* the hummingbird nest and its eggs, or *desired* to see it?

But Ndene had been clear in telling him that he must not come tonight to see her become Christian. It wasn't hard for her to reveal in her anger that she was merely doing the sagamore's bidding. And it had been easy for Lucien simply to nod, and also to show his ambivalence. In truth he had no desire that she become Christian. For one, the impossible reach of it, the incomprehension. For another — and he hoped his sin was not too great in this — for the moment it seemed needless.

The wind has died and it snows lightly as they resume their walk. Lucien is fatigued from their lovemaking, but Ndene seems little different. He admits that, since learning she was Membertou's niece — a noblewoman, in fact — he sees her newly, but in what way he does not know. He was surprised to have felt the frailest edge of scorn creep instantly into his view of her, especially when he noted her pride, or sang-froid, with him — and he traced this to his lack of respect shown his own nobles, whose unnatural arrogance at times seems less earned than any housecat's, and clearly the result of a pampered childhood, and a birthright that was nothing but chance. So, with his Ndene, he dearly hoped that he wasn't now loving her less, but he could not help but wonder if she too bore the marks of unnatural arrogance amongst her own people, and he has watched for it. She wears superior dress, the cut of her skins clean and the quillwork stitched tight and true, but that is her doing, her choice, and any other women could join her in it, had they but the skill. For indeed her hands and eyes are brilliant. She would be good as he is at his own trade. Sometimes, when her hands are on his body, he knows she would be better than he at the finer work.

And now she is a queen! He is glad that she seems to regard it as he does: a bit of theatre.

They turn downhill, toward the water, toward her people's encampment. She begins to tell him why she is angry, mostly with Membertou. First, she is angry that he insisted she be included in the Christian rite. (Lucien well knows that insistence of any kind works contrarily on her. He wonders how much force the sagamore brought to bear.) She hadn't wanted to be Christian, and now she is. She has told him before that she has her gods — in doing so Ndene looked reverently to the sky, and down into the earth, and brought invisible food to her mouth — and didn't need another. Not this god who is yours, she'd said, pointing at Lucien. To which Lucien had shrugged, though he hadn't tried to explain. How to say that, if God is God, then God is everywhere and is everyone's already?

But Ndene is also angered at Membertou's behaviour this evening. She tells and shows Lucien that he had arrived wearing a small bird tethered to his longest hair, tied by the tiny leg with three strands of it. (Lucien saw it himself, it was a type of sparrow or chickadee.) This ornament, Ndene explains now, is reserved for the grandest of weddings, and Membertou, after goblets of wine, had shouted in Mi'qmah that tonight he was being married to the god of Christians, and in his shout he meant the carnal embrace, the kind a man sometimes forces upon a woman. She seems to insinuate that Membertou's passion was a ruse, perhaps even a joke, and that his true desire was simply the ability to lay claim to the Christians' guns, hats, bread, spices, and ships. But the reddest blood of her anger lies with her uncle's bird. Three days prior it had been trapped and imprisoned for this evening's rites, and it hadn't eaten or taken water and was very weak; so though it managed to flutter up and about Membertou's head for the first portion of the evening, frightened no doubt by the lamps and smoke and noise, and lumbering humans poking at it and trying to tease it, it soon sank upon Membertou's shoulder and, not long after, died. Ndene told him it had shit its life out in fear upon her uncle's shoulder-front, and Membertou, proud and drunk and soon-to-be-Christian, had demanded, *in French*, of Poutrincourt's boy that he clean it off with wine! And then as the evening progressed and the rites were conducted, he gave no further notice to the dead bird bouncing at his chest, still an ornament, but one that had changed its nature.

Lucien grips her hand as they near her place. They can see two small fires, which appear and then disappear behind trees as they approach. They smell smoke and then see it issuing white from the tops of each of the ten or so mounded dwellings, which are black under the moon. Though it is too cold to stop, they do so now. Lucien knows it isn't the bird's death that angers her, for her people eat such creatures wantonly and by the score. It is more the manner of its death — wasteful, heedless, to adorn an act of self-aggrandizement. Some law, a law of her own gods perhaps, has been broken.

He reaches into his clothes and around to the small of his back and withdraws the small loaf he has kept for her, for they have walked far, and made love, and the night will be too cold and long to have no food to burn for one's blood. She lets the loaf cradle between their chests as they hug, the side of her forehead against his cheek. He would welcome the chance to simply walk into her family's house with her and curl up under her skins and sleep — or first make love again and fall asleep from it without fear of freezing to death. To be her natural husband. She has made clear to him that her people would not mind. Not her mother, or her three brothers, whom he knows. (Her father is long dead. A drowning.) He has made it equally clear to her that his people would do more than frown at this union of theirs, that it is dangerous to an unknown degree, and even possibly fatal. Fatal for their union, in any case. And though her people know about him, he thinks it best to remain hidden to them, lest his presence become so casual a thing that Membertou or his sons casually make mention to the nobles. Ndene has not accepted this state of secrecy and he can tell she does not yet understand. And the moment he dreads begins now.

"Ndene, Lucien," she says, touching their chests in turn. Then she points to one of the black domes. "House of Ndene." He likes that for her house she always uses the Mi'qmah word *atsonch*, while for his she uses the French. When Lucien called his abode an *atsonch*, she assured him disdainfully that that was not an *atsonch*. And of course she was right.

"I cannot," says Lucien. "No."

"Yes," she says, not smiling.

At this he merely points in the direction of the compound, which she will understand means Poutrincourt, and the King's laws, and danger. He has performed enough times before the drawing of a knife blade across his neck, which, not surprisingly, is in their lexicon of gestures too.

Ndene points to the heavens and says, simply, "God," and shrugs.

At this, Lucien cannot tell if she means that it is God's law also that prevents him from staying, or if she means that tonight, since she has become Christian, they are newly sanctioned.

"God," he agrees, nodding sadly, uncertain what he has agreed to.

"Yes?" she says to this, and pulls at him more vigorously.

"No!" he answers. He points to heaven, says yes, then points to l'Habitation and says no. Then, his catchall punctuation, he shrugs for her, his hands palm up, and in performing this gesture for her many times he has come to learn that it can mean several things. He closes his eyes and tilts his head heavenward to show that it is the meaningful, not the ironic shrug which is given with humorous eyes and lips suppressing a smile. Tonight, he also stiffens his fingers and shakes them a little, to show his yearning and sincerity and frustration.

Ndene accepts this as she always does, and with some slight anger, but they fall to embracing again, which is easiest, and it is only practical to share heat in this season, and they grow reluctant to leave the cave of each other's warmth. He hardly notes her smell now, and in the cold it is still less. Now Ndene has begun to softly moan, and Lucien can hear it is a song. It is not a tune constructed as he is used to, but he can tell it is sad. He feels it hum through the bone of her head to the bone of his face. He hears it as her talisman against what has happened to her tonight — a rite forced upon her, and wine that has worn off and drags on her spirit. He listens to her song; it's mostly in a minor key and sadly repeats, and repeats, much as monks will chant, and he hopes he is understanding in it what there is to understand. Almost sleeping on his feet, Lucien revisits the notion that, since she is now Christian, perhaps their union is — no, because now their grave sin is that they are not married. So tonight he still must leave her. And walk, cold, the long way back to the compound, shout at the gate, bear the sight of Poutrincourt's boy's sick eye through the Judas hole, climb the stairs to the men's quarters, also cold, and leap under raw blankets only to listen, while he tries to bleed some warmth into his coverings, as two — or perhaps now it is three — men moan a far sadder, colder song, as their legs ache and their teeth bleed and they try to sleep while dying.

WHEN, TIRED AND COLD, Lucien gains l'Habitation and its gate, he suffers a remarkable confrontation. He has taken but two steps inside the gate — which is unguarded, strangely — when he meets Samuel Champlain, who stands directly in his face.

"*Stop!*" the mapmaker exclaims in a hiss that is as much a whisper.

"Sir, it is only me."

"*Get out. Go back from where you came.*"

"Sir? I —" Lucien sees no evidence of drink upon the man. If anything he is calm and clear-eyed behind the hissing. He is as if performing in a play.

"*Walk off your bestial heat. Be gone, for one hour. No, for two.*"

The mapmaker stands his ground. He casts a quick glance behind him, then turns back to face Lucien with as fierce a face as before.

Lucien says nothing, and there is nothing to do but what he does. He raises his eyebrows in amazement, and then turns slowly around, and walks. He leaves the gate. Outside, he pulls his collar tightly around him and, lacking gauntlets, thrusts his fisted hands deeply into pockets. He stops, looks about, wiggles his toes to find feeling in the small ones, and he wonders where he might go.

SAMUEL WRITES BRIEFLY in his journal:

> 25 *décembre* 1606
> Joyeux Noël. Praise be to Him for giving, to us all, his Son.
> Cloud cover, and windless.

He sits and soon sees he has laid his nib against the paper, releasing ink to create a period the size of a capital O. It's all he'll write today. He has been thinking that he has yet to recruit a coffin maker. He will insist on two. He will ask Lucien his knowledge, and ask him also to train Simon. He trusts the carpenter has forgiven him now. Perhaps he has not. Samuel has not seen him since the night in question.

Samuel is not sure that he forgives himself, though he has wondered time and again what there was in his action that needs forgiveness. Because, simply, Lucien had entered the compound with Poutrincourt standing, not thirty paces away, by the well, in ill humour, discussing this very man, Lucien, and inquiring as to his relations with the savage girl. The Sieur was righteous with baptism and more than a little drunk. In any event, it would not have been opportune for the carpenter, fresh from dalliance, to encounter the Sieur at this time. Simply, Samuel had saved his friend from punishment far graver than a two-hour march.

Yes, but also, no. For guilt persists. Because Samuel also felt, and still feels, his own anger at sighting Lucien arrive there that night, at ease and content from spending time in the arms of his paramour. Was it jealousy at his own friendship with Lucien? Was it envy that this man had what Samuel lacked? Samuel prides himself on the fullness of his heart while exploring; he is not lonely. Perhaps the sight of a man, a friend, with a woman did serve to unbolt that particular door to that particular want, however briefly. For he did feel his anger soothed when he sent Lucien packing.

But nor can he explain any of this to Lucien, not without betraying his station and his avowed allegiance to their Sieur. And so the secret must stay within, even if Lucien is left to sur- mise that Samuel is less his friend than his commander.

Sadly, it is something about which two men, even two friends, cannot talk.

VERMOULU THEIR PRIEST has sickened to the point that he could not rouse himself for Mass last night. Lescarbot said some words, there being those amongst them who think that, consid- ering the times, they could and should give the Holy Sacrament to one another. And there are those who think not. Earlier in the day, Samuel had climbed to the priest's quarters, held his breath as best he could and, apologizing for the disruption, asked for a learned opinion on this vital concern. Vermoulu's shrug shocked him to the quick. Not because he took from it a meaning — he could not tell if the priest did not know, or did not care — but because it was either way a shock. After, standing outside, unmoved in the blowing snow, he did not know what news to conjure to bring back to the men, most of whom honour this priest (as he does not but dares not show it). In the end

Samuel told them he found the priest in a rare restful sleep and would not be cruel and wake him. A lie on Christmas Eve felt like mortal harm upon him, but that is what he did. And so Lescarbot leapt to his feet to say Mass of a kind.

Yet this grand day they will celebrate, and take from it and bring to it what good cheer they can. Membertou has hunted up and this morning delivered to the cookhouse three woodland birds as he long boasted he would, after hearing about this especial Christian day. One fowl he has stored overlong and in a thaw it has turned, but not badly, and Bonneville reckons a handful of juniper berries will o'ercrow it. Membertou will bring his family tonight to join them, as they wish to be all the more Christian. With their respectful visit in mind, Samuel hopes that the men — he includes himself — do not make too merry, for drunkenness may shine a bent light on how it is they honour the Birth.

There has been absolutely no wind all day and it is mild. Samuel decides that, with cloud cover so gentle and uniform, there is no weather at all.

The Metronome

HE CAME TO AT his window, checking his watch. In five minutes he had to put on his coat, shovel the drive, leave for work. He'd been watching a purple and black sunset change more from wind-pushed clouds than from a seemingly sinking sun. He watched the water too, as some crabbers rounded the point. That straggler looked like Leonard's boat but, black against the silver water, it could be anyone.

He'd been imagining Laura living here with him. It was months now and they were comfortable together — she was sitting in her chair in that corner watching him. From her perspective he saw himself staring out the window. He heard her observe, "How much time you spend staring at that water." Well, it was true. At work, he read. At home, he watched the water. Sometimes he had a book going — but he was always watching the water.

How much would he want to reveal to Laura about himself? He owned a hundred and one crazy ideas, odd inner strings that had tugged on him for years. Some were a bit lame, like how, ever since reading about magnetic fields and their subtle effects on the brain, he slept with bed pointed north. Or how he always put on left sock, shoe, sleeve first, because if he didn't, something bad would happen, and now it was a life habit. Some ideas maybe weren't as silly, for instance, his beavering out the white inner peel from grapefruit for the bioflavonoids. Or another, always taking vitamins during meals so they'd bind with the food and fool the stomach into thinking they were natural. Another, he tried his best not to eat near bedtime because the monastics of no less than a hundred percent of the major religions thought an empty stomach during sleep helped cultivate compassion itself. He also took ginseng for "masculine vigour," as well as a daily cup of green tea to prevent osteoporosis, though he knew this was an estrogen thing and told no one. He had plenty of other notions like these, and while they didn't often come to mind he saw he lived in them like clothing.

One of the larger notions was serious. Even in childhood he understood how charming water was. Wind, tide, waves, rips, patterns of breeze tickle. Logs, garbage, jumping fry, seals, tugs, unidentified floating objects that might be sea monsters. Framed in his window, no minute was like the next. No second. The Ripley Island light never stopped its rhythmic flash, a kind of counterpoint, or metronome, for the random ocean. It was quiet chaos out there, it was never not busy. Even a rare calm day was flux, the mirror sea welling up, the blue heat expanding down, birds and boats coming through on a line, for these moments a simple direction their only need.

Laura, more to the point: Gazing out the window, *he* didn't have to move because the world was doing it already. Watching the water, he felt not fulfillment exactly, but an absence of dis-content. Watching, he never felt antsy, whereas in a store, in the pub, he generally did. If at first he was troubled by how long he spent just watching the water, wasting time, over the years he'd decided it was fine to let the world do his moving, his changing, for him. Not only as minutes went by but also on the larger, more frightening scale. Years back he'd come to almost believe he didn't have to do anything as long as the world, so evident through his window, was this busy already. Laura, really: Why the hell add to it? Why even move from your chair?

Anyway, when do you reveal such notions? And how do you prepare for her verdict? She whose ambitions moved her so far away, so quickly.

SWEATING FREELY IN his fleece he shovelled the inch of snow from the considerable length of his drive, a chore undertaken more for aesthetic than practical purposes. His mother was coming for Christmas as usual and this kind of tidying up had the tone of adolescent reluctance, of cleaning up before your parents got home. In ways that counted, this was still her house.

Three in the afternoon and the light had already fallen — but odd how snow on the ground lent an able brightness from below.

Christmas in two days. Laura two days after that.

Before jumping in his car he went back and stood for a minute on the lip of his backyard, with its bonus view, as he was calling it. So far, no more land lost to acts of God. (He'd made a call to the insurance company and the agent, Brian Glenn — Andy had been in the same grade with his brother Pat — had said that land itself wasn't technically insurable, "especially in one of these standard 'act of God' things but, hey, nature takes a bite out of your house we'll be all over it. Unless it's an earthquake. Which is more, you know, 'God.' Unless you have actual earthquake insurance. Which, let's see, you don't. Would you like some?") Cliff-edge, Andy risked toeing a workboot, out into space, hanging five. Things felt solid enough. God, for the moment, had ceased acting up. Or acting out. But staring off into the approaching wall of fog, unable to see much of anything at all, he could too easily feel the melting glaciers, big rains, rogue waves, and the coming rise, and this ground falling from under his feet faster than he could backpedal. It actually made him take a backward step. This good an imagination was a potent and tricky thing. But he remembered now what was lost with that corner patch of ground. That was where Buck used to stand during windstorms. Head up, almost noble-looking. Her stance wasn't one of guarding the place, but more of trying to see what was causing that fuss beyond the trees. Maybe it was her version of sticking a head out the car window. In that rough wet weather her fur would curl into lush ringlets, revealing blonde highlights, and she'd look almost beautiful.

AFTER SNEAKING DOWN to Vancouver to catch Laura dance that one spring so long ago, Andy mailed some forms to enrol in UBC and returned that same fall. He wasn't sure why. Mostly, you were supposed to leave Prince Rupert. In his mind he thanked Laura for helping him. She was back in Toronto, but her presence on stage had warmed up the city for him.

He arrived the day classes started and there was nothing to rent near the university. Andy found a hotel downtown that rented by the month and had odd burnt-electric smells instead of cooking smells. Those first days, out his window the sirens and honks were interesting, exotic like a pushy foreign language. It was his first time living away from Beachview Drive and his first time alone, and he knew this is what adventure felt like. He could distinguish true change from one of life's non sequiturs and this was the former. He was ready for anything.

But not his constant state of want. On the floor of vast, amphitheatre classes, profs rarely said anything compelling. He could not sit still. In Biology 100 the prof showed slides of cells, using his most dramatic drone to joke that the nucleus was a cell's ego, and Andy fought to keep his eyes focused.

Andy slept all right, the traffic sounding enough like waves on gravel, but still he couldn't settle. Philosophy was another disaster, this time because of the in-class reading, something by Locke, wherein sentences tended to go for a half-page before a period. He had to ask himself honestly if it mattered to him. He stayed until the class let out because there were only a dozen in this room and it was hard for a man his height to slink. He had to admit that the only interesting thing about Philosophy 115 was that no other tall people were taking it, a question that maybe tomorrow's Psychology 104 could answer. Leaving the class it wasn't hard for Andy to accept that he would never be a great and labyrinthine thinker.

He held out most hope for English. Early to the classroom, he sat there alert as it gradually filled with women. The middle-aged professor, who identified himself as a Wordsworthian and who was handsomely square-jawed and aware of it, talked for five minutes about how hard it was to stand here and teach and not be allowed to smoke. Apparently smoking was now banned in classrooms. Andy tried to sympathize, until the prof compared himself to an English explorer returning from the dangers of the New World, who now had "to worry about having my smoker's fucking nose cut off in London." Andy watched for signs of humour, but the guy was serious. He scanned the reading list hungrily. One-third he'd already read at work, for pleasure. The other two-thirds he hadn't, because he hadn't wanted to. Now he was being forced, but not at work where he would've been paid, and the logic bothered him. Plus his appreciation would be judged by the noseless professor.

The prof ended the class telling them to march to the bookstore and buy the books. Andy joined the women in their meander through connected buildings, trying to stay interested by studying their jeans from behind, but he couldn't rise above his discontent. And then he encountered the last straw. Walking past the open doors of another amphitheatre, Andy heard an eerie, disembodied voice declare, "the *subject*, not the object of our study. Not the *object*, but the subject." Andy poked his head in, and down on the floor a thin, near-elderly woman popped the board with a wooden poker. The lone words on the board were these:

Pseudo Code Bucketsort
Running Time Bucketsort

Andy could feel his smile. His mute guffaw. No one noticed him. No women from his English class knew he was no longer following their jeans to the bookstore.

Flying over Queen Charlotte Sound, halfway home, Andy wasn't troubled by the way things had worked out. He promised himself that he would never entertain the possibility that he was a failure. One thing his buddy Leonard often said about "the Aboriginal mind" was that Natives "are really good at not doing what they don't want to do." What could be more brilliant? Why do something you don't want to do? Why read something you don't want to read? Especially when you're not getting paid union scale to read it.

Another funny thing: his name hadn't appeared on any of the class lists when they were read out, so probably he'd done something wrong and wasn't registered at the university at all. Officially he'd never been there. He'd paid fees, and could probably get them back, but didn't try. He'd work a bunch of overtime. He'd phoned before flying and was told that he'd lost seniority but his old job was there for him.

Years later, Andy had nothing left of his brief university education save for the waft of embarrassment when he thought of it, which wasn't often. He did wonder if higher education had failed him or he had failed higher education, and if the academic path would've led to a happier Andy Winslow. He also wondered what Laura's thoughts were upon hearing — because she would have heard — that Andy Winslow had left Prince Rupert but had lasted exactly a week.

The other remnant of Vancouver was Buck. Drew had a sense of occasion, and days after Andy returned from his abandoned future Drew brought him a dog. Rescued from the Terrace pound, the year-old female mutt's main feature was wildly untrusting eyes. At first Andy didn't want a dog muddying his house, but he couldn't return it to certain death in the pound. So he named her Running Time Pseudo Code Bucketsort, or Buck for short, and came to love her as much as one can a dog that bent by harm, until Buck died under the wheels of the mail truck seven years later. Andy cried as he drove Buck's blanket-wrapped body to the vet, surprising himself.

But with Buck's death, that was it for higher education and, for that matter, ever moving away from Prince Rupert, probably.

AT THE TERMINAL, under the looming bank of connected silos, he parked and locked his car, then unlocked it and left it unlocked. No one he didn't know would come by here and he wanted to keep alive at least this vestige of the old days. Maybe he'd start not locking his house again — but this thought brought to mind an image of Tsimshian gangstas lurking in bushes beyond his yard.

He walked the footbridge to the main building and saw it through her eyes, because in mere days he would bring her here. Not to justify his life but to communicate it. He liked this foot-bridge. Its thirty-foot drop, so visible through the wire grid you walked on, unnerved him just enough that he still regarded it as morning coffee for the way it woke him up. The narrow bridge was built solely to get a man across train tracks, arcing over six sets of them and the boxcars waiting to release a load from their bellies. Even if you were used to it, even if you talked about the latest YouTube madness with a hungover German named Veit (pronounced *fight*), something in your body was aware it walked on space and that was deeply wrong. No matter how dopey getting out of his car, he was awake when he punched his card.

He paused at the peak and grabbed the rail but released it, the iron hurting-cold without gloves. Below, beside a track, two ravens shared a pigeon. One stepped in, poked a few times, dragged out some gut, tossed its head forward to get the morsel to the back of its throat. The second raven hopped up to the feathered trough to stab as well. As it pulled, the pigeon followed, so the first raven put its foot on the body, holding it. Was this co-operation? They looked unhurried, unlike the riots of gulls, or even crows. Andy had seen crows kill and eat wounded pigeons and it was a savage thing to see, the stabs, flapping, ripping. Birdies. It was unclear if these ravens had killed the pigeon. Because ravens were his favourite bird, Andy liked to think they found it dead and were cleaning up the yard. Ravens were maybe even his favourite animal. The killer whale was their main competition in this, but since you almost never saw a whale's eyes, it was hard to know them.

At the door, from his workbag Andy dragged his orange safety vest out from under four or five books. Some foremen still gave you shit for not wearing it on site. About six months after 9/11, the orange vest was one of two antiterrorism measures worked out with U.S. Homeland Security. All "front-line port workers" wore them now, apparently. The other measure was a half-million-dollar, ten-foot-tall chain-link fence that ran along the rocky beach for a few hundred yards but simply ended and could be stepped around, forcing terrorists —after they'd purchased their orange vests at Harbour Rod & Gun for nine bucks — to hike a bit farther than they had to in the past. (Andy reminded himself to tell Laura he'd seen his favourite graffiti ever, pencilled on a scrap of cardboard secured to the new fence: *Heaven Attacked by the Afraid.* Funny thing is, he didn't know if it referred to terrorists or the fence.)

He punched in, nodding to a couple guys. Walking past the open lunchroom door he saw Drew, who looked up from his newspaper and called, "Little bastard came home for Christmas." Drew wore his vest inside out, showing only grey, a style favoured by him and a few other rebels.

Andy leaned into the lunchroom. "Chris is back?"

Drew couldn't keep his smile down. "Now I have to go buy a bunch of bribe presents to keep him here."

"Chris? That's so *great.*" Despite the levity of the moment, Andy couldn't help eyeing the stained and ripped plastic Santa head some cynic had nailed to the lunchroom wall and that looked, from where Andy stood, like a second head growing up out of Drew's.

"I was actually thinking of buying him a car for Christmas."

"A car?"

"Reverse psychology." Drew's mood had actually made his face redder. "As in, 'I don't want you to leave town again, so I'm buying you transportation.'"

"Seriously?" Andy was sad that he could read how his friend's happiness was already undermined by new cares. Instead of a general worry of Chris up to no good in Calgary, now Drew would know whenever he was out, and he'd wonder who with. Drew was probably wondering that now.

"An oldie. Five hundred bucks. Something he can cut holes in for speakers and whatnot. A big old pig. Paint 'anarchy' signs on the doors."

"You don't think he'll see it's a bribe?"

"I'm going to *tell* him it's a bribe."

Andy wasn't certain, but Chris seemed the type of young, dialed-in guy who'd use the phrase *carbon footprint* without irony, who wouldn't want a big pig, and it was the shits that Drew maybe wasn't seeing this.

"You know what his nickname is now?"

Andy told him no, and Drew pivoted around to get a few more guys listening.

"Pone Bus."

"Pone Bus?"

"It's like, you know how you *own* someone when you beat them at something, well the slang for that is *pown*, and bus is like he beats lots of people at once. *Pone Bus.*"

"That's great. It's sort of like Cockney rhyming slang."

Drew said he'd never been able to figure that stuff out.

"But, decent name," Andy said, tapping his wrist where a watch would be. Drew had always been in love with his son's slang. He'd loved it, for instance, when at twelve Chris said he was going to make tennis his bitch, and when he started calling high school "the taint."

HE TOOK THE EAST lift to the bin tops, choosing this clanky, open-sided, and unnerving elevator because he pictured taking Laura up here too, when a slacker supervisor was on. From this lift — a rusty cage open on two sides, a red bar your only barrier to freefall — you rose through a good view of the terminal's dank and rusty guts, all dark and hissing and banging, a chaos of heavy-duty, of industrial revolution, nothing prettied up for public viewing, no soft giant turning cogs Charlie Chaplin could ride on without getting crushed. The shape of all metal was designed for function; enough bare light bulbs dangled so eyes could just see; red paint indicated what would kill you; a lift that said *Max 5 Person* probably meant it. If you stood in one spot for a minute you might see a spectacularly plump rat trot by. Grain dust went in and out your lungs, always. And it smelled stronger than a cheap apartment block at dinnertime. Andy could hardly smell it any more but visitors said the place smelled overwhelmingly like dry pet food fermenting.

Yet not even counting the paid reading time, it wasn't bad here. He'd tell Laura that despite the American takeover the paycheques were still robust, at least for those kept on full-time. And, Laura, there have been entertaining things. In the early days up on the gallery, guys drove countless golf balls over the road as far as the blue Pacific, much laughter and money changing hands, and it went bad only when cars became targets, the poor coal-terminal bastards speeding home after their shift. Not another golf ball was hit up there after Bert Stempniak's windshield got nailed and he went into the ditch and his airbag broke his collarbone and glasses. And there was rat-plinking: guys bringing pellet guns and on their own time having contests, the laughing rationale to supers being, "For less rat part in Chinese dumpling!" There was the summer Galloway, nicknamed "Newman" after the *Seinfeld* fatty, busted a bathroom sink right off the wall while having day-shift sex with a still-unidentified woman. No one wanted to picture it and said so. There was that summer of the seven pot plants growing up on the annex against the sunny side of his tin shed, Andy swearing to a supervisor not only that they weren't his but that he didn't know whose they were, though he did. Grain dust was purportedly the best medium for growing absolutely anything, but PR apparently wasn't tropical enough and the spindly plants never got more than two feet tall, and the supervisor merely pointed at them and laughed and walked away mumbling about Charlie Brown Christmas trees.

The lift banged to a stop. With no need to please the public, the braking mechanism involved no rubber or springs and for one instant you were a hundred pounds lighter. He imagined Laura beside him, both of them leaning over the red rail to take in the two-hundred-foot drop to the dim concrete far below, feeling this same big flip in the belly.

Andy was glad he was five minutes early because he relieved Dean, one of his brasher coworkers. (Dean typically carried his coat and wore only a beater underneath, to better showcase his several heavy-metal tattoos.) This afternoon Dean brushed by him with a flat "Yahoo," where often he had a joking complaint about Andy's bookshelf lacking porn, or why weren't the rest of them allowed a TV. Dean might mock himself to Andy with a purposely mispronounced, "What do I know, ain't been to a *libary* in my life," a *sort of* compliment, but like being licked by a dog that hated you. (One time Dean had more or less called Andy a liar. A group of guys, some of them rec hockey players, were recalling funniest-ever team names they'd heard, and Andy blurted one he'd read about, "The Swastikas," and Dean had said simply, "Bullshit." Andy had to explain that it was a women's team, from Edmonton, from the '20s, before Hitler, and while some of the guys looked dubious, or impatient, possibly because he'd bothered including a women's team, he had to mumble further that swastikas were actually a religious symbol, not just in Hinduism, and...sometimes it was just too complicated to open your mouth at all.) But Dean did seem impressed once at lunch when, after marvelling over how long a glue-strip-stuck rat in B Annex had stayed alive — fucking *days* — Andy let slip that rats were the one animal that could go without water longer than camels.

He stowed his lunch, checked the screen, saw that the ship currently tied up was on a long canola fill, which would last the night. Aside from two scheduled shutdowns to let deckhands on board change holds, Andy could put his feet up and finish Lescarbot's story about the Order, an account far more complete than Champlain's, with descriptions of songs and skits performed. Lescarbot seemed to be taking most of the credit for the idea.

First Andy stepped out to stretch a bit and breathe the evening air. Laura, this wasn't too bad a job. Noisy, but the noises were expected, machines doing the hard labour, doing what your computer screen said they were. Smelly, but a body got used to anything. Like his nose, his ears had also adapted. According to his latest on-site medical, the decibels had been killing cilia — the little hairs — in his inner ear. He could see this in two ways: he had suffered a twenty percent hearing loss, or he had adapted to the noise and was now more comfortable.

Some hundred metres distant, there floated *Highlander*, a mid-sized freighter typical for its Panamanian registry and Filipino crew, and probably owned by some Russian potentate who lived in nouveau riche New Jersey. The ghost-orange halogens were already on and the vast expanse of decks was lit up so as to suggest empty midnight basketball courts in an oddly deserted city. He could see a few deckhands leaning half over the rail, literally hanging around, bored senseless, noodle-arms dangling like they wouldn't care if they just fell and got it over with. Ship duty no doubt drove these poor souls mad — less than ten miles away from a downtown with lights and bars and women. Filipino sailors generally had less pocket money than even the Chinese, but it would still be fun to walk up and down some strange streets. There on the other, seaward side of the ship, it looked like a clutch of them, at least, were fishing.

The Philippines was a Christian country, and Andy wondered what those guys down there felt about being at sea at Christmas. Probably similar to the boys here called in from layoff exactly three days before Christmas to handle fresh traffic, pissed off to work the holidays but happy for some time-and-a-half, and double time on the day itself. Rum 'n' eggnog money, right on cue. Buy Junior the latest twitch system, be a hero after all.

Andy turned to go in and read when a small plant caught his eye, growing in a wedge of grain dust gathered near the silo edge. He wondered if it could be mint. It looked like it, the classic leaf shape, with those wrinkles. He didn't like going that close to the edge, so he'd leave it be, but it would be nice just to step outside one's shack and pick something wild, wouldn't it? Did mint go with moose? He should go online to search out more spices the French had. He should be phoning Leonard. Mussels. Moose.

Andy closed the door to his shed. He swept Dean's lunch crumbs (he could smell tuna) off the metal table, feeling as he did so its odd surface, layers of thick paint over carved graffiti. Boredom's strata. But it really wasn't a bad place. He could tell her stories about some characters here, yes he could. Though some of the more high-octane stuff was troubling. Laura would have heard about Pauline's father, who fell maybe fifteen years ago now. Andy was up in his annex shack when Joe was reported missing, and he took part in the search, poking into the few nooks and crannies up on the bin tops, and peering over the edge in the spots that had safety rails. Pauline's dad was a supervisor and could be anywhere on site. Ten minutes in, Andy saw the arc lamp they'd brought to illuminate something, and then he could see Joe, lying way off, tiny and spread-eagled, two hundred feet down under Silo B. No one had a clue how Joe Mulders could make this mistake. He drank a bit but was a regular sort. There was no possible connection, but maybe the weirdest thing was that Pauline's father died a year and a day after Drew's mother had gone into the river.

Andy only heard about another one, a big prank gone wrong. Sam Cuthbert decided not to quit but get himself fired because it was easier to get pogey that way. But in the old days it was actually hard to get fired. If caught drinking or smoking dope you got suspended, which people called the unpaid vacation. Cuthbert conspired to get fired in a blaze of glory, timing everything for the toughest super, Jackson. Cuthbert had wild hair and beard and a huge flabby torso, and his better friends called him "Hogbody." Hogbody's idea: a conveyor belt cornered near the door to the general office, and if you roller-bladed against the flow, with the help of a friend's signal, Jackson would emerge to encounter a naked Hogbody skating at him hard. There was some question as to whether he'd jump on Jackson then or what. Cuthbert practised blading the belt a couple of times, and he did attempt the prank, except he was drunk on this his last day and fell after only a few strides, flew away on the belt, flipped at the bend, and got caught in the rollers. All Jackson saw was a naked man stuck in the belt fifty yards down, screaming for real though barely heard above the noise. Sam Cuthbert lost a leg mid-shin, and the pinkie and ring fingers of one hand, and it became a difficult anecdote to entertain someone with, because you could be sure Cuthbert himself has never laughed at any of it.

Then there was Andy's own first day bin-digging, the rite of passage to which they used to subject every new employee. It was horrifying, Laura! You're nervous enough, guys joke about death by methane as they strap you into a leather diaper-thing and clip it to a thin cable, and now they're sticking a weird hard hat on you, a tin one with a miner's light on it, the only light you'll have down there. Then the ratty old gas mask, which looks First World War and snaps to the hard hat with rotten leather straps; so they weren't kidding about poisonous gas. They hand you a shovel! The job is to loosen up crusted grain at the bottom of the bin, hardened from the tons of pressure. (Sort of like coal? Andy joked, nervous. Sort of like *diamond*, some wag hissed back.) They tell you that, at the bottom, some choose to step out of their harness because it's hard digging while attached to the cable, but then there's the danger of drowning in loose grain, which is *worse than quicksand*, someone adds. And because it contradicts the crusted coal image so much, you realize they're just trying to get you nervous with the worst stuff they can think of. Still, he was lowered two hundred feet, through poisonous air, in the dark, on a WWI cable. Laura — it was horrifying! But you wished new guys were still made to do it, all the same.

THAT NIGHT AT TEN, an hour left in their shift, Drew called from downstairs.

"So, yeah. We're splitting up. After New Year's I'm moving out."

"You're kidding. Where?"

"Those blue apartments on 6th, past the hospital? Third floor. Decent view."

"Holy cow."

Drew had chosen a phone call, at work, to have their heart-to-heart.

"We're thinking the weirdest part'll be that we're both still in town. I mean, we'll bump into each other. We'll hear that so-and-so was with so-and-so last night."

"Holy cow." Andy thought for a moment. "Hey, is that what happened? Does one of you already have a so-and-so?"

"No." Now Drew paused to consider. "I can't even imagine a new so-and-so. I don't even know what you do to get a so-and-so."

Drew's romantic history: two decades with the same person. Andy doubted either had ever cheated. So Drew had never dated as an adult, never been a free agent, on the hunt. But surely he wasn't now seeking advice from his best friend, whose own dating tactics apparently involved sitting around waiting almost two decades for his girlfriend to come back.

"You still splitting up even with Chris back here?"

"What's Chris got to do with it?" Drew asked, calmly. This was raw, skinless territory, and Andy could sense Drew trying to come up with something funny. "I'm paying him back. I'm running away from home. Show him what it feels like." Drew paused, and his tone shifted. "He won't even know I'm not there."

Andy shook his head at his friend's complicated pain. He remembered Pauline telling him how Drew thought *he* was depressed. Maybe when Drew saw him he saw complicated pain. But now wasn't the time for that talk. Likely there wouldn't be a time. Droning comfortably into the phone, loud enough to be heard over their respective nearby machines, they talked about little things, Christmas things. Pauline wanted Drew to help her cajole Chris into going to midnight Mass, "just once, for the experience," but Drew wasn't playing along, because there was "just no good reason to go, even to gawk." Then Drew remembered something he wanted to ask Andy, and it was whether he still had that Chinese woman's — "not the pretty one's"— phone number.

"Who, May? May E?"

"Yeah. Not the pretty one."

Andy explained that he'd given her his number, not the other way around, and asked Drew what was up.

"I guess something weird happened," Drew began, and then went on to tell Andy what his father had told him, which was that it seems "the other one, the pretty one —"

"Li."

"— had left town last week, flew back to China presumably, but called the PR police station from the airport to make a confusing complaint that sounded like sexual assault, but maybe not, and she mentioned one name — 'Danny Boy'—and described two men, and one sounded like Art Tanner."

"Did she say what they did?"

"Maybe they didn't do anything, maybe she was just pissed off in general and wanted to tell somebody that three assholes treated her like shit. I don't remember, but my dad says they both went home together. He said all proud, 'I put those two ladies in a big black taxi.'"

It sounded like Drew had slurped some eggnog in the lunch-room.

"The police pressing charges?"

"It's nothing like that. They told her to come in but she just caught her plane. The cops called my dad because I guess she mentioned his party. And now he wants to check with...?"

"May."

"He thought you had her number. Actually he hoped you'd be the one to call her."

"Would somebody fly back to China just because some guys were rude to her?"

"Who knows. Maybe she was homesick. Maybe it was the last straw."

"Maybe."

Andy remembered May telling him that the college had arranged office space for them. Rachel Hedley could help him find May's number. He told Drew to tell his dad that he'd call her to see how she was. He liked May. They had communicated, leapt over the language barrier. She might be feeling pretty lonely right now.

Drew told him a super just eyed him a second time and he had to get back at it. So they signed off, not just "later" but with some "well, okay's" too, slowly and with significant depth, letting each other know that they'd talked about some important things, that they'd just done what good friends did. Drew was definitely moving out, and he confirmed it now by asking Andy to help him take some furniture to the new place. Andy wanted to joke about women being like work, and now that Drew's shift was apparently over with Pauline, Andy was going to punch the clock with Laura, but in his head he couldn't get it to sound at all funny, plus Drew would find it pathetic in spades.

CHRISTMAS MORNING, the house smelled richly of coffee and frying bacon. As always, the day began with gifts. They were down to one apiece. After Andy and his mother started their two-person Christmas, it had taken them a few years to hold to the promise of one gift and one gift only, it being hard for her not to add "little last-minute things," often sweaters or, one time, a box holding eighteen pairs of red work socks.

Today she had just the one. Wrapped in metallic crimson paper, the box she cradled in her lap looked the size to contain a baseball. Or an orange — Andy had a favourite story from a childhood book about an impoverished rural Christmas where a boy received the sole gift of an orange and was surprised and overjoyed almost to a faint. It was a kind of emotional pornography (it was the only gift in the house, and the lone parent, his father, was dying), but the kid had never tasted an orange before, and it was a miracle not only of love but of food.

"I bet you it's gone by tonight," his mother said, pointing out the picture window at the backyard where last night's foot of pillowy snow was already half eaten into by rain. They agreed they'd had a white Christmas, which was the main thing.

Two cups of black coffee steamed on the glass coffee table. Andy's gift to her, in a shoebox wrapped in the Sunday comics, rested beside his coffee, on which floated a film of cinnamon. He sat on the couch and his mother on the matching chair, facing each other on a diagonal, both in their pyjamas and bathrobes. The ritual, unbroken since she had moved out with her three friends, was that she arrived with a suitcase on Christmas Eve, they decorated the tree, and she spent that night in the old house with Andy, waking up to Christmas morning together in this house as they always had. She slept in the old master bedroom in her old bed, the same one his father had died in while lying asleep beside her so long ago now, and Andy wondered what lively ghosts Christmas Eve must conjure for her every year.

Sometimes she volunteered a ghost or two. How well, for instance, she could remember his hair, or smell, or "his face when he was your age, Andy." Sometimes such things came in intense sudden glimpses, then were gone. She sat, sighing wistfully, confirming things such as, "He *was* a good man, your father," and "We *did* have some fun," and "It *is* such a marvellous view of the water." It became clear to Andy that this one day of the year, lasting from the evening she arrived until the next evening when she left after turkey dinner, was the time she allowed herself unabashed nostalgia of the broadest kind. It was a time they were expected to talk about his father, their house, and their lives while they'd lived here.

Some years back, after their two-person Christmas had grown stale — his mother called it "a bit precious," while he was thinking claustrophobic — they tried expanding it. They invited Leonard, but his was a large and religious family that gathered in the north village where their home church was. Another year they tried to entice Pauline and Drew, but they were with family too, and so were his mother's housemates — Marie Schultz, for instance, always flew south to be with Laura and her husband and their child. So they stopped inviting and settled back on just the two of them, and one ghost. Sometimes, watching her descend the stairs in her robe, like a sleepy child, he thought it all a little perverse. And it sparked the question, why didn't she still live here to begin with? Why doesn't family live with family? But it was a topic she'd never once raised, and the discreet air to her silence maybe had to do with the women she assumed, or hoped, he must be bringing home on a regular basis.

Andy did enjoy talking about his father. His father had built this house, or at least had a hand in the design. Sitting in it, feeling the placement of rooms and their relationship to one another, and looking out the various windows and their purposeful views, was like — so Andy imagined — sitting in his father's brain and seeing through his eyes. One of the house's features was that its living room and picture windows faced not the road, like all other houses did, but instead the backyard, and treetops and, beyond that, the ocean. Recently built houses had their main windows on the ocean too, but earlier ones didn't. Andy's father had more or less turned a house around backwards. So when you came off the road and parked in the drive beside the front yard, what you encountered was the back of the house: kitchen entrance, bedroom windows, et cetera. As his father had said, repeated now every Christmas morning by his mother, "Why would you want to sit on a sofa and face a road?" She also reminded Andy that some in the neighbourhood actually got angry with him for facing his house the opposite way to theirs.

Andy turned the frying bacon, lowered the heat, and brought in the coffee pot. He topped her up. Standing over her, bending, he could smell her. It wasn't bad, it was his mother's smell, but with a bit more oomph behind it. She looked old to him this morning. An old face really did show the night's sleep. He supposed he'd been watching her get old in her new house, while in this house he was used to a younger version.

"Merry Christmas, Mom." He slid his present at her across the table.

"You first." She held her crimson box out to him.

Despite his being ready for it, this was the sort of thing, her little commands, her insistence on running the show, that got to him still. If he'd tried to unwrap her gift first, he was fairly certain she would've corrected that too.

In any case he was looking forward to her seeing his gift. He took pride in hunting good presents, not bathrobes or perfume or something she could just get for herself. It had to be something she wouldn't have thought of, and something beyond practical. And it couldn't be radical or whimsical, that risked being stowed in a closet or hung out of guilt on a dark hallway wall. This year he'd known right away, as soon as he saw it there in the Art Gallery Store. Rich black argillite, carved in contemporary Haida style, a squatting man clenched himself at the shins in a stressful ball, the carving pretty much spherical save for his head and face lifted in sudden surprise. Whether the news, the shock, was good or bad was anyone's guess. Andy liked to think it meant that any shock was good because it got the guy out of his painful clench. It was well carved, and had the emotional clout of art rather than the safer tone of craft, and it cost only $250. He could imagine it set over the fireplace at her house, or perhaps she'd want it just for herself and make a place for it on her dresser.

He took the red box from her and held it to his ear for the obligatory joke of listening for the time bomb, then he smelled it for the rotten cheese, then shook it with quizzical eyebrows up, because maybe it was that lump of coal his father had threatened him with every year. When he heard its particular thunk, and felt a familiar heft, his stomach lifted in question, and stayed that way until he ripped off the wrapper, and opened it.

"Good God." He lifted the sleek carving to his face and stared at it.

"What's wrong, dear? Is it ugly?"

He decided not to tell her. She could have her own surprise. He sat quietly shaking his head, and when she unwrapped his identical gift she made as if she might spit coffee, then laughed and laughed, almost meaning it. She fanned her face, trying to talk.

"Don't be sad, dear, really. It isn't easy finding something unique in this town."

It irked him that she'd think he might have reason to feel sad, not her.

"And," she said, "I do have to say it: great minds do think alike."

He held both balled men steady, side by side, staring at them, trying to find something different in their faces. One's nostrils looked possibly wider. The other's eyebrows maybe up.

"I really thought there would only be one of them. I thought it was art."

"Well, I think it's funny. And I must say I never thought we had the same taste."

He hated that the carving had become less interesting and cutting edge simply because his mother had chosen it too. He should feel a little ashamed of himself for this, but he didn't.

"Andrew — if you squint — it's your lump of coal!"

They survived the gifts, and Andy actually took some comfort in knowing they would be linked by these identical objects, twin gargoyles watching over them both from mantel or sill. He and his mother began the rest of their day, preparing Christmas dinner, calling friends, taking a walk together along the beach as far as they could go, to Cow Bay in one direction and the seaplane port in the other. At one point, walking past an immense clean ling cod skeleton, one of the few remaining vestiges of the fish kill, his mother surprised him by saying she was afraid those fish hadn't been fish at all, but canaries. Glancing over, he noted her steady but elderly gait, her frail curls light as ashes, troubled by the slightest breeze. He figured that if suburban old ladies with not much life left to lose now talked this way — that is, as advocates for Greenpeace — then the planet indeed must be in trouble. The weight of this notion grounded him for the rest of the walk. Apparently each breath you took, even up here, was minutely tainted. It was eerie and B-movie, but he didn't find it hard to see everything man-made — docks, a distant ship, the houses behind them — as somehow already vacant.

At home his mother got the turkey in the oven and the vegetables and potatoes chopped and ready, while his job, as always, was the gravy. She had set the ingredients out for him — flour milk salt pepper — and she may as well have added a sign: this is it, nothing else. Always, even when his father was alive, the gravy was his to do, and he had tried different recipes, none of which caught on. His father had been almost angry with him for the smoked oysters in it the one year, and the chestnuts another, and he never seemed to believe Andy that those recipes were standard fare, from *Joy of Cooking* in fact. He'd also tried dollops of wine and pinches of curry and squeezes of lime, and it became known as Andy's danger gravy, and Andy didn't mind the playful notoriety until his mother put a stop to it by saying that variety wasn't always the spice of life and demanding that he please just make the gravy they all liked.

As usual, he skipped lunch to stay hungry for this meal, which never deviated. Turkey, mashed potatoes, his gravy, frozen peas, canned cranberry sauce (not the jelly), and yams with maple syrup. Since the banning of his danger gravy, the only variations to the meal were the moistness of the turkey, and sometimes his mother made a mistake and bought sweet potatoes, causing her to remark during the meal how starchy the yams were.

When this year's meal was ready and on the table, Andy stood and carved, as always. The food laid out before him looked as it always did. Each item was in the same serving dish as last year. His mother had the serving spoons splayed in their pattern that radiated from the centre of the table. Though there were times he felt warmed by the yearly sameness, by precisely this homey continuity, tonight for some reason he felt foolish slicing through the brown crust of skin and into the breast of the bird. They'd been clinging to these small traditions ever since his father died, but now, standing here, carving, the ritual felt worse than tired; it felt empty, or childish. Or even, he didn't know why, *cowardly*. She should be carving the turkey. Or they should be having some kind of spectacular pizza. Turkey and cranberry pizza. They should be drinking mead, or something. Bourbon, with Guinness chasers. Drew should be here. Friends. May E should be here, as should Li, who never should have left. Glowering Natives, wanting our French bread but too proud to ask. Laura's mum should be here, even. Laura should be here. Strangers. Challenging strangers. And they should all be drunk, and honest with one another, and listening to some kind of chirpy folk music in another language, something none of them had heard before. They should put on a play. A dumb show. King Neptune's Revenge.

"You're still looking overtired, dear."

The more he thought about it, the more he saw that everyone he knew was either snarling or depressed or in some kind of emergency mode, the more this party of his was a necessary idea. The seas were rising and throwing dead fish on the beach, the Third World was kindling, everyone's weather was wrong. They needed a party, time to gather and toast each other with candlelight glinting in all eyes and off smiling teeth. Time was ripe for some — good cheer. It could be for Laura. A welcome. You often read that cancer recovery was a mood thing.

Time to call Leonard.

"The turkey's a good one," his mother said, not having tasted it yet. "I like the self-basters."

"It looks great." To the knife it felt tough and it looked dry. No sheen on the white meat. A half-hour from now his mother would be dividing it up, for him and her, to use all week for sandwiches.

"Did I hear you right that you have to work tonight, dear?"

"Graveyard."

"I just don't know how you stand it. And it's Christmas."

"Double time is how we stand it."

"They should make only the more desperate work. The younger ones paying down their cars and such."

Andy didn't tell her that he had signed up. He didn't mind working holidays. The supervisors were slack and friendly, being in the same boat. Magically appearing in the lunchroom were cakes and goodies and eggnog (the rum was hidden and unofficial). Nor did he mind graveyard. He never had. He read.

"How's Mrs. Schultz doing now?"

"She's fine, dear, thank you for asking." Perhaps hearing the inanity of her words, she added, "Fine in the sense that she doesn't remember what she did. She says she remembers but you can tell she doesn't. One blessing is that you can't hold on to the bad things either."

"Right."

"Though she does have a very painful bruise on her knee where she banged something."

"Ah."

They passed food. He shook salt with indiscriminate sweeps over his full plate, if anything exaggerating his shaker action, and his mother rolled her eyes. She'd given up her salt warnings to the heart-patient-to-be some years ago. Andy noticed her sweater.

Mauve, it looked cashmere, and had what seemed like a hundred buttons up its tight front. So many buttons, little pearl-like buttons, there was as much button as space between button. It must have taken her five minutes to do up. It seemed an archaic style, like something from a royal court, yet it reminded him of the boot buttons of a saloon hooker, a name like Diamond Lil.

"Your father would be eighty-four this Christmas." Her tone was cheery and instructive.

"Holy cow."

"Well, that's where I'll be in seven."

"You'll never be old, Mom."

"And he sure did enjoy the holidays."

Did he? Andy couldn't remember. He recalled his father's look of wry amusement as gifts were passed around, like he was humouring the situation. But he also remembered his father saying he loved it when they were snowed in and the roads were quiet, and everyone inside and warm. Christmas was maybe the only time Andy saw him drink a little too much, a beer at his side waiting for him to sip it, like he flicked his safety switch off for the day. He worked for the Port Authority, and Andy never knew exactly what that meant until after he'd died: it meant he kept tabs on all the boats, ships, vessels, and craft in Prince Rupert Harbour, making it his business to know what everyone was up to. His mother had taught grade school, stopping when Andy was born and never going back. He'd never asked her why not.

During dinner his mother's conversation kept to his father, and Christmas throughout the years. She didn't talk about Marie Schultz again, or her two other friends at the house. Andy for some reason wanted her to mention Laura, or more to be asked about Laura, a mother's question about her son's girl-friend. Eventually she did ask about Rachel Hedley, who was his last long relationship, and whose duplicate library card was still hot in his pocket.

"Rachel's okay. Teaching half-time. Alexis keeps her pretty busy."

"Alexis..."

"Her daughter? She adopted a daughter three years ago?"

"Oh goodness yes. Guatemala. And she chose Guatemala because...?"

"Guatemala is one place that lets single mothers, that thinks single mothers can —"

"Yes, yes. And Alexis is...?"

"Four."

"You two haven't gotten back together I take it."

"No, Mom." It'd been ten years now. They'd gone out barely a year. Then they'd stayed friends. They'd probably always been only friends.

He noticed his plate was empty. He remembered nothing. Maybe in the first few bites there'd been some awareness, something. He stabbed some more turkey and poured gravy on it. He deliberately tasted a bite. It was dry, yes. His gravy needed salt.

"And, are you all planning some kind of *do* for Laura when she gets here?"

The sonar of mothers. And it was funny how she said it, as if there was still an "all" to plan a do with.

"I'm sure we'll do something. No idea what." Though Andy did. It involved a party, and a rotten winter, and immense boredom, and scurvy, and festering pain of all kinds. Leonard, he should call Leonard. He'd be up north. His cell doesn't work there. Tomorrow.

"You know she'll be very busy, dear, with her mother. And she's been so sick herself. I'd be careful about bothering her. She might just want to keep to herself."

"No, I know that. She's coming up here for a bit of a rest." I promise not to *bother her*.

"Well, judging from five nights ago, a rest isn't what she'll be getting."

"No." Apparently at the house they were taking turns "guarding" Mrs. Schultz, not letting her take her solitary walks, and this usually led to an argument.

"And you're going to gather her at the airport?" She smiled but her smile was fixed and her tone transparent. Not just a disapproving mother but also the friend of Marie Schultz, sounding like some kind of clumsy spy.

"Yup." He did a brief drumroll on the table with two fingers.

"You know I worry about you, dear."

Of course she did. It was the biological imperative. He waited to hear one of the dreaded, "A mother's love never ages," or, one of his all-time favourites, "An ounce of mother is worth a pound of priest." But his mom just sat there spying silently.

Andy loved his mother heartily enough to be able to admit he didn't *like* her. If they weren't related, went his logic, would he want to befriend her? Hang out with her? No.

He knew this was because they'd never talked, not really. Maybe in her view they had, maybe to her they communicated up a storm. Maybe her generation just put less pressure on it, and thought small talk and proverbs were enough. He knew the child in him still believed their lack of communication to be her fault: since she was the adult she must know how to do it, how to speak deeply about real things, and for some reason she withheld this from him, she wasn't letting him in on her secrets, or all of her knowledge. He wasn't allowed to know her. It felt almost physical, like he could only partially *see* her. His actual and adult suspicion, of course, was that she had no secrets or knowledge to share and, even worse, that *she* didn't know herself either, not at all.

257 ❦

He knew that if he had kids maybe he wouldn't be so hard on her. That is, maybe he'd stop being a child himself. Drew had told him as much. Drew who, again, found Andy's mother funny. And Drew who, yesterday on the phone at work, had told him it was in some ways worse to have Chris home again because now he was "waiting for that call," or for "the next family shit storm," and Chris leaving again. In any case, having a kid you loved so much — and here Drew's voice actually broke and it was here Andy realized that this phone call was the only way his friend could have talked about this — was automatically heartbreaking. When your child was with you, you didn't say what you dearly wanted to, and when he wasn't home, you wished you had.

Andy had told Drew, lamely, that it was too bad he and Chris couldn't have a nice heart-to-heart talk about precisely *that* stuff. Drew's snort was answer enough.

Andy eyed his mother bringing turkey dipped in gravy and cranberry carefully to her mouth, then settling her fork, tines curled down, while she chewed. No doubt she had some proverb about the transparent wall that divided Drew and Chris.

When Andy couldn't fathom his mother he sometimes thought of the incident outside the movie theatre. He was ten or eleven and they waited in a small line for tickets. He was aware even then of his mother being somehow not made for a common lineup. It wasn't her clothes — as always, she was dressed smartly, but not ostentatiously. Things matched, and were of quality. Nor was it that she *thought* a lineup beneath her — she seemed quite happy to stand in one — but more that it actually *was* beneath her, like it would be beneath a cheerful queen. There was something in her manner of standing and waiting, apart from the others' small talk, but with a friendly smile for them. Her alert posture was part of it, and so was the way she gazed easily at things, giving off a sense that she knew why things were the way they were.

In any case, on the theatre's roof that day a raven hung its tail over the edge and shat on his mother's head. She let out an uncharacteristic whoop and her shoulders shot to her ears. She didn't look up, because she knew what had happened and there was no need. She also didn't move to get out of danger, because she knew it would happen only the once. What she did do was instantly recover. There were white, wet droppings on her head above her ear, and some on her cheek. Everyone had turned to her. Her tone of voice was pleasant and clear.

"Well, it's rather surprisingly *cold*," she said. "And I can smell that it's *fishy*."

In her answering everyone's unvoiced questions, Andy didn't think his mother was trying to be funny at all. Through a mix of laughter and condolences she made her way to the ticket gate to have herself let in to use the washroom. What struck Andy most, and strikes him still, was that she had used the moment to be instructive.

They were taking last bites of turkey, not saying much, and when she cleared her throat Andy realized he'd been ignoring her overlong, staring out the window into black nothing.

"Sorry," he said, and smiled limply.

"About what, dear?" she asked, though they both knew, just as they both knew she had been as insincere as he had.

Real things. Andy would love to have a proverb-making-up session with her, about real things. "Familiarity breeds claustrophobia." "Familiarity means you don't have to talk." "Love means never having to say anything at all any more." She might even enjoy such a thing. But there's no way it would ever happen between them. How could he start such a thing without insulting her in all sorts of ways?

"Are you all right, dear?"

"Sure. Yeah. Why?"

259 ❧

"Well, I guess we all have a lot on our minds."

He took some more food, a little of everything, for lack of something better to do. He forked mashed potato and dipped it on his peas, several of which embedded themselves. Overfull, he wished he had a Scotch or something to cut through it. A cognac. No — Calvados, that French brandy made of fallen apples. He yawned and predicted his mother would mention tryptophan again, she having forgotten that, two years ago, he'd told her that turkey actually had no more of it than any other meat. People were still discovering tryptophan and loved reporting it, and at work this week he'd had to hold his tongue twice.

His mother simply said, "Well," and smiled her satisfaction. Andy imagined a quick nap while she divvied the leftovers and cleaned up, which she always insisted on doing in payment "for letting me come here for dinner." He had five hours before his shift started. In a small inner spasm that made his chest contract, he remembered the one Christmas dinner when he'd been so bored that, right about now, he'd gone off and masturbated in the upstairs bathroom, just for the contrast, for the moral danger.

But now, finally, it arrived. It was such a caricature of herself, Andy could almost see how Drew found her funny. His mother sighed, elaborately and for show, fluttered her eyelids, placed her knife and fork diagonally on her clean plate, and announced, "Well. A good Yule makes a fat churchyard."

Andy hadn't heard this one. "As in, you eat too much, you die?"

"I suppose so. Yes."

He actually liked it, perversely, for the extreme puritanical clucking: beware enjoying yourself on Christmas.

And then, after all these years, he had to know. He didn't think, he just asked. "Mom. Did you know that saying or did you look it up? You know, for today? So you could say it?"

"I looked it up, dear." She appeared not in the least perturbed by his question. She added, "Don't you think they're fun?"

"Sure." No, he didn't think they were fun. He'd never thought they were fun. Maybe they were interesting. Maybe it was fun to hear how people once thought.

"But I really have eaten too much," she said. She arched back in her chair, took a big breath, and, while still carrying her head elegantly on her neck, cradled her small belly in her hands. "Because you really do make excellent gravy."

Andy didn't know if she was trying to be funny.

FINISHING GRAVEYARD shift the next morning, he saw no sense in going home to pretend he could sleep. The Tim Hortons was open and, even more amazingly, almost full. Over steaming coffee and muffins sat a crowd of people who looked mostly at a loss as to where else they might come to spend the day after Christmas. Standing in line, Andy had to smile at himself: here he was, doing the same but he was going to judge them anyway.

Laura flew in tomorrow.

He took coffee and muffin to the lone empty table, smack in the middle of things, surrounded by people he recognized but no one he was obliged to talk to. He would have preferred a window, though the rain and cement outside were only familiar. It was more the need of an opening through which to point the eyes. If you fell into a sleepless stare here in the middle you might unknowingly target someone's breast, or wife, or eyes.

He sipped milky coffee and noted the muffin only in that it tasted like fake cherries. Was it true, the rumour that they used MSG in their coffee, to trick and addict our tongues? He did like this coffee. He could see that, outside, the rain had eased, but the low pressing clouds were of the kind that absorbed light, and things were just too dark out there for a mid-morning. In the restaurant, most everyone looked fat because lots hadn't bothered to take off their ski jackets as they blew over their coffee. Shoulder to shoulder, one couple stared out the window not knowing they did, a steadiness that aped but lacked the energy of actual thought. Streams of gossip trickled everywhere. Andy heard that Canada had won a world junior hockey game. He heard, *Heard about Simm's dog?* Yes, the friend had, and now he heard it again. In the near corner sat another lone man, an old guy, maybe seventy, but he had stayed very handsome, with ice-blue eyes and stylish hair, a rarity with old people. Andy knew his name was Charles. An artist, a sculptor. Pots, odd sculpted pots. He came from Chicago in the '80s and lived in Dodge Cove. The man looked tired and, stealing a closer look, Andy could see sleep marks cut into a cheek, like he'd slept hard on a cushion's piping. Charles made Tim Hortons feel almost cosmopolitan, but you had to wonder what he was doing here today, alone. It was odd that he and Andy had never met.

After two coffees he found himself in the Tim Hortons bathroom checking his red eyes, and then his sideburns, in the mirror. Tilting his face, trying to find five-foot-four Laura's angle of sight, he had a startle: only now did he see what in his face had changed badly since she'd last seen it. Not his cheeks, exactly, but his jaw, or even his skull — in any case his face was way rounder than it used to be. Weren't those ears almost hidden by added face? He'd seen drinkers grow round faces. He hoped she wouldn't see two decades spent in the bar. He stepped back to eye himself again, trying to see a stranger. He wondered if it wasn't the sideburns making his face look rounder. Does a line on a blank slate draw attention to, or away from, the slate?

And then it was almost like he invited people to the party by accident.

Yesterday during a dutiful Christmas call to Rachel Hedley he'd got May E's phone number. Rachel had to hunt for it, and giving it to him she berated herself and Andy and Prince Rupert for letting May and Li languish unknown for weeks, apparently with no attempts on anyone's part to befriend them. In any case, on his way back to his table, at the pay phone between the Tim Hortons double glass doors, Andy called the number.

"Yes?" she answered, with so faint an accent that Andy wasn't sure.

"Is this May?"

"Yes?" She sounded more suspicious than excited.

"This is Andy. Andy Winslow? From that — that party?" He was thinking, The party where your friend was assaulted.

"Yes?"

He was stung that her greeting wasn't warm. He thought they'd made a decent connection. He asked if things were going well and if there was anything he could do for her.

"No, not really. Thank you."

"I mean, I heard your friend, Li, had some problems, and went home, to China. Isn't that what happened?"

"Yes."

"So I wanted to see if she was okay, and if you were okay, and if I could do anything."

"I am all right. Thank you. I don't know if Li is all right. I don't know exactly what happen. Happened. The police ask me questions already."

May's pronunciation of "police" reverted into a Li-like R sound. She sounded tired and disturbed in general.

"Is she coming back?"

"No."

"Are you all right by yourself? I mean, are your studies okay? I mean, can they continue? Were you a team?"

"I can continue. It will take longer now, I think."

"Well, good. Okay." May was treating his questions like police questions. She either didn't trust him, understandably perhaps, or maybe, like some people, a foreign speaker especially, she needed to read a face to conduct a conversation. Andy decided to take a little chance, and it was here he committed himself.

In a comic voice, making the irony as loud as possible, he said, "Well, I'm phoning to invite you to *another, really fun, party.*"

"Oh, great!" she said, and laughed.

He told her it was a New Year's Eve party. She said okay, and wrote down his address, and he thought a moment and told her it was a dinner party, starting early, six o'clock. And then he immediately called Drew, who put his hand over the receiver to ask Pauline if she wanted to go to Andy's for New Year's, and he said, "Yeah, we're there," as if they weren't splitting up at all. Pauline came on to ask, "What can we bring?" Andy sadly noting how comfortably she said "we." He told them they had to bring a weird appetizer. It had to be homemade, and they can't have made it or even eaten it before. And, he added, coming to decisions on the spot, all ingredients had to be local. Pauline said she loved theme parties, and asked, "Appetizers for how many people?" Andy told her twenty, then he told her it was a little something to celebrate Laura, and she sighed an "isn't that sweet" sigh.

He slapped his pockets for quarters and almost ran to the counter to stand in line, tap his foot, and finally ask the girl for some change for his five-dollar bill.

"We can't make change," the girl told him, already turning away. Andy stood a moment before understanding she meant "won't."

"It's for the pay phone," he said to her back. She was wide, but not tall, and something in her tucked chin suggested she used whatever power she could get.

"You have to buy something," she said, so Andy swung round to indicate his table laden with coffee cups and muffin waste, but of course it had been cleared and wiped. There were likely ten easy words to make his case with, but they wouldn't come.

"A small coffee, double milk." He waved his five at her, not rudely. Her name tag, reading *Jaynie*, was pinned on a bothersome angle. "And lots of quarters please."

Next he got on the phone to Leonard, hoping five days would be enough, and Leonard said he'd see what he could do. As with others, inviting them, he found himself blurting, "I think it's a good idea." And sometimes, "All this rain." He talked fast, he felt manic. "We all need it," he said. The Tim's coffee was smooth to drink but jangle-making, unlike the darker Starbucks, which tasted like burnt toast but that, like espresso, he'd recently read, wasn't as strong.

A big party. At least they'd be entertained. Especially if Leonard came through. Andy looked down into his palm and needed to study things before determining he had a single quarter left. He thought a moment, suffered a wave of what at first felt Gandhi-like in its noble expansion, then mostly naive and corny, but he went ahead and looked up red-haired Dan Boyd's phone number. He slid in his last quarter, punched the sourly musical buttons, got a message system, told Dan Boyd about his party, and said he could bring his kids.

He found himself standing beside his Tim Hortons table, blowing into his coffee, which he soon understood was lukewarm. He sat back down.

He'd been in Tim Hortons a long time: the ski jackets were the same but the faces were different. So he was committed to it, the party. The party was for Laura too. And for his Laura *problem*. Which was, the first time he asked her out, just the two of them, could he escape the perception that he had major presumptions? In a party he could retreat, he could re-emerge. Pay attention in artful amounts. It would be his house, and if she chose to see herself as the hostess, and see people off at the door, and linger after, and stay over, having wonderful presumptions of her own, well, that would be sort of perfect. He felt there was a chance of her doing that. But it was a real party, for New Year's. It might help make amends to May E. It might even be a gesture for Pauline and Drew. And not only them — it wasn't just Pauline and Drew separating, it was everyone, everywhere, for years sliding off into isolation.

The food alone was reason enough. The Order of Good Cheer. North America's first-ever club. Andy had liked reading that "cheer" referred to food and drink. Beautiful France, where overproof stuff made from backyard pears was seen as restorative, was *water of life*. Where they brushed off dirt and straw and nibbled some outrageous cheese from some cellar in the barn. In Champlain's day they gathered for some *cheer*.

It would be excellent to eat and drink something new with Laura. A kind of exploring. Sink your front teeth in, wait for the taste, pull from the bone, such a thing, a feral thrill. Cast eyes at each other. *So, what do you think?*

HE WASN'T TOO TROUBLED that his life had peaked at eighteen, that he'd already experienced the best he ever would. This was the conclusion he'd reached. The logic was easy: making love to Laura Schultz was the best thing in life. He could even remember the best of the best: a Friday night in June, around midnight, in the attic of his parents' place, on a nest of throw rugs and winter coats, a party going on below them, one of the rare times Andy made use of his parents' being away. They did it twice, with a leisurely half-hour in between. Because the music was loud they had to put their mouths to the other's ear, and Andy could still remember the brush of her lips and her warm breath in his ear and the shivers down his spine from it. One of the rugs was the old blue and gold one from the TV room, which he knew as intimately as childhood pyjamas, and it felt like he and Laura were wrapped up in an old friend, or toy. The half-hour between sex was almost the best part. Neither wanted to be anywhere else. What was most delicious about this night, and their soft talk, lips to each other's ear, was his dawning aware-ness that this achingly adorable creature was just as shy with him, just as stricken by what he might think of her! He felt so close to her, so eye to eye and soul to soul, that sex felt almost incestuous. In any case, he knew he was truly happy, for the first time, to be alive.

And she could surprise him, her spice could trip him, as when, at the end of the interlude, he got up to pee out the top window and, more lunatic, searching for somewhere to pee, Laura went up on an elbow and spied an immense doll, stored after the visit of a cousin. She pulled its head off and squatted and held the head under her, Laura's blank-faced stare full of mischief, and Andy could see the upside-down head and shiny blonde hair hanging down as Laura peed, filling the head com-pletely. She balanced the vessel in a bunched-up sweater so it wouldn't spill and took it downstairs later to clean, hiding it behind her back, whispering that she felt like Andy Warhol. He joked that he felt like Andy Winslow, but he felt included in her nasty art.

In any case, at thirty-nine he was fine with the knowledge that he would never again enjoy a body like hers unless it *was* hers. It seemed only reasonable to be addicted to her still, so much so that sex with someone else served mostly to jostle the addiction and make her body stand out more clearly. Her thighs, her bum, all her limbs met at the apex of strength and beauty, making strength and beauty the same thing. Whenever he thought of sex with her, he could feel her strength, and he could smell her with his heart.

It wasn't because she was his first. Both had had fumbly first times with others, he with tall Sally Bevan, Laura with Doug Young, and also a drunken mistake with a twenty-five-year-old petty crook named Lawrence, who everyone called The Law. So it wasn't that. Nor in the intervening years had he sat around doing without, dwelling on what they'd had. He and tall Sally Bevan had hooked up again and lasted six months. Simone, a hippyish tree planter from Quebec who had never, not even as a child, applied makeup (why were all Québécois who came here such obvious hippies?), liked him enough to make Prince Rupert her home for two off-seasons. Then there was Rachel Hedley, with whom he'd discussed endlessly the pros and cons of living together, until they realized that if they really wanted to they would have stopped talking and just gone and done it, like animals running off to a burrow.

Animal was really the only way to make sense of something like Andy and Laura. Animal was the best explanation available to him. Her scent traps had seen him coming; her pheromones had his name on them.

But, mercy. A pull that strong and beautiful and animal had the same gravity as a wolf ripping into a big-eyed rabbit.

Andy had thought it all out, probably too much. And no matter what happened tomorrow night at the airport, none of it would be anybody's fault. As Laura herself said in her latest letter:

One more adventure, and I've had some big adventures, will be seeing you again Andy. Neither of us has a clue what it will be like. I'm actually a little afraid and I don't get very afraid anymore, except about my daughter, but that's instinct I'm guessing.

The matter of you and me — that feels alive, doesn't it? Something alive in a cave with no face. But about to come out. I know you're excited too. And we know that excitement itself is iffy, we're both smart that way, we know expectations ruin almost everything. Expectations make it likely that we'll instantly disappoint each other. Maybe knowing that is the only antidote. Who knows? I don't. Do you? Do you think you do know how we'll be together? I bet your fantasies have gone everywhere and have already done everything! Maybe I'll ruin everything by coming at all!

I'm glad you'll be at the airport. And, do you remember, it's where we last saw each other. We'll look different for about 10 seconds, and then we'll look the same, because I think our brains revert. Lucky for us, eh? Though I don't believe you for a second when you say you're hugely fat, with a grey beard down to your chest.

HE CAME TO ON the padded chrome bench in the art gallery, which was empty. His hands had trouble keeping still. It was overly bright in here and he felt too outside himself. His body felt impossible, like a cruise ship suspended by a thread.

He had to kill the afternoon, just one more. He didn't want to think of art this way but it was either here or home lying in bed. He was still in his work clothes. He could smell himself. He had invited everyone to a party.

He would bring her here too, of course. It was his other place, this new gallery hanging off the Museum of the North. This bench was where he could sit and, similar to his window on the water, do nothing. Here too he was charged with the energy of other, in this case not moving water but fixed art, a stillness that lived. Surrounded by paintings, by such concentrated vitality that could cast itself from itself, he could feel buoyed. By dropping any effort, by simply giving in to the agonizing yellow there in *Sunscape*, 1958, he could feel brilliant. The more he let go, the more brilliant he could feel.

He could relax socially too. No one from work was going to stomp through the art gallery. But no matter who came in, by definition they were now as uncool as he was. So it was a place he fitted, he could sit and say nothing, he could be himself, the blandest of the bland. His blandness was known. That tall Andy Winslow sure doesn't say much. Fine. Ever since his twenties, even since Laura left, in fact, when he stopped wrestling what adolescence shoved in his face with its mirror, he'd been relaxing into his blandness. In fact, in public he was not even shy any more. Laura, the blandness has gained confidence. In fact, he was probably now *eccentrically* bland. Which was a fine thing, that blandness could go full circle, and oxymoronic. Maybe, just in time for her, he'd be *charismatically* bland.

He was alone but smiling. Before chez Winslow and another try at sleep, he stood to scan the fifteen paintings more closely. As usual, even when other people were there, he deliberately moved counter-clockwise, against the flow, *widdershins*, the direction witches walk while casting spells. (Maybe he'd get *magically* bland.)

He was killing an afternoon. How else do you kill one?

He loved this: *A Storm*, 1971. Wildest, darkest wind and water blasted but couldn't defeat something like rock, but softer, its pinks and yellows suggesting something humbly alive. The impression Andy got was chaos threatening a human heart. Or a person's sanity. He always thought of a crucible, of the transforming fires of alchemy. He'd read that alchemy's changing lead into gold had been a secret society's metaphor — the kabbalists? the Gnostics? — for changing the self. For building a soul. Something like that. Inner change. This painting was alchemical. The small burst of excitement, before words come, surely it was minutely transforming. *All* these paintings. That woman's eyes there, *Her Birthday*, 1989, were better than eyes really were.

He stopped at the last painting by the door, *Field*, S. R. Lewis, 1953. That's all it was, a field, but a purple one, its brush strokes suggesting endless grass diminishing in the distance. It was simple, it was *bland*, and only bland, and Andy could feel nothing dangerous or challenging or alchemical about it. He probably lacked the eyes.

Laura. Tomorrow. There was alchemy in this, wasn't there? There was the churning *impatience*, but let's call it alchemy, in any love that hadn't come to a natural end.

LAURA. TODAY.

Coming off graveyard, driving home, he went into a skid on the curve near Stutz Rapids and barely held it. He slowed down, shook his head. His Mustang had never scared him before.

He wasn't hungry but decided he would make a huge breakfast — pancakes, ham, maybe a cheese omelette too — because if he ate too much he might fall asleep from it. Laura flew in at seven tonight and he was a jangly mess.

When he parked and opened his car door he heard the kitchen phone stop ringing. He knew it would be bad, not just because someone was calling before eight in the morning but because it began to ring again when he was in the hall tugging off his boots—someone was calling and calling. His stomach flipped when he realized Drew was getting home around now too, and that the phone call might be about Chris.

He was right that it was bad, but it wasn't about Chris.

The hospital was frightening, even if he wasn't there about a loved one. After graveyard, fluorescent lights were always too bright, containing tiny but extra colours, like bad spells being cast, and he felt them harsh over his head as he tried to get directions from the nurse behind her desk. Andy didn't know her, and her glasses were overtly fashionable, the arms weirdly bent, dipping down then back up, suggesting leverage, but it was all a ruse, simple arms were all that was needed, and Andy thought they looked ridiculous. She told him the east wing, fourth floor, pointing to the elevators that he could see.

"Are you related?" the nurse remembered to ask.

"Yes," said Andy, feeling the thrill of this, because it wasn't quite a lie.

"I'm not sure, but I think you should go *right* up," the nurse said, meeting his eye significantly, and what worse words could there be?

If he really had been related to Marie Schultz, he should have been able to fly to her. It surprised him that the elevator still stopped at each floor to let people on and off, the doors opening and closing with no attitude of hurry. Above, through concrete, something unknowable and life-changing was taking place, and here people chuckled, debating snow. Andy replayed his mother's words from the phone call, and how the thing she'd said first was, "I didn't want to disturb you right after work," her tone almost cheerful, her good friend dying or dead yet her worry was that Andy's routine might be disturbed. Her news came more quickly then—"We don't know if she's actually passed" and the words *massive stroke* — and hearing this Andy had found himself wondering why *massive* was the adjective they always used. Did it have to do with the physical mass of the heart, or the brain, or did it just mean big?

Here was Rita, almost blocking the entrance to the room. Rita loomed large and red-faced, her shoulders up, and she didn't appear to be breathing. Beside her hovered Doris, blinking and birdlike, unable to stop moving her hands. Beside her, his mother stood with hands folded at her solar plexus like a singer in a choir. The look on her face was placid, even pleased. Not even this had ruffled his mother's poise. It looked for all the world like she was giving her friends — Mrs. Schultz on the bed in particular — a lesson in how to be dying correctly.

Laura's mother lay dressed not in hospital garb but her pale rose nightgown. The covers were up to her armpits and her hands folded on her stomach. Morning light streamed in, its intensity and mood for some reason reminding Andy of Easter Sunday. The room was marked by its absence of emergency: no machines were blinking, no tubes ran from Mrs. Schultz, no doctors or nurses worked. The room smelled faintly of women's florid toiletries, and an earthier sour of something else. Mostly, the dominant sense in the room, and one reflected by the posture of everyone standing within it, was that there was suddenly no longer any hurry. It wasn't the lack of medical machinery but rather a palpable feeling, that time itself had been shocked and now moved in an immense new way, that told him this person was dead.

Andy went to Mrs. Schultz. He touched her bare forearm with his fingertips but quickly withdrew them because her arm was sinewy and discoloured and somehow private for that.

He thought of hugging his mother then, but didn't know if he should, or if she would not like the look of it. He was aware

273 ❄

of how stiff he felt, and how *angry*, but in confused directions. He hated this woman, but that body on the bed was this woman no longer. But he was angry at her still, and for new reasons, one of them going something like, Now you've messed up Laura's plans. And another, for making him recall when he was in a room like this, death's white noise in the air, and how he had fallen beside his father and felt the clumsy bones of his own arms hugging that body through the blankets, and his fourteen-year-old voice breaking in his ears as he moaned, *Aw? Aw?*

Andy stared at Mrs. Schultz's face. Someone had tastefully removed her pink eye patch and it lay beside her pillow, within reach should she need it. She still looked stern. A hard woman, fortified against any threat. They shouldn't use fluorescent lights in hospital rooms, it made human skin a horror. He wondered, as one must, about the span of a human life, and what it meant, if anything. And then in the midst of this ripe room, and out of his own chaos of voices, one of his mother's sayings came to him, intoning Disney-like and corny in the air. He heard, "When you judge someone, you have no time to love them." If you're doing one thing you can't do the other. And though it was Mrs. Schultz he stood beside, he hoped that, from now on when he visited his mother, who was posed helplessly in choir position behind him, he'd remember the saying and understand it.

A SMALL CAR FERRY ran from downtown Prince Rupert across the harbour to Digby Island, or "the airport island" as it was called. Scheduled for every flight, two buses crossed to pick up passengers and bring them back as part of their airline ticket. With buses on board there was deck room for only four or five cars, and this evening there was no room for a black Mustang.

A smaller car could've fit. The loading guy joked that "a Smart car would've been smart."

Nearly missing the ferry to greet Laura — which would have been absurd — Andy parked and ran back to walk on and board one of the near-empty buses, joining the scatter of other greeters. He closed his eyes. He tried a deep, calming breath and was instantly dizzy. But he thought that maybe he could finally sleep, here of all places, sitting up in a bus seat, on board a boat, going to meet a plane.

This afternoon he'd slept maybe a little in the bathtub, maybe twenty minutes if at all, because he was suddenly aware of lying in cool water. If it was sleep he'd been enjoying it was assaulted by the sudden dead face of Marie Schultz. He recalled how his father's dead face had also haunted him, for weeks and weeks, snapping him out of a doze or, if he was awake, shocking him more awake than ever, the extra clarity a kind of hell. His dad's face was yellow, almost canary yellow along the jawline, and charcoal blue around the sunken eyes, one of which stayed open just enough to give young Andy the steady glint of an eye, Dad's dead eye, a silver crescent that shone crazily while telling him nothing. For months this face with its eye would ambush and impale him, until gradually the image softened and then faded so much that he couldn't get a clear picture of it even if he tried. Though horrified to see it, he was sad when he no longer could, a link with his father gone.

This morning, Mrs. Schultz had her eyes well closed, but through a parted frown you could see a bit of yellow enamel.

Andy lurched from his seat and stepped into the aisle. The driver saw him coming in the rearview and hissed open the door and Andy stepped down into the rain to stand on deck. It was cold and the ferry's speed made it colder. His clothes would be wet and look pathetic for it, but Laura wouldn't mind because she wouldn't notice, just like she wouldn't notice his lack of a Mustang, or his decent waistline or expensive cable-knit sweater or anything else in the greet-Laura outfit — because her mother was dead. Standing with his face in the rain, Andy felt appropriately lousy for thinking, on this the day of her death, that Mrs. Schultz was doing it still, standing between them, that show of yellow tooth the hint of a fresh sneer.

Andy hunched in the gusts and moved over to the two-storey pilothouse to see if the coin was still there. It was, an old American silver dollar Krazy-Glued to the deck years ago, the source of much merriment to the skipper and deckhand up behind that window. Andy hated it and what it said about Prince Rupert, and how some people will find any cheap route to feeling superior, even if for ten seconds. Andy had been on deck once to see it for himself: a tourist, enjoying the view of the approaching port city, spots the silver dollar, sidles over, and stoops to pinch it up only to find it glued down, then hears the hoots from the wheelhouse, good old boys having themselves a time behind the smoked glass. Welcome to PR.

Andy nudged the coin with one of his new mahogany-brown casuals, which he was starting to like. The coin stayed part of the deck. He heard no hoots from behind the glass.

HE WAITED IN A building of mostly unadorned cinder block painted in pale government greens. He heard the twin-prop plane land, then taxi up. At this noise, the first real proof of their reunion, Andy realized he had no idea where she was staying tonight, or if she'd arranged something, or assumed something — though there was small chance of that. It might be difficult to broach. He would wait until they were back across the harbour, off the ferry, off the bus and in his car before a *Where to?* Now the aircraft's wing lights shone through the bank of plate glass. The engine roar ceased and he waited some more.

And here she came. It wasn't Laura, it was a woman. She had both breasts. She was dressed in a long black coat, old-fashioned looking to Andy but maybe stylish in Toronto. She was erect and buoyant in her posture, a dancer, and her walk was still Laura's, if anything more graceful, no longer in a hurry to be somewhere else. Her dirty-blonde hair was cut short, as per women of her age. She approached Andy smiling sadly, her face rich with her mother's death. But the smile was also full of greeting, and of the irony — why was it ironic? but it was — of seeing Andy Winslow again. She had room for that, she had humour for that.

They hugged. His cheek and jaw pressed her hair, and he could smell it, and her scalp, and it was Laura's smell, which was cruel. It wasn't nearly the hug he'd wanted it to be. How could it have been? He felt stunned from all directions, and he could feel her confusion too, could feel in the brief squeeze her tentative relationship to everything now. He could easily imagine her worried he was here, embarrassed for him, knowing she would soon have to turn him down — but maybe it's only sad to have a mind that imagines so well.

Andy heard himself say, "Sorry about your mom." He was determined not to say, How was your flight? He would not say that, not in a million silences.

"You know, it feels like she's given me a gift," Laura said softly, after a pause, and it sounded a bit rehearsed.

She looked at him quickly and smiled. Other travellers milled about them in the sterile room, waiting for luggage to come down the chute. Laura appeared nervous in a wary rather than vulnerable way, the way he'd hoped for. Her nervousness spoke of, What is Andy Winslow going to ask? What is he going to ask, and when's he going to ask it?

"So," said Laura Schultz, "it's good to see you."

"We both look *great*," Andy said back.

Her glance up held his eye and joined him in his humour a little, but the Laura he knew hadn't arrived, and he was still waiting for her.

The Order of Good Cheer

30 *décembre* 1606

TONIGHT, ALL IS A frightened boat, drifting backwards.

Samuel senses he is not alone in this unwanted clarity of mind. Even now, as his feet break virgin snow outside the walls, the sky so close with cloud and starless and black that he needs must keep one hand on the rough logs to guide his way, even in this quiet can he sense the minds and the open eyes of other sleepless men still in their beds yet as awake as he. This night-mind seems a mind more awake than that of day. Yet these other wakeful men — like his, their thoughts entangled willy-nilly yet cutting as razors — are more in need of sleep in this time than ever, what with the plague lurking at their innermost defences. They have six gravely ill for certain. Several more, their state still in question, share the same furtive eyes: either they are sick and not admitting it, or not sick but convinced they are. It is exceeding strange how many will search deeply in themselves for sign of sickness, and therefore find it, but not fall as truly ill.

Why then is he walking tonight? One thing Samuel has learned is that the weak and the worn do invite the scurve more eagerly than the healthy. And what one could use most, in such a winter as this, is the healthful long sleep of the bear. So why then is he, why are any of them, so wakeful? What robs their sleep? Perhaps the Night Daemon walks hand in hand with this plague, helping its arrival. Or perhaps it is one of his conniving brothers, the Lunatic. It is not encouraging to envision the Beast with a family.

He knows he should not have favourites amongst the stricken common men, but of course he worries most for Lucien. And, he won't deny it, with some guilt. Indeed, guilt that owns both the heft and the colour of gunmetal.

Clouds part and the half-moon appears, more than sufficient to light the snow and his way. Snow is silver-blue. Stumps are black. A simple landscape. In no more than fifty paces Samuel stops at the forest edge. The moonlight does not penetrate in there. He could go in, or walk the perimeter of their cleared land. He knows not what he'll do. It takes all his courage just to succumb to this wakefulness, rise from a warm bed and go walking alone in the dark. He, a man who sleeps soundly through a tempestuous sea, who admires the shrillest tunes of wind in rigging and smiles at the shocked creaking of oak, who navigates the rocks, river mouths, and tidal chaos known only to local savages. What are the dangers of a small walk on New French land? The bears run at the merest breath of a man, and in any case they sleep. Wolves, which have been heard piping from their lofty slope, engorge come winter on the snowbound moose and deer. Lions may exist, but so far they remain a rumour. In other words, Nature offers no impediment to a midnight walk. A wayward savage, starving or enraptured with hate, might offer some cause for staying within walls, but there must be few of these kind around, thanks be to those same weakened moose and to the steady guidance of Membertou.

He can admit it only to himself, but his fear caused him to place around his bare neck, right upon the skin so he can feel it sharply, the necklace of black bird bills he fashioned over the course of several months and many bad suppers. Truly, as he has overheard, in their curvature they do resemble a poor man's idea of eagle talons; and the design does travel any way it wishes; still, he grew fond of it in the making. And it seems that, lacking any particular female friend back in France, or indeed even here, to whom he might give it — it seems he has given it to himself. He has worn it more than once now, and though it feels like comedy, it does give him courage. The fearlessness of a fool! All savages make their own talismans, or are given them, and could it be that they all feel strength in them?

He skirts the edge of trees, sometimes lightly touching these trunks that are the forest's fence. If he can stay his thoughts — here, outside, tonight, is beautiful. The windless silence is purer than the crystal southern sea. He hears his breathing, and his small steps. His mind widens irresistibly beyond the confines of his skull. It feels like health itself to gain some distance from men's walls, which hold within their ragged snores, smells, and idiots' carnival of dreams. Last winter it was even worse in this regard — all too clearly can he hear the ghastly moaners. Most of those stricken, and no man knows why, chose the night to become vocal. Save for voluptuous breathing, they would lie silent through all the daylight hours and then come darkness their moans began, and gathered until the sickroom was so deep with moans that two healthy men trying to communicate between themselves would need raise their voices to be heard. Samuel doesn't think he is exaggerating this memory. Why would he? But the thunder of moaning each night caused the other men some distress, rupturing as it did their healthy sleep, and threatening weakness upon them too and then perhaps, indeed, the scurve itself. Were it not for the chance that some stricken do find their way back to health, Samuel doesn't doubt that the moaners would have been popularly dispatched with a midnight club. And he has even less doubt that, of anyone, it's the moaners themselves who most want the silence that comes with death — which, to the dying, must beckon like the longest, blackest, and purest of nights.

Samuel pauses and asks forgiveness of God for not instantly assuming Heaven for his men. It seems that these late hours fixed him with the bugging eyes that see only bleakly, and only inward.

He has reached the slight promontory on the north slope of their cleared land, and the rise is enough to show him their inner courtyard from above. He fancies he can hear snoring, but this is impossible. The courtyard is a square of bright white, scored with darker pathways indicating their daily industry. Indeed it is strange to see the compound so: a square of walls enclosing all the labours, dreams, and delusions of near fifty men, and making all of it look easily held, and small.

Though impossible because of the distance, what tries to catch his eye is the silver sovereign their Sieur had his boy attach to the post by pounding it through with a square nail, piercing it just above King Henri's hairpiece. Poutrincourt, who'd had more wine that night than was his habit, mounted the coin there after the ceremonies of savage baptismal, and his logic escaped Samuel then as it continues to escape him now. For he'd proudly announced, speaking to the French and not the savages, and jabbing at the coin, "And now in this they can see the visage of their King!" Except that the savages of New France had already been made subjects of the King, whether knowing it or not, and becoming Christians had changed their state in this regard not at all. No, if they had a new status, and a new ruler to be reminded of, it would have made some more sense to install on the post the face of Jesus! But the coin remains glinting there still, and Samuel doesn't know but that it isn't a cruel temptation to the Mi'qmah themselves, for they know well what a silver coin means, and it would take little more than a good metal blade and ten heartbeats of privacy to pry it from the post. Still, what would they do, here, with a silver coin? They could not trade it back! Even if they took it by canoe to be traded many leagues from here, word would follow that it was Poutrincourt's coin, and its ownership temporary, and injurious in the end.

Samuel wonders if maybe Poutrincourt's logic was to instill a reminder and a fear of the King in *all* of them. For the common spirit has slumped, and this in itself is, according to the letter of the law, a form of rebellion. So does King Henri's profile inspire?

No. Indeed it is not difficult for Samuel to envision one of their own men coming out in a night like this one and taking the coin for himself, even prying it with his teeth if needs be, and securing it in some nether place until he is safely home in St-Malo. Should that day ever come.

But again taking advantage of the moon to gaze into what distance makes itself available — the two mountains, the gut of sea between them, the span of west beyond — Samuel has the notion that they will never live here. It is a notion he has had before, and it is daunting in its clarity. Sometimes he has it at sea, approaching a landform, scanning it for habitability. From such a vantage, nine times out of ten there arises the certain sense that no French will occupy the shore he now holds in his eyeglass. No French grandchildren will play amongst those rocks, that slope of pine. Tonight, similarly, the sweep of moonlight lets his eyes gaze west and he has the feeling again that, though they might occupy these lands, they will never truly live here, however far west they may go. They — French or English — would never rest, at home on these slopes or plains. He sees that they will explore farther and farther inland, denuding the place of fur, and somewhat of forest, as they go, but that, gaining as much western land as is possible, all the way to the next sea, they will look about them in anxiety, and always wonder about home. Some say that France was once all under forest. That is to say, it looked just like these dark, treed lands they gaze fearfully into here. One wonders if, when similarly surrounded by forest, their forebears also could not sleep.

LUCIEN HAS LITTLE to do but stare at the lantern's flame, just out of arm's reach. They have trimmed the wick to almost nothing, so the flame is as weak as he is himself, and urine-coloured. He feels a kinship with the dirty little light.

He has heard he is the seventh. The first, Gascon, died, as has the second, Vermoulu the priest. A single cannon shot marked both funerals. Though the earth is too hard for burial. Lucien has heard that Poutrincourt's boy will be next. He has heard nothing about any one of them growing better.

He knows only that he is the seventh. Men come and stand over him as if he cannot hear and they say, "There, the seventh of us." In their voices he hears less of pity for him than fear for themselves.

Lucien was astonished that the scurve took hold of him so quickly. However, even his astonishment then became sluggish, for that is the nature of the disease. Lucien has hardly the vigour to be properly appalled at what, it seems, his body has chosen for itself.

He does think it began by entering his spirit on the long night of the natives' conversion. Following that affair there was the long walk in the snow with Ndene, and their making love, and Lucien walking back alone, tired and, for some reason, in low humour. Then arriving at the open gate, to be confronted by Samuel Champlain, no longer his democratic friend and ally, but a monster.

Champlain's face had spoken of surprise; that is, he was not lying in wait but merely passing near. It was as if, having been surprised by Lucien, he now had to respond, and he responded with an anger that Lucien could not help but make his own and carry during his entire walk. The words would not leave his ears: "Go back out and walk off your bestial heat for one hour more. *Two* hours more."

Lucien had thought the mapmaker a reasonable man, and also a friend. He does not know which of the two betrayals gives him more pain.

But so he had gone out, and walked two hours more. He walked to Ndene's encampment, saw their fire-smoke rising hardly at all, mere wisps as they weakened, untended. He had the queer suspicion she knew he was without, but because he knew this might just be his hope, and conceit, he did not wake her. And then he walked back. He felt foul, cold and ghostlike. He had no heat, none whatsoever, bestial or otherwise, to walk off. He was cold to the bone the entire time, and of spirit colder still, for Ndene was not happy he had left her, and neither Champlain, Poutrincourt, the King of France, nor God was happy he had gone to her at all. He was angered by a question that would not leave him: why weren't all the men doing as he was, that is, loving, if love presented itself? Was love not the most natural course a man could take? Didn't God grace a man with the heartiest urge to know a woman and explore her, and in the end plant his seed? Any men who would deny this are angry at themselves, and over-married to philosophy. Lucien hoped it wasn't pride telling him that, of all the men, he alone was respecting his time here.

Unfortunately, the scowling thoughts that grew in him while walking were not themselves a source of heat either. They were only right and logical and all told, they amounted less to anger than a frowning wonder at the opacity of his brothers. Perhaps he could ask Monsieur Champlain his thoughts on this night. The mapmaker had till then seemed reasonable, had seemed less bound by... certain maps. And, saddest, he had had in his eye the welcoming light of friendship, not too tainted by his rank.

No. How would such a topic be broached? This thing would never be spoken of.

Finally, l'Habitation came to view. Lucien leaned upon and spoke lightly to the gate, a growling dog and sleepy sentry let him in, he strode cold and empty through the quiet compound and fell into a cold bed that seemed to stay cold. And then he was astonished — though somehow not surprised — to wake in the morning with an ache to his legs that felt like the Devil himself had made his new home there. By evening, confirming his ailment, here was this loose flesh in his mouth and some blood in his spit.

Since that time, no one has smiled at him. Nor has he smiled himself. He knows he is likely to die.

At night, he can hear incessant moans coming from the death-boxes, as he thinks of them. They loom as large shadows at either ends of the room, impinging on the space, for they are small rooms in themselves, chambers that hold three beds apiece, built around the chimney stones in order to catch their scant warmth. It is surely God's jest that he fell sick not two days after completing their construction. It is a further jest, though not God's, that since becoming barely able to walk he has been "confined to quarters" by the Sieur Poutrincourt, for "conjugal visits with a savage." Though it has also been called other things.

So far, he has asked for and been given extra blankets. He has refused to enter either of the chimney boxes, though he knows they are warmer. Simply, no one has come out of them, save the luckless boy who bears out the chamber pots and takes the sick their scorned food, the same beef and biscuit that has been smashed fine by Bonneville's cleaver so they can mouthe and tongue it, like babies just off the breast.

He has not even the strength to read. He can perform the motions of working a book, yes, but there is no strength of interest. There is no pleasure in taking the words from off the page and making them his own.

14 janvier 1607

SAMUEL WATCHES THE painful march of the lame as they emerge
down their staircase.

Neither apothecary nor surgeon enjoys even a dream of how
to ease the sufferings of the stricken, and so in the belief that
exercise is what they need, and at Lescarbot's supercilious urging,
Poutrincourt ushers the sick men, those of them who can walk,
out of their foul beds and close dwellings to take the air and
engage in — a snowball-throwing fight! Neither good Poutrincourt nor Lescarbot has seen the scurve before now, and while
Poutrincourt looks appalled and turns greyer of face, Lescarbot
keeps up a light sporting banter, hiding his own horror.

Perhaps the news of their enforced play gives them some
hope, or confuses them, or they are simply too tired to groan as
they slowly cloak and muffle themselves, then lurch and limp
out of doors, through the courtyard, and now out from the gate
and into the abundant plains of snow. Samuel follows. There is
Lucien the carpenter, and Goddard, and Ricolet, and others.
Samuel had hoped to see Poutrincourt's boy, but apparently he
no longer can walk. As Lescarbot dances nimbly around and
cajoles and pretends fun, and now dips to prepare snow for
hurling, the sick dutifully bend to find snow as well. Samuel can
tell they do not like the touch of it, and he can also see that their

legs hurt all the more from having to step high. A few begin to toss their missiles. There are no smiles. No one responds when Lescarbot suggests they choose up sides.

One man, poor thin Boyer — having only just ventured out from the gate and pausing to squint up into what for him is a blinding light — takes a solid ball on the mouth. As snow chunks drop away, bloodied, from his face, he moves nothing of his body, not even to bring his hands to his face, and his expression changes not at all. He gathers with his tongue some dark and bad flesh that has become dislodged within his cheeks and he coughs it onto the ground, and Samuel thinks he sees some yellow teeth in his mess. He cannot look away fast enough — it is man's nature not to look closely upon sickness.

As if his duty to play is now done, and risking insubordination, poor Boyer turns tiredly away and tries to find a path back to his bed, stepping carefully in the reverse of his own two deep footprints, but then bumping the gate's post with his thin shoulder so that he almost falls and must stop and hold on to keep his feet and gain his bearings. Samuel can see that Boyer will be another to die.

When God is at His fatal work, it is not wise to find favourites, but Samuel is especially saddened to see Lucien fading so quickly. Poutrincourt has declared that wantonness has proved his undoing, for upon discovery, when he was confined to quarters, he immediately fell ill. But Samuel thinks that for the carpenter the scurve seems almost an afterthought, a kind of ornament to his captivity, which has insulted him greatly. It appears that the Sieur may wish to exercise the King's will in this case and that does not bode well for Lucien. Three winters ago, in Hochelaga, when Samuel was there, they had to hang a man (a foulest man, but a man) for forcing relations on a girl and, with a stealth known only to the most wicked, killing the brother who had not yet tried to avenge her. The hanging was necessary to keep the peace — indeed, it may have saved all of their lives, for the savage encampment that surrounded them, waiting for favours or barter, had grown into the several hundreds.

Samuel's fear is that Poutrincourt might see a similar example here, and he may well be searching for a way to free his own pent-up humours; just as, desperately tired of the wrong wind, the sea captain will slap his cabin boy or, failing that, kick the freeboard of his own good ship. It is how men manage. Though Samuel will try to speak wisely to him.

But, from the weak look of Lucien's face, freedom may not matter.

So far Samuel's own body is strong, and he gives thanks to God. Yet he grows sicker of heart at the state of l'Habitation and now must act. He is glad to have secured promises from Membertou — he will not call him Henri! — and his sons that a grand sturgeon-fish has been successfully roped ashore and well butchered and that they will have its salted eggs, and its freshly smoked flesh, as well as the head, from which the good Bonneville can extract its essence for a good Midi fisherman's stew. They have nuggets of beaver tail, which some of the men savour and others abhor, but that in itself will give rise to eating contests and perhaps a song. In the morning Samuel himself will supervise the prune and marzipan tart — beside his work desk, the prunes have bathed in Armagnac two full days.

Yes, he will harden his countenance and simply tell Sieur Poutrincourt, and Lescarbot, and whoever else has an ear, that their humour is bad and their world too dark and close, and that he fears the many corpses of St-Croix will reproduce themselves here in this spot, unless measures are taken. Namely, they will form a society of stewards, and will each take their turn provisioning a feast and providing entertainment. They must celebrate New France, and celebrate their lives here, not just on holidays but on every day. For there is the greatest need to come to see as especial, and precious, the very day they live in, now, while they still live.

Because he has whimpered certain thoughts to them at other times to no avail, he will not add that the food and drink itself might be the right tonic, for he has no science, and little proof. So he will entice them by appealing to the Sieur's vanity as a musician, and to the lawyer's as a poet.

THE NEXT DAY, he begins.

While Samuel doesn't argue with the necessity of having a man guard the wine, he does not appreciate the man's—isn't this fellow's name André? André deTou?—gaze of suspicious wonderment as Samuel secures the several gallons he needs. It is not even the good, let alone the best, vintage, and it is not Poutrincourt's own, which stands behind its own keyed gate. But the man's royal glare makes Samuel want to break Poutrincourt's lock and tilt his barrel into his mouth—just to see what this man would do.

Instead he asks, "Have you ever had hypocras, man?" He positions his first pail and then pulls the bung from the cask above.

André—tall, but with some stomach, and a poor beard— looks within, then sideways and up, and finally shrugs.

"It is wine"—Samuel gestures down to this pail that, *slosh, slosh*, fills up—"and it needn't be good wine. For into the wine, that is, into this vessel alone, I will put twenty-four dried cloves. And in this wine they will sit, reluctant. And then sometime in the dark of the night they will swell up, and gently be coaxed out, and release themselves into it." He gestures with his hand as a flower opens.

The guard looks fixedly at Champlain's hand, unsure as to how to respond.

"And I will also put in ten black peppercorns, enough to bring some water to your eyes and sweat to your nose. And I will put in enough ginger powder to cover a large sardine. And then also a full stick of cinnamon, but if the apothecary lets me, two. And then I will dump in enough sugar to make you laugh like a five-year-old. And there you have it — the recipe."

At this the guard André tosses his head a little back and snorts. But keeps his smile.

"I have not had hypocas, sir. Though maybe one Christmas at home."

"Hypo*cras*. You will taste it tomorrow night and it will make you glad. And then if you are as lucky as I am you will have bright blue and yellow dreams."

André laughs some more. Samuel hasn't recently felt so cheered and poetic. He groans happily to lift the two full pails. It's as if he's under their influence already — the twined spirits of vine and spices.

IN THE AFTERNOON, while in his rooms the wine sits gently coaxing the spice, Samuel ventures out for pine needles to dry. It is a way of cooking mussels that he saw amongst the Penobscots to the south, and so in this way he will surprise Membertou as well. In truth he enjoys the prospect of surprising not only the sagamore but also his people, whom he intends to invite. These will be men who would by nature tear into a creature uncooked, or even alive, if their fire was too far off and their hunger too great.

But as Samuel leaves the gate and turns the southeast corner of their outer wall, as if to supply more proof that some fine thing needs must be done, and soon, he encounters a clutch of men locked in violence. He approaches and sees a ring of them, six or seven keeping the two combatants within and fighting. And fighting they are: it seems the rules of sport are ignored or forgotten, for one man has the other from behind and while one arm girdles his neck the other fist pounds with near impunity on the other's face. It is hard to know whose blood is whose. They are both tired and breathing like beasts, steam and breath rising in the falling light. The various men shout encouragement, and from the supporters' eager postures Samuel can almost see the size of wager about to be won or lost. So it is sport after all. But Satan's own. When it looks like they are going to topple, the clutched fighters are given a communal shove to help them right themselves.

Samuel stops unseen and wonders what action to take. It is within his power not only to have them halt but also to see the two worst of these men in chains. The man who has the other, weaker man locked, and appears about to win, growls deeply. Two or three of his betting friends growl with him in excited unison, not even knowing that they do, or that they sound like the most automatic of beasts.

An even sadder sight presents itself over at the edge of forest. There stands the large Dédé, alone, leaning forward and gazing back upon the group with the oddest face. Samuel has heard, by turns, how the rest of the men did finally gather together in fear and disgust to shun the man or, contrarily, how Dédé has done this to himself by his own choice. But whatever the case, it seems that the brute has spoken to no one, not for some weeks, finishing his labours and then keeping his own company. And there he stands now, leaning forward, the look on his face not unlike an open-mouthed baby's, and there is clearly envy and bloodlust in it too.

Samuel backtracks softly and retakes the corner of their compound. He knows of another close stand of pine. The needles need but dry a single day. Any more and their savoury resin is lost into the ether, and not into the orange flesh of that strangest of clams.

HE KNOWS SHE IS there because he can smell her, her fur wet from snowmelt, his favourite dog, the brown and blonde bitch. She lies just below his bed frame and he has only to let his arm hang down and it rests on her neck. She comes here most days and it seems she has learned to set herself in the spot most advantageous for a scratch. Which Lucien does, though it's sometimes only a bare spasm of a squeeze. When he scratches her, though, he feels the smallest tide, a rise in his heart, that he's giving pleasure. He knows why so many keep dogs, beyond the practical purposes, and it is that one can give the beast so small a treat as a scratch and yet fill the creature's need and be blessed by its adoration.

He scratches her almost vigorously and can hear her tail tap the bed leg. Would that be heresy, to claim one can be blessed by a dog?

But he can feel the cure in it too. He knows he isn't in his ordinary mind, but in giving the beast pleasure and being blessed by it in return he can feel lifted up, and he knows that if he stays lifted up, and is lifted up again and again and always, he would stay this high, and as long as he stays this high, he will stay cured, and not die.

NOW FRANÇOIS, THE rough carpenter, comes with the day's wine and some news. He sits on the edge of Lucien's bed frame, and

Lucien wonders if the unlucky man can smell him. He knows it is poor François's assigned duty to help Lucien up to toilet and to ensure he is clean at the end of it, and these crimes against Lucien's modesty are what most make him see death as a route one might choose as the most reasonable path left to him. He sees that with a secretive foot Francois has pushed Lucien's chamber pot well away from them and more over into the centre of the room.

François proffers the cup of watered wine and the reed through which Lucien can more ably drink it, and Lucien sucks — he thinks of the word *suckles* — as heartily as he can, for he would like to make himself drunk, if only he had the energy, and if only the wine weren't watered. And something in the wine tastes strangely excellent, if only because strange. He can taste pepper, and fruit.

But, the news. François offers it all ahush but voiced quickly and with some excitement, for things of import are taking place, and in some absurd way François in his excited posture reminds Lucien of his own sister talking to her friends.

First, his woman, the savage he has so famously befriended — François struggles to say the name — anyway, she has been here, to bring him —

"Ndene," Lucien says, softly, and he feels an ache of another kind.

— to bring him some medicine. She was not allowed through the gate, at Poutrincourt's instructions, and then the apothecary d'Amboise claimed he wanted first to study the medicine, and he burned and breathed some of it and mixed some with snow and with ice, and also mixed it with his own remedies and cures. It is said, and here François leans in closer and speaks lower, that the apothecary was making letters and words and shapes with the roots and herbs, and speaking over it, and "to

299 ✳

all appearances, experimenting in Darkness." When discovered, he made as if he would perhaps throw it all out, but Monsieur Champlain simply took it away from the apothecary, who has been ever more and more strange, and told Bonneville to see if it would taste well in a soup.

"The mapmaker said it was powders and ashes all amix. He says he doesn't know if your woman's dried things are in there or not. But he also put it in some special wine-drink for a feast, and you are drinking it now. Whatever it might be."

Lucien pulls back from the cup but it is too dark to see into it. He returns his lips to the reed and sucks harder, with a new hunger, and he thinks, *Ndene*. And, yes, the wine tastes both good and bad as medicines do.

"This was two days ago," says François. "You have been sleeping a lot. Which I have heard might be for the good."

It is the only good.

"And then this morning the strangest event of all. Some savage boys came upon the apothecary in the snow. Seated in the snow." He waits as if for Lucien's response, and none comes. "He was waiting, only that. He was up to nothing else. He was not asleep. He had placed himself in back, up near the trees, away from public view. At the edge of the graveyard."

"We have a graveyard?"

"East of the storehouse." François points east. He holds his arm up while he speaks. He seems reluctant to say more, but appears to know how it is that a sick man needs any detail about his future, whether it entails health or the other. "Not truly a graveyard. The ground is frozen, of course. So, at this point, the men, the three who..."

"They lie waiting in the snow."

"For spring, yes. And then"—François's tone gains assurance, as if filled with happy news—"they will be given proper burial, deep and safe in the ground. And already they have good crosses marking where they are. And they are guarded, dawn and dusk."

"Guarded?"

Lucien smiles gently in asking this but François has closed his eyes and shakes his head. He has said too much and will not consider Lucien's question, the answer to which involves wild beasts nosing frozen bodies and ripping them to pieces. Lucien touches François on the arm by way of apology, and to ask him to please continue his story, which he does.

"In any case, there in the snow the apothecary sits, choosing where he did as if perhaps to sit bedside with them still, or perhaps feeling remorse that he had not cured them. Who can say? But he was sitting in the snow, resembling a stump, indeed he wore some new snow on his shoulders, and he was almost dead, but healthy otherwise — that is, his own choice sat him down and not some accident. Some say he was that far out of his head and was choosing this way to die."

"Is he" — Lucien gestures with a loose wrist to indicate his own body — "is he sick?"

"With scurve, no. At least, there is no appearance of it. Monsieur Champlain has let it be known that, exactly this time after Yule last winter, on St-Croix, one man made himself drown, by taking a canoe far out into the bay and tipping it."

"Yes..."

François speaks more quickly. "It is a secret to which he has held firm, until now. I believe he is concerned for all of us, and wants us to be alert to any urges."

"Yes..."

"The apothecary is confined to his rooms, where he was given the full taste of Monsieur Poutrincourt's anger. We could all hear the shouting. The window glass shook in the Sieur's wind."

"I think I heard it too. A curious... cure."

"He is not in good spirits. He is well angered, red with it. His... Well, his boy has died, you see, and —"

"I think I knew that." Did he? For hadn't that particular moaning note, that lighter and less manly tune, issuing there from the corner, ceased?

"— and as you know, some men's sadness burns, and shows itself in fighting."

"Yes..."

"And so, Lucien?"

"Yes?"

"You should know that the Sieur is also most angered at you."

Lucien nods once, merely. The Sieur is but a small part of that which is angered at him.

"You must know that, should you become better, still you might not be free."

Lucien smiles darkly at this. He thinks, *None of you are free.*

François says that he should be going, calls him "friend," and squeezes his shoulder. He takes Lucien's cup, which is empty, which Lucien has sucked dry with a hope so tired that it can hardly be called hope.

Standing, François lingers, tells him how he feels guilt to announce this, but that they will be having this grand party, a feast, tomorrow evening at supper, involving great food and a butt of the superior wine, and also surprises, and an entertainment. Not for the nobles only, but for all of the men, even some savages. François promises to sing so heartily that Lucien will hear it from here.

"François..."

Lucien spoke, but too softly, to the rough carpenter's back, and the man keeps walking until he is gone. He wanted to ask if the surgeon has cut into any of the men who have died. He heard the surgeon Guillaume speaking of this early in autumn, when the scurve was still but a rumour, was a subject that aroused debate and interest, and the man had said that, like the surgeon at St-Croix had done, he too would cut into the sore legs and the loose faces of the newly dead, so to explore the ill humour to its source. Guillaume had heard that the blood is black in the legs but didn't believe this, and in any case his desire is to seek out the source of the disease and, once finding it, intuit its cure. Guillaume, from Honfleur, Lucien doesn't like. He is a man who almost never talks, and his face looks always hungry with something secretive. Lucien has seen him cut apart a pig, with brow knit, adjudging the mixture of fat and table meat. With that same temperament of face he will dissect a man, looking — for what?

Lucien wanted to tell his friend François not to let that stupid man come near his legs.

Lucien wonders if he will see his St-Malo home again. Then he wonders at his certainty, for he knows now that he won't.

AND SO THE FESTIVE night arrives!

It begins with the mapmaker Samuel Champlain shouting, *"Please! To your feet!"* and, to a man, those assembled are excitable, smiling with rumours, made young simply because something new, something they don't yet know about, is unfolding, breaking their habits in half, and Samuel sees this and is glad, because this is truly all he wanted. And now, as men finish rising and silence is once more gained, Ricou takes his fiddle to the peak of a haunting solemnity, and Membertou's young niece, no more than nine years old, and looking even younger in height, wearing someone's elegant blue linen tunic, eyes focused on her freight and tongue protruding with effort, bears the first dish into the dining hall, a platter heavy with the comically homely nose of a moose, upright with nostrils attempting to sniff the better odours of heaven. The roomful of men — even the nobles — had been restive and eager, waiting to learn the nature of this evening and its celebration, and because the appearance of the girl is a surprise, and her load a humorous one, and the music so bright behind her, the room bursts into laughter and applause. There is perhaps some nervousness too, for though none have eaten moose nose themselves, they are aware that savages enjoy it, and now they have come to understand that, tonight, so will they.

While jugs of hypocras are passed and emptied, Samuel directs the platter of moose nose be placed centre table and then he calls Monsieur Lescarbot forward. When the poet is standing quizzical in front of him, Samuel addresses the roomful of men, which includes, in the corner, Membertou and his main family.

"My good Sieur, and gentlemen all," shouts Samuel, "on this night we gather at the warm hearth of King Henri"— Samuel gestures at the blaze; the room is jammed with bodies and it grows quickly too hot —"far from our home. But we celebrate, tonight, our new home, and our own good company, and the good cheer that God provides"— he gestures both to the brimming jugs of superior Bordeaux wine and to the table that now bears other dishes too, namely root vegetables, the tureen of stew juices from the moose's cooking, and the salted eggs from the great sturgeon —"in such bounty. And, so, in the spirit that 'tis a sin not to enjoy His available feast, I do proclaim a new order of fellowship, commencing tonight but continuing through each night until the coming of the first green of spring, and I call our fellowship ... the Order of Good Cheer."

The dining hall shakes with affirmative bellowing and goblets are thrust high with such lack of care that hypocras breaches many a rim, and Samuel catches sight of Membertou's sons shrinking back in possible dismay, for of course they have not minded a word of his speech and are dreadfully surprised. At the height of cheering, men fling open the several parchment windows, for it has got thick and hot, and the effect of casting open the frames is a not unpleasant though rather immodest one of lending their shouts beyond l'Habitation to all the ears of New France. Then a breeze carries some coolness in, and the room is at once smarter for it.

"Fellows!" The men are so eagerly in accord that their silence is instant. "Given that I, your humble son of Brouage, Samuel Champlain, am steward of this first night, I would now like to confer upon *tomorrow* eve's steward, this collar of the Order of Good Cheer."

Amid more lusty cheering, Samuel removes from his own throat the loose, red-ruffled collar, with its three dangling bronze amulets, lifts it high, pauses long enough to catch Monsieur Lescarbot's eye, waits for the man to dip his head, and then drapes it on. And the hall finds yet another full lung for shouting its approval.

It still feels right to have done this, that is, to choose a successor now, for the next night, though this one has yet even to begin. What he wants is for the men to know that it is not this night only, and not the next night only, but rather a feast that does not stop. A state of lifted humour, of thanks and of appreciation, ongoing in its effect. As well, he hopes this gives spirit to the others, most of them savages, and their women and children, who did not fit in this night's shoulder-against-shoulder dining hall, that they may well take their turn here tomorrow, or the next night.

In bestowing the collar on his nemesis Marc Lescarbot, he does it as much to challenge an enemy as to offer a wreath of forgiveness to a friend. And he sees from the gleam in the lawyer's eye that it is taken more as a challenge. Also, indeed, the lawyer no doubt knows that accepting the collar — and how could he refuse! — means that tomorrow morning, instead of nursing hypocras' head with the rest of them, he needs must be up planning, rehearsing, and procuring new and better cheer. As for tonight, Samuel already has the lawyer's promise that later, before the course of sweets, he will recite several of his poems, one of them lengthy, making pretty about wine and venison and flowers — so Lescarbot will have to look farther for his main entertainment for tomorrow. (Perhaps he will hasten to resurrect his Neptune play!) Nor can Lescarbot call upon Poutrincourt to play his flute, for the Sieur is already doing so tonight, before the meat course; nor can he ask Ricou to compose yet another three-part song to be sung, for that is commencing now.

It is a beautiful tune! Ricou has begun with a trill of fiddle and, when he stops and tucks it under his arm, both Branchaud and the pilot Champdoré step up beside him and they three sing a simple melody but in three different voices, or keys — Samuel is not adept at music — one voice feminine, another middling, and Champdoré's a deep bass, and they do not hurry to reach the next note but linger, and then bend the note so that it rises rather than stops, and the effect is lovely — though not so lovely that the men fail to notice the evening's pièce de résistance: the grand sturgeon-fish, longer than a man and near as thick, lying on a plank fresh milled from a grand birch, borne now to table by Bonneville the cook and two others. Though the fish is no secret to anyone, for it has spent two full days hanging in the smokehouse, to be peered at by yet another small crowd when-ever the door was opened to add more wood, and perhaps they have heard his own rumours of the fish's excellence, for he has tasted it prepared this way in Hochelaga, and he let slip out that in the mouth it will feel more like pudding than like flesh; and indeed this is the same beast from which an entire cask of sleek beige eggs has been scooped and pickled; still the sight of it now resting freshly and well cooked upon the table is enough to bring the men once more to their feet, and they applaud yet again — not so much a bellowing this time, but rather a reverent murmuring, and hands well struck and at length, and, in some cases, noble rings rapped earnestly against pewter.

HE HEARS THEM. Mouth limp and half open, lying only on his back, tits up, he hears them down those impossible stairs and across the courtyard and through the open windows of the dining hall. Singing, shouting. He can hear individual speeches bellowed, sometimes even some of the words. He can hear the trained, blade-sharp tone of the lawyer proudly giving dramatic voice to one of his own poetic compositions.

Their glad noise makes him more lonely than silence has ever done.

In years to come, all they will find, he thinks, all that will outlast his bones, is his cup here, and the brass buttons from his shirt up on that nail. They might mention his name, if his name is remembered by anyone at all, when — to Poutrincourt's future children perhaps — they point out the well-joined handrail, with the curl and simple fish head carved at its bottom end. A carpenter named Lucien did that fine work, someone might say. And, look at how tight this frame is around the window glass. But that would be the sum of it. Of his life made visible, that would be it.

He knows he should have done more while he owned his life, but this could be his fever's voice. Still, he remembers, upon seeing the short height of the proposed ceiling in this same common room in which he lies, his urge to say it should be taller. The tall men, like Lucien himself, true, but Dédé especially, almost are made to stoop, and what does this to their moods? And does it not lower how they value themselves? He even had a joke ready — Surely now, let's have a few more inches! A higher ceiling will give us a small taste of Heaven and not scrape the hair from our heads! — but he was timid to say it to the Sieur, Poutrincourt himself, who stood there saying yes and no over plans for the building, one of which he held and read upside down.

Heaven, yes. Here, it may already be Hell. Here, what will stay here are his cup, and buttons, and tools — awl, plane, and six good drill bits — that are his father's, and not yet paid back, so not even yet his. All the wooden rest-of-it, and all this sore flesh, will change colours and become other than itself, and then mud. He will leave this ache, this red phlegm, and this falling tissue behind, its foulness accepted into the bestial ground, while his fresh soul flies, on a perfect route, in Heaven.

And what of Ndene? How long will it still live, her wondering after him? She seemed always so proud and happy to walk beside him, turning no eye to any of the young Mi'qmah who could otherwise be her suitors, and who, indeed, were not shy to eye her. How long would her love stay her from the embrace of others?

Cup, buttons — otherwise, nothing. Upon his death his father's tools will be taken back aboard the first ship, for that was written down.

As such thoughts scrape through him, they soon fade to become ghosts of themselves. Often he lacks strength for these more brashly coloured thoughts, and he can wrestle only the grey wisps; and then sometimes the biggest part of him is breath. A breath is loud, and then it happens again, and then again, and it saves his life every time. Though he knows he sometimes moans, the breath is constant, and loud enough in his ears.

Maybe breath is itself the middle place, is Purgatory. Breath marking time, while we are mortally judged. Time will continue, a breath will rise again, and then probably again, but then there will be … a last one. And never another. That moment *will* come. In this truth, he has the company of every soul now living. It is hollow comfort, but a comfort.

One more thought is muscular as it rises: that final breath will be the biggest proof that we were ever alive.

HIS SLEEP IS PILES of dirty gossamer, and through it he hears laughter and some refrains of song. But Lucien comes back to his mind and understands his plight only when he hears Dédé laugh. This man the size of a door, this man who has grown wider these past months while the other men shrink, who has gone silent as well; whose head hair has begun to fall out while his fetid beard grows dense and tangled, this man whose smell has not once abated — he has entered the sickroom and stands robustly as ever. This man with whom Lucien once licked molasses, and suffered his wink; the man who stood in line behind him and tortured his ribs with a knuckle, and twice slapped his book right from his hands.

Lucien lies on his front with his face against the wall. Now with no small effort he lifts his head and pivots it to face the room and his visitor. At this, Dédé laughs a louder, welcoming laugh, somewhat surprised, it seems, that Lucien is awake. He whispers, but only to himself, *Ah, bonjour.*

Lucien hears himself moan. He knows what Dédé is about. And in his moan he can hear the past moans of others, in particular the moans of Poutrincourt's boy, who had lived his last days alone in the chimney box. Indeed, Lucien thinks now that he once saw Dédé slink in there, as much as slinking is possible for that man, and at the time he may have thought it a dream. But Poutrincourt's boy also would have known why the beast had come, and it was a brilliant plan of Dédé's to visit himself upon the sick in this way, because in this room any moan was just another moan and he could do what he did with impunity.

This evening the foul man's plan is more brilliant still: below them, further covering the beast's noise, rise the laughter and song of a feast that has grown louder and more thoughtless with the hours.

Lucien has turned his head back away, but he hears the drunken mumble:

"O your bitch she's a shiny bug."

He feels the hand, damp and thick as a haunch, press cruelly on the back of his neck. It doesn't close off his breathing, but it hurts enough and is a warning. He hears:

"You shut up."

Another paw flings off the blanket and begins to rip down his breeches. The cold air assaults him first, his legs especially, adding rudely to their ache. But Lucien knows that is nothing. What has happened so far is nothing. He wonders who is alive still in the chimney box, and if they might hear him if he shouted words. Or if they would move, or could move, if they heard. Or if they'd care, or if they weren't already familiar themselves with what is about to happen to him. Now he hears:

"I'll have her through your back."

The hand comes off his neck but is replaced with the full weight of the fellow lying on the length of him, and thrashing, cleaving Lucien's legs apart, trying for purchase, moving quick as a devil. Lucien feels several ribs bend, and break. A nether pain begins, and he knows it's but the beginnings of this pain, and he hears:

"I am fucking her now."

But then, through his fright and thirsting for breath, he hears confused commotion, and shouts, and now Dédé has leapt off him, and Lucien sees he has also been pulled, and now two men hold him down in a sitting position, and another — it is Samuel Champlain — stands apart from the scene, breathing fiercely through his widened nose, his small sabre out, looking like he wants to use it. At his feet, a good pewter plate, heaped with the oddest family of foodstuffs, as well as a goblet that steams with spice. Lucien can smell clove.

Monsieur Champlain had come up here to see him fed.

SAMUEL SITS PONDERING his sketches, unable to add artful ink to them, full as he is with good cheer. Also, reveries stay his pen. It is a fortnight now since the first celebration.

Lescarbot's night went well, despite the lawyer taking every opportunity to describe, in verse, each dish as it got carried to table. But there was a fine beaver tail made in a pie, with such addition of garlic and salt and butter that it could have been as exquisite as aspic of escargots. And he introduced a right clever song, to be sung in rounds, as an addendum to his Neptune play, which he did recomprise. He challenged the men to compose lyrics in the very moment, right where they sat. But since wine makes many different creatures at table, the lyrics shouted out were often leagues apart in meaning from the line that preceded it, or too rough-hewn. In any case, Lescarbot enjoyed playing judge, or in truth emperor, with his thumb up or, more frequently, thumb down, and the lyric was killed.

Following that, Ricou's feast was worthy too, particularly the cranberry marmalade that did well to overcrow the moose kidneys and tripe, the bulk of which was passed out of the dining room and into the other rooms where it seems every savage in the territory now awaits a morsel. But the evening settled into diligent labour at getting Lescarbot's song well turned out, and at last they agreed to entitle it "Without Doubt Mermaids Heed This Our Song." No singer, Samuel stood in back and aimed soft moans toward his feet. But he finds it both ennobling and fun to build a good song together.

Next, the apothecary d'Amboisee, whom Samuel understands was passed the steward's collar as an act of compassion and intelligence, for "never fall idle, never go mad," as is said. The spitted otter was delicious, its crust of burnt herbs not the medicinal abomination some had feared. And the lobster crème that began the evening was the perfect goad to their healthful appetites. The lone curious spice the apothecary added to the affair was his request — more a command, truly, and lacking in any mirth at all, with nary a wink from him — that all men be served according to height, from tallest and then next tallest, et cetera, which was a lunacy bland enough but lunacy all the same. Samuel knew it also threatened their appetites by bringing too clearly to their minds the absence of the towering Dédé, who otherwise would have, for the first time in his life, been served first, before nobility. But the monster is in Poutrincourt's gaol for the rest of his stay here.

This same Sieur, whom the men have perhaps been too shy to ask and encollar, has finally tonight, through waving comically at Gagne, making his availability known, received the red collar, and tomorrow will bestow his feast. It is rumoured that in the morning he will perform his own hunting, accompanied by a small party of Mi'qmah.

To date, Fougeray de Vitre has supplied a night, as has Champdoré and it seems any man of means amongst them, those who have a knife to trade for a rare haunch. But the collar will circulate the stewardship throughout the common men too, as they have been told that good cheer is not necessarily of any expense at all, but can come of their own labour at hunting, or favours for the savages. And all they needs must do is put forth some effort at leading the toasts, and song.

He sees he has as good as ruined a sketch of the fields and forest trees up the River Eel, so he flips the sheet to write on its back. His mood is again unlike that of wanting to record events in his ship's log. He moves the feather on his lips for more of its sweet tickle. He will write his true thoughts down, much like an assessment of damage done by a storm, and of progress made despite it.

21 *janvier* 1607 (*to burn*)
IT GOES WELL ENOUGH. We are depleting our good wine, and much of our spice, not to mention a goodly number of knives, blankets, and nails in exchange for the best and freshest and hardest-to-procure game, and with insistence of an exact day of deliverance to us — even so, Poutrincourt and the others would not for a moment argue that the Order of Good Cheer is not a godsend for its remarkable lifting of our common humour. Not to mention our health, in particular those with the scurve.

I confess that I did very much savour the time when Poutrincourt himself remarked upon their changes: their skin gaining back robust colour and their night noises ceasing, and then their blackmouth losing its odour and then beginning, after the bad flesh fell out, to heal instead of fester anew. I waited until I was certain these changes were good ones and true, and only then did I confess to the Sieur to having secreted food — the freshest, and the organs especially, and broth most rife with herbs — to their bedsides each day and each night. At first Poutrincourt answered with thoughtful silence, and Lescarbot snorted, though warily, while watching the Sieur, and then the Sieur said, "It's likely good, then." So dull and vague a statement was this I could take it to mean permission at least to continue the medicine. In any case, Bonneville is now pleased he need no longer prepare plates in secret, this having made him anxious because, though he was carrying out my orders, my rank is not the highest.

I have instructed poor d'Amboise to cease his struggles in the sickroom. The apothecary's fumigations of vinegar brought forth only needless tears. The elaborate poultices of bread grated and mixed with strong powdered lead caused only a new kind of festering to the leg sores, wounds not pacified but made more angry; plus it appeared to make the men fall stupid. Though it marked his failure, d'Amboise appeared relieved to be released from this duty.

The beast Dédé and the good carpenter Lucien are both charged with crimes against God, and confined to their separate rooms within the compound. After Poutrincourt made this most obscure decree, and saw me linger while the other men left, he read what was on my face and held his palm up against me speaking. He told me, simply, that he acted solely on what had been witnessed and that upon our regaining France in summer there would be a fitting trial, and innocence would come out, if indeed any existed. I believe this is when I raised my voice at him, but before three words were out he shouted, and I held my tongue. I know that his logic lies in the carpenter not defending himself against his assailant, not even to voice his displeasure. I suspect he knows full well that Lucien is innocent of the crime. Perhaps he is using this facsimile of a crime to put a stamp of greater certainty on the other crime, of loving a savage. Or, perhaps something in Poutrincourt's ordinary good nature can simply not fathom, cannot bring to mind or to words, that any man could take carnal knowledge of another man who lay that sickly and that near death. Perhaps to admit Lucien's innocence would also be to admit the awful truth about Dédé, whose life is one of God's mysteries.

But the men know, of course, what we stupid nobles do not know, or will not know. Though it sorrows my soul that I cannot be seen to disagree with the Sieur's censure, the regular men visit Lucien frequently with gossip and songs, and once, I've been told, they put on a play for him, rehearsing it for the feast later that evening. They also, I believe, bring small treasures from his girl, one of them a bone ornament he wears openly, that is, defiantly, from around his throat. (Perhaps some proof that the Sieur knows him innocent is that Dédé is by comparison kept shunned in his own especial gaol, the sail room, where he waits patiently. What is left of his hair is apparently becoming grey, a sure sign of some extreme unease.)

I myself informed Lucien of the Sieur's decree — and that he is now twice confined — and at this redundancy Lucien weakly though bitterly smiled, and his chest buckled in what was part laughter, part spasm, for he is not yet well. But nearly so. Yes, nearly so, for that is what I climbed the stairs to see, and that is cause for joy. If not his, then at least mine.

The Party

ANDY RATTLED OPEN the old French door to his mudroom, reached in and squeezed a pine bough to feel the needles for dryness. They felt as turgid with sap as ever. The room smelled like a version of his father's aftershave. Did anyone still use aftershave? Online yesterday he'd learned that this was a kind of white pine, which he thought an interesting coincidence. It was a broth made of white pine needles, *annedda*, that Cham-plain had seen cure scurvy in Quebec but couldn't find in Port Royal.

In any case the needles were for smoking the mussels tonight — Jesus, his party was *tonight* — and the mudroom was a three-dimensional maze of boughs, impossible to walk through. He'd chainsawed them off his blown-down tree and it was clear that even if the needles shrank and shrank he'd have far more than needed. He'd got carried away with the fun of bucking the branches. With the upright root-ball clinging to the edge of his yard and the tree aiming down, its tip resting on the gravel beach, he'd balanced himself on the trunk as he sawed off the big bottom branches first and then gradually scaled down the tree, or actually up, taking off branch after branch, climbing the tree upside down, as it were, until, near the tip, he jumped to the gravel. What he now had, besides all the branches to haul, was a cool ladder back up to his yard, an apparatus he would have loved playing on as a boy. He wondered who he knew with kids the right age to enjoy such a toy, and couldn't think of anyone.

At his feet, tucked just inside the mudroom, was the big blue cooler. Leonard's scrawled note lay on the lid: *Went to Terrace for moose, maybe a fish.* Andy lifted the lid again to appreciate, under melting crushed ice, the biggest mussels he'd ever seen.

From down the hall he heard Laura's seventeen-year-old daughter, Amelia, flush the toilet, a sound he found a little thrilling, except he was afraid of her. It was Amelia's fault that, all day, his world felt off-kilter. It was almost a visual thing. Even here in his house the space between objects felt tilted, iffy. Her presence made him think of "time out of joint." You feel like you might fall on your face, but you don't. It was probably just graveyard shift and sleeplessness. If you kept a dog awake four days it would die. He had probably only a bit of that. Tibetans, they had a feeling they called *diagonal-line hell* — what would that be like?

Over two days he'd spent more time with Amelia than her mother. The day after Laura's arrival, while she worked at death certificates and funeral arrangements, he'd ferried over again to greet Amelia this time, and it was just one more oddity among many lately, welcoming this younger version of Laura. She'd said "nice car" climbing into the Mustang, and the way she said it made Andy like his car a little less. He had to keep himself from staring as he tried to parse her father's features from her mother's. She was stunning, truly, in a classic feline way. The father must have been kind of pretty himself, Slavic or even Asian, or at least a Johnny Depp. In any case great cheekbones and jaw. He talked with her as casually as he could; she seemed a typical teenager. She let slip that she was missing a skiing holiday with friends, and getting back to Vancouver only a day before the start of term was the shits too. He sussed that she hadn't been fond of her grandmother and was here more out of duty to her mother.

This morning they'd been at the funeral together, Amelia seated between Laura and Andy. It was just the way they ended up in the row. Andy's mother and Marie Schultz's other friends comprised the row behind them, and Andy could smell their intense perfumes wafting at him due to two large fans at the back (he had the grisly thought that these fans were to drive any waft-of-*body* away from the audience), and he wondered if he wasn't becoming sensitive to chemical scent, as people apparently were. He'd read that most perfumes and deodorants now used a highly allergenic enhancer chemical that helped fragrance knife into the olfactory nerves more efficiently, saving a company money.

It was an open-casket affair, and while most people lined up to peer in, or pat a folded hand, or bend to kiss, Andy was happy to sit and wait it out. He could see her well enough from there, her auburn hair with its new 'do, the coffin's white satin lining puffed out like heaven's own comforts. Mrs. Schultz was made up to barely resemble herself. In fact Andy jerked awake staring at that face, and an odd vision he'd been enjoying of her. Perhaps it was the tan makeup, but in death she looked vaguely Native, and in his vision Andy saw three hummingbirds tied with black thread to her hair. He'd read about this rare spectacle, of a Haida chief's favoured wife entering a ceremony so adorned, making a once-in-a-decade splash with this highest peak of fashion. And it *was* the best ornament, these three tethered hummingbirds—three seemed perfect. He could almost see the birds buzzing, straining along the farthest arc of their tether, and he could hear the three-part thrumming, a beautiful little chaos of orderly sound, and he almost liked Marie Schultz now because of it. He could admit she'd had a nobility about her. Though he did note that, on either side of him, neither Laura nor Amelia was crying.

For reasons she kept to herself, Amelia refused to go to the graveyard for the burial, telling her mother, "I just can't do it," and Andy said he was fine with hanging around with her till after.

So he asked if Amelia wanted to see some sights and she said sure. First he drove her up to the hospital grounds for the view (it was momentarily odd because he could see the hearse and funeral procession moving east through town, though he didn't point this out to her). He indicated the various islands, and the directions things lay, like the airport, and Japan, and the Charlottes if you could see their mountains through the mist. Amelia stood hunched overdramatically in what was barely rain, nodding dully, her gaze more inward than out. So they drove back downtown to do the waterfront.

They trod the short boardwalk in front of the tourism building, Andy pointing out the last fish plant — a crab cannery — the cruise-ship dock, the bald-eagle tree, and the long slips where cruising billionaires tied their three-storey yachts. As her eyes followed his knowledgeable pointing arm, he felt content with his city and proud to be this closely linked to such a beautiful young person. He wondered if it would feel much different being her father.

"What are you taking at UBC?"

"Um. I'm not exactly majoring yet, but I think environmental studies."

"Ah." That was a program? He flicked his hand out at the water. "Out just past those islands," Andy told her, "they made one of the first discoveries of 'deep ecology.' Know about that?" When her silence told him she didn't, he told her how these waters once swarmed with sea otters, wiped out two hundred years ago to make hats for Paris and Moscow. The otters lived in the vast kelp beds that, from here to San Francisco, also protected the beaches from surf. Then the strangest thing happened — when the otters went, the kelp disappeared too! Then the newly pounding surf washed the sand away. The beaches could no longer launch canoes, so that was it for lots of villages. Plus, with no kelp, the herring couldn't spawn, so they left, then the salmon did too. Some figured it was evil magic, but the scientists who came found that the kelp had been eaten by a suddenly huge population of sea urchin. The otter had been the sea urchins' only predator. "It's a funny logic," Andy said. "If you make otter hats, the sand washes away and villages die!"

Amelia had half turned from him and might have stopped listening, so Andy ceased stabbing in the direction of the outer islands where all of this was discovered. Maybe she felt lectured to. Maybe she owned a fur hat.

He wanted to joke to her, So if they keep shipping grapes up from Chile, would his backyard fall into the sea?

He didn't tell her about the mystical Queen Charlottes out there too, untouched by the last ice age, an unglaciated *refugium* for animals found nowhere else — he understood that this was simply more stuff he'd been saving up for Laura, stuff he'd read, since she'd been gone, about their home.

They headed uphill to the municipal grounds. Silence grew quickly weird so he described how in summer when a cruise ship came in, this side of this street was crammed with vendors' stalls, and though most sold six-inch totems and vacu-pak smoked salmon and little necklaces, some were colourful, like the old Norwegian guy in his seventies who wore spats and busked, playing hymns on his fiddle, ending each with a long baritone "Ahhhmennn." And here was where a friend of Rachel Hadley's — Magda? Magma? — set up a table under a "Wiccan Fortunes" shingle, and she read people's lives with tarot cards, or by holding their two hands in hers. Andy had spent a few evenings beside her in the pub, and she hadn't seemed, well, "wise." Though how much wisdom did it take to read a face and say, "You've had it rough, but you can begin trusting life again," to make you happy enough to part with twenty bucks.

"It's the closest thing we have to a farmers' market," Andy explained. "Except there's no farmers, or vegetables."

"The tourists couldn't cook vegetables back on their ship anyway," Amelia instructed him, unsmiling, and Andy wondered if she was mean or if she really hadn't understood his quiet little joke. He thought of her grandmother, and how genetic traits often leapt a generation.

Enthusiasm stunted, he pointed out the spot where one vendor sold T-shirts, some with typical "I Survived Prince Rupert Rain" logos, but others with weird Photoshopped creations, Andy's favourite being a monster, the Thing from the Fantastic Four, but with three heads: Bill Gates, the Dalai Lama, and Michael Stipe.

"Do you have a favourite band?" he found himself asking her. Saying Michael Stipe's name had made him feel contemporary, until he remembered R.E.M. had had hits before she was born.

"A few, sure."

"Who?"

"You wouldn't know them, I don't think."

"Probably not, no."

They reached the grounds where, in behind the antique locomotive, in a clearing of maples, stood a decent totem pole. Most poles got painted these days, but this was ash-grey untreated cedar, which was how they were in the old photographs and in Emily Carr paintings. The animals and faces depicted weren't the usual ones either. Andy read the small plaque under glass and tapped it with his finger.

"Eagle Person. The Uncle. White Marten. Split Person. Small Humans. Gitksan Crest."

"Wow. Look at The Uncle."

She pointed to a face that was the embodiment of goofy, one you could imagine Jim Carrey straining for. When Andy asked Leonard about Split Person, a carving that suggested two faces uncomfortably conjoined above and below, anticipating Picasso by centuries, Leonard eyed him dismissively and said, "White people don't even *know* crazy." Leonard went on to tell him about the ancient villages and their degrees of banishment for degrees of mental illness. There was a specific kind of permanent insanity ascribed to surviving a tipped canoe in winter.

"Were you very close to your grandmother?" he asked Amelia.

Amelia looked down, then squinted back up at the pole. "I don't know. She didn't seem to open up much. Couldn't relate to...I don't know."

"Couldn't stoop to your level?"

She picked her head up, smiling. "Exactly."

"There's something about that generation that's really stuck," he said, insinuating that there was nothing stuck about his, and she could open up if she felt the need.

"I guess. My granddad on my dad's side is pretty cool. He's really cool, actually. He's a painter. Lives mostly in Prague."

"Holy cow. Prague. Prague's the new Paris."

"You like Prague? I didn't at all. It was all like dirty and rusty. And how taxis try and cheat you as much as they possibly can?"

"Well, I've only read about it." Read a lot about it, he wanted to add. Not that it would help his case that he knew their system of parliament, or Vaclav Havel's brand of cigarettes.

"But that's not why I didn't do the graveyard," Amelia insisted. "I just don't like the whole burial thing. It totally scares me."

"I'm not a fan either."

"The whole death thing really gets to me," she added. "Her body lying there like that? It's so unnecessary."

"I totally agree." Maybe not totally. It was closure for some, seeing the body.

"You know that like, North America's the only place that does the whole embalming thing? You know Europe doesn't?"

"That's right."

"What's with putting preservative in your veins, and then *burying* you? I mean, it delays the whole 'getting eaten by worms' deal, but so okay what's *that* about?"

"Well exactly." Though no one is buried alive, a primal fear. Only a hundred years ago the best-selling coffins came with an interior handle you could yank that made a little flag pop up and tell any passersby to please start digging.

"You know they did an autopsy?" Her shoulders hunched, as if she was cold. Andy made a motion with his hand and they started walking back to the car. "She was old, old people die."

"They do." But that explained her new 'do, which might be a wig. Someone had taken her brain out to weigh it and puzzle over Alzheimer's. Andy pictured a brow-knit grad student toothpicking at a pocked brain, hunting aluminum.

They walked down the hill. Andy could not help but steal glances at her mellifluous stride, and then he made himself not look.

"So you get to see your mom dance much? When she was still dancing?" He pictured Laura on that stage in Vancouver, in a skintight, skin-coloured body suit, that odd and funny pas de deux with another female.

"I was pretty small. She mostly, you know..."

"Choreographs." The other dancer ran her hands over Laura's whole body, but always exactly an inch away, never touching, just followed the contour, intimate but always a perfect inch away. Laura smiling mildly, but still as a rock.

"And teaches, yeah." She shook her head, seeing something. "At home I watch her doing little moves, working on something. It's amazing."

"You ever dance yourself?"

Sharp-eyed, she laughed. "Of course not!"

And here was his Mustang, Amelia waiting at her door. "So, you went to high school with my mom."

"Yes, I did." He pointed his fat key and beeped it, and four magical locks rose.

"She said it was really weird growing up here."

"We were pretty close," he found himself saying at the same time.

"No offence," she said, smiling and pulling open her door, like she hadn't heard him either.

He drove them back up the hill, faster than necessary. He was afraid of her now. Her nose was so clean and perfect, and so was her hair, curled to suggest wind, even indoors. She felt like some kind of bright malignancy beside him. Partly because she was so pretty, and partly because she couldn't communicate, at least not with him. But it was mostly because sitting in the seat beside him was something that Laura had made with her life. It had nothing at all to do with him. And he had nothing like this to show, for his years alone, that had nothing to do with her.

HE STOPPED BY HIS place to check on his needles and the mussels and also because Amelia needed "a bathroom really badly," which made him wonder if her standoffishness had actually been a holding in of urine, and he felt better about her, especially

329

when she truly seemed to like his house. He dropped her back at the hotel to rejoin her mother, and when he called out the window, "See you tonight," her quizzical and wary look as she walked away said she'd forgotten all about his party, and he decided to dislike her again.

He headed home to tend the simmering base for the stew, add the prunes, and the mace he'd finally found. He would add the moose, if it was there yet. It was reflex that made him turn up his mother's street. He approached her house and then just kept going, hoping no one saw him. He'd dropped in yesterday and had far too much to do for tonight. He'd love to grab a nap but he had to dig the firepit, and ready the pine needles, and taste the hypocras. But as he motored past, he knew he was avoiding her and her house like one naturally flees the sick.

Visiting yesterday he'd had a disturbing talk with her. Slumped on the couch, she wouldn't even answer Doris's wave as Doris tottered birdlike out the door, off to buy some "French red wine," because that's what Andy had suggested after she insisted she bring something to drink for tomorrow night. For food, he'd told her to bring an appetizer she'd never had before because sure, it was indeed sort of a theme party. He was asked what theme exactly, and Andy came up with, "It's 'let's try something new.'"

"Oh, I can't think of an appetizer I've never had," his mother had said, more to herself. Then, looking up to him, "Why would I think of an appetizer I've never *had*?" Then down again, looking strained and upset.

"Mom, forget it. There'll be lots of food. Don't bother. Please. You're tired."

"*You* look tired, Andy. And now this party. I worry about you." But she gazed off to the side, worrying about something else.

The mix was weird enough already, and now three old ladies were coming. The day before, he'd told Laura, innocently enough —

but also, yes, trying to entice her further — that the party could be seen as a wake for her mother and then, naturally enough, Laura asked if her mother's friends were coming. Andy said he would invite them, and now he had, and now they were. It felt so Old World to be inviting your mother to a party. Next you'd expect accordion players and a church pastor and kids smelling of lye soap, whatever that smelled like.

What would happen when Drew got drunk and put on some growliest Tom Waits and cranked it? You don't want to invite somebody only to drive them away. But for a dinner party, and theme party no less, it was turning into an unchoreographed affair. Some Leonard-relatives were coming whose names he didn't even know. Drew and Pauline's Chris might even come. What had happened was, when Andy phoned Pauline about serving bowls, Chris answered and, almost as a joke, Andy asked him what he was doing New Year's. When Chris didn't outright laugh or refuse, Andy described things a bit and Chris had grunted, sounding somewhat seduced by the concept of free wine as well as by the "we're actually going to conduct a living sacrifice," which Andy would say no more about. (What he'd meant was *odori*, which was more an experience of live sushi, and which would take place only if Leonard's friend came through.) And Rachel Hedley was coming, with her girlfriend, and the way she said it did sound like *girlfriend*, and it was none other than white witch Magma, or Magda. Rachel had dropped a hint or two, it seems, and Andy had heard a rumour, and sure he'd had suspicions since way back when, but here it was. To think that he and Rachel had once talked, albeit dispassionately over tea, about getting married.

"I didn't tell you because I didn't want to upset you," Andy's mother was saying, looking at her hands, "but Rita's cancer is back. And they suspect her liver. It seems it's lodged there as well."

"That's — really sad." It really was. "Is she — Is she coming tomorrow night?" Andy didn't know what else to say, and why had she decided to tell him now?

"Yes. But we might not make it all the way to midnight, dear."

"No, it's great that you're coming at all."

"We can cab it when she gets tired." Perhaps envisioning their arrival back, she looked around her as if assessing. "Andrew, I just don't know what's going to *happen* now."

"To your house?" Andy gestured with a palm and his mother blinked deeply. He was going to ask something lame about finding another roommate, but obviously things had passed this stage. Her news about Rita sounded like another vacancy. This house was too big for his mother and Doris to rattle around in, and Andy had always thought his mother wasn't much more than tolerant of Doris. But then she'd never seemed that fond of Marie Schultz either, and look at her now, all beaten up over it.

"To *me*, Andy. I don't know what's going to happen to *me*."

She enunciated so crisply that Andy's neck hair shivered and stood. She'd never said anything this raw to him before.

"It's a strange time," he offered.

"I just don't know." His mother looked frightened, and on the verge of a violent pout, like she might stamp a foot.

It was here that Andy saw a sudden future rise up, fully formed. He knew that he must ask her to move back into their family house, and he knew that she must accept. And he realized how victorious Mrs. Schultz was in her hate for him, for somehow the woman had conspired with fate to come up with a perfect ironic finish: her dying meant that Laura was free to be in the world, while he, not her, would be the one in Prince Rupert looking after a mother.

Andy waited for a maxim about death or the future, but none was coming. His mother gazed out the front window, which offered only some snow and the uniform trunks of what used to be a cedar hedge, now sizeable trees. One hand absently rubbed the couch arm, hard enough, he could tell, to scour the fabric's texture into her palm.

"You could move back to our place, Mom," he said, and the proof that his suggestion was no surprise to her, and that she had already accepted it, was her unexcited gaze that didn't rupture, and her rubbing hand that didn't miss a beat.

"It would be expensive," she said, still pouty. "We'd have to suite it."

He knew she said this to save face, to make it seem like she was demanding privacy, protection from all the young ladies he would be bringing home. Saying it, she had never seemed older to him. Her hair looked dead, like fine brittle wood. A line of powder ended in the middle of a cheek. He could see in her acceptance of his offer the acceptance also of a new helplessness. For the first time, he saw the face of her coming decline, saw the route she would take into warbling uncertainty, and the fog she'd wander in stubbornly.

"Mom, this party tomorrow? It's for you and your friends too. It really is."

WHEN ANDY GOT BACK from delivering Amelia to her grieving mother, he saw that Leonard had indeed delivered moose. There was so much to do. He managed no nap, no shower even. People had been asked to arrive at six, and it began snowing at five. Andy was glad that, out back, he'd thrown a tarp over the firepit and small woodpile and two buckets of pine needles. Snow hadn't been forecast; it had called for lots of rain and a good blow from the southeast. But for now a gentle snow. And when the first couple arrived — Rachel Hedley holding mittened hands with her Wiccan girlfriend Magda or Magma — the driveway and yard were white and pristine, and when he flicked his driveway spotlights and lit everything up, it wasn't unlike a moonlit Christmas card.

As often seemed to happen at parties, these first guests weren't vital guests but fringe guests. Though he liked Rachel well enough he didn't care for Magda (not Magma; he told himself to remember this time). After sitting with them for a minute in the living room, careful to show nothing remotely like surprise that the two women were "together," Andy was glad he could bolt and attend to his list of chores. And the list was growing because time had become a factor: the curd pie needed testing, somehow, for doneness, and the moose needed poking with a fork. He did these things, as well as taste the stew again and add the salal berries, and yet more salt, then he uncorked the dozen bottles of wine to let them breathe (though he'd read that this perpetrated a myth, and that wine breathed properly only when sitting in a snifter-shaped glass), then he called Drew to see how many coffee mugs he could bring, but only mugs of solid colour, no patterns or goofy captions on them, like some Drew had, his Colbert "truthiness" mugs or melting-clock Dali series.

"Why just solid?" Drew asked, sounding irritated but like he had to know. He'd been working the same shift as Andy.

"It's for wine, actually," Andy said. "I want the closest thing to clunky goblets. Like, you know, the French used."

"I'll bring my set of pewter quaffing vessels," Drew said softly, and because Drew did have that old, failed basement pub, stocked with who knows what, it took Andy a second to know he was being mocked. Andy didn't tell Drew about the wine he'd bought, clearing out the store's stock after consulting a map of France. The idea was to find something resembling what they actually drank in l'Habitation, to recreate the same buzz, to think and to feel like a confined French settler. He found a Château Rennes, after noting that Rennes was near St-Malo, where they'd provisioned the ship and sailed from. And the wine was organic, which sealed the deal, seeing how they didn't know what a chemical was in 1606.

Before hanging up, Drew remembered something he needed to ask and it was that Chris might actually come tonight, but could he bring a couple of friends. Andy said of course. He could hear in Drew's voice a nervous amazement about the Chris possibility, though no thrill about the friends.

Next Andy unboxed the candles and asked Rachel and Magda to help place them strategically about the main rooms. They were three-inch-thick and self-standing, all of them beige. He'd considered white too unnaturally pure, their effect suggesting a kind of holiness or sanctity. Beige gave more the sense of the rough-hewn, of impure tallow. Anyway the idea was to have a night lit as much as possible without electricity.

As if on cue, with candles lit and electric lights freshly flicked off, three old women climbed out of the taxi at the head of the drive and, arm in arm, made their careful way down the slight incline, stepping high through the quarter-inch of snow. Once in, removing their coats to reveal they were dressed mostly in mourning black, they remarked on the loveliness of the candlelight, though Andy's mother went instantly to any candles Magda had put on the floor, despite their being out of the way and not likely to be kicked over. "Sorry, dear," she said, meaning Andy, "but these simply aren't wise," and she moved through the offending rooms quickly, knowing her house well, and found ledges and sills for them.

People began arriving in a flurry, as if the weather had found them and chased them in off the streets, for rain had started and so had a heavy wind. May E ran lightly down the drive, both hands on her bare head, hoping to keep her hair dry, and when he opened the door for her, here came Drew and Pauline and son Chris and a friend, James his name was, who looked in, saw all the candles and said, "Cool," with no attempt at toning down the sassy irony.

Andy took May's coat and half listened to her exclamations over his "lovely house," May still proud of her Ls and overdoing them. He also checked out Drew and Pauline, who, though they'd arrived together, and slept last night in the same house, and stood within elbowing distance of each other now, would tomorrow morning go their separate ways. They didn't look any different; they never did dote on each other. Drew seemed obviously tired, but he always did working this shift. Pauline helped take Chris's and his friend's coats. As if anticipating their early departure she told them she was "just going to fling them on the bed in the bedroom over there." She told them to make themselves at home but turned back to waggle a finger and say but not *too* much at home. She returned from flinging the coats and it was just Pauline and Andy in the hall. She sighed, her work done, and she nodded and whispered to herself, "Party," remembering why she was here.

"Par*tay*," Andy corrected. Pauline turned, only now aware of him, and though she smiled, her eyes intended deep sadness.

"You okay?" she asked, trying to catch and keep his eye.

"*Ça va très, très bien*," he said, fiddling with an umbrella handle extruding from the tall bronze bucket.

"Okay," she said. "Partay."

May E had run, girlish, to the living room. She acted like she'd just been let out of a cage, and Andy wondered how bored she'd been. She seemed different, without her unfortunate cohort beside her, and Andy could see that they hadn't been close, likely the opposite. Though she didn't have to, she stood on tiptoes to look out the blackness of the picture window and exclaim and laugh about the view, "due west" and "all the way to China." She caught Andy's eye to deliver her punchline, that she could see her house from here.

Now Leonard shouted a grunt and shouldered open the carport door to the kitchen, holding one end of a six-foot Styrofoam cooler. His nephew, who for some reason was wearing those same catering whites, hefted the other end. Both men grunted while shuffling their feet under the burden, which they took directly into the mudroom. On their heels came Leonard's glum wine-pouring niece, whose eyes were heavily enrimmed with kohl, and who smiled sweetly but insincerely for Andy this time; and then came two more Natives, one a prematurely hunched woman of perhaps sixty, the other a boy of ten or eleven.

Andy followed the cooler into the mudroom. "You gotta see this sucker," Leonard told him over his shoulder. He did a private double take and then added, "Actually it *is* sort of a sucker."

The fish, much alive and looking unconcerned as it hovered in its close confinement, did look like a sucker. On the underside of its head, its mouth was for vacuuming bottom stuff. A fleshy whisker, its base as thick as a finger, ran back from either side of its mouth, no doubt a sensor for the lovely rotting flesh of corpses, or for dangerous shards of beer bottle glass. Its shark-shaped body was knobby-sided and vaguely armoured, in shades of grey and tan that, against the white Styrofoam, looked black. Its nose and tail both stayed an inch away from their respective ends of the cooler. The fish was as long as a boy and as thick as a man's leg.

"That's a sturgeon," Andy said.

"A youngster," Leonard said. "Probably less than fifty years old."

"Really?" asked Andy.

"It'd be around that," Leonard said, nodding. "It was seren-dipity. They're pretty rare up here. It was in a guy's weir, upriver. He didn't know what to do with it. I think down south they smoke them."

"In the mouth," Andy said softly, "more pudding than flesh…"

"You've had sturgeon?"

"Not really. No." Sometimes he had trouble knowing what he'd had and not had. "But I'm not sure I wanted a sturgeon."

"You said you wanted something alive," Leonard said, stab-bing a finger at the fish. His relatives surrounded the cooler, staring down at it. "A sturgeon can stay alive forever, man. They've been beached for hours and then thrown back and they swim away. They have almost no metabolism."

Andy watched the fish hang suspended, the picture of patience, and he could not put the sight of this creature together with *odori*, with eating it alive, the dance of cells, of spirit, as its flesh became his flesh. Looking at it he felt absolutely no hunger. He could not even joke about sturgeon sushi. In his imaginings a salmon, the bullet of the sea, had always come to mind. Salmon ran in mindless uniform schools and got harvested like grain. This fish looked goofy, and somehow kind. He had the not unpleasant fantasy that this fish was, like him thirty-nine.

"How you gonna kill it?" Leonard asked.

"I don't know yet."

Leonard nudged Andy's gut with an elbow and whispered, "You actually going to cook that nose?"

Andy put a finger to his lips.

The ten-year-old boy, whose name was Alex, wanted to feed the sturgeon a mussel and Leonard said why the hell not, grabbed a mussel from the other cooler, crunched it under his foot and handed it to Alex, who fingered out the raw orange flesh and dropped it in near the sturgeon's head. The big stoic fish appeared not to notice. But of course, Andy understood, it was impossible to know anything about a fish that lacked face muscles and couldn't blink. For all he knew, that sturgeon thought the mussel meat was an attack from above and it was frozen with panic, it was hysterical.

"Eat it," Alex said, and gave the cooler a kick. Leonard grabbed the boy's shoulder and told him firmly "no," but the kick resulted in an instant powerful flick of the sturgeon's tail, which drove the fish's bony snout into the cooler. Andy could see a dent there in the Styrofoam, but it didn't look new. And now he saw the boy's hand, shooting out of a long sleeve, where he kept it hidden, to scratch under his nose. At first Andy thought it deformed, but saw it was missing half its thumb and most of its index finger, a messy rather than clean injury. How had it happened? Alex seemed the kind of kid who'd stick his hands in anything and wouldn't stop, even now. It was his right hand, probably his writing hand, his everything hand.

Oh, he was tired, too tired for any of this. He left the mud-room for now, deciding not to decide. Humans killed and ate things all the time. That fish was tonight's pièce de résistance. It was the party's raison d'être and joie de vivre, *non*?

But here, finally, came Laura and Amelia down the drive. Only when he saw them did he understand that he'd been spending any snatch of free time at the kitchen window. He'd been stirring stew, sipping wine, greeting friends, but mostly he'd been waiting.

THE NIGHT HE MET her at the airport he'd taken her straight to her hotel, not even that good a hotel, the Aurora. She'd booked it, she explained, "online in some airport a few hours ago, I think." She was on eastern time, for her it was the wee hours and she was "half dead." Indeed in the car and on the ferry ride she appeared to doze a bit, and she cried once, briefly, and their only conversations involved glancing at each other and then shaking their heads saying, "This is too amazing. Look at you. I can't believe this." As he dropped her off she apologized for "not being up to a proper reunion with you," and she said she'd call tomorrow and "we'll do it then," if that was okay with him.

After working all that night, aflood with what "do it" might conceivably mean, when he got home he managed only the most fitful sleep. Nested in a pillow, his head held a carousel of notions. "Do it" couldn't possibly mean do *it*, could it? To calm himself he had to slap the juvenile side of hope hard in the face. It would be unrealistic and also ungainly and even a bit gross for her to want to jump into bed with him after eighteen years, one day after her mother dies. But there *was* a syndrome wherein a stricken person confuses grief for lust, and you did see it in movies, but it didn't make sense in this case, in his and Laura's case. And so he did manage to convince himself that not sleeping with her right away was a good thing. But first he had to agree with his adult, unslapped side of hope, that nothing in her signals tonight had ruled out jumping in bed *eventually*. He'd always known, without really knowing it till now, that their eventual uniting would not resemble the teenage version. Their eventual jumping into bed would involve no jumping at all and it would be mature, patient, and burnished. Staring up from his pillow, picturing Laura here at last, but across town in a pastel hotel, aroused all sorts of such notions that had to be wrestled with and understood. A mantra-like one being: *her mother just died she's not in the mood.* He leapt up more than once for a cup of green tea, which no doubt didn't help his sleeplessness, and then the bathroom urge woke him when he did finally lose consciousness, and when her call came at one the next afternoon, even after his quick shower he felt yellow-eyed and bejittered. He donned his Johnny Cash suit and felt ridiculous.

On the phone she said she'd already had lunch — being three hours ahead of Prince Rupert — but she asked him over "for dessert or something. Let's meet in the café here." And entering the café, seeing her sitting alone in a red leatherette booth, this short-haired and womanish replica of Laura, wearing a mature, patient, and burnished smile, nearly two decade's worth of questions came back to him in a nutshell: there might not be anything left after this long, but why wouldn't there be? We didn't burn it out, we'd only got started. We were ripped apart — wouldn't two bloody severed ends recognize each other and want to reattach?

He sat and ordered green tea from the young waitress, who was one of the Jenkins kids, and who said she'd have to check to see if they had any of that. When Andy told her they did have it, Laura laughed and asked for the same. She smiled at him as if to say she knew not only him again, but also the workings of this town.

"So, sleep okay?" It was like asking how was her flight. He could hardly look at her.

"Not bad. It felt wrong to get up when it was still pitch-black, though."

You should have called me right then. Better yet, you should have been with me in the first place. But he talked instead about northern latitudes and S.A.D., and as they waited for the tea he became thuddingly disappointed to see them entering into a pleasant catching up. Obviously she was labouring under her mother's death — she told him it made her "not know what death *means*"— and she looked a little relieved to talk about mindless things. He asked about her dance career and he got the condensed version. As to her health, she was long in remission and thinking positively. With this type of breast cancer, two more years and she would be considered cured. Laura rapped the table with soft knuckles. Andy found this sort of talk so unlike their letters, which somehow leaped over news altogether and went to ideas. He wanted to tell her this — and telling her this would be more like the nature of their letters — but he didn't know how.

"You miss performing?" he asked.

"Half of me does."

"Which half?" Andy leaned in at her for a comic appraisal of one side of her face and then the other.

"The half that daydreams all the time."

"Ah, that half." Andy nodded. He wondered if that side of him didn't take up more than just half.

"Actually it was *unfortunate* that getting sick was what made me have to stop. It's worse that way, it's like an injury. The career-ending injury. Instead of, you know, it being your own choice." Laura nodded sadly, but the comic glint rose in her eye. "It's just like with athletes. Those really embarrassing comeback attempts. I've been trying to resist one of those."

Andy pictured her again in Vancouver, and wondered when the time would be to tell her about it.

He flinched as she slid her hand toward his, across the Formica. "Give me your hand."

He held out his hand and she took it, gently but firmly. As she pulled it across the table toward her, he knew he was being given a lesson, she had seen something in his face and she was correcting things; but mostly he was aware that he was being touched, touched by Laura Schultz. Laura Schultz had him by the hand, Laura Schultz was pulling.

"Stick out your finger."

He stuck out his pointer finger and she grabbed the finger's knuckle and guided the finger in so it touched her left breast, through her burnt-orange sweater. She pulled it in harder, an inch deep, looking him in the eye, then prodded herself with it rhythmically, in and out, what felt like sponge rubber.

She held his eye and might as well have said, That was then, this is now, snap out of it. Andy simply nodded to her. He tried to look chastised. Laura manoeuvred it to the topic of dance.

"It wouldn't look like the other one. Or move like the other one. And I won't just take it off, because I'm too chicken to make that statement." She released his hand. Then smiled again. "Easier to stay retired."

Andy wanted to reciprocate, to offer something he thought important, something about his life without her, but he couldn't. Laura described the main two schools of modern dance she'd followed and performed, Graham and Limón, and raised her eyebrows when Andy knew about both of them. He decided not to reveal how much he knew, because she might see it as either pathetic or a form of stalking, and anyway there was so much else to talk about. She asked him about his work, not letting him pooh-pooh it that easily and making him expand on some details, so he did. He said it would make for an entertaining hour's tour for her, entertaining if she liked Charles Dickens, that is, and she laughed. She talked about arrangements for her mother's funeral, and how bureaucracy had its unfeeling finger everywhere (Andy didn't like this image, given how he'd just touched her), and she gently cried, at which point she slid her hand out to be held and he did so, brotherly. Nothing was said of her plans beyond these next few days. Nothing about her, nothing about him. Nothing about here. He couldn't broach such a thing unilaterally. Any segue to that here in this café would feel as natural as him ripping off his shirt and yodelling. He was happy to have the excuse that now was just not the time.

But he stared at her, deeply. He supposed he was telling her that her breast-poking gesture hadn't worked on him, not really. Sure, this is now, but it isn't much different, Laura. She met his gaze only fleetingly. She was beautiful to him still, but he didn't feel overwhelmed. It was here he mentioned his party, one he said he'd planned around her arrival, "to get some people together for you," but now it could also be a wake. If she liked.

"Thanks," she said. "I'm not sure how jovial I'll be."

She looked to be trying, but for now the pall of her mother was a constant, clumsy weight over everything they could possibly say or do. It made his tea only bitter, without taste. It made the teary spark in her eyes an empty thing, a reflection of fluorescent lights on irises. And now she was asking him if he would mind ferrying out to the airport that afternoon to pick up her daughter while she attended to necessary business. He said of course, but wondered aloud about her not greeting her daughter in person, and she told him she'd left her only yesterday, they'd been visiting for Christmas. He realized, again, that he knew nothing about her life, not the details anyway. He asked himself how much the details mattered.

He had to leave right then if he was going to make the ferry. He reached into his pocket for his wallet and Laura waved at this almost violently and said she'd charge it to her room. So he stood facing her. He smiled, paused, and shrugged rather emphatically. Andy wasn't sure himself what he meant by it — then she smiled and shrugged identically back.

"Sorry, Andy, we —"

He put a hand up to stop her talking. "It's okay."

As he left the café he hoped he wasn't the gangly fool he felt like. He didn't know what had just transpired, only that they still hadn't had their reunion.

EVERYONE WHO WAS drinking tonight had one in hand. Drew, who Andy made music master for the night, had put on the *Goldberg Variations*, a heady but good early choice if only because there was no forced fun in it. The fire out back had burned down almost to coals so it was time to get out there and smoke the mussels. Climbing into his black rain-gear, he saw he'd forgotten to change his clothes for tonight's big to-do, which was funny given the shopping spree and all the rest of it. Here he was wearing worn-out blue jeans and an old sweater, comfy brown wool with a yellow and olive Aztec sort of thing going on. He pinched up the ribbed hem and brushed off what looked like pastry flour. It was good he was dressed for action. He had these mussels to smoke. Later he'd be butchering a five-foot fish.

He knew he was being watched through the wall of picture windows as he humped the mussel cooler to the firepit. He didn't mind the audience, the attention, maybe because it was in his own yard. It felt like a current of water that moved him along. Leaning back, elbows out, he waddled side to side and understood that from behind he looked like a tall penguin. Though there was no snow underfoot. The rain had taken care of it. His workboots felt cruel on the lush grass, richly bejewelled even from the living-room candlelight. It was good to be outside, no longer buffeted by people and talk. In this solitude, where he could hear nothing but the wind and his own grunts, he could feel how busy he had been and how tired he was. He really hadn't slept much lately at all. Things had edged beyond the numb and into the vivid, where indefinite rabbit-like creatures spring out from the legs of coffee tables or from shrubbery. He hoped tonight's measured doses of wine would steady him.

He was starting things off with the "mussels smoked under pine needles," one of the supposedly authentic Order of Good Cheer recipes he'd found. He was changing only one thing. The recipe called for the dried needles to be placed on *top* of the mussels, and then lit, and when the needles had finished burning, the mussels would have opened by themselves and be done. Well, theoretically the mussels got cooked and smoked enough sitting under the burning needles, but Andy didn't believe they would. Plus, as they opened, wouldn't all the pine ash fall into the exposed meat? It sounded so wrong that Andy suspected a failure in the translation he'd read. So, out here in his yard, he did it the more logical way. He poured two bucketsful of pine needles on the coals, dumped the mussels on a sheet of chicken wire, and lifted them onto the smoking needles. As he did so, applause broke out from behind the living-room windows, and through the billowing smoke, which still reminded him of his father's aftershave, he could make out his cheering guests. May E laughed at something, her own joke probably, and Pauline smiled in her ear, nodding. His mother and Doris and Rita stood shoulder to shoulder as though in support, and his mother looked only concerned, perhaps about the smouldering hole in her lawn, perhaps about the neighbours. Off to the side, Laura was lifting her wine mug to him. Beside her, Amelia neither cheered nor lifted a glass, but appeared to be checking him out. Chris and his friend James lurked in the darkness behind her, their eyes probably on the prize. Leonard was vigorously waving him in and yelling, but then Andy looked to his right and saw it was little Alex being waved to, no coat on, arms wrapped around himself, staring at the black shells as big as dance slippers like he wanted to get in there and grab something. Andy wedged his body in front of Alex's. And in the time it took to become aware of his own patience, one by one the mussels began to ease apart. As they did, the fire hissed with their juice, and to the pine smoke was added the smell of living ocean.

TEN PEOPLE SQUEEZED around the dining-room table and others sat randomly in the living room, appetizer plates and mugs in their laps. During an ebb in the conversations, Rachel Hedley asked, "Andy, so what's this about? It's *great* I mean, but..."

She sat across the table from him. Vivaldi was energetic on the stereo and she spoke loudly so that everyone in the room could hear, and inclined her head toward Magda, as if asking on her behalf. She was using an empty mussel shell to scoop some of the cognac pâté that Doris had brought. He hadn't remembered to ask everyone to bring "an appetizer you've never tried," but someone had brought mushroom caps stuffed with anchovy and sun-dried tomato, and another some jalapeño hummus. May E had brought, of her own accord, a block of that English cheese with the festive red marbling, and there was also a little tub of baba ghanoush. As a joke someone, likely Drew, had plunked down a can of smoked oysters and box of Ritz crackers. Otherwise, Andy had positioned on the table two bowls of coarse salt for pinching up with one's dirty French fingers. No other condiments allowed.

The "mussels smoked under pine needles" were so-so, tasting too resinous, too much like gin, making the gentle seafood bitter. Maybe if he had put the needles on top, as written. But each creature was as big as a fat man's thumb, and the flesh so bright orange that each bite was startling. More than one person suggested squirting lemon on them, which would have improved them, yes, but Andy had to go find the two lemons he had and hide them under some apples. At l'Habitation, lemon was one thing they famously and fatally didn't have.

"So you going to tell us what all this is about? I mean"— Rachel lifted her eyebrows in feigned horror in Magda's direction — "apparently we're not only eating moose tonight but we're eating it for a reason."

Andy told them about a cluster of claustrophobic men under short ceilings, a dark winter, and depression, and scurvy, and Samuel Champlain, and the Order of Good Cheer. From over in the living room's darkest corner Rita shouted that she remembered that from grade-eight history, and some others thought they'd heard of it too.

Magda piped in that Christmas was originally a pagan festival of light held, for good reason, at the gloomiest time of year. It was because of Magda, and also because for some reason Andy wanted everyone to *like* Champlain, that he didn't tell them he'd read how Pierre Berton called Champlain "that assassin." Or that, after his sailing days were done, Champlain went back and married a twelve-year-old girl. And somewhere along the line he added the pretentious "de" to his name. But theses things seemed like gossip, and didn't properly sum the man up. Who knew anything about him? It was funny, but not an hour earlier Drew had thrown on The Tragically Hip, and at the "He's thirty-eight years old, never kissed a girl," Andy instantly pictured Samuel Champlain standing arms akimbo on deck, face into the wind of a new sea, and he wondered what the man's mind felt like.

Nor did Andy say what he'd been thinking, which was that, whatever this night was, it didn't seem to be working, at least not for him. In fact he thought he might be losing it. Sitting at the table, he found if he relaxed too much in a certain way, the space around people, but not the people themselves, gained a humming sort of richness, so much so that people didn't feel important any more at all, didn't feel like the main thing. He could also blink rapidly and feel Laura three seats down from him, and he could feel his mother over in the corner by the window, and he could feel the vast night out there, and the water below it, his moving water that he watched daily, and not only could he hold all of this in his mind, he couldn't shake it.

Sitting with her shoulder pressed to Rachel's, Magda announced that the festival of light was common to every civilization in the northern latitudes. "Anyone," she said, "who had the solstice and the shortest day figured out."

"They're all calling, 'Hey, Andy,'" Rachel coughed out, "'*turn on some fricken' lights*!' Just kidding. We like the candles." Rachel looked a little drunk already.

Andy wondered if he'd be kissing Rachel tonight at midnight. It had been part of New Year's parties ever since high school. At midnight you kissed your girlfriend but then every other girl too. Sometimes there were little extramarital displays, kisses that lingered or dared some tongue. Sometimes you kissed someone you didn't want to, and how many girls had suffered the same with him? But it was a ritual lasting into their twenties. Maybe it continued still; Andy had been to New Year's parties only sporadically and rarely saw any of the old gang, possibly because they didn't live here any more. But he remembered Drew yelling once, after his Pauline-kiss was over, "Time for some *wives*."

Maybe he'd kiss Magda tonight too. Why not? He checked out her thin mouth. She had what Rachel herself used to call chicken lips.

"So you're curing our scurvy?" This from Drew. His head down, he mindlessly diddled two forks on the tablecloth. He was wearing his grey hoodie, up. He must have been outside for a smoke. He hadn't acknowledged Andy much all evening.

Andy matched his tone, which had sounded a little angry. "Just yours."

Diddling his forks, his anger almost palpable now, Drew pointed his chin at the table and its scatter of mussel shells and half-eaten appetizers and snorted.

"Well, whatever," Andy said. "I thought it was a good idea at the time." What was with Drew? From around the table came eruptions of "No, this is good," and "Hey, great party," and the like, and Andy was embarrassed he'd fallen defensive. But he understood Drew's irritation. Drew would bristle at the supreme arrogance of his intentions and was simply letting him know. Or — maybe Drew was only mocking Andy's ulterior motive, to worm his way into a certain someone's embrace.

Deus ex machina, the timer rang for the curd pies and Andy leapt up. He also saw it was time to open a few more bottles to breathe.

He let the two pies cool on the stovetop and meantime stirred the stew and its bulbous piece of moose in the middle. He was opening more wine when here was Pauline at his side.

"Don't take Mr. Dickhead personally," she whispered. "I don't know what he's so damn *cheer*-ful about." Pauline, on the other hand, seemed quite energetically happy.

"Really not a problem." And it wasn't.

"Well, actually I do know what it is."

"It's understandable. The guy's moving out tomorrow."

"Well, that's another thing. He isn't. We decided he shouldn't. Chris. The timing is just — You know, Chris moves back in, dad moves out, it sort of sends the wrong, you know..."

"Ahh."

"So we're going to try it out for a while. The happy family."

Andy turned to her. No wonder she was happy. "Well, that's great." And it was, it partly was. But he did understand Drew now. Drew had tried to change his life and he had failed.

"But anyway he's pissed off because of Chris tonight."

Studying the knife coming out of the curd pie, Andy checked for doneness, not sure what to look for. "Why?"

"I hope you're not bothered by it too, but Chris and James took mushrooms."

"Mushrooms." Andy stopped and turned to her full on. "Holy cow."

"They were laughing so much in the garage, and Drew said something, and James made some crack about 'the 'shrooms,' because he thinks we're cool about everything, I guess Chris gave him that impression, but Drew sort of went all quiet on them, so. I mean he should be happy when Chris is open with us, don't you think?"

"Maybe there's the whole drug thing he's worried about in general."

"Well, *he* certainly did mushrooms. They're no worse than pot. You did mushrooms with us too that time, didn't you?"

A hundred years ago. Laura had been there too, it was the four of them. He'd felt a bit uneasy and then, for maybe an hour, on the verge of a giggle that never came. Mostly just sort of fuzzy. Pauline was right, it was no biggie. And he couldn't help but feel a tad proud that here were two kids on a head romp who thought his house and his party might be a good place to be. He hoped it was. Anyway, it wasn't mushrooms Drew was mad about.

"Is Chris going to school?"

"He's agreed to go back to school."

"Grade eleven, right?"

"Grade eleven. And we worked out that as long as he keeps a B average, he gets his freedom. Pretty much. Curfews and stuff."

"That sounds fair, I'd say."

They left the kitchen each bearing a curd pie, Pauline using the oven mitts, Andy a towel.

Placing their pies on the buffet to the exclamations of others, though they merely looked like pies, Pauline said to Andy under her breath, "I'm just trying to enjoy everything about him."

"Sounds good," Andy said, just as hushed. He stooped at the buffet cupboard for some small plates, and Pauline joined him.

She paused in their chore to squeeze his arm. "Anyway, Andy, sorry about Laura."

"I know. It's sad."

"Wednesday, eh?"

"Wednesday what?"

"She leaves Wednesday? Her flight?"

Andy's hands froze on the stack of plates.

"Right." Right, yes, how stupid of me, it slipped my mind. Wednesday?

"Now she gets to be nearer her daughter."

"That's right." That would be, let's see, two more days. Here I was hoping it might be a tad longer.

"Can't blame her on that one."

"We can't," he whispered.

"What a complete *knockout*, eh? Is Amelia gorgeous or what?"

"Boo-yes."

Andy knew now what Pauline's sad, sad look there at the front door had been about. It hadn't been big-eyed sadness for herself and Drew, but for him and Laura.

He rested a moment more, his hand on the plates. And now Pauline had his arm in a firmer squeeze, maybe because of what was on his face.

Andy was glad to see Leonard lean out from the kitchen, arm around his niece, nodding vigorously at him, mouthing, *The moose? The moose?* An hour earlier Leonard, good old Leonard, had taken him by the soft of the inner elbow and in his deep, Tsimshian tones suggested that his niece serve this main course, under the guise of giving her more training. Maybe he'd seen Andy's edgy state, his sleeplessness, the nerves he couldn't shake, the pressures of hosting, and of Laura, and yard tumble and glacial melt and looming scurvy and his mother, and also maybe a glass of wine too many.

Leonard hissed that it was not only ready, it was all plattered up. Beside him, his niece stood wearing her cousin's chef hat, around which was tied a broad red ribbon decorated with sprigs of pine.

Andy considered getting up and joining the procession in, but didn't. At l'Habitation, the main dish was brought in to great fanfare and shouts of praise, and sometimes even a hymn.

So Leonard's niece bore the silver platter, actually an old tea tray of his mother's, walking slowly. On it the moose nose, a massive and awkward nub, its nostrils pointing up like two cavernous eye sockets atop a brainless and hairless head. Everything about it — the shape, the mud colour, the pocks from plucked bristles — was homely and absurd. Surrounding it, a crudely decorative collar of potatoes, carrots, and parsnips. Following with the tureen of stew, Leonard for some reason hummed "Here Comes the Bride." He stared fondly at the moose nose, his smile growing.

Leonard's niece's arrival with the platter sparked sounds of delight or disgust or incredulity as it dawned on people what part of what beast this was, and she rather proudly set it down, centre table. Poor Doris knocked her chair back as she rose to her feet to get away. May E looked simply pleased, in her smile no awareness that this wasn't traditional holiday fare. Drew couldn't help laughing at first sight of it.

Others were mostly laughing too as Andy went to the kitchen for his carving utensils and the ladle. He glanced at Laura, who appraised him in a lovely, significant way, eye to eye, no words needed. Here she was. Andy took an involuntary breath. It was like the last twenty years of his life brightly watching him. He wanted to run, to leave. How was that look of hers even possible? He tested the absurd notion that this night was working magic and she would now not be leaving town after all, but this hope made him feel pathetic. From the kitchen, rooting in the implement drawer, he could hear Leonard answering the moose questions, the where it came from and the how it got here. Returning appropriately armed, Andy confronted the moose with a carving pose just as Chris and his friend came guffawing in from the backyard, having learned of the nose and enamoured with it already, and Amelia followed behind them, brow knit and newly unsure.

Andy began to carve. He decided on thin slices, he didn't know why, it just seemed better than big country chunks. The texture as felt through the handle of the knife resembled the beef tongue he'd had once, but there was an unappealing sponginess to this nose, sponge was the word, no doubt about it, though the bubbles were a little finer.

They would try it, he was pretty sure. In the spirit of the night they'd give it a go. Especially anyone who had learned, like he just had, that this party, this night of Good Cheer, was meant for every one of them.

So he paused in the carving for a taste of something he'd never tasted before. He hacked off not an exploratory sample but a hearty square, an inch back from the nostril. Some people were watching, others weren't. He lifted it in the pinching tips of carving knife and fork and into his mouth it went. He chewed, tall and brave, a big dumb moose himself, and his teeth crushed it to release a brown rainbow of alien flavours. This nose meat wasn't organ meat but its own unique not-quite-meat. He could taste its snuffling proximity to fungus and mud and the swampy roots of reeds. He could sense a decade's worth of oddest breath droning lungfully through it, and though his instinct was to ignore exactly this taste, it was what woke him up, this was his medicine.

GRATEFUL TO PAUSE, and do something simple, he put his hands in the soapy hot water and let them hang there a moment. He liked that he'd insisted on candlelight in the kitchen too. It lent a soft contentment to the room that seemed to go well with this smell of soap and the underwater clunking of dishes. As happened at any party he'd ever been to, people were gathered here in the kitchen, but they spoke more softly and seemed to enjoy the atmosphere too as they watched him work. Enough dirty cups and glasses had to be washed to serve everyone the Napoleon brandy. He was insisting that everyone at least put their pursed French lips to it and have a sip, because he wanted to make a toast or two. And then maybe try to get everyone to sing, or dance, or a game. Some kind of homegrown entertainment. He had a pretty decent guitar in his room. He wondered if anyone played besides Drew, who he knew wouldn't go near that thing tonight, not for a million dollars.

He circulated with a tray of glasses. His mother, Doris, and poor hefty Rita looked dithery and lost, and it dawned on Andy that of course Marie Schultz had been their leader, the planet within whose stern gravitational pull they'd gathered. To look at them now, though they were standing grouped, they stood less chest to chest than back to back, pointing their gaze out into the room. It seemed like they had no focus, and might easily drift away one by one, with no goodbyes, and be gone.

Andy put glasses into their reluctant hands, saying, "Just a sip, just a sip." Hidden in behind them, but part of their faltering conversation, was the older Native woman, whose name Andy had learned was Gloria Tait. Only Rita, whose past included years of front-line social work, looked at ease with her. Andy wouldn't call his mother a racist, but she would be a little too aware that she was standing there, at a party, in her own house, talking to a Native.

No, he should give her more credit. She was stilted and queenly with everyone; her bigotry was universal. Leaving the women to their talk, he heard his mother say, "Well, of course, home is where the heart is." Maybe she referred to Gloria Tait leaving her village, or maybe it was about Laura leaving on Wednesday. Or, maybe she was talking about herself. That his mother had stooped to such a humble maxim didn't bother him as much as the question it raised: was she talking about her old house, that is, this house, or the one she would soon be leaving? He understood that the answer could hurt him.

Outside, the promised storm was picking up, mostly the wind, gusts of which could sometimes be heard over the music, except when Chris succeeded in putting Death Cab or Modest Mouse on again, CDs he'd smuggled in. Because there was a storm, in the kitchen the clutch of people — Leonard and his niece, Rachel Hedley and Magda, and Laura — decided that the brandy should be warmed, so Andy complied, putting the bottle in a pot of water on the stove. It should be warmed "in *honour* of the storm," not because of it, Laura added, and Andy liked that. He had the sense she was in the kitchen because he was. He wanted to tell her about storms and tides and show her the yard he'd lost. She knew his yard, she'd see the difference.

Leonard tilted his head at the platter and what was left of the nose. The stew had actually been good, and lots got eaten, same with the cheese-curd pies, with their cranberry relish. But though people put on a brave front with the nose, Andy had spotted most of it in the garbage.

"So," Leonard said to the half-nose that was left, "that's Micmac medicine?"

"Yes. I think so." It was properly pronounced *Meekmah*, but Andy kept mum. You don't tell a Texan about their Alamo. "For the French, anyway."

At this, Leonard plucked the brandy bottle from the pot, uncapped it, and took a quick pull. Rachel Hedley laughed, "Excuse me?" and Leonard, calmly smoothing back his ponytail and dangling feather, said without looking at her, "No worries, antiseptic." His niece stood beside him staring into space, perhaps listening but likely not. She had a bovine's contentment, and it looked like any company would do.

Leonard turned, again businesslike, to Andy. "So, eating a fish alive is a cure for —?"

Andy put a comic finger to his lips, because the sturgeon was still supposed to be a secret. He said, "Global warming." Somehow he meant it, too, he didn't know quite how, and his smile probably conveyed the opposite, so he added, "I'm almost serious."

"I know. This is kind of fun." Leonard indicated with a sweep of his hand the kitchen and beyond, to the whole party.

"It's actually a cure for depression." Andy shrugged to tell him that he was serious about this one.

"How does that work, exactly?"

"Eating a nose sort of jostles you." In the good fire of the moment, no problem can live.

"And eating a live, rare —?"

"They aren't so rare, they just aren't caught much around here." The sturgeon, the noble hermit grandfather of all fish. The one in the mudroom, Andy knew, was a green sturgeon. Smaller and less tasty than its big white cousin to the south.

"But, that's it?"

"I think so." And walls come down between one breath and another.

Rachel Hedley was waggling a finger in Andy's face.

"So, am I understanding it right, that Leonard got you a moose, and a sturgeon, and that both are, what, out of season?"

"Well, I don't know if there's —"

Leonard interrupted. "A moose *nose*. The *moose* was hunted, dead, butchered, and on its way to its new home in the freezer. The nose would have been thrown away."

"Still, the Native, you know, the Native fishery isn't supposed to be —"

"Or used for dog food. Sometimes —"

"— it's supposed to be for Natives only, so —"

"*Some*times —" Leonard tilted himself at Rachel in a way Andy didn't like the looks of.

"— dey freeze the nose and the guts too, eh? Dey freeze the cocks and the tits, and the egg hoops and de shit hoops, freeze 'er up for de dogs, eh? Especially if dey got a friend with doze sled dogs. Cock's a fuckin' *steak* to doze sled dogs."

"Fine," said Rachel, unperturbed. "It's bad enough that it's poached, out of season —"

"You'll have to stop saying that." Leonard drew himself to his full height. He sucked in his gut and out came his chest, and Andy couldn't tell if he was fooling around. It was one of the times Leonard might not know either. "I am a status Indian. There are no hunting *seasons*. We take food for our survival. We take it when we need it."

"Leonard. Come on. You have a business. You have an SUV outside. Those are — Look at those shoes you're wearing."

"Are you saying I don't have a right to —"

"You know as well as I do you're allowed to hunt and fish but you're not allowed to sell it to white man here"— she jerked her head Andy's way—"and when you say 'survival' it burns me a little when I think of, oh, I don't know, just a few people in Africa to whom that word actually applies."

It was an impressive display, and because neither Leonard nor Rachel had raised their voices or twitched even an eyebrow in anger, their audience felt safe to merely nod, or adopt an expression that weighed the questions.

Magda, laughing lightly, said, "Here's a different thing. I'm a vegetarian? So, for me, *everything alive* is 'out of season.' So pooh-pooh on both of you."

"Anyway," said Leonard, smiling easily, nodding to Rachel, "point taken. But please also take my point, which is that I mean 'survival of culture.' Okay?" He didn't wait for Rachel's response but turned briefly to Magda. "And pooh-pooh taken."

"But you know," said Magda, to Andy now, "if that sturgeon is really fifty years old, just think for a second."

"It's thirty-nine," said Andy.

"You know how much metal's sitting in that thing? Mercury? What else is up here? Lead? Aluminum!"

Leonard looked at Andy too. "Jesus, she's right."

Magda said to Leonard, "You don't eat the big old halibut, right?"

Leonard was shaking his head. "We've actually been *warning* customers when they get one over forty, fifty pounds. And they're nowhere near fifty years old." He laughed. "And neither are the halibut!" He grabbed for the brandy bottle but yanked his hand back because it was too hot.

It was all the out Andy needed. He didn't want his garbage can full of raw uneaten sturgeon in the morning, he really wouldn't be able to bear that. He pictured the sturgeon's gnomish face and gentle ways. Though wasn't the spirit of sacrifice about love, and loss? Didn't you have to kill and *waste* something?

They got the brandy cooled down enough to serve. Out in the living room, when everyone had a drink in hand, after a toast thanking Andy for his party, and then a sadder toast, from Pauline to Laura over the loss of her mom but also to welcome her back for this brief time — Andy announced the imminent release of a live sturgeon back into its ocean home.

BECAUSE LOTS OF PEOPLE wanted to go down to the beach and because the storm was worse than when they'd arrived, Andy went to the attic for parkas and rain-gear he thought were stashed there. He climbed to the second floor, and in the hall-way pulled down the collapsible, spring-loaded ladder. And here was Laura, at his side.

"Where you off to?"

Her cheeks were flush with wine and she looked forgetful of anything dire in her life. It was like she had, as of now, decided to enjoy herself. And it was the closest she had come, so far, to looking eighteen again.

"I'm getting coats and stuff. Attic." His pointed his chin at the ladder, which he'd already pulled halfway down.

"Can I help?"

He said sure, and was instantly excited. They were going up to the attic together, and Laura couldn't not remember, as well as he did, every detail of that time. As he followed her up the ladder, face a foot from her jeans, he got so excited that he was a bit worried for himself. It meant nothing, she was merely help-ing. Her daughter was bored a floor below them and her mother had just died, he was an idiot. And there was no way in the world he could let himself make some putridly lame move on her once they were alone up here and — But here she was pulling the spring-loaded trapdoor up behind them and closing it.

"Shut the noise out," she said, and when she turned to him her little smile dropped. "It'd be nice to say hi to each other. We haven't really done that. You have a minute?"

"Sure do."

Her eyes were Laura's eyes but set in a wider, more experienced face. Her smile was a little professional, maybe. Her breasts were perfect wonders, under a fuzzy sweater that would feel like the belly fur of some baby mammal.

Andy opened his arms to her, said, "Can I?" Her lack of hesitation was thrilling, as Laura met his step forward with one of her own and they were hugging.

He could feel her, her moderate pressure answering his, along the length of his body. It was all he could do not to try taking things further.

"It's a weird time, isn't it?" Andy whispered.

"I'm an orphan."

Andy didn't try to imagine how that might be for her. He could only revel in the hug that might be the only time they touched, and might be over any instant.

He said after a moment, "I hope the party's okay. Sorry it's a little goofy. Considering it's..."

"It's a perfect distraction."

Andy held on a moment more, but the hug had gone over-ripe. He sighed "okay," and he broke the hug himself, leaning back but keeping his hands on her shoulders.

"What?" Laura asked. It must have been on his face.

"Pauline told me you're leaving Wednesday."

"I didn't want to tell you. I sort of chickened out."

"Why?"

She didn't meet his eye. "Sorry."

"Were you just going to leave?"

"I don't know. It's just that — You had expectations, Andy."

"Maybe some. Sure."

"Well, no, you did. And so did I. I mean, I was going to be here. You were going to be here. We were going to test the waters." She flicked a hand between her stomach and his.

If you're stuck in Hicksville, might as well test a local yokel. He almost said this. Maybe he still would.

"But now I'm free to live where Amelia lives, and she's... Especially now, she's by far the most important thing in my life. I'm sorry, but..." Sorry but, childless, you couldn't understand and I won't even try to explain. We who play the children card never have to.

"But you can visit." Laura placed her hands where, before his diet, his love handles used to be. He could see in her face her enthusiasm. "Andy, really — you could visit."

"And test the waters?"

"Yeah."

So he went in for the kiss. She saw him coming and wasn't moving away. And he was astonished by what was coming, the finality of it: in seconds he would know his entire future. The feel of a kiss would bring their worlds together, or seal something cold.

WITH THE EXCEPTION of the older women, who wished them well, almost the entire party bundled up for the release of the big fish. They had four flashlights between them and followed Andy, Leonard, and Drew, who laboured under the long cooler and its load of water and sturgeon. Young Alex was instructed to light the ground just before their feet so they could see where to step, and not twenty seconds went by before Leonard had to bark again at the boy for his inattentive beam.

As they neared the edge of his lawn and the start of the path down, Andy shouted over a gust of wind to Laura, "There's the corner of yard I lost."

The makeshift rock and root steps were slow going, but they made the beach. Alex lifted the lid and shone his flashlight in while the three men caught their breath. The fierce wind and thigh-high crashing waves made the dark gravel beach feel unwelcome, even dangerous, and though that was only an illusion, it forced an urgency on things and made the ceremony a quick one. Andy had his own reasons for haste: in the mudroom when he took a look at the sturgeon he noticed it starting to loll, indiscriminately to one side then the other, belly up, and he knew enough about fish to understand it was almost dead. He saw Leonard watching it too and they met eyes.

"Ceremony" wasn't really the word for it. The three men, helped by the religiously stoned teenagers James and Chris, who looked frantic, almost weepy in their helping, walked the cooler into the building waves and lowered it down, almost submerging it. And then they carefully pulled and punched the cooler apart. Hunks of broken Styrofoam bobbed around them, and as Alex yelped and ran up to get in some kicks himself, all the others took up a simple chant of "Good, bye, old, fish!" Andy saw that many of them had refilled their brandies to bring along.

When there were no longer any sides to the cooler, and the sturgeon was given a hand to move it forward, and another to show it how to move its tail, the fish of its own accord swam lethargically out of flashlight beam into instant darkness. The chant held up for another ten seconds and stopped as soon as it began to fade. Waves hitting him to the waist, chanting simply "Fish! Fish!" in a small voice barely heard above the wind, Alex stood pitching rocks in the fish's general direction until Leonard tugged him gently ashore by the hand.

The party made its way back up the short path. The brief and minimal shelter of trees felt like a haven and the wind malevolent. It was exactly this kind of night, a tryst between high wind and a tide that would peak in an hour or so, that had gouged Andy's yard and toppled trees. Trudging the slope, he felt almost overcome, not so much drunk as exhausted, but he lacked the energy to care about his yard; he had thoughts about it but no feeling. The memory of his bed, the imagined smell and feel of his pillow, almost had him asleep as he walked.

He sensed rather than saw Drew's hooded head approach from behind. His friend didn't seem all that drunk, but Drew pressed his forehead against Andy's temple and then a little hiss, "So you get *lucky* up there?"

Did he get lucky up there? He wasn't sure if the word applied. He still wasn't clear on what had happened. In one sense, it simply fit this colourful night, adding to its choreography. Another wonky crescendo. Did he get lucky? Laura did meet him halfway in his grotesque lurch at her, going in for his kiss. All he'd really needed was that kiss, and for it to reveal what he had to know. Even her refusing to kiss back would have done that job perfectly well. What he didn't want was another question mark. He didn't want lips that left him uncertain. He was ready for her to turn her head away, even — he was ready for that final cheek.

But he was also ready to be met halfway, and he was. He could feel her equal passion, and the unconfident, searching vigour in her lips. Lips are sweetest when unsure. Ah, it made him happy, to be kissing her like before. This would have been enough. Because then it grew mostly awkward to be tugging down each other's pants, Andy wondering if her urge in this was still equal. They were both smiling and even laughing a bit, whispering, "This is amazing, isn't it?" like they had on the drive in from the airport, but they weren't laughing or smiling as honestly it seemed, there was a dark eye on the whole transaction and he knew something wasn't getting said; but then they were on the floor in the heap of coats Andy hastily flung down. It was against the wall opposite to where they last had been, on that pile of carpets, removed years ago now, and this time Laura didn't take off her sweater.

Andy still hadn't answered Drew, who just now prodded him in the back with a knuckle, wanting one.

"Yeah, right," Andy said, turning to give him the side of his face and what he hoped was a defeated smile.

Did he get lucky? It was amazing, his body some kind of automatic animal, taut yet fluid in everything it did, all its hungers being met, beautiful, what feels better in life? She even smelled as before, wine and venison and flowers, which almost made it end too quickly. Even as he took businesslike steps to distract himself, directing his attention to the wood grain and imperfections of the plywood floor, he shook his head, though maybe not physically, at the low comic irony of making love with Laura at last yet trying to think of other things! It was something he would tell her about later, because it was the kind of thing they could talk about, and this as much as anything else was why he'd always loved her. He asked her then, feeling both businesslike and also profound, if he could come inside her, and she said "sure can," and maybe it was this that sobered him, her easy way of saying it, maybe meaning she was on the pill, but in any case implying that his coming inside her was of no consequence. It used to be such a problem for them, an urgent concern always, and met with cobbled-together precautions.

But of course a long-married woman would have found a stable answer for conception. For most people out there the problem maybe wasn't profound. In fact for other people sex itself was maybe not that profound. Other people, they had affairs to escape its routine, to find some shock and profundity again. How many affairs had Laura had? Her "sure can" maybe said something about her social life. For lots of people sex was probably just complicated entertainment. Maybe, for dancers, it was a post-rehearsal cool-down, casual, while taking sips from their tinted plastic water bottles. Laura, he knew so little about her, her details — But his evidence was flimsy and unfair and, mostly, what was he doing in daydreams about Laura *now*?

He got out of his thoughts and found his animal pleasure again. They kept making love, gently rocking in the coats he would soon be bringing down for his Order of Good Cheer guests to wear to the beach. Tom Waits was roaring through the floorboards, almost like Drew's sent message. Chest on chest with her, he could feel the difference she feared, the ordinary flatness of her right breast versus the lack of give on her left side, the inhuman foam, and he could feel her awareness of it, an awareness that probably rarely left her, and he could also glimpse in this her fear, and her humiliation at being mortal. Up here in the attic, Laura was letting him know her again and it was heaven for this. What wasn't heaven, what wasn't *lucky*, was his certain sense that Laura was holding something back, was keeping a part closed to him. Even if she didn't know it herself. It wasn't physical, it felt bigger and more certain than that. What she was keeping closed to him was her future. He could feel that, for Laura, this gesture in his attic was an act of punctuation. This was another kind of death to take care of here in Prince Rupert. He could feel it, was certain of it: moving under him, rejoining him in their world of pleasure, after eighteen years, this was, finally, her proper goodbye.

Laura appeared to reach her peak and finish. And then it was funny, a little: maybe twenty seconds before Andy finished too, someone downstairs stopped the music. In those last moments the new silence was haunting, as if his labours were watched and appraised not just by patient Laura but by something surrounding him, something larger even than his attic and his house.

ANDY NEVER WOULD find out whose idea the moose dance was. Likely Gloria Tait. But it also could have been Leonard, because he always promoted such things, or it could even have been little Alex. It could have been anybody.

Andy was in from the beach with the others and had just descended from his bedroom where he'd put on dry pants. Drew was up there now looking for some too; Leonard hadn't bothered, waving off Andy's offer with, "You're way too skinny for me." Instead, Leonard turned on the oven and stood in his boxer shorts by its open door, and there he quietly sipped a beer.

Andy wandered, prospecting for a cozy spot to sit while waiting for people to leave, because he was ready for that. He moved from kitchen to couch to dark corner, but found no vacant chair appealing. He realized that what repelled him was the candlelight itself. Its effect had shifted from churchy to ghoulish, from sombre to gloomy. For one thing, it lit faces from below, a non-stop flashlight held under the chin of everyone. Andy had to resist going to the light switch. The flickering chiaroscuro made everyone eerily not themselves. Andy walked past his mother, for instance, and she sent him a little wave that unsettled him, the light and dark on her face a kind of duplicity she somehow seemed aware of, and she was having him on, perhaps truly witchy, her little wave maybe a curse. John Lennon's soft "So this is Christmas..." couldn't be trusted in this flickering light either. And now he remembered with a downward lurch in the gut that he had invited red-haired Dan Boyd to this party tonight, he'd left that message, and Boyd might walk in, any second. Andy didn't want him here. Dan Boyd's smile, lit by this wavering candlelight, could mean any number of things, and most were bad.

Andy found himself staring at his front door, pleading that no more people come through it. But then he knew it was all him, he was only tired and stupid. Plus he knew that Boyd wouldn't be showing up tonight; sometimes you could simply trust that your enemies would stay your enemies. But as he turned on his heel to go sit down beside his mother after all, his new mood made him reconsider l'Habitation, and spending an entire winter in light like this. Long greasy black hair, heavily moustachioed faces, ill lit, from below. The stink of whale oil and tallow smoke, the walls and ceiling heavy with soot. Faces bobbed and wavered, not to be trusted in such light; you could be cursed by both Catholics and Indians many times a night and not know it and —

From the group at the couch rang a new eagerness of voices, outshouting Lennon, about a "moose dance." A moose dance was about to begin in the backyard, around the firepit. It was Gloria Tait being consulted, from the looks of things, and she had risen off the couch wearing a palpable pride. Her head was back, her face stern and commanding, and she stood two inches taller. She said something to those around her, and little Alex shouted, "*Wounded*-moose dance! *Wounded*-moose dance!" An odd smile lifted one side of Gloria Tait's face as she approached

the glass doors to the yard, and Andy didn't know if a traditional dance was forthcoming or if she'd made a little joke. She
wore braids and seemed girlish and unpredictable for them, and
she didn't seem drunk, though you never knew. May E did make
a joke out of it, proclaiming, "Wounded-moose-*with-no-nose*
dance," and when no one laughed she said it again, and a few
people did.

People climbed back into the same coats. The old ladies
came out this time, because Gloria Tait was leading. Everyone
came out. It was the end of the party and everyone knew it.
Some carried another refill of brandy. Pauline lugged her own
full bottle of expensive French wine that she and Drew had
brought. Some clomped in wet boots over his living-room wall-
to-wall. Leonard wore a parka but below the waist only his
boxer shorts, and he was bringing out the rest of the nose to
cremate and explained to his niece that this needed to be done.
Rachel Hedley and Magda were blatantly holding hands. Drew
put on and turned up that sassy Pogues Christmas song Andy
could never remember the name of, and after he'd gone out
through the double doors, Andy's mother went back in and
turned it down.

On the way up from the beach Andy had thrown the remaining wood onto the bonfire and now it was high, and when
smacked with a gust it added its roar to the wind's. Because of
the surrounding trees, and house, the yard was a bowl that
caught the wind and swirled it, and the fire's orange arms flailed
out in supplication, or sudden punches, and the fire seemed
conscious of its own melodrama.

Gloria Tait said nothing, no instructions, she simply began
to dance, moving at a slower-than-walking pace in a wide circle
well out from the fire but close enough to feel some of its blowing heat. As a dancer she was deceptive and odd. She merely

walked, but with no movement in the hips, no sway, just a sliding forward, the rock 'n' roll duckwalk, all in the knees and thighs, head cruising steady as a hunting cat's, eyes forward. Even from behind you could tell that Gloria Tait wasn't blinking. A moose would be the last animal you'd guess.

Then, every five steps, Gloria Tait dipped at the knees, collapsing and then catching herself after a fall of two or three inches.

And that was it. People fell into line in the circle and followed, walking smoothly, without blinking, and they dipped in rhythm with Gloria Tait. The moose dance. The wounded-moose dance. Wounded-moose-with-no-nose dance. Andy enjoyed it, it was mindless and easy. Around and around they would go, where they'd stop, nobody knew. Between each gust and the fire's answering roar, you could hear some faint Pogues.

He'd just about completed one slow circuit when he noticed people laughing, a few nervous titters, a few guffaws. He watched Gloria Tait again and saw why. He counted five, six, seven steps, and she dipped. Some people had dipped at five, and now they quickly dipped again, too late. Gloria stepped two more steps, and dipped. Andy could see that some dancers were frustrated, turning to complain over a shoulder to a friend that that woman couldn't count. Others found it funny, thinking Gloria Tait a comic. But whatever the idea, people settled in, if randomness can be settled into, dipping whenever they wanted to, which Andy was pretty certain was Gloria Tait's intention from the start. Her wounded moose was a random moose.

But here they all were. It was heartwarming for Andy to see, in his dark yard, following in the circle, the bulky form of old Rita — wise-cracking, cancerous, game for anything, using her cane to keep steady, having a finer time than anyone in her condition could have. Instead of a dip from the knees, she performed it quite gracefully with a bob of her head. Behind her, Leonard's niece didn't dip at all but merely walked, obediently putting up with adults, likely trying to stay on the good side of Uncle Leonard, who walked, dipping proudly in his boxer shorts, behind her. Then came Andy's mother, who dipped not randomly but every third step, making it a waltz, and he knew her smile would be fixed and tolerant, and perhaps she wanted Gloria Tait to watch and learn from her. Then came Rachel Hedley, who was drunk and getting in some shoulder rolls and hip-hop moves, dancing to music of her own. On her heels was Magda, who looked all-knowing and who stepped, if anything, like a patient sorceress. Behind her bounced young Chris, and it was amazing he had stayed, because when the dance began Andy heard him say to his buddy James, in a dead voice beyond ironic, "This is the entertainment." Chris walked in a chain of odd intention made up of James, who had his hands on Amelia's shoulders, and Amelia, who had her hands on Chris's, each of them looking too alert. Maybe they'd got Amelia to eat some mushrooms. Then followed May E, happily dipping, apparently content to be included in what she took to be a typical New Year's night. May E, always trying to be funny, probably lonely, maybe about the same as him, and Andy wondered what it would be like to have her as a girlfriend, Chinese, her childhood as unknowable to him as art to an ape — Now little Alex zoomed past at a furious speed around the outside of their circle, enjoying his bigger, faster one, sometimes dipping so deep he slapped his palms on the ground, sometimes kicking and throwing punches at the air, a perfect little kid with a steep future.

Finally Andy felt guilty for spying on people.

But here right in front of him was Drew, his best friend, hooded like a monk, not sober under his cowl, beaten back because he had tried to leave his life but couldn't, but now maybe his son loved him, and he plodded on, dipping with the dance only because he knew Andy wanted him to, because after all, above all, he was a friend. Andy didn't know if Drew knew his back was being watched, but now in that clairvoyance of theirs, which never really stopped, Drew brought his flared hands up and stuck thumbs to his head to give himself moose antlers. With no pause he slowly pivoted one down, so the antler dangled and pointed to the ground and swung limply. It was from a cartoon they'd once watched somewhere, some time, and the little miracle was not only that Drew knew Andy would remember but also — it was a wounded moose.

Drew having forgiven his party, Andy went back to mindless walking, dipping. The music was harder to hear over the rising wind, which now blew intentionally into the maw of the firepit, brightening it in pulses and launching sparks that flew in brief curves before dying. When he passed leeward of the fire he could smell charred shellfish, and an earthy spice of what must be burning nose.

He wondered how long they should keep the dance going. At first in its silent solemnity it had felt somehow important on a New Year's night, even apocalyptic in such a wind, but this had passed. It was hard to tell who was invisibly grumbling and hanging on, and who was amused, and who might actually be in the spirit of things. Whatever that spirit might be. To each his own spirit. He glanced up again. Most looked, if anything, quietly happy, all part of this single possible animal, a herky-jerky snake mouthing its tail. In any case no one was shooting him looks, he sensed no mutiny, everyone was here, dipping around the fire, because he had asked them to be. He caught a small guffaw coming up; then his swelling heart in his throat; he loved these people.

This could let him stay here. This could let him stay here.

He hopped and spun comically high in the air and landed walking backwards, and here walked Pauline. She waved at him but looked mostly tired, her wine bottle bouncing off her thigh. Behind her came skittery Doris, who would do this all night if she thought she was supposed to, and then finally there she was, there was Laura, striding and dipping beautifully, just look at her move. The word *dance* applied and it hadn't before. Andy could see that she was doing nothing extra, just that all of her was in on it and all of her was smooth. She was doing it for him though her mother had died. She was doing it though she'd leave on Wednesday and neither of them knew if he would ever visit.

Andy hopped back around and caught himself in a stagger. He didn't want to stagger. He smiled slyly in the dark. They were out here walking off their good French wine. They were outside l'Habitation's buggy wooden walls, dancing a wounded routine in the snow, the wide dark unknown their —

He laughed at a sudden daydream image that came unbidden and flowered out of control. It was another Order of Good Cheer night, not four hundred years in the past but four hundred years in the future. Exactly four hundred years from tonight. But tonight was the new solstice, because Earth's axis has shifted a bit, due to something heating up, or because more of the planet's surface is water again. Somewhere — it's in the exact centre of the continent, it's in North Dakota, on the shore of a vast inland sea, it's eerily dark, though not yet night, and a ceremony is unfolding around a man, his name Lu. Lu's hands are bound behind him. Good Cheer Night is the new Christmas, and the whole remaining world is its Order. It's a world where food is grey buttery meat grown in vats, and delivered in beaten plastic pails, themselves centuries old. Wild food is almost unknown now, it is so achingly rare it has become demonically sacred, and bound Lu kneels, waiting while a hushed crowd of unseen

thousands watches from all sides from the seats of a dark amphitheatre he can't see. He kneels teetering on the lip of a twenty-foot
steel bowl. And now, with the sound of rusty grating and groan-
ing, out of a steel wall (everything is steel, not stainless but Soviet
steel, oxidized in shades of gun and black) grinds a ten-foot steel
phallus, at the tip of which is a single, gleaming wild berry tiny
and bright as a chipmunk's eye. The phallus head stops over the
centre of the bowl, the inflexible yoni bowl, and after several
seconds of the amphitheatre's held breath, the crimson berry
drops from the tip, into the bowl, lands with an unheard *tick*,
and Lu is at that moment shoved in too. He slides down on his
side, then quickly finds his knees. He knows he is a sacrifice but
he's eager, he wants that berry more than his own life and he
scrambles in the dim light and snorts and huffs and noses it
around and finally tongues and lips it up and with no room for
thought eats this wild bright living taste that he's never ever —
And then he is killed. And, after being cooked, he's eaten too,
because, well, he contains the sacred berry.

Smiling at himself, at his talent for dreams, Andy woke to
the backyard wind's next assault, a howler that blew the flame
horizontal. The fire's roar grew momentarily louder than the
wind's, and then came an even stronger gust, and the wind won.
Some hats flew, hitting the house or off into the trees, gone, and
Andy was fairly certain he would lose some land to waves, even
as they danced. But no one left the circle yet. They seemed to
know what a south wind was, how it was lunatic, and why it was
this warm, and what it could and couldn't do. They seemed
brave beyond their drunkenness, because even if they didn't
know the future in its details, in its entirety they did.

What Andy Winslow knew of tomorrow was, he would sleep
well, he would go in and start two weeks of afternoon shift at
the grain terminal, and he would read.

One thing he wanted to read about, though he dreaded it, was an aspect of marine biology having to do with fish (now he remembered the word might be *diadromous*, he'd look up diadromous fish), specifically any fish that lived in both salt and fresh water. Because, the thing was, tonight while releasing the sturgeon, with everybody chanting drunkenly and feeling good about having saved a noble creature, its tail waving languorously to them as it pushed itself into deeper murk to disappear — well, Andy had felt horrible. He'd remembered that salmon, coming in from the sea to spawn and entering the brackish river mouths of their childhood, needed a period of adjustment to get their tissues used to the fresh water. If you dropped a young one into salt, or a salty adult into fresh, they died as if by poison. Was it the same for that sturgeon? It'd been caught one hundred miles up the Skeena River. Watching the fish swim off, Andy couldn't help imagining its next moments, which might be its last, the old guy writhing in toxic freedom.

New World

1 *mars* 1607

WHILE STILL COLD, the days grow resplendently longer. Samuel finds himself standing quietly on the boards of the palisade, watching the world beyond their brief walls. His bare hand cups the arched black metal of a cannon, warmed by a sun that is barely into its strength. It is odd that metal, that a cannon, is the only warmed thing.

He watches for one in particular, but knows he will not see him.

The Order has proved beneficial, but that is enough of it. All have gained good humour and strength, and now they needs must spend it in the labours to come, with spring not far off. All the men are eager to break from winter's damming confines. Samuel knows that all of them dream (though no one dares mention it, fearful of bad luck) of little more than seeing the ship, whose arrival in weeks can now be counted on two hands.

Those who o'ercame grave disease, such is their joy that it brings joy to the rest. Samuel tries not to take a special, private gladness from it, for this would be a pride unwarranted. Though he may have calculated properly, it is God after all who made him a scientist.

In any case he has noticed, especially this year, that after surviving such illness a man becomes changed. The passion of one who is once more made alive is such that normalcy is now plenty. Simple light of day. The taste of modest broth. Rainfall. Even the itch of a chigger's bite Samuel has seen draw forth gladness and laughter! The man made newly well knows no lack, is desirous of nothing more than *this*. A homely world clung to and nursed upon, perhaps he lives in hidden fear that some new thing may turn foul and once again bring Hell through the door. But in any case they appear happy, and more thankful than babes.

All save Lucien, whose anger deepened, and who is now gone.

The more the carpenter grew in health, the more he scowled. He became short-tempered even with his friends, and of course with Samuel. Lucien could never be at ease with the knowledge that he was twice imprisoned, and that both crimes — who won't admit? — were less than crimes. To be riven by such as Dédé and then to be punished for it is to be riven once more.

Another thing: as soon as Lucien found his legs, the slight joy at walking again was at the same time dashed by his not being allowed to take himself beyond the stinking walls of the sick quarters, now otherwise empty.

His plea to Samuel was less plea than command. It was the simple, *Let me go*.

Samuel did. They all did. Samuel believes that even Poutrincourt, while unaware of the details, knows the heart of the deception, his show of ignorance an easily won means of saving face, all the while satisfying the just demands of what is, after all, his good heart. In any event it was a sad pleasure for Samuel to conspire with Lucien's friends and get him out under dark of night, with as many things as he could carry while still weak. But he had not many things: a book, three of his father's tools. And in the morning came their grave announcement of his dying in the middle of the night, and the marking of his interment in the snow, and the funeral rites, which Poutrincourt himself conducted, as usual. (Try as Samuel might, he could not read if the Sieur's dour visage was the face of guilt at having helped kill a man, or that of lying, saying God's words over a feigned corpse.) When the thaw arrives and they undertake the true burial of six bodies, and one is found absent, they will blame wolves, and that will be that. Perhaps they will construct a proper head-marker for Lucien, perhaps they will not bother.

So Lucien is gone from l'Habitation these past few days. He must be weak still, and either he is alive or he is dead, perhaps killed by savages, some of whom will be his rivals. These Mi'qmah are more peaceable than most, but there are those in any tribe who will kill who they can.

In any case he is gone. And here Samuel will admit — he must turn and see himself to admit it — that Lucien's leaving has made him sick with emptiness inside. He discovers only now that the carpenter is the closest man to a friend he has had in New France. Perhaps elsewhere. His leaving has shown not just how alone he is in these days but, more so, how alone he has been throughout this life.

His friend is out there somewhere, beyond these walls.

And Samuel finds himself envious of Lucien in this regard. They of l'Habitation will likely not stay here, not even in New France. None of them. Even the Sieur Poutrincourt, whose dream was to raise his children on this very land, is saying now that he may not, it is too hard, the winters too harsh and long, the land itself dangerous if only for its vastness. All will go home, if not this summer, then the next. Samuel himself will find new virgin shore, and make new maps, but first must await, as always, a benefactor with dreams, or a newly whimsical king. It is Lucien alone who will remain here, in Port-Royal, this darkly beautiful land, with its calm bay.

Samuel notes the islet across the way, white with birds along its shore, their shared cacophony a single ragged note. And he cannot help but contemplate — still envious — that though the scope of Lucien's world is small, circumnavigated by paddle in a tiny craft, or on foot, Lucien's explorations will outdo Samuel's own by leagues and leagues. For though his body will travel the least of any of them, the journey of needs undertaken by his head and by his heart is unfathomable. Lucien must wilfully become as the Mi'qmah. He must win a brutal new life.

The cook signals the midday meal. Samuel feels no hunger but he will go and eat with the men. There is gladness in their planning. Gardens, apparently, will be everywhere. Lescarbot whispers rhymes to himself about the firmness and lustre of his *haricots verts*. The men speak of women and their throats swell closed. The Sieur wonders about the size of the Cross still to be milled and placed, magnificent, on the North Mountain.

Before Samuel goes in, he angles his face fully into the sun, seeking some small heat, and for the first time finds some. So, after eating, he will scrape his cheeks free of winter beard, and be the first of the men to do this.

11 *mai* 1607

KNEELING BEHIND, in the canoe belonging to Ndene's brother, he watches the turn and flex of her body in its paddle stroke, sees the poetry in that skill. He watches her hips for signs of swelling, but of course it is too early for that. She quietly vomited — *soqotemun* — again this morning. Twice there has been no blood — *maltew* — during her time of moon. She will not say the word for fear of turning their luck, but he has heard it from all the other women, always said through a smile, and the word is *teleg*. It is all too much to think about. It is easier to simply learn the words.

He's learning their language in part because Ndene has decided there is no need now for her to learn his. So be it. Her finality is not cruel, it is plainly honest, and he has never known her to be wrong. But with similar small regret did he burn the pages of his sole book, the Homer, to use as ripest kindling for his own and Ndene's brothers' fires, and in so doing gained their friendship, for paper is not only rare to them, it is so beyond their reach as to be almost a kind of magic. And in not many weeks the book was gone. Burning it took his breath away, but it also made him laugh. The leather cover he uses for a stiff window flap in the house, if it can be called a house, one that Lucien, with much argumentative and often useless help, cobbled up in a hurry. The carpenter in him was disgusted at having to use mostly bark; its lack of uniformity made him almost nauseous. He had to learn to laugh at himself, learning what seemed a child's trade. Ndene, finally and properly angry with him and what she took to be his French arrogance, asked him if his new house didn't keep out the draft as well the more pompous walls of l'Habitation, and in the end Lucien had to admit that it did.

This morning they paddle to the farthest upper reaches of the bay, where he has been but twice, and he is excited to see it again, and in green bloom. But the paddle will tire him. He is not yet himself, though his legs have regained some thickness. Perhaps all that can still be seen of his disease is when he speaks, having lost three teeth, companions to one another, so that now there is a gap in the bottom front corner of his mouth, a place where Lucien has taken to resting his crude pipe, however infrequently it is filled.

It is full spring now, *siggw*, and with it the people are happy, their bodies eager to move, to work for as long as the sun is up. He helps as he can, and most are friendly as they teach him. But he finds it a trial to be away from Ndene for long, a half-day is almost too much, and no one minds this of him. To be alone — Lucien insists on the French habit of being alone to make love — they walk a trail together, or more often as they gain this warmer weather take a canoe to the grassy fields, like these they approach at the head of the bay. Today, as on others, they have with them her basket for any curled shoots of fern they might find and pluck (he so craves these, and even more so the small onions, though both need be well cooked). As well, pointed at the sky and useful as a cane when his legs weaken, he carries a long spear for the eels that any time now will come onto the muddy shallows, where they lose sight of danger as they twine and couple, just as Lucien and Ndene are about to do.

He aims for a rockless groove in the mud, then sculls with paddle, slowing their glide. As one they both stab the mud with a paddle, halting the canoe before it beaches. He enjoys how little they need speak. Few tasks need more than pointing, sometimes with a finger, or even a blink. First Ndene and then Lucien steps out into icy water. The blonde bitch, which followed Lucien away from l'Habitation simply because he'd whispered a whistle to her, leaps into the water barking, thinking it play. Ndene named her Stag, which is funny to Lucien, but these people don't see the sex of creatures in the same way, and Ndene smiled at his queries and said only that the dog has the same lift to her head as a stag does.

They carry the canoe high, well above any rocks, and take it up to rest on the grass. A canoe with a hidden hole can mean not surviving a trip across this very bay, and since it is the season of watery sap, not yet the good gum — *sqmugualaw* — and holes can take an entire afternoon to repair, why not take care and win that time for exploring these grass fields, and each other?

Canoe secure, Ndene begins the brisk walk upriver, taking what is almost a path. First Lucien stands to peer back across the water, in the direction of l'Habitation, for here is a most complete view of that entire shore. He sees the tall thread of their smoke. He feels a kind of homesickness, though not the full swollen heart that wants St-Malo and his sister Babette, and Mother, and his old bed. (He thinks Simon might try getting word to them of his true condition, but he isn't sure.) Whenever he eyes the distant smoke from their wet-wood fires he feels mostly a hollow loathing, though he does miss his friends. Simon, and François, and Leduc, and Bonneville, who so loved to feed them. The mapmaker too, in a way. And now, as testament to what remains of them in his heart, he wears the necklace — so noisy with rattles it is no good for hunting, so misshapen it is no good to trade — that

Monsieur Champlain forced tearfully into his palm as they stood in the snow. For this, they'd taken him just beyond the gate and the knowing eye of the Judas hole, a furtive and hasty farewell and then — he was alone.

Once, a fortnight ago, in the dark, after the moon set, he paddled past, not a stone's throw offshore, so close that the hair rose on his neck, for he could see the sentry move when his paddle was heard. The sentry called a warning — it sounded like Leblanc — and in his excitement Lucien wanted to shout back a jibe, a comedic bird call, anything, to let his friends know he was here and alive, perhaps as happy as they were, perhaps more so. But he quelled an equal urge to shout something obscene, and a list of names for Satan to take for his use. Neither kind of theatre won out; silence was and still needs must be uppermost in Lucien's relations with them.

Has he changed? He bathes more than he used to. He eats less. Some days he eats nothing, and some days, like a dog, he eats until he sleeps. He can speak with his new people but not well, and many of them still think he is stupid. The children pretend that he is, for they enjoy his teasing and know he is not. And though Ndene has decided that there is no need for him to teach her any more French, he is teaching it to Ndoxun, Member-tou's grandson, who in truth is the sagamore's great-nephew. Lucien sees that Ndoxun, who might be his own age, will become his closest friend.

Lucien is sometimes content. He has discovered that he feels relief for a world become smaller. In this life he might see little beyond this bay, or a few leagues inland from it, where apparently this summer they will hunt certain birds and roving deer and porcupine — he has seen one, it is real — and trap de Monts's precious beaver, and collect vegetables for drying. He will learn from Ndene's people how they make their houses, and with his several tools he has shown them some small things too, but not much. He will not frame himself, nor anyone else, as Sieur in a fine French house.

Living in marriage with Ndene he has known children were forthcoming, but this speed is almost too much, he isn't sure he has the strength to witness, let alone partake in, what's to come. No, he is excited: it feels not unlike yet another voyage! Perhaps the main mystery in this is how many, and will he love them so well as to be subsumed by them, as many fathers are and his own father was not. And would he then spend his years of fatherhood quietly smiling, as though, somehow, naught can now go wrong? He does know this is merely romantic, as is: each child would grow up as rich with private thoughts as a book has pages, and they would grow well beyond his body as well, peopling the lands west of this bay. This vision is so clear it is like he has always had these offspring and has only to make their acquaintance. Again, Ndene will speak of none of it, wary of dashing their luck.

He catches up to her. Waiting for him, she stands just off the trail, her hand fondly embracing a young tree. She turns when he comes, smiling, pats the trunk, and says, "*Malip qwanj.*" It is the nut tree he has heard of, with nuts that are sweet, *seggw*.

She continues walking. Trails, when they exist, are never wide enough for two, but he is happy to follow her, for it has become her custom to walk before him and point out leaves or objects and say their names. To make sure he is listening, she might call a mushroom an armpit. One time, she called a hummingbird a penis. (There is always some slight poetry to her ruse.) Then, some weeks afterwards, he called his penis a hummingbird and she laughed, remembering, and they paused and saw into each other's eyes to know once more how much they are together in mind. And also now, more and more, how they are in the other's memory.

In this same way, Lucien can see that, soon enough, this day will be in their past. And sometimes, when he thinks of his life here, his future so tightly enmapped, his days and nights so closely twined with these new people, he feels vastly alone and he grows afraid. Yet he seems to have found remedy for this dark humour. He calls it kindness. He gives it to himself most of all. He may have won this notion from his reading, he does not know, but when he gives it, kindness, it eases his blood and also goes beyond his blood. He knows that if he ever doubts this remedy he will begin to cause harm.

Today, as on some other days, they do not get to their destination — to check a weir for early river herring — right away. They are but half the distance upstream when Ndene bends to pluck a sprout, *saqaliag*, and brings it to his mouth. It is delicious, the mixed bitter and sweet of endive. And now they spot a clearing with some sun on it, and she pulls him by the hand, or perhaps he pushes her, and they fall to the warm ground, making honeyed songs in their throats, a wordless moaning language that they have learned together and is possibly theirs alone.

And so it goes. A first blackfly of the season fights the breeze for purchase on the carpenter's neck. Lying on the earth, the breeze and the bug in a dance on his bare skin, Lucien feels, again, all there is to feel. It could be any place. All he knows is that, as he goes into Ndene, in the push of entrance itself, all other routes are vanished and there is only this one. It might be the only thing he knows. It is a moment that, after firmly held breath, two souls trumpet with a gasp — a vast thing. As he enters her, there is no more need. All maps and questions are burnt. When he enters her, and she him, the road is clear as one already taken, the acorn is already the oak. It is as if they have been long, long dead and come to life only now.